A STUDY IN CRIMSON

K.C. NORTON

RILEY ROOKHOUSE

Cover illustration by Hannah Elizabeth, HannahElizabeth.ca

Cover lettering by James T. Egan, BookflyDesign.com

Managing editor: Diane Callahan, QuotidianWriter.com

Copy editor: Angela Traficante, LambdaEditing.com

Sign up for notifications of upcoming releases by Riley Rookhouse at RileyRookhouse.com

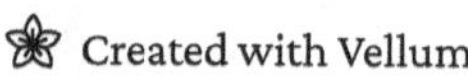 Created with Vellum

To the entire Story Garden publishing family. We love you all.

A FATAL AFFAIR

CHAPTER ONE

The Emerald Flame—my father, friend, mentor, and creator all in one—raised the collar of his black wool coat against the winter wind as he stomped through the streets of Kinmore. Each breath curled in a plume of white smoke between the shorn-off stumps of his tusks, and his gray-green skin had darkened to a ruddy hue in the frigid air.

"Pulchradune's useless *nips,* it's cold," he grumbled.

"Then wear a hat." To drive my point home, I adjusted mine.

The sidelong look he gave me would have curdled fresh milk. It was possible, however unlikely, that I was being just the *tiniest* bit insensitive to his plight. After all, the cold made no difference to me whatsoever.

It did provide me with an excellent excuse to dream up a new wardrobe, though, and for that, I was grateful.

Before leaving the Lute and Goose, I had rearranged myself into my usual shape as Simone, the one I'd worn most often since arriving in Kinmore. A few people had seen me in my more masculine form early on, but when we'd decided to take up residence at the

Lute and Goose, I'd lost the freedom to change my appearance on a whim.

Keeping my more feminine figure, I'd abandoned the reds and golds of my autumn wardrobe and, in celebration of my first-ever snowfall, wreathed myself in white. A square fur cap featured a small lace veil that half-obscured my scarlet eyebrows. My fitted white trousers and knee-high black boots were almost entirely covered by a massive fur coat that appeared to be made of white and silver fox fur. I had tucked my white-gloved hands into a fashionable feather muff adored with the heads of the birds who might have grown those feathers, had they not been mere tricks of the light, just as I was. The only pop of color, other than my red hair, was the brooch I wore pinned to my cap: the red-and-black emblem of the Middling Godlet, my unofficial patron.

Emerald rolled his eyes as I adjusted the fall of the lace veil. *[You look like an idiot.]*

"I look magnificent," I corrected him, with all the aplomb of one who is secure in their fashion choices. "*You're* the one who looks like an idiot, freezing those massive ears of yours off in the snow. A hat really would help, you know. I'm sure we could find one boorish enough to suit your needs."

Emerald grunted. *['M fine.]*

"Suit yourself." I finished fussing with my cap and returned my hand to my muff, trotting along beside him through the snow. I didn't leave footprints, but enough people took these roads that the pristine snowfall of the morning was already tamped down by hundreds of pairs of feet.

The snow had transformed Kinmore from a gray, unappealing port city into something out of a fairytale. My young friend, Sister Svelte, was able to summon winter using her Arctician *Aidea*, and she had once transformed our old dormitory into a similar snowy scene. That had been lovely. *This* was spectacular.

"Why are you gawking?" Emerald demanded. He didn't bother to look back at me.

I snapped my mouth shut at once. *[I wasn't gawking.]*
[Were too.]

I puffed out my cheeks and let my gaze wander back to the spires of the high city. *[It's the light. It's like the snow chases away darkness. Underwrites shadows. And the ice. Look at the ice, Emerald! The way it sends the light scattering into rainbows...]*

"Mm," Emerald grunted. "Lovely." He did not sound impressed.

I made a sound to mimic the clicking of a tongue—easier said than done, given that I didn't have one. "One would think a Light-weaver would be more enamored with that particular sort of beauty."

"Maybe I'm unimpressed because I could do it better. Ever think of that?"

"I *know* you've done better." I waved a hand at myself and smirked.

He made a rude noise and averted his gaze.

"I don't know *why* you're so disagreeable today."

"Lots of reasons," Emerald muttered.

I followed the turn of his head, and my good mood melted like snow before a fireplace. While I had been marveling at the buildings in the wealthy heart of the city, Emerald had been studying the docks and rowhouses. One did not have to look far in Kinmore to see proof that not everyone in the city lived a life of luxury. In the lower city, the fresh snow was already turning to a gray, downtrodden approximation of mud, mixed in with the dirt and grime of everyday living.

"Oh," I murmured. A handful of street urchins clustered in the road along the tenement wall, talking to each other in low tones. When they caught me looking, they fell silent, staring back at me through narrowed eyes. Their patched and tattered clothing revealed skinny limbs turning shades of pink in the wintery air.

I did not hold Emerald's fashion sense in high regard, but I could see how *they* might think I looked like an idiot. I certainly felt it; if my outfit had been real, it would have cost more money than any of them would likely see in their whole lives.

[Can we... give them something?] I was thinking of Tala, the dwarf girl who lived back in Upper Bound, who'd called me a mingy hedgepig. I wondered how she kept warm in the ever-lengthening nights.

[Like what? A few coins? A new home? We've already taken in three strays, Crimson.] Emerald was still moving, and I was in imminent danger of being left behind.

Still, I hesitated, lifting one hand in greeting and offering the children a hesitant smile.

They scattered at my movement, disappearing into doorways and alleys that looked so uninviting, I could not imagine that anyone called them *home.*

[They have no one to look after them,] a voice in the back of my mind hissed. *[They have no one to care for them. The city grinds them under its bootheel like the carcasses of all its other vermin. They are unwanted, Crimson. But we could help them.]*

I shuddered and turned away, lengthening my stride to keep up with Emerald's. I was not sure how to respond to the thing that had made its home in the eaves of my mind-cottage, and I had no response. My best defense was to pretend that I hadn't heard it in the first place.

The squalor of the lower city was not the only thing that put my friend off-kilter. Ever since we'd returned from our tenure at the Brotherhood of Guise, Emerald had been spending his days at the Conjury headquarters, doing odd jobs for an organization we neither liked nor trusted.

As we approached the marble steps of Kinmore's Conjury head-quarters, a familiar young man in a silver-and-purple coat approached from the opposite direction. When he saw Emerald, he tipped his nose in the air and slipped by us, only to stop directly in the doorway and spend a solid minute knocking the snow from his boots in the entryway. Emerald and I waited behind him.

[He is being rude to your creator. We could punish him. We could make him pay. If only you would let me out...]

I pretended to clear my throat.

[Don't bother,] Emerald thought glumly. ***[He knows exactly what he is doing.]***

I didn't bother to explain that I was more concerned about the monster that lived in my head than the snitty Conjury secretary. I had tried to tell Emerald about my passenger, Innocent, more than once. Unfortunately, Emerald was incapable of remembering anything I told him about the shadow-beast, thanks to Harmony's meddling with his memory.

My life had gotten a great deal more complicated since arriving in Kinmore, and I was the only one who could remember why.

The secretary finally moved on, allowing us access to the main lobby. We passed the bust of Henda that stood inside and continued down the hall without a word to any of the other Conjury employees.

In the weeks since Emerald had started working with Commander Finch, I had met a handful of Castcadesmen, half a dozen secretaries, and a score of state-sanctioned bankers and tax collectors. For the most part, however, Emerald kept to himself, and he answered directly to Finch.

"Inspector." Finch glanced up from her reports as we entered. Her golden eyes tracked Emerald's movement through the room, and her ears flicked back in what I was beginning to recognize as an involuntary sign of suspicion. Finch was always careful around us, more so than others. I had the nasty feeling that she suspected me of being something other than, as Emerald put it, a magical dummy. If the Conjury found out that I was a mystical aberration rather than a simple lightweaving, the consequences for both Emerald and me could be dire.

So far, she had no proof that I was different. Still, her clever eyes made me nervous.

Sure enough, when I followed Emerald into her office, her

whiskers twitched. "Your illusion is rather... overdressed, don't you think?"

I would have loved to set her straight on that matter, but when Emerald and I were in Commander Finch's presence, I never spoke. To do so would have been to invite unwelcome questions. Instead, I stared straight ahead, playing the part of an empty husk.

[Why pretend? We could kill her, if we wanted. You and I, we would do wonders together.]

As usual, I ignored Innocent.

"I was feeling whimsical this morning," Emerald lied. Gods bless him, the fellow had probably never had a whimsical thought in his life. He dropped down into the seat across the desk from Finch and held out one huge hand. "What have you got for me?"

Finch smirked at me again before reaching for a stack of loosely bound folios before her. "The last of the cases. I must say, your efforts are making my life much easier."

"That's why they keep paying me, isn't it?" Emerald took the folios and dropped the stack in his lap, then opened the top one. There were perhaps two dozen sets of notes altogether, but I knew from experience that this wouldn't be enough to keep him occupied for long.

His green eyes skimmed the notes until, with a snort, he tossed it onto the desk in front of him. "Accident," he said.

"You're sure?" Finch didn't have eyebrows per se, but there were darker patches of fur on her forehead that served much the same function when it came to conveying her emotions. They rose as she reached for the discarded papers. "I thought the bloodstain on the candelabra might suggest foul play."

"Wrong kind of wound," Emerald said, already moving onto the next case. "Head injuries are prone to excessive bleeding, and if he'd been struck but the base of the candelabra, the skin would have broken. He was holding the candelabra when he fell, but the wound itself was from the stairs."

I braced myself for another tedious conversation. In theory,

Emerald's job was to solve mysteries involving the *Aidea*, but relatively few of Kinmore's crimes and tragedies were magical in nature. The presence of the Conjury served as a deterrent, and most of the mysteries Finch had presented to Emerald over the last few months were relatively mundane. In fact, many of them hadn't been crimes at all.

"Oh, now *this* is interesti—no, I take it back." Emerald tossed the second folio aside. "Accident."

"How can you be sure?"

"It's obviously an allergy. There was nothing the wife could have done." Emerald's mouth twitched toward a smile before settling back into a flat line. "Unless you're suggesting that she *coerced* a bee into stinging him?"

Finch pursed her lips. "I suppose that is rather unlikely."

Perhaps I was wrong. He could muster whimsy when called upon, but only of a grim variety.

"Hm." Emerald paused a moment to study the notes from the next folio. Through our connection, I felt a surge of excitement. Here, perhaps, was a real case, something to occupy his mind for a few days and help him forget what he'd left behind on Kovin Isle.

Just as suddenly as it had come, his excitement vanished. "Butler did it," he grumbled, and the folio followed the others onto the table. *Thump.* "You'll find the ruby in the lining of his coat, if he hasn't sold it by now."

He proceeded to make his way through the rest of the pile. Each time, Finch snatched the folio up to scribble a few hasty notes in the margins.

"Accidental drowning." *Thump.* "Intentional poisoning, check with the cook, I bet you anything it was the mushrooms." *Thump.* "Snake." *Thump.* "Oh, *obviously* the husband is to blame, that's hardly a mystery..."

"Hold on." Finch looked up from her notes. "Did you say *snake*?"

"Mm." Emerald tapped his thumb against his lips. "Most definitely. Now, this one..."

Finch blinked at him. When he did not elaborate, she spelled out the word *snake* in tidy letters, followed by a trio of question marks.

"...this one is curious. They never found the body?"

Finch craned her neck to see what he was reading. "That fellow from the party, you mean? No, no sign of him."

"Might not be dead at all, then." Emerald set this folio on the desk with a bit more care, leaving it aside from the others. "Or he might have gotten drunk and walked off the pier in the dead of night. I can't tell from the notes."

The mention of someone stepping off a pier into dark water made me shiver. It was less than a year since Emerald had done much the same, and it was my constant fear that his prolonged absence from Dyrne might lead to a relapse. So far, he had kept himself together, but I could feel him fraying at the edges, just as I was.

"I'll have someone look into it." Finch set the folio aside. I might have imagined that her eyes were on me when she spoke. Had she noticed some change in my demeanor?

I was sometimes tempted to stay away during these meetings, but I didn't want to miss anything of consequence. If and when Emerald stumbled across a new mystery worth solving, I wanted to be there from the beginning.

Besides, I didn't like leaving him alone.

"Accident." *Thump.* "Accident." *Thump.* "Son did it." *Thump.* "Accident." *Thump.* "Snake."

"Another snake?" Finch asked. "Or the same one?"

"Different, probably. Not that it matters. Ooh." Emerald shuddered. "Definitely *not* an accident. You're looking for a Sonicist with that one. Poor bastard, what a way to go, bleeding from the *ears.*"

"His partner is a Sonicist." Finch made another note. "She went missing at the time of his death."

"No real mystery there, then." To Emerald's dismay, he reached the bottom of the pile with nothing particularly arresting to show for his efforts.

"Is that all you have?" he asked hopefully, as if Finch might have a difficult puzzle set aside for him, like a treat saved until he'd eaten all his vegetables.

"Indeed." Finch set the annotated folios aside, setting the one containing information on the missing partygoer on top. "I appreciate your help."

Emerald drummed his fingers on the arm of his chair. His dissatisfaction was building by the day, and I worried that it would sour into a desire to drink his troubles away. We'd been down that road before, and I hoped never to repeat the experience.

"Anytime," he said at last. With a frustrated sigh, he pushed himself to his feet. Instead of turning toward the door, he hovered there for a long moment. "Finch, let's say I wanted... someone to help me answer a research question. Where would I go?"

Finch cocked her head. "Research? On what topic?"

"A theoretical question about lightweaving."

I stiffened. This was part of the reason we'd chosen to stay on the mainland: the hope that we might be able to learn more about what I was, how I had come to be sentient, and most importantly, how I might someday be able to become my own being, rather than a dependent of my creator. In short, what if I could summon *myself*?

Finch's whiskers twitched again, her ears flicking back toward her skull. "I would have thought you an expert on the subject." She studied me as she spoke. "I don't know of any Lightweavers in the city more skilled than you, but a number of our patricians keep extensive personal libraries. The king's archives would be the most extensive, of course, but you would have to contact his court directly, and it would be up to them to give you access. If it's a consultation you want, though, I'd point you in the direction of Venta Bulgarum."

Emerald huffed. "I was afraid of that. Well, maybe when we're ready to move on, we'll head there next."

"Any idea when that will be?" Finch asked.

Emerald shook his head. "Not yet."

Finch nodded. Emerald turned his back on her and made for the door, so he didn't see the look she gave me as we departed.

I wondered if she noticed, as I had, that when Emerald spoke of his plans, he had said *we.*

OUR WALK back to the inn where we had set up temporary headquarters was conducted primarily in silence. Emerald, I suspected, was wallowing in his boredom, and his perpetual desire to return to the town of Dyrne an ocean away. He'd been parted from Tincrown for more than three months, and I knew—even if he had never voiced the thought aloud—that the idea of spending his winter evenings holed up in his room doing whatever sweethearts did in private would have been a far more appealing way to pass the time. He was restless, and having seen for myself the conditions in which he'd grown up, I suspected that it was a *new* sort of restlessness than he'd known before.

Emerald had spent most of his life running away from who he was. Meeting Tincrown had set him on a new track, one where he longed to run *toward* the person he might be. Alas, we could not return to Dyrne without raising the Conjury's suspicions. Not yet, at least.

I had my own troubles to contend with, not the least of them being Innocent's constant presence and near-constant badgering. Neither of us had been in good spirits since we departed the Brotherhood that fall, and the weight of our worries was beginning to take its toll on both of us.

As usual, I was the one to break the silence, though I waited until we were strolling through the lanes near the Lute and Goose before doing so.

"Perhaps we ought to see about visiting the king's library," I suggested.

Emerald snorted. "Good luck with that."

I cocked my head. "Surely you're clever enough to find a way to grease those particular wheels?" My jibes about his grooming habits never landed, but the one thing Emerald would not abide was the implication that his intelligence was lacking. Perhaps this challenge would provide the diversion we both needed.

Alas, I had miscalculated once again. Emerald waved to his own face. "It's not a matter of cleverness, Crimson. Feynlish's relationship with the Conjury is on shaky ground, and in case you've forgotten, people like me aren't exactly *popular* around here."

I bit my lip. He was right, of course. Humans in general seemed mistrustful of jotunn, and my friend's mixed parentage often meant that he didn't fit in anywhere. "Perhaps another patrician could be convinced?" I pressed, reluctant to give up on our lead so easily. "Maybe one of them has a problem we could help with in order to win their favor."

"Right." Emerald rolled his eyes. "I'll just go around knocking on castle doors and asking if anyone needs a mystery solved in exchange for a week poking around their library."

"You could at least *try*," I mumbled.

Emerald snorted. "Do you really think I haven't tried? I submitted a petition to the crown the first day we were here, and I haven't heard back. I don't expect to, either. It's been *weeks*. We'll need another plan, Crim, and I'm tired of being shut out, so *please* just let it go."

I huffed, letting the illusion of my own frozen breath drift between my lips. Around us, the simple farmhouses were utterly picturesque in the waning light. Days were so short in the winter, although Emerald had promised that they would lengthen again after the equinox. In the meantime, the windows of the farmhouses glinted gold, refracting firelight into the gathering dusk.

I wondered what it would feel like to belong somewhere. To call someplace home. To surround myself with living things, to reap and sow and let the earth lie fallow.

At least the Lute and Goose waited to welcome us with open, if temporary, arms. Emerald shouldered through the door of the inn.

The dining room was empty, as were all the rooms upstairs besides the two we rented from Yerik: one for Emerald, and one for the three children who had lately come into our care.

"Home sweet home," Emerald grumbled as he knocked the snow from his boots.

I glanced sidelong at the massive portrait of his rival and some-times-friend Coirpre that loomed over the bar. "Indeed."

Emerald shrugged out of his coat. "Never seen it this quiet. People must be avoiding the weather, although I could have sworn there were cart tracks in the snow outside."

"Were there?" I asked. "I didn't notice."

Emerald hung his coat on a peg by the door. "You ought to pay more attention to your surroundings, Crim. You never know when—"

"*Emerald!*" A high-pitched voice sounded from the back room, followed by the thumping of two pairs of small, stockinged feet and one pair of hooves. Three children all but bowled over each other as they flew down the stairs. Svelte took the lead, with her red hair flying behind her. Gangly Blare followed at her heels, just outpacing the lambkin, Quell. Svelte collided with Emerald and threw her arms around his waist. I felt his surprise, followed by a wave of affection. Ostensibly, he'd become these childrens' temporary guardian as a favor to me, but I knew he privately adored them.

It was the closest thing he'd come to having a family in a very long time.

"Emerald, guess what!" Svelte lifted her head to beam at him.

Blare's hands flew faster than she could speak, signing out the news. *There were visitors earlier, looking for you!*

"You should have seen them!" Quell had given up his Sonicist *Aidea* weeks ago, but his voice was still astonishingly loud, given his size. "They were wearing these uniforms, Crimson, with these gold buttons... so many buttons, Crimson, some of which didn't even *go* to anything, they were just there to sparkle, you would have *loved* it! And there was gold braid on their coats, too..."

"They let me feed apples to their horses!" Svelte clapped her hands to her freckled cheeks, her eyes glittering like a pair of jeweled buttons in their own right. "They weren't like the draft horses we see out here. They were big and sleek and black as midnight. I want to ride horses like that someday…"

They were looking for you! Blare added, signing over Svelte, who was turned away from him.

Emerald held up his hands, gesturing for the three of them to settle down. When he spoke, he also used the same sign language Blare had, to make sure all three of them could understand. "One at a time. Who were these people?"

"Dunno," Quell said, doing an excited little dance in place. "But they were *rich*, Broth—Emerald." It had taken the children a while to get used to calling us by our real names, rather than the ones we'd used when we visited the Brotherhood, and they still forgot sometimes.

They left you a letter, though, Blare added.

"A letter?" I repeated.

"I have it here." Our host, Yerik, had emerged from the back of the inn, bearing a cream-colored envelope in one hand. His usually frizzy hair, which he kept tied back when the inn was busy, was freshly oiled and now fell around his shoulders in a wave of corkscrew curls. I had the sneaking suspicion that he was making an extra effort with his appearance now that Emerald was living under the same roof.

He held out the letter to Emerald. Across the front, in burgundy ink, someone with impeccable penmanship had labored over our full prominence titles: *Crimson Smoke and the Emerald Flame.*

"Hm." He flipped the envelope over and froze.

"What?" Svelte stood on her toes, trying to see what Emerald was staring at so intently. "Does it say who it's from?"

"After a fashion." Emerald's green eyes flicked toward me. He held up the envelope for inspection.

On the back of the envelope, covering the flap, was a large seal stamped in sunflower-colored wax, which had been sprinkled in gold leaf. I squinted at the emblem, which showed a lion bearing a sword, surrounded by stripes.

"Should I know who that's from?" I asked.

"I told you, Crimson," Emerald said as he slid one finger beneath the flap of the envelope. "You need to pay more attention."

"I don't—" I began, before realizing that I *did* know the image. I'd seen it everywhere since we'd arrived in Kinmore, in the pennants hanging from the eaves of houses and businesses all over the city. I'd noticed the red-and-gold coloring but taken the iconography for granted.

"This," Emerald said, even as I came to the same realization, "is the sigil of the Kingdom of Feynlish."

CHAPTER TWO

The five of us crowded around Emerald as he opened the letter. The children made no attempts to hide their curiosity, but Yerik seemed torn about asking impertinent questions. In the end, however, he joined us at one of the inn's round tables, while I hovered over Emerald's shoulder.

"Hmm." Emerald tugged a letter from the envelope and raised his eyebrows when it was accompanied by several smaller pieces of heavy paper, one of which appeared to be made of pressed linen. "I wonder..."

"What does it say?" Quell stood on the seat of his chair and braced his arms against the tabletop, straining to read the letter upside down from across the table.

Emerald scanned the page, and his expression grew more surprised with each passing line. His silence only added to the children's excitement. After a moment, he slid the page to Svelte.

"You can read it aloud, if you like," he said.

"Why does *she* get to read it?" Quell whined.

"Because I'm older." Svelte snapped up the page, cleared her throat extravagantly, and lifted her chin. "*Dear Sir and Madame... Oh,* they've got it wrong already." She lowered the letter a fraction to look at me. "They called you a *madame*, Crimson. That's not right."

"Close enough," I told her. "I don't mind, really. Calling me *sir* would be no worse or better, and I've let people think I'm a woman."

She huffed. Her indignance on my behalf made me feel... seen, perhaps, in a way that I often wasn't. I didn't know many people who were the both-and-neither, in-between thing I was, and I'd made no effort to advertise it. The people who knew me understood. That was good enough.

"Fine, then." Svelte cleared her throat once again and started over. "*Dear Sir and Madame, The palace is holding its winter ball in celebration of the crown prince's engagement. It is the crown's hope that you might attend, not only to demonstrate that the common folk of Kinmore can and will rise to prominence when necessary, but also to offer necessary assistance to the crown itself. We trust you will be discreet, and we look forward to meeting a fellow master of illusion. Yours In Need and Sincerity, The Future Crown of Feynlish.*" She lowered the letter again, frowning down at the signature. "What does *that* mean?"

"It means that Crimson and I have been invited to a party." Emerald held up the sheet of linen paper for me to see. Sure enough, our names were inked into the invitation.

"A party. At the palace." I raised my eyebrows meaningfully. *[See? There is a way to ingratiate ourselves with the crown of Feynlish after all. Maybe that library isn't as out of reach as you thought.]*

[Maybe.] Emerald stroked his chin. "Did you see that there's a dress code?"

"Oh!" I bent over his shoulder, hungry for inspiration. I'd never attended a royal event before, at least not since I'd gained sentience. This would be the perfect opportunity to dream up an outfit worthy of a princess, something so marvelous that even Emerald would have to admit that my taste was impeccable.

Then I saw the last line of the dress code, and I let out a quiet moan of distress. "No. *No.* Can they *do* that?"

"Of course they can," Emerald said. "The crown can do whatever it likes."

The crown, I decided, was unworthy of the title. What kind of disturbed person would insist that the guests wear, of all things, *yellow*?

Still, I would do what I had to do for the sake of the investigation, even if it turned my metaphorical stomach.

THE EVENT IN QUESTION, it turned out, was only three days away. The morning after the letter's arrival, Emerald went into town alone to tell Finch he wouldn't be available for a few days, and to arrange for the delivery of a new outfit.

"I ought to go with you," I said as he pulled on his boots.

He let out a derisive snort. "I suppose you want a say in what I wear, but I'm afraid that you'll have to trust me this time."

"It isn't that." I wrung my hands and paced back and forth through the still-empty dining room. It had snowed again in the night, and the usual lunch crowd was still holed up in their homes. "You're going to look terrible no matter what—yellow *really* isn't your color any more than it is mine..."

"Exactly." Emerald rose from the chair and reached for his coat. "And I'll barely be speaking to Finch, so you won't miss anything. I just need a moment to myself for once, Crim."

I fretted all the way toward the door. His hand was on the doorknob before I finally blurted, "Promise me you won't drink!"

He stopped in his tracks and turned to face me. "I beg your pardon?"

"I just... every time you *needed a moment alone* in Upper Bound, you really meant you wanted a drink, and I know it's terrible being away from Tincrown, but I need you to promise me that you won't do anything foolish out there on your own." I shuffled from foot to foot, filled with a nervous energy that mounted with each additional second that he stared at me. "I promised him I'd look after you."

Emerald's gruff expression softened. "Crimson," he said. "I promise, I won't do anything you'd disapprove of."

"Other than buying a yellow outfit," I amended. "I can hardly *approve* of that, but I understand the necessity."

He laughed, a real belly-laugh that eased my nerves a fraction. "I promise I won't do anything I can't take back."

That was what I'd *really* needed to hear. Ever since he'd mentioned the missing partygoer walking off the pier, I'd wondered if the prospect of doing so had been on his mind. We shared a connection, but even with our mental link, there were doors in Emerald's head that even I couldn't open. Some that even *he* couldn't open.

With one last reassuring smile, Emerald stepped out the door into the snow and was gone.

In his absence, I let out a deep sigh and rubbed my temples. Things had been going as well as could be expected since we left the Brotherhood, but I couldn't shake the feeling that something would give eventually, and I was worried what would happen when one of us finally snapped.

I hadn't realized we had an audience until Yerik said my name, and I nearly jumped. That would have raised some questions, given that I was more than capable of flying through the ceiling if I wanted to.

"Sorry!" I yelped, although I could not have said why I was apologizing.

"I didn't mean to overhear." Yerik stepped behind the bar and began his daily cleaning ritual, despite the fact that he hadn't hosted a single patron in two days. "Are the children awake?"

"Not yet," I told him.

"Mm." He wiped the bar with a damp cloth, working in neat circles so as not to miss an inch. "Who's Tincrown?"

"Er..." I knew, although Emerald did not, that Yerik had harbored feelings for my friend when they were younger. Besides, how was I supposed to explain the fact that Emerald loved a man who he'd left behind, without being able to offer a satisfactory explanation for why he had done so?

Yerik chuckled at my awkwardness. "Right. A lover, then. Funny, I always thought he and Coirpre might be... you know. More than friends."

"Er," I said again, looking up at the grinning portrait of the bard in question. Emerald and Coirpre were both less *and* more than friends, inasmuch as I understood their relationship.

"Really?" Yerik looked up at the painting, too. "Good for him."

I didn't know of which *him* he was referring to, and I decided I was happier that way. The goose in the painting watched Coirpre with sycophantic, almost lovesick eyes. Given that Yerik had painted the picture himself, I wondered how much he and the goose had in common.

"I'm glad you're looking out for him," Yerik said, turning back to the bar. "When we were younger, something... happened to him. Back at the Brotherhood."

"I know," I said. We'd solved that mystery earlier in the year.

Yerik looked up at me sharply. "He told you?"

The answer was on the tip of my tongue, but there was something in Yerik's expression that gave me pause. "Are we talking about Reticent?" I asked.

Yerik cocked his head. "Reticent?"

"Never mind," I said. "What are *you* talking about?"

Yerik bit his bottom lip, and the hand that held the cloth stilled. "It's not my place to say. But I think it's the reason he started, ah..." Yerik tilted his arm subtly, indicating the inside of his wrist. I knew what he meant, and I'd seen enough of Emerald's memories to remember that he'd been making those little marks on his own arms long before Reticent died.

"Oh," I said sadly. "Yes. Right. And no, he hasn't told me about... that."

Yerik winced. "I shouldn't have said anything."

"No, it's all right." I twisted my fingers together. "I know more than he'd like me to, but I'd never use it against him. And I know he helped *you* more than once."

A rueful smile stole over Yerik's features. He leaned forward on the bar, resting his elbows against the glossy wood. "You know, when he first came back in the fall, I let myself believe for just a moment that he might have come back for me. I think I'd built him up in my head as this larger-than-life hero, and I think I wanted him to come whisk me away to an adventure. But it turns out, I like where I am. And I'm glad to hear that he has people looking out for him now. You're good for him, and I hope this Tincrown fellow is, too."

I stood there, lost for words, as Yerik began cleaning again. If I could have hugged him, I would.

There were times I wished that I could embrace every single person who had thought kindly of my friend, because they would never know how desperately he needed it.

"Dear gods," I said in horror, staggering back from Emerald as he adjusted his new coat, "I hope you didn't pay *money* for that."

Emerald glared at me, although the effect was somewhat diminished by the absurdity of his garments. "Of course I paid money for it. That's how commerce works."

Convincing my friend to spend any amount of his hard-earned coin on clothing was a struggle at the best of times. He was happy to wear boots until the soles gave way, and his threadbare shirts were the bane of my existence. The only satisfactory thing about his dress was his taste in coats, but despite my general frustration regarding his wardrobe, all those complaints paled in light of the abomination before me.

An unflattering jacquard vest in two shades of eye-searing yellow clasped over a loose-sleeved shirt in canary gold. Matching leggings hugged his calves and vanished into ankle-high, heeled, lemon-hued leather boots with brass buckles. Worse of all was the collar, which stood straight out from his throat. At first glance, it appeared to be made of white lace, but once I steeled myself for closer examination, I discovered that it was actually a shade of eggshell that, with creative license, might have been considered yellow as well.

"Good heavens and cursed hells." I covered my face with my hands and shuddered. "*Five* different shades. I might be sick."

"Six, if you count the brass." He tried to look down at his boots, found that the collar blocked the view, and held up one foot as evidence. "It's ghastly, isn't it? What about you?"

I had delayed donning my party appearance until the last possible second, but now that the time was upon us, I rearranged myself into the only outfit I had been able to stomach during all my hours of obsessive experimentation.

Emerald's eyebrows rose. "You call that yellow?"

My layered skirt was closer to the color of fresh cream than true yellow, with gold and bronze accents. My bright-red hair coiled over my shoulder in three princess curls, held in place with ornamented gold pins. Citrine buttons held the back of the gown in place. "I call it as close to yellow as I can get without falling into a stupor," I told him.

Emerald rolled his eyes even as he shoved the door open. "Fine. Let's just hope that the footmen let you in—and that you aren't accused of treason for failing to follow the dress code."

If anything, *he* should have been the one people looked at askance, but I didn't taunt him. After all, he was the one who had to go around looking like a sickly daffodil all night.

I had wondered if we'd be making the walk into Kinmore, dressed as we were, which wouldn't have done his outfit any favors. Instead, there was a conveyance waiting at the door for us. The side of the carriage was emblazoned with the kingdom's leonine seal and pulled by two black horses that were everything Svelte had described.

The children were already outside, bundled up in their winter coats, feeding apple slices to the horses with open palms.

"You see the buttons?" Quell whispered, pointing to the driver. "What did I tell you? Gold!"

Yerik stood with them, watching intently to make sure they came to no harm. His russet skin was tinged pink with cold. When he saw Emerald, the flush spread to his cheeks, and he covered his mouth with one hand in a vain attempt to stifle his laughter.

"Yes, yes," Emerald grumbled. "Very funny."

"You look, um..." Yerik choked on another laugh. "All dressed up and ready for a party."

"You're too kind," I assured him as I slipped past Emerald and into the open carriage door.

My companion lumbered after me, shaking his head even as he smiled to himself. We waved out the window as the carriage pulled away, bearing us toward the heart of the city.

"You're in a remarkably good mood," I observed, hovering just over the seat.

Emerald, by contrast, was being jostled all over the place as the carriage wheels hit potholes and stones. All the same, his smile only widened.

"Of course I'm in a good mood," he told me. "Aren't you? After weeks of resting on our laurels, we finally have a *case*."

CHAPTER THREE

Feynlish Castle was little more than a silhouette by the time we pulled up to the front gate, but it made a striking silhouette indeed. The building was even older than Fenguard Keep, and far larger, its walls hewn from stones so massive it must have taken the assistance of *Aidea* to convey them from whatever quarry that had produced them.

"Oh." I pressed my face to the window of the carriage, careful to not push through the glass, marveling at the buttresses and towers and crenellations on the wall. "It's like a city *inside* a city."

"Mm." Emerald was staring at the castle through slitted eyes. "You could live inside the walls and never leave. Never want for anything." He lowered his voice. "Never have to confront the way your subjects are living, or what *they* might need."

I pulled away from the window. "Hold on. Is the king to blame for how his people live, or the Conjury?"

[You might want to be careful when and where you utter treason,] Emerald warned. *[And it's both their faults. The Conjury is responsible for taxation and oversight, but the king imposes sepa-*

rate taxes on the people as well, and arguably does even less for them in the long run.]

I thought of Yerik, and the small farms surrounding the inn. Of the street urchins glaring daggers at my fur coat. *[They're taxed twice over?]*

[The Conjury needs money to fund its growth and oversight, while the crown needs money to fund... this.] Emerald waved dismissively at the castle. *[Where did you think it all came from?]*

To be perfectly frank, I hadn't thought about it at all. Money wasn't something I'd ever had to consider deeply, since I couldn't even handle coins. Everything I needed, I produced myself with little more than a thought and an effort of will. But of course, the Conjury paid Emerald, operated its headquarters, and employed scouts and Castcadesmen all over Dregandresal. To do that, they must have a way to fill their coffers.

Not for the first time, I thought of the Fenguards, who had shed blood in order to stay young for centuries. I had been horrified by their selfish actions, but I was starting to see that they really had done the best they could for their people.

The world was not as clear-cut as I'd once believed, and I missed the simplicity of right and wrong, even if that simplicity was the result of my own ignorance.

We waited in a long line of carriages until we were deposited by the front entrance of the castle. There, we waited in *another* line, while footmen compared swatches of approved colors against the outfits of the other guests. When one woman was informed that her pale cream-colored dress was insufficiently yellow, I cursed under my breath.

"Told you," Emerald whispered out of the side of his mouth.

[I thought you were joking! What is **wrong with these people?]**
Fortunately, the area where we waited was not well-lit, so I was able to rearrange the colors of my gown without anyone noticing. By the time I was done, my dress was decidedly amber. The footmen took one look at us and waved us through the door; Emerald's suit was

such an eye-searing shade of yarrow that no swatches were required. We left the woman who'd been turned away crying against the wall, while her husband tried his best to console her.

The grandest room I'd ever personally encountered was the hall in Fenguard Keep. That room had been massive, bordering on cavernous, but the king's hall was ever larger. It was three stories high, with balconies at every level overlooking the festivities. Columns thicker than the masts of sailing ships supported the honeycomb vaults of the ceiling, braced by entablature hewn with faces of snarling lions. Saffron-yellow banners spanned the pillars like autumn limbs, illuminated by dancing lights that twinkled as brightly as free-falling stars.

[Is a Lightweaver casting those?] I asked, worried that I might be called upon to answer some unfortunate questions about my nature.

[What, those?] Emerald scratched his chin, nonplussed by the astonishing display. *[Nah, they're an enchantment. A Lightweaver probably made them, but that's simple stuff.]*

[An enchantment? Like the one you taught Nechtan to cast over Dyrne?]

[Exactly. Objects imbued with Aidea can hold a spell for months, if not years. They probably have to refresh 'em every few weeks, but it wouldn't take a Lightweaver to do that. See there?] Emerald pointed to one of the pillars above us, where an elaborate geometric carving stood proud on the stone surface. "That's clever work. The king must have paid through the nose for that commission, but it'll last for years. Decades, even, so long as it gets a little jolt of *Aidea* now and then. Doesn't even have to be a Lightweaver to do it."

I thought of the gloves that Tincrown had worn back on Kovin Isle when he was checking to see how Bilk Deepvein had died. For someone who was made of *Aidea*, I had very little sense of how it all worked.

I was on the brink of asking more questions when a passing

gentleman doubled back on his path to speak with us.

"I beg your pardon," he said in a voice as smooth as the silk wall-hangings around us. "I didn't mean to eavesdrop, but it sounds as if you are proficient in the *Aidea*, and I can't help but wonder... are you the gentleman known as the Emerald Flame?"

Emerald's eyes widened in surprise. "I am."

The gentleman bowed with a little flourish of one hand. "Such a pleasure to make your acquaintance in person."

From Emerald's far side, I sized the newcomer up. Like everyone else, he was dressed in yellow, but it suited him better than the vast majority of the crowd. Most of the material was silk cut through with burnt-orange stripes. Subtle embroidery patterns glittered when the citrine seed beads threaded amidst the stitching caught the light. A half-cape covered one shoulder and accented his broad shoulders, while the nipped waist of his jacket was a distinctly feminine style. As my gaze traveled to the floor, I realized that he was wearing a *skirt.*

I could not help but stare. It was the sort of outfit that I would have dreamed up in the mind-cottage, or even donned in the privacy of my rooms, but I wouldn't have dared wear it to an event like this, and certainly *not* when I wore Simon's face. The stranger had not shaved his jaw, although his trimmed beard made it quite clear that he was careful in his grooming.

If I'd had lungs, I would have held my breath. I did not know his name, but I envied his boldness.

He caught me staring and turned to me, a smile playing over his full lips. All that yellow brought out warm tones in his dark complexion. He was *beautiful.* There was no other word for it.

"And you must be Crimson Smoke, by extension," he added.

I nodded, clutching at my skirts. If only he did not have to see me in yellow. If only I could have changed my outfit like plumage, then and there, to let him see that I was the same.

The thought gave me pause. *What does that even mean?*

In moments where I did not understand my own thoughts, I

often found that they came from Emerald's mind. When I flicked a glance toward my friend, however, he was frowning at me in bewilderment.

Ah. So the thoughts were mine alone, then. Not sure what to make of my intense surge of emotion, I pretended to reach onto some secret fold of my dress and produced a fan, just so that I would have something to do with my hands. "I am indeed," I told him, several beats too late. "And who might I have the pleasure of addressing?"

The man bowed again, evidently pleased by my reaction. "Forgive the faux pas. I am called Serkadis."

"Of Kinmore?" I asked.

Serkadis winked. "Oh, my dear, if you mean to draw attention to the fact that I have no prominence title, I'm afraid you will find me quite lukewarm on the matter. I have done nothing of real import in my life, and I have no intention of starting now. I shall leave the heroics to my betters."

"You flatter us." Emerald's voice was flat and cold.

"No," I said, fluttering my fan so that the yellow lace obscured the lower half of my face. "He mocks us."

Serkadis shook his head. There was laughter in his dark eyes, but no malice. "Quite the opposite. I have heard tales of your exploits, and you have my highest admiration. I know how difficult it is to make your way through the world as an outsider."

Emerald couldn't keep in a dismissive huff as he cut his eyes away.

Serkadis's wide brows wrinkled. "You may not believe me, Emerald Flame, but I do. Come, I see we've started off on the wrong foot. Let me make it up to you."

He flagged down one of the uniformed footmen and swiped two flutes of some fizzy drink off of the tray he carried. He offered one to Emerald.

If I could, I would have slapped the drink away. Serkadis didn't know what he was offering. I would *not* sit by and watch Emerald slip into his cups again.

To my relief, my friend shook his head. "Thank you, but I don't... imbibe." He sounded calm, but I saw him press his palms to his silk-spangled thighs, wiping away a sheen of sweat.

I should have realized that this party would test his resolve, but the thought had not occurred to me until that very moment.

"Ah." Serkadis nodded in understanding. "I see. My apologies. Overindulgence makes monsters of us all. I avoid meat for that very reason—I find that it warps the mind. Alas, I cannot give up all my vices."

His reference to monsters brought out my claws, so to speak. I bared my teeth behind my fan.

[Are you really going to let him speak to your master like that?] Innocent's voice grated in my head. *[Are you going to let him call Emerald names right to his face? We could hurt him, if you wanted, slice that pretty face to ribbons, make him mewl and bawl and bleed, make him beg for forgiveness and show him none...]*

I pressed my fingers to my forehead and closed my eyes, grounding myself in the only thing that was unassailably real to me: myself. When I looked up again, Innocent was silent, and Emerald was staring at Serkadis, his lips slightly parted.

"*Oh,*" was all he said. "I see."

I certainly didn't, but given that Innocent had been howling in my ears only moments before, I was reluctant to speak to Emerald through our mental link.

Serkadis turned to me and proffered the second flute of sparkling wine. "Do you drink?" he asked.

I shook my head, not trusting myself enough to open my mouth.

"Well, then." Serkadis winced. "I see that I've made a mess of this whole exchange. Perhaps we can speak another time. In a less public setting, where we may be freer with our words." He downed one flute of wine, quickly followed by the other, as he hurried away.

"*Ass,*" I muttered in his wake.

"Nah," Emerald said. He watched Serkadis as the man disappeared into the crowd. "He's no Dirkus, I'll tell you that. Come on, let's get something to eat." He held out one arm, and I made every pretense of taking it.

As my form overlapped with his, I got a sudden glimpse of our surroundings as seen through his eyes. For a moment, I breathed deep, reveling in the smells wafting from the long table along the wall. Roasted meat, braised vegetables, fresh bread, sauces both savory and sweet, the buttery crusts of pies, the perfume of herbs and spices... I could never taste any of it, of course, but the smell was an astonishing delight.

Emerald collected a gilt plate from one end of the long buffet and made his way along the spread, selecting dishes as he went. I hung back. Since the maids and footmen were serving each guest individual portions, I had no way to *pretend* to accept anything. I would simply have to wait until Emerald was done and then conjure the illusion of my own plate from thin air, so that I could pick at a phantom meal.

I was still fantasizing about the smells I'd briefly experienced when a feminine voice spoke in my ear.

"It's dreadful, isn't it? All this food, and I can't eat a bite, or I'd risk bursting at the seams."

I turned to my left and found a plump, sweet-faced young woman hovering at my elbow. Heat rose in her cheeks as I studied her. She was taller than I was, with a full figure that, judging by the dismissive glances from the passing crowd, was not the fashion in Kinmore. Her long, wheat-gold curls were bound up in an elaborate style, and freckles peppered her rosy cheeks. The longer I stared at her, the redder those cheeks became, and despite her height, she seemed to shrink before me.

"Sorry," she blurted. "I didn't mean to bother you—"

"You didn't," I said hastily. "Bother me, I mean. Have we met?" I was quite sure we hadn't, but I was *equally* unsure of the etiquette regarding formal introductions.

"Not yet." Her cheeks darkened further still, and she twisted her hands in front of her. "I'm Rubi. Er, that is, I'm Rubigold Stonewall,

Thirteenth Heir of the House of Thorns, Future Wardeness of Fallow Lakes. But my friends call me Rubi."

"A pleasure, Rubi. I'm known as Crimson Smoke, but *my* friends call me..." I was about to say *Simone*, but I caught myself. I had a prominence title, after all. What did I need my given name for? Why couldn't I just be myself, the way Serkadis had been, regardless of social expectations? "...Crimson. For short. Where is Fallow Lakes? I've never heard of it." As the words left my mouth, I grimaced. At best, admitting that I didn't know the place might make it sound like I was ignorant of geography. At worst, it might sound like a slight.

But Rubi only laughed and tucked a stray curl behind one ear. "That's no surprise. It's an old title, and it isn't even called that anymore. You know these old families, though, we just *love* our titles." She rolled her eyes and tittered before lowering her voice. "I know all about you. Well, not everything, of course, but I've heard *all* the songs."

I pressed my lips together and arched one eyebrow. "Once again, Coirpre precedes us."

Rubi laughed again. It wasn't a delicate, affected giggle, but one that carried enough to turn a few heads and draw the attention of nearby courtiers. She immediately pressed one hand to her mouth.

"Sorry," she began, "I know that my manners aren't exactly—"

"Are the rumors true?" Another young woman strode over, with two of her friends in tow. She ignored Rubi altogether and smirked at me. "They say that jotunn don't make for good conversationalists, but he must have some *hidden* qualities that make him worth keeping around." Even as she came to a stop before me, she turned her attention to Emerald, her mouth pursed in a nasty little sneer. "Is he obedient, at least?"

I gawked at her, while Innocent's low growl started up again. *[Wretch, scum, filth... I could split her open like a sack of rubies if you let me. Turn this party red instead of yellow. You'd like that, wouldn't you?]*

Even as Innocent spoke, the girl turned toward me. "What?" Her smile widened. "Don't be coy, now. They say that you're one of the cleverest investigators in the Conjury, Crimson Smoke. But we women have our needs, don't we? Perhaps you can lend him to me for the night so that I can see for myself?"

[Bend her. Break her. She deserves it.]

I found my voice at last, and shoved Innocent away. If I was going to eviscerate this newcomer, I would do it *my* way. Instead of snarling at her, I let my eyes sweep over her, cool and slow.

"Rubi," I asked, "do you know this girl?"

A muscle jumped in Rubi's jaw. "I do indeed. This is Lady Isabella of Tenbridge Sound, Fifteenth Heir of the Lower Tidelands, and Future Wardeness of—"

I cut her off with a yawn. "So nobody important, then?"

Rubi choked on another laugh, and the smile was instantly wiped from Lady Isabella's face.

"A pity." I looked over Isabella again. "That particular shade of mustard *really* doesn't suit her, and yet from now on, I shall never be able to imagine her in anything else."

Isabella's lip curled. "How *dare* you—"

I flicked my fan shut, remembering to add a loud *snap!* to accompany the illusion. "Quiet, child," I said. "Adults are speaking. If you're bored, perhaps you can wander off and find a stray dog or two to play with. I'm told that if a cur is desperate enough for company, it'll befriend *anyone,* so I really do think that's your best bet." I offered her a simpering smile and turned my back on her, blinking up into Rubi's astonished face. "Now, Rubi, you must tell me *all about* Fallow Lakes. It sounds *fascinating.*"

Rubi's face contorted with barely suppressed glee. Behind me, the harsh *clack* of heels on stone told me that Isabella was beating a retreat.

"She's awful, isn't she?" Rubi whispered. "I've never seen anyone talk to her like that, though."

"What would she hope to get out of insulting my friend to my face?" I asked. I didn't know Rubi well enough to guess her intentions for approaching me, but I wasn't particularly interested in impressing her, anyway. If she said something awful, I would happily turn my ire on her.

"There is some... speculation." Rubi shifted from foot to foot. "About the nature of your arrangement. Knowing Isabella, she probably wanted to appear worldly. You'd be surprised how many people find her bluntness amusing. Oh, look!" She pointed to the long buffet. "They're about to open the babblebird pie!"

An immense, uncut piecrust had been wheeled out on a special cart large enough that two people had to work in tandem to pull it. As Rubi and I watched, one of the footmen unveiled a massive ornamental spoon, which he lifted above his head before bringing it down on the brittle crust like a woodman's ax.

The pastry shattered, and at least a score of live babblebirds burst free, fluttering around the room as they cried, "Long live the king!"

Some of the partygoers, like Rubi, applauded in delight. Others seemed less impressed with the display. Many of the guests didn't look up at all, as if such events were commonplace and not worthy of their attention.

In that moment, I saw the party as Emerald must have seen it. The buffet, bearing enough food to nourish half the city, picked over by guests who discarded heaping plates that they had barely touched. The banners, made of fine silk that could not be reused at the next party should the hosts decide that purple was preferable to marigold. All those handsome costumes, tailored just for tonight, would be tucked away in the wee hours and likely never worn again, while children in the lower city huddled in damp rags against the cold.

Overindulgence makes monsters of us all, Serkadis had said.

And he was right.

CHAPTER FOUR

[If you're going to sulk, you could at least try to be less obvious about it,] Emerald suggested. When he'd returned with his plate, Rubi had made her excuses and scurried away, although I couldn't gauge if her discomfort was on account of his presence or Isabella's comments. I had spent the last twenty minutes watching the crowd from behind my fan, wondering what *really* went on in their heads. My mood had irreparably soured.

"I'm not sulking," I murmured. "What are we *doing* here, Em?"

"Waiting." *[Whoever sent us that letter was a member of the royal family, and since none of them have shown their faces yet, we must be patient. We can't go barging around in their private chambers, can we?]*

[One can only imagine the sort of rumors that would spark,] I thought dismally.

Em paused with a bite of some rare meat halfway to his lips. It was pale pink in the center, the color of a fresh wound. *[Rumors?]*

[I was talking to some awful girl earlier. Or rather, she was talking to me.]

[Ah. I assume she impugned your honor?]

[I would argue that she impugned yours.]

Emerald smirked. *[I hope you talked me up. If I'm going to have a reputation as a scoundrel, I'd rather leave them jealous and intrigued.]*

I rolled my eyes at him. *[I told her that if she wanted a detailed and lyrical account of your bawdy exploits, she'd be better served by asking Coirpre.]*

Emerald choked so hard he nearly dropped his plate, and he was still trying to clear his throat when trumpets sounded from on high. Every voice in the hall fell silent, and the crowd turned as one toward the thrones deep in the cavernous room. A rather short and stocky man with a graying ginger beard mounted the steps. Unlike every other guest in attendance, he was dressed in scarlet velvet.

I didn't need Emerald to tell me that I was looking at the king of Feynlish. It was obvious: the red set him apart from the rest of us.

[Red as blood,] Innocent growled. *[Red for what he's done to this city.]*

I ignored the shadow-beast, but rather than calling me to action as it normally did, Innocent seemed to be speaking to itself.

[Under a better ruler, my mistress's mother might have lived. Reticent might not have been sent away to the Brotherhood. There might be schools for those born with Aidea. If you let me free, I would not kill him. Not right away. I would build him a prison in his own mind and make him live the life he condemns so many others to, one of hunger and helplessness and despair. I would drive him to madness. I would convince him to brick himself into some little corner of the catacombs and die slowly, from thirst and hunger, as so many others have during his reign.]

I flicked my fan a little faster, unsettled by Innocent's vehemence. This was more than a reflection of its usual anger. Even more disturbing, I thought the king might deserve it.

Maybe not the bit with the bricks, but...

The king of Feynlish settled into his throne and waved for his yellow-clad cupbearer to follow. The boy handed him a drinking horn, and the king raised it above his head.

"Good people," he said. His words carried throughout the room, either by the application of some enchantment or a clever trick of the architecture. "Ever since the passing of my late wife, your beloved queen, there has been a pall upon the castle. Her loss weighs heavy on my heart. My children are dear to me, and when they are old enough to be presented at court, they shall be dear to you—but nothing and no one can replace her. Let us have a moment of silence for those who cannot be with us today."

All around me, people bowed their heads. Couples reached for one another, clasping hands, as if afraid they would be parted on the spot. I wrinkled my nose at the display, thinking of all the people who suffered in the streets at that very moment. So much tragedy might be averted if these people used their money to improve the city rather than whiling away the winter nights throwing grand fetes.

Beside me, Emerald let out a pained sigh. *[Those who can't be here with us...]* The absence of so many people he held dear weighed on him constantly.

People like Tincrown.

Like Reticent.

Perhaps I should not be so quick to judge the people around me harshly. They were not all Isabellas, and despising them on principle would only make me more like Innocent.

The king's voice rang out again, shattering the silence. "Today, we are not here to mourn our losses. We are here to celebrate a new union. After many years as an errant bachelor, my brother, Prince Efrain, is prepared to announce his engagement. Tonight, it is my pleasure to introduce you to Mercedes of Kinmore, my future sister-in-law!"

A delighted gasp echoed through the audience, followed by a cheer that began in one corner of the room and rippled outward. A second man, perhaps thirty-five or forty years of age, strolled out from some hidden alcove with one arm lifted high above his head. He, too, was dressed in red.

It was the woman on his arm, however, who drew my eye. She was young, no more than twenty, with a river of black hair that spilled over her shoulders, obscuring her face. The underskirt of her dress was a deep claret, layered with yellow lace that climbed the bodice.

I had long viewed clothes as a means of self-expression, and it seemed the people of Feynlish felt the same. Like Serkadis's garments, this young woman's attire told a story, one that anyone in that room could understand at a glance. The monarchs of Feynlish wore one color, the lower classes another.

Only this woman wore both. This whole party had been designed around this moment, this image, this message.

The common folk of Kinmore can and will rise to prominence when necessary, our invitation had said. There had been a code in that letter, one that only made sense as I watched the future princess cross the tiles. Unlike Rubi, she had no title reaching back generations. She was the one who had summoned us to her debut, although I still did not know why.

As if she could read my thoughts, the young woman lifted her face to scan the crowd. Her eyes fixed on me and Emerald, and she nodded our way before acknowledging the room at large with a hesitant wave. An eruption of cheers greeted this small gesture.

I was so engrossed in the scene before me that at first I failed to realize the drama unfolding near the entrance of the hall. A frisson of disapproval passed through the partygoers as raised voices drew attention away from the guests of honor.

"Out of my way!" someone boomed. "Step aside, if you please. I have business with the prince, and I will not be delayed!"

"You can't carry *weapons* in the king's presence!" A harried page scurried along in the widening aisle formed by the guests as they moved aside to make room for... whoever the intruder was.

[Can you see?] I asked Emerald.

Despite looming head and shoulders above the average guest, he shrugged. *[It must be someone short...]*

He cut himself off as the intruder strutted into view. A bandolier hung over either shoulder, each supporting a shortsword. Aside from that, he was completely naked, without a stitch of yellow in sight, or anything else besides.

"He's a *krub*," I blurted.

The amphibious gentleman brandished one sticky finger toward the crown prince. "Halt there, good sir!" he cried. "Unhand that woman! She is not some prize for you to claim."

The prince glowered at him, but the rest of the party seemed delighted by this turn of events.

"It's better than a play," one man next to me murmured to his companion. "I *knew* that paying for this silly outfit would be worth it. This is going to be the talk of the season."

"I bet you thirty hogs the king has him boiled alive in front of us," his friend whispered back. "The *audacity*."

"Where did he even come from?"

"Even if he doesn't boil the krub, that blasted pageboy will find himself in hot water..."

Half a dozen guards followed in the krub's wake, looking murderous. Courtiers scrambled out of their way, but the krub ignored them entirely. He only had eyes for the prince.

Amid the rising hubbub of the court, Prince Efrain slammed his foot down on the dais. "*Silence!*" he bellowed.

The courtiers fell quiet. Efrain deposited his sad-eyed bride-to-be in one of the chairs beside the throne. Then he turned on his silk heels and trotted back down the steps to the main floor. The crowd parted in anticipation of his arrival, giving me and Emerald a front-row view of the conversation that followed. A single gesture from the prince brought the guards to a halt as well.

"Who are you?" Efrain demanded. "This is a royal event. Commoners are not welcome here."

The krub drew himself up to his full height, which was not particularly impressive; he was not the largest of his kind I'd ever encountered, and even with his muscular legs fully extended, the green dome of his head barely reached the prince's waist.

"I," he said, with all the gravitas of royalty, "am Squampf. My father was the greatest swordsman in all of Dregandresal. I may not have been invited, but I am hardly a commoner." His accent was unfamiliar to me. There was resonance on each consonant that made it sound almost as if he was keeping live bees in his cheeks.

The prince's brow wrinkled, and the fire in his eyes intensified. "You are mistaken. There are no krubs in the court of Feynlish."

I expected the interloper to retort that he was the king of some body of water within city limits. My only experience with krubs was my friendship with the king—or rather, in light of all that had occurred, the *queen*—of the Black Hollow, Burp. Krub lineage and royalty was not as fixed as that of the dry people.

Squampf made no such claims, however. Instead, he puffed out his chest. "My father is no krub, your highness. My father is Neandor of Ebreus."

[Neandor?] Emerald perked up slightly.

[Friend of yours?]

[Nah, but I've heard of him. Even met him, back in the day.] Emerald popped a small egg tart into his mouth and chewed thoughtfully. It seemed that the events unfolding before us hadn't put a damper on his appetite. *[All the best fighters pass through Venta Bulgarum sooner or later. Pretty sure he's past his prime these days. Heard a rumor he'd been injured pretty badly during a tournament a few years back.]*

The prince stood there for a long moment, glaring down at the green fellow before him. His mouth trembled with what I thought must be rage. One word, and he could have the krub's head struck from his shoulders.

"Why have you come?" Prince Efrain hissed.

"Because you, sir, have laid claim to my ladylove." Squampf gestured one three-fingered hand toward the dais. "And I cannot stand by and watch her wed another. I mean to challenge you to a *duel.*"

I had misread the prince's emotions. He was not shaking with anger, but with mirth. At this last pronouncement, he could not help himself any longer, and burst out laughing. He laughed so hard that he nearly toppled over, and tears streamed down his cheeks.

His amusement was echoed in the faces of the onlookers, who began to laugh as well. Squampf stood resolute in the midst of their mockery.

I did not laugh, and when I turned back to Emerald, he was not laughing, either. His gaze was fixed toward the front of the room, where even the king was mocking his uninvited guest.

Mercedes of Kinmore sat upright in her chair, her face a mask of solemnity, her eyes unfocused.

She is pretending to be somewhere else, I thought, although I couldn't say with any certainty how I knew that. *She has gone as far away as she possibly can.*

"You mean to challenge *me?*" The prince dabbed tears from the corners of his eyes with one scarlet sleeve. "By Celestriona's crown, what am I to make of that? I didn't know that Neandor had some spittle-flecked foundling son in his care. And you think you'll be a match for me?"

"I have killed four men before you," Squampf announced coldly. "I am more than capable."

The prince swiveled back toward his bride-to-be. "My lady, do you know this... fellow?" The mocking lilt on the last word made it clear that this was a further insult.

Mercedes's expression did not change. "Yes, my lord."

"And do you wish to marry him?"

"No, my lord." Her words were soft but bell-clear. Many members of the audience snickered. I wondered if they could not see how sad she was, or if they simply did not care.

"Does that not settle the matter?" Efrain asked.

Squampf shook his head. "Of course not, your highness. What else could she say? Could she defy you, knowing what it would cost her? Of course not. But I am a fighter, sir. She and I were friends when we were children, and friendship grew to love, before you stole her away. I will not allow it, sir. So again, I challenge you. Only a coward would decline."

If anything, this only made the prince laugh harder. "How could I decline such a request?" he exclaimed. "Squampf, son of Neandor, of the stinking city of Ebreus." He addressed the room at large, spinning on the spot to encompass the whole crowd. "What say ye? Would you like to see how a krub fights?"

Any words uttered by individual tongues were lost in the swell of bellowed assent that rose from the crowd.

"In that case, I have one condition." Efrain whirled back to face his uninvited guest. "Our contest will be to the death."

Squampf raised his chin. "I would have it no other way, Your Highness, so long as you agree to fight with blades."

Efrain clapped his hands. "Three days hence, in the gardens, at midday. Let's make a party of it."

[Not another one of these stupid color parties, I hope,] Emerald muttered into my head.

"Three days hence." Squampf flared his slitted nostrils at Efrain, then bowed twice toward the distant dais. "Until then, my king. My lady." With that, he turned back to the door and strode away, with the pageboy still chasing after him in an attempt to herd him toward the door at last.

THE PARTY CARRIED on after that, but it wasn't long before Emerald deposited his empty plate with one of the many servants and strode toward the door.

[Leaving already?] I asked as I hurried after him. *[We didn't even get a chance to speak to Mercedes. Er, the princess. Or whatever you want to call her...]*

[Nor will we. She'll be the center of attention all night. We'll find an opportunity to talk to her soon, never fear.]

He was right, I supposed, but I still hated to leave her without a single word of greeting, or even a kind gesture to indicate that someone had seen her reaction to the night's events.

Efrain had returned to her side and was talking and laughing with the courtiers who had come to wish them well. I spotted Isabella among their simpering number. Mercedes nodded and spoke and never once smiled.

Emerald was right. We would have no opportunity to speak to her plainly, not with Efrain at her side. I followed my friend out of the castle and back to where the coach waited.

The driver had wrapped his coat tight in our absence and turned his collar up to ward off the chill. The sturdy black horses at the front of the carriage stomped their hooves and shifted in their traces, which made the muscles ripple beneath their velvet fur. Each huff and exhalation sent plumes of mist rising from their nostrils.

"Leaving already?" the driver asked with some surprise.

"I'm not one for parties," Emerald grumbled back, and heaved himself up into the interior with such force that the whole conveyance rocked sideways. I followed after him without, of course, affecting the balance of the vehicle at all.

The moment we were inside, Emerald ripped the stiff lace collar from his neck and tossed it to the carriage floor. "Gods," he grumbled, "what a miserable night."

I didn't reply. The coach jerked into motion, but I sat perfectly still, staring at the window, but seeing only the blank, defeated expression on Mercedes of Kinmore's face.

CHAPTER FIVE

The morning after the king's party, Emerald found me downstairs, seated by one of the Lute and Goose's windows at a round table suitable for two. There was frost on the pane, and despite the early hour, a handful of guests populated the dining room. Most of them were local laborers who, according to their conversation with Yerik, had been up since dawn and, I quote, "*Damn near frozen our arses off clearin' 'em roads.*" They'd come for breakfast and were lingering by the fire, chatting about sheep and weirlings and how much grain they had put by for the winter.

In an attempt to blend in with the local color, I had conjured myself a mug of my own, as well as the wafts of steam that rose above its surface. Occasionally, I took a sip, just to sell the illusion. I wished that it tasted like *something*, but I had little enough experience with taste that I couldn't effectively imagine what drinking a hot beverage might be like.

"So." Emerald dropped into the chair across from me with such force that the legs creaked. "I've been thinking. We ought to talk to both of them."

I glanced up sharply from my steaming mug. "Who is *both*?"

"Mercedes and Squampf," Emerald clarified. "And I suspect that it will be easier to find time alone with the latter than with the former."

[As long as you don't mean Prince Efrain,] I thought. Innocent had been suspiciously quiet since we left the party, but I didn't think it would be a good idea for me to seek out the prince's company, in part because I was inclined to agree with Innocent's unflattering assessment of the royal family.

Someone ought to teach them a lesson.

Right on cue, Innocent chimed in. *[And who better than us? We are a phantom, Crimson Smoke. We can come and go as we please. You know what I am capable of... only imagine what the two of us might do together...]*

"Aster's sake, no." Emerald snorted. "But I think we could learn something from the krub." **[And settle down with that steam, Crim, there's no way a cup would stay hot that long even if it was boiling when it arrived.]**

I pretended to blow on my cup and dismissed the steam as I did. I should have realized that—I could still *see* how tea behaved in the real world, even if I couldn't experience it for myself. It always annoyed me when I got the details wrong.

"What do you hope to learn from Squampf?" I asked.

Emerald sat back in his chair and threw one arm over the backrest. He managed to lounge *and* hunch at the same time. Truly, my friend was a man of many talents. "It might be a coincidence that we were invited to an exclusive party the same night that a krub challenged the prince to a duel to the death. Then again, it might not. Either way, talking to Squampf will be educational, if nothing else."

Yerik emerged from the kitchen with another plate of pastries and was greeted with a cheer from his patrons. When he saw Emerald, he excused himself and hurried over to our corner.

"Are you hungry?" he asked, in a slightly breathless voice. "Can I get you anything?"

Emerald shook his head. "No, but maybe you can tell us something. Ever heard of a fellow named Neandor?"

"The swordsman?" Yerik's smile faded. "Of course. Even met him a few times. He used to come around for a drink, when he first moved in, but he's... well, I expect you'll want to talk to him, if you're asking. Is it for a case?"

Emerald and I nodded in tandem.

"I'll tell you where to find him, then," Yerik said. "But I can't guarantee a warm reception."

In the course of my short life, I had come to the conclusion that people lived in one of three main conditions: the wealthy, like the King of Feynlish and Laird Fenguard, who reveled in finery and extravagance; those like Yerik, Tincrown, the farmers on the fringes of Kinmore, and the folk of Dyrne, who lived modestly but wanted for little; and others, far too numerous, whose livelihoods were hand-to-mouth, and whose means were not sufficient to ensure their comfort, or even their survival.

Neandor's home was of a different kind. It was set far away from the road, along the banks of the river that bordered Kinmore to the west and fed into Bracken Bay. The surrounding farmlands were well-kept, with small, neat houses and freshly painted outbuildings half buried in snowfall. Yerik's directions took us past the farmlands and into a grove of spindly, barren trees.

Emerald crunched through the iced-over snow, but I stopped at the roadside.

"Surely he doesn't mean *there*," I said, wrinkling my nose at the hut that lay beyond. It slanted to one side, and the roof balanced on top of the pockmarked boards at an unsettling angle. I would have thought the place abandoned if not for the smoke that rose from the crumbling chimney.

"Yerik warned us about the state of things." Emerald pressed on without waiting for me.

With some reluctance, I followed. At least I'd had the sense to adopt a less conspicuous appearance than usual, although even my woolen greatcoat and burgundy walking dress were out of place in that grim copse.

Emerald knocked on the door three times and waited, with his hands cupped around his mouth for warmth, exhaling loudly with each breath.

[Gloves exist, you know. And you still don't own a hat.]

He glared at me. *[Thank you for the reminder, mum.]*

[A cap might ruin your air of brooding mystery, but those massive ears of yours are liable to freeze off if you don't cover them. I suppose Tincrown might still love you if you had blackened nubs on either side of your head, but why take the risk?]

Emerald opened his mouth to protest at the same moment that the door was yanked wide, nearly coming off its hinges in the process.

The man on the other side was very thin, almost skeletally so, with dark and haunted eyes that stared out from his shrunken face. Despite his emaciated state, he held a sword in one hand, its tip level with Emerald's gut.

"Go away," he snarled. "There's nothing to steal."

Emerald looked from the man to the blade and back again. "Is Squampf home?"

The man in the door reeled back a pace. "Who are you?"

"Did the prince send you?" another voice called from within.

Emerald and I exchanged a glance. "No," I called back. "We're... friends of Mercedes?"

Emerald raised an eyebrow at me, but it seemed that this was the correct response. Neandor let the tip of his blade fall to the weathered floorboards and stepped aside to let us pass. "If you lay a hand on anything," he muttered, "I'll spit you both like daw-hares."

[Let him try to spit us,] Innocent growled. *[Let him see what happens...]*

I could not imagine wanting to touch anything in that house. I slipped through the door, with Emerald just behind me, and tried not to grimace at the state of things. The condition of the hut, if it could even be called that, reminded me too much of the room Emerald had rented in Upper Bound at his lowest point. Empty bottles were clustered in heaps around the place, and what little food there was had been left out to mold. A bed stood in one corner, with tatty sheets arranged like a nest on the threadbare mattress. The only welcoming aspect of the place was the fire burning in the kitchen hearth.

Next to the fire stood a large copper kettle, in which Squampf was ensconced. His skinny arms dangled over the sides, and his head lolled against the rim of the pot. The twin bandoliers and the swords they contained hung from an iron hook nearby.

Unlike Neandor, Squampf exuded an aura of utter relaxation. For the man, such living conditions suggested malaise. For the krub, they contained everything one might need: standing water, a fire to keep that water from freezing over, and a ready source of flies and pests that would provide valuable nourishment.

Seeing the silver lining of their arrangement somehow made the house even more depressing than before.

"Mercedes sent you?" Squampf sat up so quickly that a bit of his bathwater splashed over the edge of the pot.

"Not exactly," I conceded. "She reached out to us for help, and since it seems that you and she are an item—"

"This nonsense again?" Neandor snorted. He slid the blade into the sheath at his belt and limped over to his bed, the edge of which provided the only seating in the room. The way he moved suggested that the injury that had cut his career short, so to speak, had not healed properly. He raked his greasy hair out of his eyes and glared at us. "Putting ideas in his head, are you?" Had he spat at our feet, his disgust could not have been more apparent.

"I'm going to save her," Squampf insisted.

Neandor snorted. "Royals take what they want, boy. You really think they'll let her leave? That the prince will risk his life in a fair and honest duel? Those royal pricks will stab you in the back and congratulate themselves for having done so."

[Yes, yes,] Innocent purred, *[that's why it's best to stab them first…]*

I shifted nervously and cleared my throat.

Neandor's eyes snapped back to my face. "Aye, you heard me. Call it treason if you like, I don't care. Report me. You're Conjury folk. Don't lie, I remember *you*." He jerked his chin toward Emerald. "Met you before, Inspector, though I doubt you recall it."

Emerald nudged an empty bottle with the toe of his boot. "I remember."

"Then you know how far a man can fall. How much he can lose. If the prince wants my head for speaking ill of him, he'll take that, too."

Squampf sighed. I suspected that this was not the first time he'd heard Neandor speak against the crown. "I know," he said. "But a man's got to fight for what he believes in…"

"Else he's not a man at all." The sharp angles of Neandor's face softened slightly as he returned his attention to the krub. "You're a good lad, Squampf. I hate to see you throw your life away, but I can't fault you for doing what you must." He waved one hand at us. "Ask your questions, then."

My job, as usual, was to open doors. Having done so, I deferred to Emerald for the investigative portion of the conversation.

"What can you tell me," Emerald asked, "about Mercedes?"

Squampf's eyes took on the distant, dreamy quality that Burp's had when my friend spoke of the Black Hollow. "I've known her since we were children," he sighed. "I've loved her since… oh, since the first moment I laid eyes on her! Neandor taught me everything a man must know, but to watch her plait the strands of a fishing net, or speak the names of the constellations, or list the uses of common plants and point out local birds, *that* is something special." He sighed again and paddled his webbed feet behind him. "She makes me long to be a better version of myself."

I snuck Emerald a sidelong glance and found him prodding the bottle with his toe again. I didn't need a mental link to know what face the krub's lovesick monologue brought to mind.

"Poor boy's besotted," Neandor sighed. "I've tried to convince him it's useless, but—"

"She doesn't want to marry him!" Squampf cried. "At the very least, she shouldn't have to marry a man just because he can afford to wear a gold hat!"

"Crown," Neandor protested.

"It's the same thing," the krub retorted. "The only difference is that people *believe* there's a difference."

"And the people who believe it are willing to kill those who disagree, so watch your tongue, boy." I suspected that they were so used to being the only two people in the room that they'd forgotten our presence entirely.

"How did you two..." I pointed between them and tried to find a diplomatic way to ask my question. The basics of biology were still a mystery to me, but I was fairly certain that krubs and humans were not... compatible.

"Found him as a krubibie," Neandor said fondly. "All alone, swept downstream from a hatching pool, I reckon. Didn't know much about krubs, or babies of any kind for that matter, but he didn't seem to mind. Only thing he could say in those days was his name. Took him to the vernal pond and waited; come that summer, he'd gotten legs, and here we are."

The krub didn't seem sad about his lot in life. I wondered if, far upstream, some worried krub-mother fretted over the fate of her lost son, or if she'd taken her lot in the same stride as Squampf took his. I didn't know many mothers, and a mere one of them was a krub. I could only speculate as to the general attitudes of the species.

I did know one thing: hearing their story made me view Neandor in a new light. He might not have the wherewithal to care for himself, but he'd extended kindness to something small and helpless when he didn't have to. I respected that more than any tale of bloodshed and swordplay he could have recounted.

"Where would you take Mercedes, if the two of you left?" I asked. I doubted the answer would have any bearing on our investigation, but I wanted to know for my own sake. "Let's say you defeat the prince and the king honors his word." Emerald and Neandor both uttered skeptical grunts. The swordsman glanced at my friend in surprise, reassessing him. I pressed on. "*If* that happened, where would you go?"

Squampf braced one elbow on the edge of the tub, cradled his chin in his hand, and stared off into the distance. "Wherever she wanted. Wherever we could be together. I only want to save her."

Neandor averted his eyes from the krub's face and pushed himself to his feet. "We're done here. Out with you, Emerald Flame, we all know whose side you're on."

I could feel Emerald's burning desire to protest his loyalties, but there was nothing to be gained—and much to lose—by revealing his personal politics to a stranger. A stranger who would, I was sure, sell us out wholesale if he thought it would help his son. He let Neandor crowd him toward the door without protest.

I hung back, which didn't seem to bother our host. With the two of them gone, I was able to speak to Squampf on my own for a moment.

"Have you really killed four men?" I asked.

Squampf's demeanor changed abruptly. He raised his blunt little chin in defiance. "I have," he said, and from the cold flash in his gold-limned eyes, I believed him. "I may look like a krub, but my father raised me as a man, and a man does what he must."

"Ah." I nubbled my bottom lip. In the walls of my mind-cottage, Innocent let out a bark of approval. [*This one understands... the price of living is blood, and someone else must be made to pay it.*]

I made to move away, but I stopped before I reached the open door. "Master Squampf?"

He squinted at me. "Yes, Inspector?"

I licked my lips and wondered how much treason I was willing to commit. In that shabby, slantwise cottage, it was hard to feel reverence for an indifferent crown. A golden hat, as Squampf had called it. I was inclined to agree.

"We saw you last night," I said. "At the palace. When you challenged the prince."

Squampf's eyes narrow further still.

"I just wanted you to know..." I stuffed my hands into the pockets of my greatcoat. "We didn't laugh."

An expression of startled surprise settled onto Squampf's blunt features. He soon composed himself, but I had seen his relief, and that my words mattered even if he would prefer they didn't.

"That's kind of you to say, Inspector."

"Good luck," I said, knowing full well that his good fortune would mean the prince's death.

[And? Let him bleed. Too many have paid the price for his lavish lifestyle. Let me out, Crimson Smoke, let me help. We will make him suffer, as his kind made my mistress suffer, as the sharp-tongued bastards and bastardesses of the court wish upon your master...]

I did my best to ignore Innocent's ravings as I stepped back out into the snow. Neandor and Emerald stood a few dozen paces from the hut, speaking in low voices.

"—know he doesn't stand a chance," Emerald said as I approached.

"You think I don't know that?" Neandor demanded. He gestured sharply toward the city, where the outline of the castle stood stark against the gray winter sky. "You think I don't *realize* what they're capable of?" This time, he really *did* spit into the snow at Emerald's feet. "The Conjury, the kingdom, what does it matter? They only see us as resources they can burn through like fuel. That poor girl doesn't stand a chance, either, but someone needs to stand up to them, to remind them that they're not all-powerful. To remind the *people* that the royals aren't gods."

Emerald held up his hands. "I hear you. All I'm saying is, there might be another way..."

"Your way?" Neandor spat. His voice had risen to a volume that frightened the birds out of the barren trees. "Bow and scrape and take their coin? Rebuild the system from the inside? Is that your plan?"

Emerald opened his mouth, but Neandor cut him off.

"And here I thought you were supposed to be a smart one, Inspector. Scales of Dekaios, you're as bad as all the rest." He whirled away and shuffled past me, back toward the door of his hut. He slammed it behind him with such force that the walls rattled and a heap of snow slid off the uneven roof.

[Yerik was right about the greeting,] I thought.

[Yeah, well.] Emerald turned away and began the trek back to the main road. *[When I'm in his shoes, I expect I'll feel the same way.]*

It was disconcertingly easy to imagine a future in which Emerald, fallen from what little grace the Conjury had offered him, was holed up alone in some dilapidated hut with only wine for company.

Not now, I promised us both. *Not now that I can help. If the Conjury lets him go, we'll return to Dyrne. He won't end up like this.*

Even so, Neandor's parting words weighed on my friend all the way back to the Lute and Goose. Insults like the ones hurled by Isabella of Tenbridge Sound, or by Dirkus of wherever-he-came-from, were bad enough, but at least they were born out of malice rather than truth.

Neandor's words cut deeper, in part because we both suspected he was right.

CHAPTER SIX

"Have you heard about this nonsense with the royal duel?" Commander Finch asked.

Emerald glanced up from the paperwork she'd laid before him. "Between the prince and the krub, you mean?"

Finch growled. I'd heard Emerald make a similar sound of annoyance before, but her Leonhite anatomy made her capable of particularly deep and resonant rumblings. "Don't know why he agreed to it. The whole city's losing their collective minds. The crown can provide their own security, but I don't think they've got any sense of how much work this makes for us."

[What is she talking about?] I asked Emerald. As usual in Finch's presence, I had spent the last hour or so staring at the wall without speaking to anyone.

Finch was making notes on her own files. Her fur was more rumpled than usual, and her tail twitched every few seconds, belying her agitation.

"I take it the populace has a vested interest in the outcome?" Emerald asked, partly in answer to my own query.

"Gods, yes." Finch rumbled again and tugged at one feline ear.

"As if they weren't riled up enough by the announcement of his engagement to a *peasant.*"

Emerald sat back and folded his hands over his stomach. "You don't approve."

Finch flicked both ears back and lifted her eyes from the paperwork at last. "It's not my place to approve or disapprove of the crown," she snapped. "The Conjury has no say over the king or the prince's behavior."

Emerald gazed across the table at her with the same blank expression that I'd adopted all morning.

"...but I would prefer," Finch eventually added, "if the royal family would resist the urge to rile up the populace. He could have sent the krub away. Locked him up for a few days as punishment. Hell after hell, *banish* him for all I care. This, however, is madness."

"Because the people are taking the krub's side?" Emerald asked.

Finch's nostrils flared and her ears pressed flat to her skull. "What do you think? That his plan to elevate an ordinary person will win over the Pruvs, or endear him to the beggars scraping by in the Hives?"

I didn't know what a Pruv was, but I knew what she meant by "the Hives." The poorest districts in Kinmore looked more like honeycombs than houses.

Emerald nudged one of the files with his finger and examined Finch. Neither of us knew quite what to make of her. On one hand, she was an agent of the Conjury and could destroy Emerald's career —and possibly his life—if he revealed too much to her. On the other, occasional conversations of this nature suggested that she was not entirely loyal to the cause.

I felt the moment when my friend decided to risk a dose of honesty. "I doubt that the crown cares very much about the attitudes of the people, as opposed to the feelings of the court. If they continue to believe that the king respects them, and might elevate them at a whim, they'll side with him."

"Which still doesn't explain why his brother has agreed to a brawl with a spitlick," Finch muttered. "And if the Hives rise up and cause mayhem? Whose hide do you think *that'll* come out of?"

The conversation was cut short when the door of Finch's office swung open to reveal one of the many purple-clad Conjury secretaries who staffed the offices. "Pardon me, Captain, but there's another shipment of goods heading north that want inspecting."

"Lemda's bloody bandages, another one?" Finch groaned as she pushed to her feet. "One Conjury member gets it into his head that someone's smuggling intel north, and now there's another job on my plate..."

She stomped off, still grumbling, and slammed the door in her wake.

The instant she was gone, I let myself relax and wriggled around a bit. I was bored nearly to the point of madness. *[How much longer do we have to be here?]*

[Until dark, at least.]

I stifled a groan. *[Will it really take you another few hours?]*

Emerald rubbed his eyes. *[No. I could have given her answers an hour ago, if I wanted. Another snakebite... another jealous lover... this fellow was killed by a rival luthier... this woman was clearly poisoned, most likely by the wine, although I can't be sure, and anyway she's made a full recovery... as for this one? Simple. Dirt steak.]*

I blinked at him. *[I beg your pardon?]*

[It's ambiguous,] came the terse reply.

His agitation was obvious, and since I had no idea what in Aster's name he was talking about, I moved on. *[Then why not tell her that?]*

[Aren't you listening?] Emerald snorted and rolled his eyes at me. *[The crown has increased their security. If we're going to sneak onto the palace grounds, better to do so under cover of darkness. I can't cast a proper illusion on myself without dispelling you, and I know how you hate that, so we'll have to improvise.]*

My irritation at his useless answers faded. Emerald might be in a sour mood, but he was taking precautions to avoid abusing my trust.

I appreciated that more than words could convey.

Night fell early in midwinter. The clerks and secretaries were still wrapping up their final tasks of the evening when Emerald and I finally made our departure.

"I appreciate your dedication," Finch told Emerald as he passed the last of the files back to her. He was out of his chair and reaching for his coat before she spoke again. "May I ask you something? Out of professional curiosity."

My friend shrugged on his greatcoat. "Is this off the record, then?"

Finch's black lips twitched upward to bare her canines. Leonhite smiles were unsettling, to say the least. "Of course. I just wonder... why keep your illusion present? Why not dispel it when you're here?"

Emerald took his time adjusting the collar of his coat. "It would look odd, wouldn't it, if the two of us walked in and this one suddenly vanished." He tipped his chin toward me. "You've got staff that come and go. Surely not *all* of them know what we are."

Finch hummed her agreement and spared me a once-over before returning to her papers.

Being referred to as "*it*" bothered me. Finch's comment wasn't meant to wound; she thought she knew what I was, and she had every reason to believe that I was nothing more than a construct of air and light. In her mind, she could no more offend me than she might offend a rainbow, or a waft of steam rising from her soup.

I should have been glad, given that our safety depended on her continued ignorance. I should have worn that "*it*" like a badge of pride.

That, at any rate, was what I told myself as I followed Emerald out of the Conjury's offices and into the street.

[We'll start out as though we're headed back to the inn, then

circle around toward the castle. I'm not sure how close I can get, but as long as we're close enough to keep our tether intact, that shouldn't be an issue... you'll have to be the one to speak with her.]

He didn't seem to have noticed my mood, and knowing how people spoke to him, I decided against complaining. He'd weathered worse than a single, accidental insult. Asking him to comfort me would hardly have been fair.

[If you need to free up your Lightweaving, I'll wait in the mind-cottage,] I told him. *[I don't mind, so long as we discuss it first.]*

[Duly noted. For now, though, I don't think that will be necessary. For all Finch's complaining, there wasn't much security on the castle grounds the other night. The building itself is another matter; I wouldn't make it three paces without setting off one of their enchantments, but I expect it's hard to maintain that level of security on the grounds at large.]

[Is this entirely speculation?] I asked.

Emerald cast me a disgruntled glare. *[Of course not. While you were busy gossiping with the other guests, I was paying attention. That krub wouldn't have been able to sail through the doors on any other night, but the wards were disabled for the party. That's why they had to hire all those extra Augurs as security. Didn't you notice?]*

[Well...]

[I swear, Crimson, if I still doubted that you had a mind of your own, your consistent disinterest in the relevant details would serve as proof.]

I bit back a smile. So Emerald *had* noticed that something was off after our conversation with Finch. Gods forbid he try to make me feel better by being *nice*... but insults worked, when they came from him. Let Finch think of me as a mindless poppet. At least my friends knew better.

[Someday,] I promised him, *[one of our cases will hinge on an intimate knowledge of fashion, and you'll eat your words.]*

Ahead of me, in the darkness, Emerald snorted. *[Whatever you have to tell yourself.]*

The sky was clear, with no clouds to block our view of the frozen stars, and no fresh snow to preserve Emerald's bootprints. Not a soul who could help it was out in that bitter cold. Even Emerald, whose bulk—as well as, I suspected, his jotunn nature—usually rendered him indifferent to the cold, shivered in the frigid wind.

We reached the low wall that surrounded the castle gardens and crouched beside it.

[Check the other side,] Emerald told me.

I rearranged myself into that of a small red fox and slipped through the wall. There was a guard hut not too far away, and I padded over the frozen ground where two soldiers dressed in the scarlet and saffron of the Feynlish flag were stationed.

"Gods-cursed wind cuts right through you," one of them grumbled. He was a younger man, hardly a man at all. A bowless was strapped to one shoulder, but unlike Emerald, he'd been smart enough to don thick gloves and a frumpy knit cap that looked as though a child had made it.

His companion was an older woman, though only her face was visible beneath her many warming layers. Judging by their hunched postures, the small fire that burned between them wasn't enough to stave off the biting chill.

"You get used to it," she said. "Here, Shona sent me off with a canister of hot bone broth. That'll warm you right up."

She poured them each a mug of the thin liquid.

[If you come over the wall now, I don't think they'll notice,] I told Emerald. *[They're a good way off and preoccupied for the moment.]*

The boy accepted a cup of broth and sighed. "Oh, that's good. Wish I had a wife at home to cook for me..."

The woman snorted. "Well, you can't have mine, but let me know if you want another cup. There's plenty."

Behind me, Emerald grunted as he heaved himself over the wall.

A moment later, he landed with a dull thump. Both guards tensed and reached for their weapons.

"What was that?" the boy asked.

His counterpart snatched up a torch and plunged it into their little fire. Once it was lit, she held it out, squinting into the darkness. I stretched my legs and turned my head, letting my eyes flash as if they reflected the firelight.

"Just a fox," she said with a chuckle. "Poor thing, it's awfully small. Here, kit, are you hungry? Not much to eat this time of year. Why aren't you in your burrow?"

I could sense Emerald moving away along the wall behind me, just another shadow among the garden hedges. I took a step closer to the guard, feigning wariness, in the hopes that she would fix her attention on me.

She walked away from the fire, still holding the torch aloft. Halfway to me, she squatted down and nestled her cup upright in the snow, then retreated a few steps. Her eyes never left me.

"That'll warm your belly, if you want it. Come on, kit. There's marrow in there, and salt, too."

I advanced again and made a show of sniffing the cup, watching her the way a wild beast might have done.

[I'm clear,] Emerald told me.

I spun away and bolted into the darkness of the gardens. The young guard's voice echoed behind me. "Off it goes! Dunno what you thought would happen, Mav, or why you'd want to waste good food like that."

"It's cold," Mav replied. "And the poor little devil looked half-starved…"

Their voices faded behind me as I fled deeper into the gardens. Emerald was waiting for me along the castle wall.

[Good distraction,] he thought. *[Glad I didn't dispel you earlier, by the way. I don't know if you've noticed the wards. If I tried to summon my Aidea here, it would snuff out my casting and bring every guard in place running. That's clever of them. Makes it so*

that their charms and protections work just fine, but stops anyone from casting unauthorized magic on the grounds...]

He babbled on for a bit about the mechanics of the wards. My mind, however, lingered on the two guards. They were just... people. Ordinary people, decent people, who were willing to share what little they had while the royals squatted in their castle, draped in gold and drowning in excess.

Life would be easier, I mused, *if people were less complicated.*

From within the recess of my mind, Innocent chuckled. *[Everyone has secrets. Everyone has darkness inside them.]*

As if I was any exception, when I played host to a monster.

My usual form as a redwing blackbird might have aroused suspicion if I was spotted, given the season. When I adjusted myself into a creature with wings, therefore, I chose the form of a small, red-feathered owl.

[I'll be down here,] Emerald told me, *[squatting in the herb garden.]* The rest of the grounds lay dormant, but some clever Vulcanist had laid a warming enchantment over the cook's garden, and the poisoner's garden beyond. I wondered if the gardener who tended the beds was an Augur, like Amaya, who had grown many of the same herbs back on Kovin Isle.

While Emerald lurked, I took to the skies and circled the castle in search of the princess-to-be. This was easier said than done, given the sprawling layout of the architecture. It took me the better part of an hour to find the rooms set aside for Mercedes of Kinmore.

[There.] I swooped down onto the edge of a balcony. Through the large, mullioned windows, I could just make out a familiar silhouette. Mercedes was hunched on a chaise by the fire, with her knees drawn up to her chin and her black hair spilling around her shoulders in untamed waves. *[I've found her. Any suggestions for how to approach without scaring her half to death?]*

[I'm the one with the brains, you're the one with charisma. Figure it out.]

[Rude,] I scolded.

[And now I'm the one freezing my arse off while you fiddle about!]

I perched there for a moment, considering my options. Popping into her room in any of my human forms was out of the questions, but in my many animal forms, I couldn't speak.

But why not? I thought suddenly. *A cat, for example, doesn't have the anatomy to speak, but I don't have anatomy at* all. *What's stopping me?*

One of the peculiarities of my condition was that my limitations were often self-imposed. The laws of *Aidea* dictated certain things I could do. Or could *not* do, such as engage in touch, taste, or other forms of interaction with the world around me. On the other hand, as a human, I could do many things that other humans could not. Why shouldn't the same logic apply to my other forms?

Might as well test that theory. I sprang off the railing, contorting myself into a different shape as I did so.

Mercedes did not notice the fat, bright-red toad that hopped through the doors separating her room to the balcony. She did not notice the improbable leap that toad made from the floor to the arm of her *chaise.* She did not notice me at all, in fact, until I said, "Mercedes?"

Her tear-dampened face whipped toward me, and she let out a yelp of shock. This was followed by a spasm of her limbs that sent her tumbling to the floor.

"Sorry," I said sheepishly. "I didn't mean to startle you."

Mercedes brushed her hair away from her face and sat up to study me. In the high hall, during her introduction, she had seemed an almost otherworldly beauty. Up close, in a plain white nightdress, with her hair loose and no makeup or glamor to augment her, I could make out the pimples on her chin, the dark hollows under her eyes, the puffiness of her eyelids. She did not look like a queen. She looked like a girl, and a frightened one at that. A girl who had spent the evening crying. Alone.

[How's it going?] Emerald asked.

[Extremely well,] I fibbed. *[Give me a minute.]*

Mercedes inched closer. "Who are you?" she asked. "*What* are you?"

"I'm Crimson Smoke," I said. "You, um, you wrote to us. For help, I think."

"You got my letter." Her dark eyes widened. "You understood. When you left the party, I thought... well, it doesn't matter what I thought. You're here! Can you help me get away?"

"That's the plan!" I spoke with conviction, despite the fact that Emerald and I had yet to formulate anything resembling a plan to facilitate her escape. "We can get you out of here, reunite you with Squampf, and then—"

"Squampf?" Mercedes wrinkled her nose.

"Yesssss..." I drew the word out, wondering what I'd missed. "We spoke to him yesterday. Aren't you, um..."

"Madly in love?" Mercedes buried her face in her hands. "That's what he told you, isn't it."

"That was the gist of the conversation, yes." I tipped my head to the side. "Am I wrong?"

"Squampf is my friend," she said. "Nothing more."

"Since childhood?"

She dropped her hands. "*His* childhood. Neandor found him last summer. I was sixteen, and he was—" Mercedes gestured helplessly.

"He was a boneless little tadpole of a fellow," I supplied.

"He didn't even have legs!" She flopped sideways against the chaise. "And then he got bigger, and if you've met Neandor, you know how *he* is. All he ever talks about is fighting and being a man. It isn't right, being raised like that. My own da was..." Mercedes sniffed and rubbed the lace sleeve of her nightdress beneath her nose. "Hard. Not cruel, but not kind either. And Squampf had *never* known kindness."

"So you pitied him?" I asked, still trying to smooth out the rough edges of my understanding.

"No." She sniffled again. "I understood him. He's dear to me, that's true enough, but it's not *love*. Not for me. If I stay here, the prince will—" She shook her head. "I know what he'll do. He'll do whatever he likes, because there's no one to stop him. But with Squampf, I was practically a mother, and now he wants me as a wife. Krubs only live so long. I'd become his caretaker before the end, and then be left alone." Mercedes took a few shuddering breaths. "I don't want to spend my whole life in the role of either a trinket or a nurse-maid. I want to decide things for myself. I want to go to, oh, to one of the bardic colleges! Or apprentice as an herbalist! I want to choose what I do, and who I do it with." She let out a sob. "Not let two men battle over who gets to decide my future!"

I hopped closer. "I understand that. Well, not the part with men battling over me. But I do know what it's like to be beholden to someone. Even if you love him, being beholden forever is a dismal prospect."

Mercedes wiped her eyes and sat up straighter. "Does that mean you'll still help me?"

"Of course." Silently, I added, *[Did you get all that, Em?]*

[All of it.] My friend sounded slightly disgruntled. *[Bardic college? Aster's sake, she really* is *a child. The last thing Dregandresal needs is another Coirpre galivanting around. That's her affair, though. As for how to get her out, I have an idea, but you'll need to ask her something.]*

"Mercedes," I asked aloud, paraphrasing Emerald's query, "is there anyone in the castle you can trust? Someone loyal who won't report you to the king?"

She nodded. "I'm a follower of Lemda. Efrain says she's a peasant's goddess, but he brought in one of her priestesses so that I may continue to honor my patroness."

"And this priestess—"

"Her name is Oreia, and she's the only person in the castle I can trust." A shy smile stole onto Mercedes's face. "Except for you, I suppose."

[A priestess of Lemda? That's lucky. And perfect. I need you to repeat everything I'm about to say, and to do it very carefully. That means you need to pay attention to the details, Crim.]

[I'm listening.]

Over the course of the next quarter of an hour, I explained Emerald's plan to Mercedes in excruciating detail. By the time I left, the girl was weeping again, not in despair, but in relief.

CHAPTER SEVEN

Emerald spent the morning of the duel huddled in the corner table that was well on its way to becoming our usual haunt. The morning brought the sun with it, and the icicles that trailed from the inn's roof had already begun to melt in the gray winter light.

Every chair in the inn was full, and Yerik, Svelte, and Quell were frantically shuttling a steady supply of hot drinks, pastries, and what looked like porridge out of the kitchen and onto the tables. Blare had confined himself to the kitchen; some of the regulars had learned the hand signs that were his primary form of communication, but on busy days, guests who didn't know better sometimes shouted orders as he passed without giving him the chance to read their lips. When the inn was full, he preferred to help from the back of the house.

The sun had been up for nearly an hour when a new guest stumbled through the door.

"The princess," he gasped. "The princess! Have you heard?"

Those seated closest to the door turned to face him. One woman got to her feet and offered him her chair, although it became clear at once that she expected gossip in exchange.

"Catch your breath, love," she said. "What's this about the princess? Fainted before the duel, has she? Scales of Dekaios, can you imagine having two men come to blows over your hand? Even if one of them *is* more animal than human."

"Aye," snorted one of her companions, "and the other's a krub."

A wave of raucous laughter swept the room, and even Emerald chuckled, although he disguised it by taking a sip of the tea he'd been nursing all morning.

The newcomer only sobbed. "She's dead."

The laughter ended abruptly. "Who's dead?" the woman asked.

"The princess. They found her in her chambers this morning, not breathing, heart stopped, cold to the touch. Poisoned."

"Mere rumors!" the woman spat. "Can't be true."

"'Ent rumors," the newcomer insisted. "My niece works in the castle. She saw the body with her own eyes."

"That poor thing." I didn't see the speaker, but their sentiment was echoed across the room by a dozen other voices.

"Just a girl. 'Ent right."

"She was one of us."

"Still *is* one of us. You think she did it herself?"

"*I* would, if it's a choice between a grave and the prince's bed."

"Unless the prince *did it*..."

At the suggestion of murder, every patron of the inn began speaking at once. In the midst of the hubbub, Emerald got to his feet and made for the door. I followed close behind.

[It sounds like it worked,] I told him.

[So far,] Emerald agreed. **[Now we just need to warn Squampf and head to the castle.]**

In the light of the winter sun and the relief of our burgeoning success, our walk to Neandor's hut seemed to take half the time it had before. Just before we reached the copse of trees, however, Emerald stopped short.

"What?" I peered over his shoulder. "What's the ma—"

The word died before I could finish it, and it took my satisfaction with it. Neandor's hut was gone. The copse was empty. The only sign that it had ever stood there was a trampled pile of old, splintered boards, shredded rags, and muddy bootprints in the swiftly melting snow.

*[I should have reached **out last night,**]* Emerald thought. He had taken up residence on one of the benches in the palace gardens. The gates were thrown wide, and a crush of observers filled every walkway. Layman, nobles, scholars from the guild colleges, Conjury officials, and guards rubbed elbows. Enchanted braziers full of *Aidea*-fueled fire provided some warmth and added a touch of festive cheer at odds with the tense atmosphere. Mercedes's name was on everyone's lips, and rumors about Prince Efrain were passed from mouth to ear in an endless and untraceable chain.

Nobody was concerned with Squampf.

[When would we have gone? It was nearly midnight by the time we returned to the inn, never mind the hours you spent in the kitchen making sure this plan would work. You couldn't have done more.] I hovered alongside my friend in a muted gray coat that would, I hoped, draw no attention.

Emerald wrinkled his nose. ***[You're telling me you** don't *feel* **guilty?]***

I did not reply, which was in and of itself an answer.

The whispers around us faded, and people stood a little straighter, looking toward the castle door even before the prince entered their line sight. By the time he came into view, the courtyard was eerily silent. There was no sign of the king.

[Because he knows that unrest among the people only ends when heads roll,] Innocent purred.

I brushed at my shoulder, as if the motion might shoo the voice away. Innocent sounded closer than usual. It was as if the walls of the mind-cottage had suddenly thinned, and rather than speaking through a brick wall, Innocent could address me through open bars.

[You know that this is wrong, Crimson Smoke. You know what is coming. I told you: the price of living is blood, and the people require a sacrifice. Did you really think the prince would foot the bill? No, you're smarter than that. You're naive, not stupid.]

My throat bobbed as the prince mounted the stone steps of a raised platform in the center of the garden, in full view of the assembly. The structure reminded me of the mud mound upon which Squelch and Burp had battled for the title of king. That struggle had been born of honor and ended in unity.

I doubted this battle would conclude so happily. Assuming Squampf was even still alive.

"Citizens of Feynlish," Efrain bellowed. "By now, you must have heard the news. My beloved bride-to-be was murdered in the night."

The assembly gasped, and Emerald covered his face with one hand. ***[Gods curse it, I should have known...]***

"The royal inquisitors have discovered the culprit." Efrain waved a hand behind him.

I pressed my hand to my mouth as Squampf was dragged up the steps in the prince's wake. He was indeed still alive, but his bright green skin was mottled with dark bruises, and one of his eyes was swollen shut. The guards dragged him by his armpits and deposited him in a quivering heap on the stones at the prince's feet.

"This treasonous wretch poisoned my future bride," the prince snarled. "He has betrayed the crown, he has betrayed his so-called lover, he has betrayed common decency. He knew he could not have her, so he had made it so no one could..."

"Mercedes," the krub croaked.

Efrain paused with one hand raised for emphasis. For a moment, he seemed to have been turned to stone.

"You speak of her as property." Squampf raised his head. He was shaking, either from the beating or from the cold air on his unprotected skin. Perhaps both. "But you have not uttered her name. *Mercedes.*"

Efrian whirled toward the krub and bent low to deliver a backhand blow.

I did not hear a single word uttered around me, and yet I could *feel* the sentiment of the collective crowd as clearly as I could feel Emerald's emotions through our link, or Innocent's bloodthirsty impulses. They—*we*—were on Squampf's side.

I closed my eyes, just for a moment, and Innocent pushed forward. I saw the scene play out as if it were real: the crowd turning against the prince, swarming the walls, forcing their way through the wards and guards and tearing the castle down brick by brick, with their bare hands if need be. Efrain's power, the *crown's* power, relied on the collective obedience and support of the people.

[Imagine it,] Innocent hissed. *[Imagine the whole palace demolished as thoroughly as Neandor's hut.]*

I did imagine it. More importantly, I imagined what might come after. What Kinmore could be without the crown's boot on its neck. The city that could rise from Kinmore's ashes.

When I opened my eyes again, Squampf had struggled to his feet. He lifted his gelid chin in defiance. "My honor is at stake here, sir. My good name. You agreed to cross swords with me, and I will have my satisfaction, or every member of this audience will see what a coward you truly are."

Efrain's lips peeled back from his teeth in a smile even a Leonhite would have found disturbing. "Swords," he snapped, and held out one hand.

The guards who had dragged Squampf in exchanged a wary glance. As they did, I recognized one of them: Mav, the woman who'd tried to offer me a cup of broth the night before. Without her hood, in full daylight, I hadn't realized it was her.

Efrain's hand twitched, and the guards surrendered their blades. Efrain took one; Squampf, the other. With the hilt of the sword in hand, the krub stood a little straighter. His whole posture changed.

He held the blade aloft and bowed to the prince, then turned his back. Efrain did the same, although his answering bow was barely a nod. The two of them stood there, only a few paces apart, blades at the ready.

"On three," Efrain said. "One."

The stillness that descended over the crowded gardens was absolute. I would not have believed that such a large number of people could be so utterly silent. If I listened hard enough, I swore I could hear their beating hearts.

[They could fall on him like a tide,] Innocent whispered. *[Tear the prince apart by the handful, scoop his flesh from his bones, pry his joints apart, transmute him from man to meat in the span of a few seconds.]*

"Two."

[Let me out, Crimson Smoke. Let me show you what we could do together. Let us show them what we are capable of.]

"Three."

[Let me—]

Innocent fell silent. I had been so focused on Squampf's blade, on the bloodthirsty silence of the crowd, that I had failed to see Mav raise her bowless. The bolt cut through Squampf so cleanly that at first I thought she'd missed and only hit the stones. He stood there as if in shock before toppling sideways.

[Gods.] Emerald flinched away. ***[I knew it was coming, but...]***

I hadn't known. Innocent was wrong about me: I was both naive *and* stupid. I had sincerely believed that Efrain would meet Squampf in battle and trust his strength and skill to save him.

The crowd was silent, and that silence stretched taut. When it snapped, when we all snapped together, Efrain would be the one standing in our sights.

Only, it never happened. The prince sneered down at the fallen krub. "Idiot," he snarled, although Squampf was beyond hearing. "As if you ever stood a chance." He stormed back to the steps and loped away toward the castle with the guards close behind him.

And the crowd let him go.

Instead of breaking like a dam in a flood, the tension dissipated. Members of the crowd split off and filed away. The intensity that only moments before had posed a threat to the castle simply... ended. Vanished.

[*Cowards,*] Innocent rumbled. [*They're afraid.*]

"Gods above." Emerald pressed his palms to his eyes. "Gods below." After a pause, he added, "Shit."

[*I told you, Crimson Smoke. You should have let me out.*]

The worst part was, I almost wished I had.

The procession that bore Mercedes and Squampf away from the castle was small and subdued. The royal family made no appearance, and most of the witnesses to the krub's death had dispersed. Only a few dozen solemn faces surrounded us as we followed the caskets to the temple of Lemda for their last rites. Mercedes was on full display, dressed in her red-and-gold gown from the party where we'd first met. Her hair had been oiled and arranged in glossy waves around her shoulders; her skin, once the rich golden-brown hue of burnished einwood, had taken on a bluish and pallid hue.

Squampf, mercifully, was covered. I could not imagine having to look at him, knowing that we might have averted his untimely death.

The little party arrived at the doors of Lemda's temple just as twilight stole over the city. The bodies were carried inside, and the rest of us were left to mill about in the square outside until, like the audience in the garden, people gradually dispersed. Emerald and I waited until the square was nearly empty, then we wandered down a side street along the temple wall. We circled around to the back entrance, where Emerald knocked three times.

"Emerald Flame?" The door opened, and a woman robed in white peered out at us.

Emerald nodded. "Oreia, I presume?"

The priestess of Lemda waved us through and hastened to latch the door behind us. "You might have left the matter to us."

"You'll forgive me if I want to see the outcome for myself," Emerald said. He tucked his chin into the collar of his coat. "This day hasn't all gone according to plan. If anything goes wrong, I want to help."

"You're referring to the krub." The priestess nodded. "It is a shame, but we'll see to him as well. He may not have worshiped Lemda in life, but his death was an injustice, and we will not forget it. Come." The priestess strode deeper into the temple, gesturing for us to follow. A soft rattling accompanied each step, suggesting that she wore mail beneath her robes.

There was no sign of Squampf's remains in the room where Oreia led us, only a simple cot and a few plain articles of furniture. Mercedes had been moved to the bed, and another white-robed acolyte waited with her.

Oreia extended one hand to my friend. "You have the antidote?"

Emerald dug into an inner pocket of his greatcoat and removed the phial within. I'd watched him decant the contents in the wee hours of the morning. The poisonous leaves of Gwalgofethsbane from the poisoner's garden had been enough to send the girl into a deathlike stupor, but the antidote had been brewed with care, and required a far more nuanced understanding of herbalism.

With great care, Oreia removed the stopper. She knelt by the bed and opened the girl's mouth with one hand while pouring out the antidote with the other. When she was done, she set the phial aside.

We waited.

[How long is it supposed to take?] I asked.

[Not long. Look, she's already moving.]

Sure enough, Mercedes stirred, and her brow wrinkled slightly. The color gradually returned to her cheeks.

"Impressive." Oreia sat back on the edge of the bed and scrutinized my friend. "I was wondering how we might spirit her away and keep her out of Efrain's grasp. It never occurred to me that he might *surrender* her to us, although I suppose that's for the best. Lemda is not the subtlest of goddesses. I have more knowledge of blades than of books." She rose in one smooth motion and nodded to the acolyte. "Fetch a pitcher of water and a glass. And some acolyte's robes. She can't wear *that* and go unnoticed."

The acolyte hurried away, and Oreia returned her attention to us. "I'll make sure she's safe. She can stay here for a while, with us, and then decide where to go next. We'll see to it."

I looked from the priestess to Emerald and back. "Are you really comfortable defying the crown?"

Oreia chuckled, and Emerald glanced at me sidelong. "I've never met a priestess of Lemda who was afraid to go against the law," he said.

"I respect the laws," Oreia told me, "when they are *just*. Laws that protect the people should be upheld. Laws that result in an imbalance of power, or in active harm, are nothing more than the selfish whims of selfish men. Why would I respect them? I serve a daughter of Driaweep, and vengeance—like death—comes for all who tempt its hand. Eventually."

Mercedes coughed and sat up on the cot. Oreia swooped back to her side and helped her sit up.

"Mercedes?" Her gentleness surprised me. "Breathe, child. Breathe."

The girl relaxed a little and drew a few deep breaths before opening her eyes.

"Oreia," she said in a hoarse voice. Her eyes roamed the room until they found my face. "*Crimson*. Is that... you?"

I nodded.

She coughed again. "Odd. I thought... you were... a toad."

The acolyte returned with water. Oreia filled a glass from the pitcher. Without looking up from her ministrations, she said, "Show them out. The girl is in our care now. We will tell her what she needs to know when she's ready to hear it."

I was glad that we wouldn't be present when she learned

Squampf's fate, and I was ashamed of my relief. Emerald must have felt the same, because he let the acolyte lead us back to the street without protest.

Night had brought clouds with it, which made the sky feel crowded and close. We made our way back through the city in silence, both knowing we had done something of value, and wishing we had done more.

CHAPTER EIGHT

Five days after Squampf's death and Mercedes's resurrection, Emerald was roused from sleep by Yerik pounding on the door. I was sitting in the chair by the window, puzzling over a file that Emerald had brought back from the Conjury offices, as I had been all night. He had already solved it, of course, but the long and lonely nights troubled me and left me with too much time to think. Studying the pages of the file, which he had laid out in order since I couldn't turn them myself, helped pass the time and keep my mind occupied.

"Aster's breath." Emerald yanked one of the pillows over his head. "It's not even dawn yet, is it?"

"No," Yerik replied from the hallway, "but there's someone here to see you, and it can't wait."

Muttering a series of foul oaths under his breath, Emerald rolled out of bed and yanked on yesterday's trousers and a rumpled shirt. He stomped to the door barefoot and yanked hauled it open.

"Lead the way," he grumbled. If it had been anyone else, I had no doubt that he'd have been harsher, but even he found it difficult to berate Yerik.

The dining room was empty. Yerik led us through the doors to the kitchen. The cloaked figure waiting by the back entrance wasn't immediately familiar to me, but when the man lowered his hood, Emerald and I winced in tandem.

"Neandor," Emerald said. "I wasn't expecting you."

The despair in Neandor's expression was heartbreaking. The man had once been a master swordsman until his agility was taken from him. Then he'd been a father of sorts, but that role was taken, too. Even his ramshackle hut was gone. What was left?

"I'll, um..." Yerik bounced on the balls of his feet. "I'll just, um, I've got to..." When it was obvious that he had no real excuse, and that no one was listening to him anyway, he fled the room, leaving the three of us in awkward silence.

Neandor sighed and ran one hand through his greasy hair. "I wanted to thank you."

I squinted at him. "*Thank* us? For what? We didn't warn you in time—"

"I've talked to Oreia," Neandor interrupted. "She let me see him before... Squampf, I mean." He cleared his throat a few times. "She told me what you did. For the girl. His *ladylove*." The sound that followed might have been laughter, but there was no joy in it. "And I wanted you to know, there was nothing you could have done. They came the same night you visited us. What did he think would happen? They were never going to let him fight, never going to give him a chance." He shuddered and slumped forward against the counter, as if the weight of his grief was a physical burden that bore him down.

Emerald held out a hand. "I'm sorry—"

"*Not your fault.*" Neandor slapped his hand away. "What did I just say? Without you, he'd have died for nothing. He'd have vanished, and that girl would still be trapped. Instead, she has a life ahead of her. And my boy died a hero, with a sword in his hand. With *honor.* There's no better death than that." He straightened up and made a visible effort to pull himself together. "Anyway. Thought you ought to know."

Emerald licked his lips and tried again. "If there's anything we can do—"

"You're still going to take the Conjury's money, aren't you?" Neandor sneered at him. "Still going to serve the king and his coffers, and those greedy bastards in Venta Bulgarum, high on their hill? You're no hero, Emerald Flame. Nor you." He jerked his chin toward me. "You'll defy them, so long as you can do so in hiding. If you were half the man my son was, you'd tell them all to go to their own private hells." He spun toward the door and limped away, moving even more slowly than before. I wondered what the king's soldiers had done to him when they leveled his hut and took his boy.

I wondered how it was that he was free, not confined to the king's cells.

I wondered if his anger was meant for us, or for himself.

The door slammed in his wake, and Emerald and I stood there for a long moment, staring at nothing. Emerald sucked his teeth; his eyes pointed toward the door, but I could tell his mind was elsewhere, perhaps miles away.

"Crimson," he said at last, "have you managed to make sense of that file I brought back?"

If he wanted to change the topic, so be it. "I'm not sure, but I have a few theories."

"Walk me through them," he said. "I'd be a shite mentor if I gave away the answer every time. Ask Yerik if he'd be kind enough to make some tea while I run up and grab the paperwork."

Given that I had no more desire that he did to dwell on Neandor's words or my own lingering guilt, I did exactly as he asked.

As for my hopes of ever visiting the king's library, they were thoroughly dashed. That shouldn't have bothered me, in light of everything else. I kept my disappointment private. After everything that Squampf and Neandor had lost, my fleeting hope of becoming my own creature was a small enough price to pay.

THE TALE OF THE EMERALD PENDANT

CHAPTER ONE

CHAPTER ONE

The worst of winter was behind us, according to Emerald, when I finally met my first Pruv.

In all honesty, I had likely encountered them before. People came and went through the Lute and Goose all the time, and many of them had the rough accent unique to their settlement along the Sprinit River.

I knew nothing of the geography, however, on the day when a stranger approached our usual table in the corner, dragged an extra chair up to it, and settled in between us.

"Ah," he grunted, "must be f' Emerald an' fe Smoke. 'At you?" He pointed one massive finger at me and narrowed his eyes. "Red hair, red name. *Ah*. Clever."

I stared down the finger that was pointed right between my eyes. "That's me," I affirmed. "Crimson Smoke, at your service."

Emerald had frozen with his mug halfway to his lips. His green eyes studied the newcomer with more intensity than usual. Mostly, he took one look at people, assessed the details, and moved on. His interest in this newcomer surprised me.

Not that I could blame him. The man was big, not just in the gut or the shoulders or in his stature, but in *every* direction. If I hadn't known better, I'd have wondered if there was a bit of jotunn in his family tree, but other than his size there was nothing to indicate that he was anything but human. His hair was the same glossy brown as the burnished tabletop. He reminded me of someone, but I couldn't think who. Regardless, I didn't believe we'd met before.

"I've heard fings," our new acquaintance said. "Not all good, but mostly so. My cousin says you're ar'aight, anyhow, 'n he's seen more'n fe world as I have."

"I'm... sorry?" I glanced at Emerald, thinking that the stranger's cousin must be an old acquaintance of his. It didn't help that the man's thick accent and odd turns of phrase made him largely unintelligible.

Emerald lowered his mug. "Your cousin knows us?"

"Ah, 'n he c'n spot a sour turnip from fe bunch, he c'n." The man nodded sagely. "If he says we c'n trust a Conjury muskrat, *well*." He kept nodding as he sat back, as if he had imparted some great wisdom upon which we could all agree.

"Oh!" I cried, not because I knew the first thing about turnips or muskrats, but because I'd finally placed him. "You mean Boo!"

In my peripheral vision, Emerald's eyebrows rose, but the stranger was nodding. "He says you're not bad, for a fribble."

I let out a bark of laughter and turned my attention back to my bemused companion. "You remember Boudreaux, don't you, Emerald? Marsha's, er..." I hesitated as I searched for the word to describe the relationship between Boo and the Mistress of Midtown. Friend? Lover? Partner?

"Doormat," the visitor supplied.

I choked on a laugh, and Emerald's eyes lit up with recognition. "Ah, yes. I remember." He raked one hand through his black hair and bit back a smile. "I have to admit, I never made the connection, but of course Boo is Pruvhathayn."

I cocked my head at the odd word. Once again, the stranger nodded.

"Boy lost his vowels, has he? Well, 'at's no surprise. Once fey leave Pruvhathayn'He'Vhu, you c'n count 'em out of the flock. Gods-damned shame. Wish it weren't so, but never mind. Apologies, I didn't say mine. I'm Marf." He held out a hand toward Emerald, who shook it. "'N may I say, nice to meet one of your lot who knows fe name. Most Conjury stick to fe regions inked over fe map."

"Most people are ignorant," Emerald replied.

Marf let out a laugh and slapped his thigh in obvious delight. "Fey are, fey are! Ah, you're just as I'd hoped. But you..." Marf's eyes strayed to mine. "You're a mite different 'an what Boo said to expect."

I tried not to appear self-conscious and almost certainly failed. On our earlier cases, I'd been able to be Simon in one place and Simone in the next, depending on what the case required. I hadn't initially planned to stay at the Lute and Goose for months, and I had made a miscalculation when it came to deciding my appearance. For most—but by no means all—of the small cases we'd worked during our time in Kinmore, I had appeared in some variation of my femi-nine form. In Upper Bound, however, I had spent the vast majority of my time as Simon.

Marf's eyes flicked over me. He shrugged. "Odd boy, 'at one. Anyhow." He pressed his palms against his thighs and lifted his chin. The shift in his posture suggested that we were about to get into the true purpose of his visit. "I'm here on business. Dumplin wants to meet."

I smiled politely. *[Dumplin? Is that another funny word choice, or...?]*

[No idea.] Emerald braced his elbow against the table and rested his chin in his palm. *[But this is interesting, isn't it?]*

I knew that look. Over the winter, Emerald had grown cooped up and bored. Poring over the files Finch gave him provided little in the way of diversion, and neither of us had quite recovered from the grim events surrounding Squampf's death. A compelling case might be exactly what we needed.

"I don't mean to be rude," I said, "but who or what is Dumplin?"

Marf sucked in a breath. "You don't know *Dumplin*?"

"I'm afraid I don't." I tried to inject a touch of regret into my expression.

"Dumplin is…" Marf lifted his eyes toward the beams above and sighed. "Dumplin is fe most gorgeous woman known to man. Ah." He shook his head dreamily. "She's kind 'n generous 'n… well." Color rose in his cheeks, and he scrubbed his finger beneath his nose as if scratching an itch.

"She's persuasive," I suggested.

"And… popular?" Emerald asked. "With the gentlemen?"

I squinted at him, not sure how to interpret the tickle of amusement that passed through our mental link.

"Not just gennlemen," Marf mumbled. "Everyone loves Dumplin. She's no Pruv, but she's one of ours, if you follow."

[I most certainly do not,] I thought.

Emerald licked his lips. *[I'll explain when you're older.]*

I whipped around to face him, a gesture which I suppose Marf may have found unexpected. *[What?]*

"I look forward to making her acquaintance," Emerald said aloud, ignoring my bewildered stare. "She sounds like quite an interesting person."

"Oh, ah." Marf bobbed his head a few times. "None like her in fe 'ole kingdom. She's a plum among crabapples." He reached into his pocket for a ragged scrap of what might, in another life, have been paper, before it was bent and crumpled and squashed into a small and rather dirty wad. "'At's her. She 'n her boys are round 'ere most days."

With those parting words, he got to his feet and set out for the door. Yerik was on his way to greet us, presumably to offer his guest a hot drink and platter of breakfast as he usually did. Marf bowed his head in greeting on his way past.

"Huh." Yerik meandered our way and rested one hand on the back of Marf's borrowed chair. "What was Marth doing here?"

"Marth?" I repeated. "I thought he said *Marf.*"

"It's his accent," Emerald explained. "Pruvhathayn has a different linguistic root than Osmarian. I'm given to understand it has something to do with vowel qualities and where the accents in words fall, but anyway, you can usually tell a Pruv by the way they talk. They have a tendency to sort of... squish words together. I doubt he speaks Osmarian at home, either. I suspect Marth's either a nickname or a foreshortened version of an older name passed down through his family tree."

I settled in for what I feared would be a long and very dull explanation of language mechanics, but to my surprise, Emerald let the subject drop. Instead, he glanced up thoughtfully at Yerik. "Ever heard of someone called Dumplin?"

The grin that stole over Yerik's face was nothing short of wicked. "I have indeed. Don't tell me she's reached out to you?"

Emerald's thick eyebrows shot toward the beams above. "Is that a... bad thing? Is she trouble?"

"Gods, yes." Yerik chuckled. The longer he stared at Emerald, the more his amusement multiplied. "Don't worry, she's not a bad apple or anything."

"I hear she's a plum among crabapples, actually," I interjected.

"The Pruvs love her," Yerik said. "By all accounts, she's not a fan of the Conjury, though. So be careful."

FOLLOWING our hours in Finch's office, Emerald and I entered the depths of the city.

The address scrawled on Marth's scrap of paper drew us to a place I had never visited before. Emerald, however, seemed to have no trouble at all finding his way.

"This is awfully close to the Hives," I observed as we wound our way through the narrow streets. I was glad that I'd chosen to wear a somewhat more feminine version of the same outfit Emerald preferred. It wasn't flashy, but that was the point.

[Why awful?] he asked.

I stepped around a pile of refuse that might once have been something living—a skipgull, perhaps, though I could not have said that with any degree of certainty. I didn't want to know what, if anything, I would feel if I happened to pass through it. *[What do you mean?]*

[You said we're awfully close. *Why that word?]*

[It's the same word I'd choose if we were getting dangerously close to anything else. Like the guards, when we broke into the castle grounds.] As soon as I thought it, I regretted any reference to that ill-fated journey. Mercedes was freed, but I could hardly call that case an unblemished success.

[But we're not trying to avoid the Hives, are we?]

Personally, I rather *was,* although I somehow felt that it would be wrong to say so. *[Why do you ask?]*

[Because I made you, more or less. Which means that I'm responsible for your education, doesn't it? And learning how to look for clues is all well and good, but I know how you are with fine things, Crim. And I don't like that you put so much stock in them.]

I frowned at the cobblestones beneath us. *[Just say what you mean, Em.]*

[You've got this idea about the Hives as being someplace awful and unsightly. Someplace pathetic. Someplace to avoid. Or maybe someplace where people end up when they've got nowhere else to go. But it's their home, *Crim. Yes, I wish things were better for the people who live there, but not because it's* unsightly.*]*

[That's not what I—] I cut myself off. His words bothered me, if only because there was a nugget of truth in them. I *did* want to avoid the Hives, not out of fear but or disgust but... pity, maybe? Which didn't seem much better. Though I'd never verbalized the full extent

of my feelings on the subject, I had certainly painted the inhabitants of the Hives with a broad brush and in a rather unflattering light, as if they had no agency of their own. If anything, I had assumed that the king held all the power and that the residents of the Hives had none at all.

What a limited, condescending way to think of people I didn't know.

Emerald stopped so abruptly that I nearly walked through him. *[I didn't expect it to be so crowded this early.]*

I peered around him. Sure enough, although it was barely sundown—and wintertime sundown at that—the address Marth had given us boasted such a large and boisterous crowd that it had spilled over into the street. A cluster of unusually tall men, clad in layers of irregular clothing that appeared to be handmade, clutched large and lumpy glazed mugs that had a similarly hand-crafted appearance. Several of them held long pipes from which wafted thin clouds of smoke. Not one of them was speaking Osmarian.

In the past, whenever I encountered languages that Emerald knew, I found it easy enough to understand, based on the link that threaded between his mind and mine. The conversation of the Pruvs, however, was largely unintelligible. I could catch a fragment of meaning, but not enough for me to follow the conversation.

[I thought you spoke Pruvhathayn?] I asked.

[Only a few words here and there, not at this speed. Pruvs stick to themselves, for the most part. Never found anyone willing to teach me, and their written language is notoriously hard to parse. Can't blame them for being secretive. They were here before the kingdom of Feynlish was established, and the crown has never done right by them.] He scratched the beginnings of stubble on his jaw. *[Nor the Conjury, for that matter.]*

I was about to urge him onward when something occurred to me. *[I don't think I'll be able to go inside, Em. The likelihood of someone putting an elbow through me is much too high.]*

[Or worse,] Emerald agreed. **[It's probably best if you hang back. You don't mind waiting?]**

[What does it matter if I mind?] I asked. **[It's the smart choice.]** Aloud, I said, "Go on without me. I'll meet you back at the inn." I wasn't sure if my tether would allow me to travel that far, but hanging around in the street for gods-knew-how-long would only make people curious, and I couldn't very well rearrange myself in the street.

"I'll catch you up on everything you miss," Emerald promised.

I turned back the way we'd come and set off, while Emerald headed toward the door of Dumplin's establishment. I hadn't even reached the end of the street when Innocent began to laugh.

[Crimson Smoke, haven't you learned anything? What a poor caregiver you are, letting your master wander off like that.]

I clenched my hands into fists and kept moving. *[He's fine. What am I meant to protect him from, anyway? I'm not like you, I'm not going to kill anyone. He can handle himself.]*

[Can he? Look again.]

I paused to glance over my shoulder. Emerald had approached the door and was speaking, presumably in Osmarian, with one of the Pruvs. *[They don't seem hostile.]* I hated asking my unwelcome passenger for advice, but I hated the idea of failing Emerald even more. After a long moment of indecision, I gave in. *[Do you think it's a trap?]*

[It doesn't have to be, Crimson Smoke,] Innocent purred. *[What do you think is in those mugs?]*

If I'd had legs, I could have kicked myself. I should have thought of that... I'd seen how drink affected my friend, *felt* the depths to which he plunged at his lowest points. To my knowledge, he hadn't swallowed a drop of anything stronger than tea since we left Upper Bound, but he hadn't been left unattended in a tavern, either.

Innocent was right. I'd need to find a way in.

CHAPTER TWO

CHAPTER TWO

It was easy enough to slip into an alleyway. Once I was reasonably certain that nobody was watching me, I crouched down behind a bin overflowing with refuse. It was a matter of mere moments to rearrange myself into that of a ginger rat.

I had seen a great number of rats during our tenure in Kinmore, although they tended to be some variation of gray or black. I had no intention of being spotted, however, and if I was, a ginger rat was less likely to draw attention than a red-haired woman who could walk through walls.

I followed the back alley until I reached the raucous building and slipped through a hole in the wall. A *real* rat might have found the passageway uncomfortably tight, but I was only using it for the appearance's sake, anyway. I passed into the wall but not out the other side, following the foundation instead. Through the plaster that separated me from the main rooms, I could hear the thrum of voices speaking Pruvhathayn as well as Osmarian.

Once I'd made my way back around toward the front of the

building, I paused. A rat might not draw attention in the streets, but I doubted I'd be welcome on the tavern floor. Perhaps instead of scurrying between the feet of the patrons, I could try something a little more discreet. Something smaller.

Within seconds, I became a round-bellied, eight-legged spider.

The experience of having eight eyes was momentarily disorienting. It hadn't even crossed my mind that spiders would *have* that many, but Emerald must have known, because it had seeped into my subconscious somehow. Once the world, or at least the insulation, came back into focus, I climbed up through the beams and old straw that comprised the interior walls of Dumplin's establishment. Once I'd reached the seam where the ceiling and the wall intersected, I carefully tiptoed my many legs into the open room so that I hung inverted from the ceiling. If anyone below happened to be watching, I hoped it would look as though I'd merely slipped through a crack in the plaster.

I had been wise not to wander into the establishment in human form. The walkways between the low tables were so narrow that most of the people present were forced to stand in tight clusters rather than employ chairs, which would have made the room impassable. I wondered why the owner had not furnished the place with standing tables; there were a few in the Lute and Goose, for those who preferred to stop for a quick drink rather than allow themselves to get comfortable. These tables were uncommonly short, and as many of the patrons were uncommonly *tall,* the resulting tableau was somewhat odd.

I had thought it strange that the business boasted no sign out front. Inside, there was a plaque over the bar, but I couldn't read the words. I assumed that it was written in Pruvhathayn.

Emerald had begun the tedious process of squeezing between the tables. He appeared to be headed for the bar. On his way, he bumped into a man standing at a packed table. The man glanced over his shoulder, then did a double take. From my awkward angle, I could not see his expression, nor did I recognize the song the man immediately began to hum. A few of his drinking fellows joined in, and Emerald paused as if frozen in place.

"'At's you, innit?" one of them asked. "Fe Emerald Flame?"

Emerald nodded. Too late, I realized that I *had* heard the song before, if only in part. It was one of Coirpre's.

"Move over, move over!" The oldest man at the table, an elder with a shaggy white beard and a few errant wisps of hair still clinging to his scalp, shooed the others aside. It was a tight squeeze, but when Emerald hesitantly approached, there was just enough available space to accommodate him.

"Didn't realize I had that much of a reputation," he murmured.

"It's fe music." The old man tapped his temple. "Sticks in fe mind."

Emerald grimaced. "Of course it does."

"Here!" One of the other drinkers thrust a mug in Emerald's direction. "Drink up!"

Emerald lifted his hands and shook his head. "No, I don't... partake..."

"It's not hard drink, lad. Called *vhingdlathuch*. It'll put hair on your chest. Not sayin' *you* need it, but..." The man looked Emerald over and took a sly sip from his own mug.

Emerald pulled the mug closer and took a sniff. He wasn't *trying* to communicate with me, but the stomach-churning nausea he experienced at the scent was so physical that I emitted a tiny spider-gasp. Whatever was in that mug wasn't wine or liquor, as I'd assumed, and it *certainly* didn't hold the same power over him.

Even from my remote vantage point, I could see that Emerald's eyes were watering. He looked around the table at the expectant faces of the men and women watching him. He must have decided that it was worthwhile to win their trust, because he lifted the mug to his lips and drained it in one long gulp.

He coughed and sputtered on the aftertaste, and his nose began to run. I shivered at the secondhand discomfort and wiggled my mouthparts in sympathetic disgust.

The Pruvs at his table burst out laughing, and the old man slapped him on the back. "Quite fe flavor, innit? C'n't stomach liquor myself, but 'at'll clear you *right* out. Ever had fermented sheep's milk before?"

Emerald's voice cracked when he answered, "No."

It wasn't the first time I'd seen him sample the local cuisine. In Dyrne, he'd suffered through *hagbraggh*, a sort of chewy boiled sausage. He'd eaten it, I thought, mostly to be polite. I wasn't sure if his swig of *vhingdlathuch* was out of a simple attempt to bond with the locals, or out of genuine curiosity. Perhaps a bit of both.

If he was attempting to curry favor with the Pruvs, it worked. The group of them lapsed into easy conversation, mostly in Osmarian, which made it easy to follow their lines of conversation.

"Here to see Dumplin?" the old man asked. "Patience, lad. She's a busy woman."

A chorus of laughter rose from the table, accompanied by the jostling of elbows and knowing looks.

"She'll eat you up like cake in fe pigpen," one of the women assured Emerald. "You're her type." This pronouncement was followed by a jaunty wink.

Emerald studied the group. He seemed more at ease with strangers than he usually did, perhaps because the Pruvs seemed indifferent to the things that people were usually quick to point out: his height, his heritage, his *otherness.* "I'm a bit surprised to see so many Pruvs in this part of the city. Are you just here for...?" He waved one hand to encompass the room.

"Nah," one of the men grunted. "Come for fe dock. I work fe warehouses. 'Ere's farming up norf, but my family needs fe coin. How else c'n I pay taxes?"

"C'n't pay in seed," another said.

"Or nightly favors." The woman who'd winked at Emerald rolled her hips against the table, and they burst out laughing again.

"Always a mind in fe gutter, Parla." The man to her left jostled her with his elbow; she jostled him right back.

"I trust our Dumplin." The old man waggled a finger near Emerald's nose. "But look out for her, ah? She's a good'un. Our home away from home."

"She's like our ma," one of the younger men added.

Parla cackled. "Ah, what do you get up to wif *yer* ma, Olen?"

Olen's cheeks darkened and he hunched lower over the table. "You know what I mean."

"What do *you* get up to wif Dumplin?" another asked.

The cocky grin slipped from Parla's face. "A hard ride 'n a wet retreat," she mumbled.

"Ah, go on, we're not impressed," her friend replied. "It's fe same for all of us. We know fe truf."

Emerald opened his mouth to ask something. Before he could, the noise level in the room dropped off sharply, starting near the stairs beside the bar. Another large man moved through the crowd, and the patrons were quick to make room for him. They didn't seem frightened of him, more... respectful. They parted for him as he walked, and they left the path behind him open.

The newcomer marched over to Emerald, looked him up and down, and nodded. "She'll see you," he said.

That was all. He turned on his heels and strode back toward the stairs with long, loping strides.

I wasn't sure where the two of them were headed, but I had no intention of losing track of my friend. I dropped from the ceiling, rearranging myself as I fell into the form of a fly. Admittedly, the red tint to my abdomen would have drawn attention from other members of the species, but it was winter, and I wasn't much worried about the opinions of flies anyway. I flew after Emerald, making sure that he never left my sight.

There were three stories to the building, and Emerald's guide walked him all the way up. I flitted silently from wall to wall, mindful of anything that might be a trap. In my head, Innocent had gone silent. I had no idea if that was a good thing or a bad one.

The upper floors of the establishment were quiet. Aside from the echoes of the rowdy gathering below and the tread of two large pairs of boots on the stairs, everything was quiet. Emerald was shown to a door on the hallway of the third floor, where his guide knocked twice.

"Show him in," said a soft, feminine voice from within.

Emerald entered the room alone, or alone *enough*. I dipped through the wall above him, leaving the Pruv in the hall outside.

I nearly gave myself away with a noise of surprise when I saw the room's interior. I had been there before... or at least, I had been someplace so extraordinarily similar that it boggled the mind. Trinkets and curios lined the walls, worn but elegant carpets covered patches of the floor, and an assortment of plush chairs was scattered about the room's interior. Lamps of every conceivable variety hung from the ceiling. The focus of the room was a small chaise with bright-purple upholstery, beside which stood a cart brimming with decanters and delicate floral cups.

In detail, the room was unique. At first glance, however, it perfectly matched the chamber belonging to Marsha of Midtown.

"Emerald Flame," that sultry voice purred. "I'm so glad to meet you in the flesh. Please, take a seat."

Emerald looked around. In the midst of all the bric-à-brac, I hadn't registered the three-paneled folding screen in the corner of the room, but that was clearly the source of the voice. After a brief deliberation, he settled into one of the larger chairs, lowering himself gingerly into the seat lest the legs give way.

[If it can hold a Pruv, it can hold you,] I thought.

Emerald's legs shot out from under him, and he looked around sharply until he spotted me on the edge of an enormous, gilded portrait of a country landscape. *[Didn't realize you'd come along for the ride.]*

[I figured someone ought to keep an eye on you.] I fluttered my iridescent wings. *[Keep you out of trouble, and all that.]*

[Right, because trouble never follows you.] Emerald shook his

head, leaned into the armrests, and turned back toward the folding screen.

"I got your invitation," he said. "Although Marth failed to explain your interests."

"That's because he didn't know them. A girl can't reveal everything, especially not to her... clients." A high-pitched giggle accompanied this last word.

"I'm afraid I disagree. Since it seems you'll be a client of mine, and I'd prefer you to be as transparent as possible."

"What? Don't you like surprises?" The screen shifted. If gravity had any hold over me, I would have dropped to the floor in shock.

Dumplin was dressed in a lavender silk robe tied about the waist. Her thick, honey-colored curls floated in a cloud around her face, through which her brilliant blue eyes shone like sapphires. Her bare feet tapped against the floorboards, only to be muffled by the carpet as she approached. Her sturdy horns had been worn smooth in the place where they curved back toward her shoulders.

Not one person who'd sung Dumplin's praises had thought to mention that she was a lambkin.

She sashayed over to the chaise and hoisted herself into the deep-purple cushion. When she was seated, her cloven hooves dangled above the floor. She took her time, leaning back on her palms and rearranging her robe so that it showed a peek of one fluffy thigh.

"You never answered the question."

Emerald's face was blank as a cliffside stone. "I like to know the facts," he said. "Like what a businesswoman such as yourself wants from a Conjury investigator."

Dumplin's smile widened. "You get right to the point, don't you, love? That's just as well. I've got a little problem, and I'm hoping you can help me. Drink?"

"I've had my fill of *vhingdlathuch*, and I've sworn off the bottle."

"That about covers all your bases, doesn't it? Suit yourself." Dumplin reached over to the private bar and poured herself a tipple of some dark-brown liquid. She swirled her glass several times in slow deliberation, drawing out the tension.

I had the sense that she was trying to learn what enticed my friend, and that she found it in that moment: he loved a mystery, the sweet anticipation of a challenge not yet laid out for review.

"As you can see, I'm something of a collector." Dumplin settled herself back on the chaise and gestured around the room. "A girl needs her creature comforts, and I think I've earned a few indulgences. Part of my collection consists—or perhaps I should say *used* to consist—of some fine jewelry. Nothing too fancy, mind you, nothing those birds in the king's court would bother with, but I worked hard for what I have." A storm cloud passed over her hitherto sweet face, and her blue eyes flashed. "And I don't like it when people steal from me."

Emerald's disappointment jolted through me. "Theft?" he asked. "I hate to say it, madame, but when it comes to matters like this, it's best to look close to home."

"*Madame.*" Dumplin giggled. "Listen to you. Nice manners you've got, love." She took a sip of her drink. "Everyone thinks you big boys are all muscle and no brains, but I know better. People underestimate your intelligence and *overestimate* your capacity for cruelty. Am I close?"

Emerald didn't so much as blink. "You were telling me about your missing jewels?"

"Look at you, all business and no play. Quite the tough customer." Dumplin sipped her drink again. "Fine, we'll stick to the facts. My display box was there." She pointed to a long dresser. There wasn't a speck of dust anywhere in the room as far as I could see, but there was a slightly darker patch of wood visible against the glossy grain, as though something had been sitting there for a long time and only recently been moved.

"And whoever robbed you took the whole box?" Emerald asked.

"They sure did." Dumplin stuck out her bottom lip and pouted. "Probably because they couldn't unlock it." She lifted one hand to her neck and pulled on a thin silver chain until a key slipped free of her neckline. "I've still got it right here."

"May I?" Emerald leaned forward and held out a hand.

Dumplin frowned, then shrugged one shoulder. "I suppose. It's not like you can use it now, with the box being gone and all." She unclasped the chain and passed the necklace over.

Emerald studied the key closely. "Fine craftsmanship," he said at last. "Odd, though, that you didn't mention the unique nature of the lock."

[What makes a lock unique?] I asked. *[Or rather, aren't most locks unique, unless they take a skeleton key?]*

[Sure. When the locks aren't magic.]

Dumplin's face lit up with a wicked grin. "Think of it as a little test. I know your reputation, but I wanted to see it for myself. How did you know? Can you sense it with your...?" Dumplin wiggled her fingers in the air in a poor imitation of someone casting the *Aidea*.

"No, but I recognize the theory." Emerald flicked one finger against the metal. "The sigil in the filigree was made by an Automatist. Whoever took it will never manage to pick the lock unless they've got some *Aidea* of their own. Do any of your employees have *Aidea*?"

"I'm afraid not, honey. Not unless they're great at hiding it."

"They could deliver the box to someone who does," Emerald mused. "I assume it can't simply be broken either."

"What would be the purpose in investing in a charmed lock, otherwise?" Dumplin fluttered her eyelashes.

Emerald ran his thumb over the bright metal in his palm. "What else can you tell me? About the jewelry itself, perhaps?"

"The centerpiece is a gem the size of my palm." Dumplin held up one petite hand, barely a third the scale of Emerald's. "It's purple. Not the most valuable stone, but..." She indicated her robe, then her chaise. "It's my favorite color, and it makes me feel like a queen when I'm wearing it. The settings are silver..."

"Like the key," Emerald said.

Dumplin nodded. I noticed a slight shiftiness in her eyes, and I suspected that Emerald did, too. "Gold's beyond my means, love. Besides, silver suits my complexion better."

"When did it go missing?"

"Yesterday," Dumplin said. "Since it's right out in the open, it's hard to miss. I was at dinner, downstairs, drinking with some of my regulars. The box is big enough that I would have noticed if someone carried it out, but that's the funny thing—nobody came upstairs that whole while. My boys were guarding the stairway, and even if I didn't trust them as much as I do, I trust my own eyes. They were there the whole time."

"Who would have been on the second floor? Or in the other rooms up here?"

"Nobody." Dumplin shook her head. "The whole third floor is mine. I've got my personal rooms, and then my..." She fluttered her eyelashes. "My business rooms. The only time they're occupied is when I'm in there with my clientele. And my boys, Poke and Doodah, they have rooms on the second floor. All the kitchen storage and the bar's cellar are *down*stairs, so there wouldn't have been anyone coming and going for business. It just..." She held up both hands and fluttered her eyelashes innocently. "It just *vanished.*"

"Hm." Emerald surveyed the room. "Do you mind if I look around?"

"Suit yourself," she said.

Emerald took stock of the room; with a little nudge from him, I took off as well to see what I could glean.

[How would I recognize a clue amidst all this clutter?] I asked. *[Short of finding footprints or a splash of blood, I wouldn't know what I was looking for. Also, what are the names of her two employees? I can't have heard her right.]*

[Curious that in a room full of objects, a thief would take the one thing that's locked up,] Emerald mused. "Was anything else removed?" he asked aloud.

"Not that I've noticed," Dumplin said. "And believe it or not, I think I would be able to tell if there were."

[She's lying,] Innocent whispered.

I landed on the surface of a tall mirror. *[What do you mean? You think something else was taken?]* I immediately regretted asking. That was twice in one day that I'd asked Innocent a question, and I didn't want to make a habit of it.

[No,] it said, but that was all.

[Emerald?] I loathed giving credence to my dark passenger, but Innocent's interest unsettled me. ***[Do you think... do you think Dumplin might be lying?]***

[About what?] he asked as he prodded the windowpane. "This was latched last night, I take it?"

"Always. I take my security seriously. Why do you ask?"

"Because it isn't latched now."

Dumplin said something in another language. It didn't sound like Pruvhathayn, but it had the tone of a curse. "It *isn't*? But I checked." Her hands flew to her mouth. "Oh, *no*. Do you think the thief was *here* last night? That whoever it was got in while I was at dinner and... *stayed?*"

"And left *after* you realized the necklace was missing," Emerald confirmed.

My experience of Dumplin was limited and brief, but I was positive that her horror was genuine and absolute. There was no girlish tremor in her voice, no coquettish play. I realized then how small she was. How vulnerable.

Emerald often went out of his way to appear smaller than he was. Dumplin did the opposite: she had made herself seem larger by amassing a loyal following of big, strong people who adored her.

How easily all that might be taken away by one lone thief biding his time in the night.

"I'm afraid so," Emerald said.

"Oh, golly." Dumplin stumbled back a few paces and wrapped her arms around herself. She rubbed her palms up her arms. In an instant, she pulled herself together, and she was the mistress of the house again.

But I had seen the frightened lambkin beneath that cool veneer, and having seen, I could not *unsee*.

"I suppose this just gives me more incentive to find the thief." She squared her shoulders and lifted her chin. "If you'll help me, I've got a full purse with your name on it. And a private session, assuming your lady friend doesn't mind."

"I'll stick to the purse," Emerald said drily. "I'll look around the rest of the building. And before we leave, I'll speak to... Poke and Doodah."

Dumplin nodded her approval. At an opportune moment, I flew into Emerald's lapel and rode along while he examined the rest of the building, then engaged in a deeply unhelpful questioning of Dumplin's two henchman. Poke, the one who'd led us upstairs, had ears that looked like small heads of cauliflower, and spoke mostly in grunts and one-word answers. Doodah had a mop of dull black hair that looked as though it might be a wig, and once he discovered that Dumplin had been endangered on his watch, he started crying and didn't stop.

In the end, we learned nothing new, and I was left with Innocent's words echoing in my head.

She's lying.

Perhaps. But what was she lying about?

CHAPTER THREE

For the first time in several weeks, Emerald and I did not start our workday with a visit to Finch's offices.

"She'll be fine," Emerald promised. "There's nothing she has me doing in there that can't wait another day at least. Besides, I'm only a *consultant* for the Conjury. I'm allowed to take my own cases so long as I'm not neglecting their orders."

Restored to my form as Simone, and at Emerald's behest, I robed myself in purple and silver. Once again, I opted for trousers, but in a more opulent style than before. After a few false starts, I layered on a long purple coat in the same colors.

"I liked the other style better," I whined when Emerald insisted I change.

"Nobody would be wearing a light jacket this time of year, Crimson." Emerald rolled his eyes. "If you were a human woman, you'd freeze your tits off."

"Anything for fashion," I muttered, but I conceded the point.

Our excursion for the day brought us into a part of the city which I had never had the chance to properly explore. West of the Hives and the middle-class residential areas they abutted lay the market district.

It was *huge*.

[This is spectacular,] I told Emerald as we navigated the streets. A handcart loaded with skinned goat's heads stood across from a venerable bookshop. *[Why don't we spend more time here?]*

[Hoping to buy some sheep skulls, were you?] Emerald asked drily.

[No, but it's fun to look...]

[Not so fun when every merchant watches your hands like you're a thief,] he retorted. *[The only time they don't hover is when they think I work for you, which is bad enough now, but before you were you... It was humiliating. Besides, our needs are more than adequately met. We're not like Dumplin. We don't have rooms to fill with useless junk.]*

I fell silent. I appreciated the honesty with which he'd spoken, and I'd seen for myself the way people treated him. Still, I wished I could explain to him how much I loved seeing new things for the first time. He'd traveled extensively and observed large swathes of the world; I was still discovering new things around every corner.

Even watching the people left me fascinated. There were humans with skin the color of polished einwood haggling with the narrow, upright forms of alder elves. One woman wore her hair wrapped up in a brightly colored scarf... why, I wondered? Did the patterns on it have meanings, or was it simply beautiful? A trio of heavily tattooed dwarves studied an array of herbs and spices laid out on a rotund Teguan's folding table. A Leonhite—the first I'd seen in the city, aside from Finch—was showing off a group of patterned baskets to a cluster of curious lambkins. There were even a few people with jotunn ancestry who nodded to Emerald as we passed. He nodded back, but never stopped to talk.

[Quit gawking,] he scolded when I stopped to admire a stall brimming with handmade clothes. The colors were eye-catching, but I was more interested in the two women running the shop. The

younger of the two looked extraordinarily like Tincrown, and I wondered if she was from the Nomad Gamut.

[Sorry, sorry. I'm just curious! All these people have lived lives so different from ours.]

Emerald waited while I rushed to catch up with him. There was a funny tilt to his mouth, as if he didn't quite know what to make of my enthusiasm.

[What?] I demanded.

[Nothing. I just forget how young you are sometimes.] He turned back to the street. *[Can't remember if I was ever that young.]*

Our first destination for the day was a pawnshop. Emerald held the door for me while I stepped inside. The assortment of goods on the shelves reminded me a little of Dumplin's collection, but without the cheer that accompanied it. She loved her strange hodgepodge of possessions, while these items had been abandoned.

On second thought, it reminded me more of Brother Harmony's collection, or the toys and memories stashed beneath the floorboards of the Brotherhood. A reliquary.

"What can I do for you, miss?" The elf behind the counter looked up from his book and studied me as I approached. I was keenly aware that he didn't give Emerald the time of day.

I smiled at him with only a fraction of Dumplin's charm. "Hello there. I do *so* hope you can help me. A dear friend of mine fell upon hard times recently and was forced to sell a family heirloom. She was too embarrassed to tell me of her troubles, poor thing, but I'm hoping I can track it down and buy it back. Money, of course, is no object, and any leads would be *greatly* appreciated."

Light flashed in the elf's eyes, like the distant gleam of unspent silver. "Is that so? What does this heirloom look like?"

I described the necklace, per Dumplin's description, though at Emerald's request I made no mention of the enchanted display box. The elf took notes, despite the fact that he claimed no such object was in his possession. He was the very picture of helpfulness, although he was visibly reluctant to offer the names of his competitors.

[How do we know that whoever took the necklace will have sold it?] I asked when we left.

[We don't. But anyplace that will pay coin without asking too many questions is the best place to start. Don't think that fellow bought your story, either.]

[Then why tell it at all?]

[Because if he finds it, it'll give him *an opportunity to say that he tracked it down out of some noble impulse without having to admit to any potentially shady business dealings.]* Emerald led me through the bustling market to our next destination. *[If you'd told him the truth, he'd have battened down faster than a ship's hatch in a winter storm. You set the terms of your acquaintance. You gave him plausible deniability.]*

I nodded, trying to make sense of what he'd told me. All the while, though, I kept thinking of Innocent's warning.

She's lying.

What frustrated me the most was that Innocent had seen exactly as much as I did, which meant that I had failed to notice something.

Unless somehow my passenger had inside information to which I wasn't privy.

Throughout the late morning and into the afternoon, I batted my eyelashes and implied that there was money to be made should anyone be able to help me recover my "friend's" necklace, but to no avail. As the late afternoon sun began to rearrange the shadows of the buildings, Emerald paid a few small coins for a paper sack full of vegetable handpies and sat on a stone wall to eat them.

[I'm not sure what we've accomplished today,] I complained.

Emerald chewed placidly. *[Not much, yet. But if anyone tries to fence that necklace, we've got a decent chance of hearing about it. There's another avenue we might pursue, though.]*

I reached into his paper bag and pretended to retrieve a pie of my own. I nibbled on the phantom crust. *[Emerald? How much is an enchanted display box likely to cost?]*

[Depends where it came from. It's possible she befriended—or blackmailed—an Automatist to make it specially for her. If she bought it new...] He bobbled his head back and forth. *[Judging by the quality of that key, it's fine workmanship, but not so fine that I find it suspicious.]*

Still, once the question had occurred to me, I couldn't let it go. I had spent the day telling shopkeepers that I was looking for an item, the value of which was primarily sentimental. It was, in effect, much the same story Dumplin had told us the night before. She had played the necklace off as relatively unimportant.

But I knew enough of finance, and of magic, to realize that she wouldn't have housed a cheap bauble in an expensive box just because she liked the color of the pendant. And no thief would have gone to the trouble of squatting in her private rooms for hours just so that they could steal a sentimental trinket trapped in an unbreakable magic box.

That necklace was of greater value than Dumplin had admitted.

[Good,] Innocent whispered. *[You're getting smarter.]*

"Ever seen a key like this?" Emerald laid an illusion of the key Dumplin had shown us on the workbench.

The dwarven Automatist adjusted the array of lenses that sprouted from her hat in droves. She studied it for a long moment. "Hard to say without seeing it in person. It would be nice if I could *feel* it, you know? It would give me a better sense of the enchantments, but..."

"But you know something?" I prompted.

The dwarf lifted her head and grinned at me. She held out one calloused hand. "I don't give knowledge away for free, do I?"

Emerald lifted one eyebrow. "Not even to a Conjury employee?"

"Hells, no." The dwarf laughed. "If this was all aboveboard, you wouldn't be coming to *me*, you'd be asking one of the Cast-cadesmen rather than a member of the Smith's Guild, wouldn't you?"

"I'm only willing to pay for *useful* information," Emerald warned.

The dwarf wiggled her fingers. "An' I promise you'll get as much intel as your money is worth."

With a weary sigh, Emerald reached into an inner pocket of his coat and produced five coins. He ignored the dwarf's hand and laid them out on the counter. "How about you tell me what you know, and I decide what it's worth to me?"

The dwarf rolled her eyes at me. "Is he always like this?"

"Stingy?" I asked. "I'm afraid so, Miss..."

"You can call me Mel." She turned back to Emerald. "My folk are from the Clanstone Mountains, so I don't need anyone telling me who *you* are."

[What does that mean?] I asked.

[Got my prominence title from the king of the Clanstone dwarves,] Emerald thought curtly. ***[Reckon I have a bit of a reputation up that way.]***

I desperately wanted to ask for details, but Mel had her eye on the coins. She pointed down at the illusory key. "First fact: this is Automatist work, but I don't know the maker."

Emerald snorted. "Thanks. That's *really* useful."

"It is when you consider that I've lived in the city all my life, and I've been working for the guild for most of it." Mel rested her elbows on the counter and grinned. "If I don't know the maker, it means that whoever it belongs to had to have gotten it made elsewhere. Maybe that doesn't mean much if they're just passing through, but if they're a local...?"

"Mm." Emerald drummed his fingers on the counter. "And how long would you say you've been working for the guild?"

Mel's eyes drifted toward the ceiling and her fingers twitched as if she were counting off the years. "Forty-one years. Thirty-eight, if you don't want to count my apprenticeship."

[And from what I've gathered, lambkins don't live a terribly long time,] I mused.

Emerald grunted. He lifted one index finger and flicked a single coin toward Mel.

She pursed her lips as she scooped it up. "And here I thought that would be worth something to you. All right, how about this: it's not guild-crafted, either."

"You already said you didn't know the maker," I pointed out. "How's that different?"

"This tells you more about who it *isn't*. There are guild members all over the continent, and thanks to Conjury regulations, we all use standardized enchantments. The same symbols, the same shapes, all of that. We work from the same instructive texts during our apprenticeships."

"Wouldn't that make it easier for someone to learn how to break them?" I asked.

"Not really. You can use the symbols in all sorts of combinations. It's like..." Mel wrinkled her nose. "Like an alphabet, I suppose. Or rather, a cipher. Being able to read Osmarian doesn't mean you automatically know every possible sentence you can construct with it, but at least you're all on the same page. Only, whoever made this ain't writing Osmarian. They're writing in... I dunno, Draconic?"

Emerald's eyes widened. "So whoever it belongs to would have had to find an Automatist who was..."

"Working without a guild license, yeah. Probably without a Conjury permit, either." Mel's eyes flicked from Emerald's face to the pile of coins and back.

He flicked another her way. "Anything else?"

"Sure." Mel hunched her shoulders and lowered her voice to a stage whisper. "Just because we don't get *trained* in other sigils doesn't mean I've never seen 'em before. And these?" She pointed to the key. "These signify a two-way street."

I followed her lead and lowered my voice as well. "What does *that* mean?"

"Means whatever this key belongs to isn't just made to keep folks out." Mel beckoned me closer before adding. "It's meant to keep something in, too."

"Something like what?" I asked, before I realized that I already knew the answer. "Something like *Aidea*?"

Mel nodded. "For example."

We both stepped back. Mel looked a great deal more satisfied than I felt. I had gotten to the answer eventually, but *much* too slowly for my liking. Why hadn't I thought of it earlier? We'd all speculated how a thief could sneak into Dumplin's private rooms undetected, and all the while I'd been hiding there, proof positive that there were no wards protecting the place from magic.

And whoever had snuck in had done so not because they wanted to steal something they could pawn... they wanted something they could *use*.

"Hmm." Emerald waved his hand, and the illusion of the key disappeared. His expression gave nothing away, not even when he pushed the last three coins toward Mel.

She swept them off the edge of the counter and into her palm with a triumphant smile. "See? I'm useful when I want to be. Anything else I can do for you?"

"If someone approached you about opening a box like this..." Emerald began.

"Wouldn't do it," Mel said at once. "Not for nonstandard enchantments like this one. There'd be *loads* of paperwork, I'd have to file a report with my superior, it'd be a bleedin' nightmare."

I fiddled absently with the lapel of my coat. "And if I wanted to bribe you, how much would I have to pay?"

Mel stood up straighter. "You think you could buy me off? Listen, I'll take a coin here and there to answer Conjury questions, but if you're testing the waters for bribery, you can show yourself out."

I shook my head. "Just wondering how hard it would be for someone to get around the enchantment. How much it would have to be worth to them."

She eyed me warily. "Well... any guild Automatist would be risking their license and the backing of the union. I'm not saying *nobody* would take the risk, but I don't know anyone who would for mere coin. But not every Automatist can work their way into an apprenticeship, and not every apprentice earns a position."

I watched Emerald out of the corner of my eye. I didn't need our mental link to know what he was thinking, because I was thinking it, too.

If one renegade Automatist was all that stood between the thief and whatever was inside that box, we might soon find ourselves at the center of a very nasty business indeed.

BY THE TIME we left the Smith's Guild, it was already getting dark. The bustle of the day had given way to the quiet of early evening. Peddlers were packing up their wares, and while the streets weren't as empty as they had been after nightfall in deep winter, we passed very few people as we headed back to the edges of town.

[Wish we'd done things the other way around.] Emerald kicked a loose cobble in irritation. *[I thought I was so clever for recognizing the work of an Inciter... Why in every hell didn't Dumplin mention that there was* Aidea *involved?]*

[Maybe she didn't want you to know?]

[She must have realized we'd figure it out sooner or later!] Emerald stuffed his hands in the massive pockets of his coat and hunched over like a sullen child. *[It would have been one thing if I was interrogating her, but she's the one who called us in. And given that we work for the Conjury, I think she'd be worried about calling us in and revealing that she had something illeg—oh.]* He stopped short. *[Oh, of course. But how would she...? Of course, Marsha...]*

I had lost the thread of his runaway monologue and would have demanded answers if another, much softer voice hadn't hissed:

[Look out.]

I spun in a circle, instantly on guard. I had only a moment to be embarrassed by how easily Innocent could put me on edge. The creature could easily be playing with me, driving me to maddening distraction.

Only, there *was* someone watching us.

"Emerald," I snapped. "Over there."

"Huh?" He shook himself like a dog shaking off rainwater. "What am I looking at, exactly?"

"Him." I took a step toward the young man who had just emerged from a nearby alleyway. He was short and slim, with the patchy beginnings of a beard that marked him as more youth than adult. He was dressed in black, from his boots to the hood that was pulled up around his moon-pale face. He looked like an ordinary human, until he turned his eyes. Then, they glinted silver and flat, like those of an owl on the hunt or a cat watching its prey.

Emerald weighed easily three times as much as he did. So why was I afraid?

"Crimson, don't point at people on the street, it's rude," Emerald said. "He's only—"

The boy burst into motion, charging forward with his hands spread as if he were carrying something the size of Emerald's skull between them, but there was nothing there. Nothing, at least, that I could see, but I could *feel* it pulling at me, stretching me, *thinning* me...

I didn't know what he was doing, but it involved the *Aidea*.

Emerald dropped into a crouch. A few passersby stopped to watch, their mouths falling open, but if they spoke, I couldn't hear them. All I could hear was the hum. It was so loud that I instinctively lifted my hands to cover my ears, although of course my intangible palms did nothing to block the sound. It wasn't coming from outside of me, anyway, but from within, as if the whole world was vibrating to match the frequency of the power cradled in the boy's hands.

The boy was only three strides away when the world exploded.

Everything happened at once.

Emerald swung a fist at the boy's head and sent him sprawling; and Emerald swung wide and lost his footing so that he crashed into our assailant; and Emerald stumbled backward and clamped his hands over his ears, only to trip over the curb while the boy attacked. It was as if I was watching dozens of possible realities play out at the same time, with dozens of Emeralds and dozens of boys and dozens of *mes* all colliding in every permutation of possible outcomes.

The hum ended abruptly, and it took the dizzying sensation of possibility with it, consolidating into a single reality in which Emerald fell backward, cracked his head on the cobbles, and went still. The boy was on him at once, clawing at his neck with all the ferocity of a mother griffin protecting her nest.

Emerald's pendant flashed in the boy's palm. There was nothing I could do but cry out in vain as the boy yanked the chain so hard that the clasp broke, and I vanished.

CHAPTER FOUR

[*Too bad,*] Innocent whispered. [*I was hoping this might be my chance.*]

I lay on my back staring up at the star-spangled ceiling of the mind-cottage. Everything had happened so fast that I could barely make sense of the chain of events which led me to be trapped in my own private reality.

"What *happened?*" I mumbled.

[*A Kineticist attacked us. Or perhaps a Cosmic? It can be so hard to tell when their magic doesn't fit the rules.*] There was a crack in the ceiling, the twin of the one in Emerald's old bedroom through which I had first glimpsed the shadow-beast. That didn't bode well. A crack might widen over time.

A crack might eventually become a means of escape.

Things in the mind-cottage never quite followed the rules of the world outside. It wasn't a physical space, and as such, nothing should have existed outside of it. And yet, even as I watched, a rippling shadow moved on the far side.

"Why are you saying that the person who attacked us was a cast-off?" I asked. *Aidea* users generally fell into one of about thirty different classifications, but there were some whose abilities were so specialized or unusual that they didn't fall into any known category at all. According to the knowledge I'd inherited from Emerald, cast-offs were particularly dangerous, if only because they were so unpredictable.

[Is it?] Above me, the darkness shifted. *[Is that what I'm saying, Crimson Smoke? There is a great deal that the Conjury doesn't know, that their scholars have failed to analyze.]* An eye appeared in the gap above me. *[You and I are proof of that.]*

The eye flashed in the sourceless light of my mind-cottage, and I gasped. It was flat and reflective, just like—

"Crimson?" Emerald's voice was frantic. "Crimson, are you all right?"

I blinked a few times. I wasn't sure when it had happened, but I was no longer in the mind-cottage. Instead, I was lying on the floor of a familiar kitchen. Five worried faces stared down at me. Quell, Blare, and Svelte had obviously been crying; Yerik wore the unflappable expression of someone who had chosen *not* to have a panic attack, thank you very much; and Emerald, looking somewhat greener than usual, was kneeling next to me.

As a matter of fact, *everything* had a greenish tint to it.

"What's happening?" I asked. My voice didn't sound right. I tried to get up and failed utterly.

A drunkard might have tripped over his own feet and sprawled on his face. I tripped over my feet and burst into a prism of light, scrawling rainbows across the kitchen floor as I fractured into the individual components of myself.

"Steady, steady." Yerik laid a hand on Emerald's shoulder and squeezed. "I think it's working."

"It's not," said the red bits that were usually my favorite part of being Crimson Smoke. "I've just realized that one seventh of me is yellow, and I may never get over the shock."

Emerald let out a wordless sob and pressed the back of his hand to his mouth. His other hand shifted a bit, and I was back to being

Crimson, or close enough. Breaking apart didn't hurt, but I didn't like it one bit.

"I'm sorry, Crim." Emerald opened his fist to show me the smashed-off bottom of a green wine bottle. "I know you hate being sent away. I didn't mean to."

"Emerald." I made another attempt to stand. "You were *attacked.* You can't possibly think I'd be mad about—*oh help!*" I stumbled sideways and tried to catch myself against the freestanding cutting board only to fall *through* it and break back into a disordered and disgruntled prism.

[*This is not a sustainable means of existence,*] I complained.

"It's because I don't have my necklace," Emerald said. He shifted the fragment of the bottle again. "It's not ideal."

Blare's eyes widened. He clapped his hands to get our attention before signing, *What did he say the problem is? That it's flat?*

Svelte shook her head. *Sorry,* she signed, *I should have been signing the whole time. He said the glass is not ideal, but he didn't say…*

He doesn't have an affinity for it. Blare bit his bottom lip and stared, not at Emerald, but at the mess I had become. At least I was whole for the moment. Judging by how I felt, though, I probably looked pathetic.

I think I can help, he signed, and bolted toward the door.

"Any idea what that's about?" Quell asked.

Svelte sucked her teeth. "He doesn't tell me *everything,* you know."

Yerik slumped back against the counter and scrubbed his hands across his face. "Well," he said, "this has been quite the revelation."

Emerald, still crouched on the floor, hunched his shoulders further still. "I'm sorry. I should have told you about Crimson, I just…"

"That they're a lightweaving? It's not entirely surprising." Yerik's laugh was slightly manic, but there was real humor in it. "Emerald, please, give me a bit of credit. I've seen you do lightweaving before, you were a Castcadesman for the Conjury, your best friend is a Lightweaver—"

"Best friend?" Emerald asked.

"Coirpre," Yerik explained.

I coughed into my fist.

"And then you show up with this—this person." Yerik waved a hand at me. "Who never looks the same twice, but who *can* have conversations without you. No, I figured out what they are early on. What I didn't know for certain until tonight is that Crimson is *real*. You wouldn't be in a panic otherwise. At the very least, you would have let me bandage your head properly before you started casting."

Emerald bit his bottom lip and lifted one hand to probe at the back of his skull. He hissed when his fingers made contact. "Fair enough."

"You're smart," Quell told Yerik. "*I* thought they were a ghost."

"Does the Conjury know about Crimson?" Yerik asked.

I shook my head. "Not the important parts."

"All right." Yerik squeezed his eyes shut and took a deep breath. "So. How can I help?"

Emerald's shoulders sagged with relief. "I wish I knew."

The patter of feet on the stairs heralded Blare's return. He shoved through the door, cradling something in his hands, which he offered to Emerald.

My friend's brow crinkled in confusion as he accepted the large green marble. "What's this?" he asked. "I think I've seen it before."

I took it from the Brotherhood, Blare signed. *Crimson said it used to be yours.*

Many of Emerald's childhood memories had been sealed away in the depths of his subconscious by his old mentor. In some ways, I was glad that Brother Harmony had spared Emerald all the pain and guilt that would have come with remembering. On the other hand, it meant that some conversations simply wouldn't stick in his brain no matter how many times we had them.

"Was it?" Emerald frowned at the marble for what seemed to me a very long time before twisting it and the chunk of glass in his palm. The resulting sensation was terribly strange, but the relief that followed was immediate. The world became clearer, and when I took a hesitant step to one side, I retained my shape.

"Seems like it was," Emerald mused. "Thank you, Blare." He set the disc of glass on the counter and got to his feet. "That's very helpful."

"Wonderful." Yerik clapped his hands together. "Now, I want you all out in the dining room. We're going to have some dinner, I'm going to clean that injury of yours, and then you're going to tell us exactly what's going on."

THE LUTE and Goose was quiet that night. While Yerik hurried around getting everything in order, the children explained what I'd missed. Emerald had staggered into the inn halfway through the evening in a state of disarray. Yerik had shooed all the diners out and locked the door behind them, and Emerald had rushed around like a madman in search of something suitable for spellcasting.

"I thought he was going to cry," Svelte whispered. "I've never seen him like that. He was *scared*."

"I didn't know people that big could get that scared," Quell added. The lambkin wrapped his arms around himself and shivered. "Yerik was brilliant, though. He was like a general, telling everyone what to do."

I'm glad you're all right, Blare said. *How do you feel now?*

"Better," I told him, signing as I spoke. "I'm lucky you thought to bring that marble with you."

He bit his lip and nodded as Yerik hauled Emerald over and sat him down in one of the empty chairs. "Wait here," the innkeeper commanded.

The children seemed reluctant to talk with Emerald present. He kept poking the back of his head and frowning at the table.

[This is you, isn't it, Crim?] he asked.

I cocked my head. *[What do you mean?]*

[Back in Upper Bound, I made something that... wasn't you. I thought it was, but it wasn't.]

I knew exactly what he was talking about, although recalling the experience was just as awful for me as it was for him. *[It's me,]* I assured him. *[I don't know how I'd prove it, all things considered, but it's me. You'll just have to take my word for it.]*

Someone knocked on the front door, and Svelte leapt to her feet, crying, "I'll get it!" just a bit too loudly. "I'll tell 'em we're closed."

"No." Emerald lurched upright. "I don't know who attacked me, but if they followed me back here, I don't want you getting in the way."

Svelte sank back into her chair as Emerald headed toward the door, her brows pulled tight together.

"He didn't mean it like that," I said. "You wouldn't be *in the way*. You'd be in danger, and he wants to avoid that."

"Yeah," Svelte murmured, signing along for Blare's benefit. "That's the weird part. Grown-ups don't usually want to protect me. Even Brother Harmony wasn't... paternal. Not really."

Blare nodded. *Yerik cares. Emerald cares. You* care. *It's weird.*

As their words sunk in, Yerik emerged from the kitchen with a giant tray of cold cuts, pastries, fruit, and tea. "Oh, Aster's gardens. Where's he gone now?"

Emerald returned with three figures in tow and a scowl on his face. "I was greeting our guests. Looks like we're about to get an explanation."

"I think that's warranted." The smallest of the three figures lowered her indigo hood and fluffed out the mass of honey-blond curls beneath. Quell let out a squeak of surprise.

"Dumplin." I crossed my arms and glared at her, along with her two cronies. "To what do we owe the pleasure?"

. . .

Dumplin blew on the cup of tea that Yerik had poured for her. "The first thing you need to know about me is that my reputation isn't quite what it seems."

"Yeah," Emerald said. "I worked that out. Most brothels aren't one-woman affairs, and between *your* size and *their* size"—he nodded to the Pruv guards who were standing guard at either door —"the math doesn't add up. No offense to your stamina."

Yerik grimaced. "Emerald, please, there are children present."

"One of my neighbors worked in a brothel, back before I was sent to the Brotherhood," Svelte said. "She was really nice."

I wrinkled my nose at her. "What exactly *is* a brothel?" I tried to find an answer in Emerald's memories, but they were strangely closed off.

Svelte smirked. "I'll tell you when you're older."

Emerald cleared his throat. "*Anyway.* After what we learned in the guild, I take it you're a Lightweaver?"

Dumplin shook her head. "Not exactly."

Emerald blinked a few times. I could almost hear him sifting back through the clues we'd gathered. "But... but the necklace you're using is Lightweaver magic. No other branch of the *Aidea* uses gems as a focus, and that's what the necklace is. You're using an amethyst dragon scale to let your clients experience anything they want. To live out their fantasies."

"No, honey, but you're very close." Dumplin set her cup down on the table and leaned forward conspiratorially. "I'm not a Lightweaver. I'm not much of anything. I know enough about the art to realize what *you* were doing..." She shot me a pointed look. "But the necklace itself is enchanted. The silver settings are made from..."

"*Silver* dragon scales." Emerald's eyes widened. "And the key, too. Gods above, how much did you pay for magic like that?"

"I have connections," Dumplin said. "And you'll forgive me if I don't disclose all my secrets to a Conjury stooge. I know exactly how powerful that necklace is... and how illegal it is for me to own it. It's a pretty bit of jewelry, though, and I think you're the kind of man who could fully appreciate the level of artisanship that went into the making of it. The silver settings work as a source of energy to power the gem's illusions, using the wearer as a sort of muse."

"Oh, my." Yerik looked as if he'd been struck about the head several times in quick succession. He lifted both hands to rub his temples. "Dragon scales? Even *I* know that's bad. The lengths the Conjury would go to if it meant they could get their hands on *dragon* magic..."

"Are dragons that powerful?" I asked.

Every head in the room swiveled toward me. Even Quell, who was barely three, seemed disturbed by my ignorance. I shrunk in my seat. "Sorry for asking," I mumbled. ***[Thanks for nothing, Em. You could just* tell *me these things...]***

"Dragon magic is tricky," Emerald said aloud, mostly for my benefit. "It's like cast-off magic, only... more. Dragons can pull magic from the very air. They're almost extinct now, but one rogue dragon could easily wipe out a city, if it was old enough and powerful enough. The Conjury isn't exactly forgiving when it comes to dabbling in dragon magic."

"I understand that." Dumplin let her fingertips drift over the silver chain at her throat. "In the right hands, it could be dangerous. Hence the box."

"If it's so dangerous, why are you using it at all?" Quell asked. The young lambkin had given up his *Aidea* only a few months before, and I knew that he'd wrestled with the question of power in the past.

Dumplin smiled sadly. "Because I happen to believe that I can use it for good. I don't want to build an army and topple the kingdom. I don't want to make myself a queen. I just want to feel *safe*, for once. I use the magic for profit, yes, but I do it by providing my clients with a perfect fantasy. Some want to speak final words to loved ones who are gone. Some want a sense of closure with those who have wronged them. Some want to live the most perfect moments of their lives over again, just as vividly as they lived them the first time."

"So you lie to them," Emerald said.

Dumplin's cheeks flushed. "It's not that simple. What I do requires trust. I can't create those moments without knowing my clients intimately. As I said, I'm the architect of those moments. I have to be able to guide them through those fantasies, and to do it in a way that brings them *peace*, rather than feeding an addiction. Do you have any idea how many clients I turn away? How many requests I deny? I give my clients something they can't get anywhere else, and I'm *supremely* careful to do it in a way that respects their minds, emotions, and autonomy. Do you really think the Conjury would do the same?"

Emerald drummed his fingers on the table and reluctantly shook his head. "No."

"So, are you going to report me?" Dumplin demanded.

"...no."

"Then I guess you had better figure out who stole my necklace." Dumplin leaned back in her chair. "I had no idea that they'd target you, but when I heard someone had jumped you in the street, I figured I'd better come clean. Because if the thefts are related, there's now a very powerful Kineticist running around the city with two pieces of magical jewelry, and I don't think that bodes well for anyone."

"Or a Cosmic," I blurted.

Emerald tilted his head to one side. "Why do you say that?"

"Just a hunch," I lied. "Since their magic is so weird, it could be either, couldn't it?"

After some consideration, Emerald nodded, confirming Innocent's earlier assertion. "I suppose."

Between Dumplin's revelations and Innocent's little hints, I had begun to form a theory of my own. I had tried to explain the situation with Innocent to Emerald in the past, but his mental block meant that the shadow-beast's existence was one of the things he couldn't remember. Instead, I was forced to choose my words carefully so that Emerald would be able to understand my idea.

"If this is the same person," I said slowly, "they've now stolen at least two objects that are capable of casting... nontraditional illusions. What if that's the goal?"

Emerald's brow furrowed. "Elaborate."

"Let's say there was something magical that didn't belong here. That defied the laws of magic. Something that needed *more* magic in order to manifest on this plane."

"Like you," Quell said.

Blare gulped. *Or the shadow-man.*

"Precisely," I said.

"Shadow-man?" Emerald asked.

Yerik's eyes were huge. "Are you suggesting that someone is trying to conjure a *demon*?"

Emerald snorted. "Don't be superstitious, Yerik. Outsiders are hardly 'demons.' That's something you picked up from Modest's old lectures."

"The Brotherhood aren't the only ones who talk about demonic beings," Yerik retorted. "Call them Outsiders if it makes you feel better, but they're real, and the harm they can do is real, too. They can possess people."

"You make it sound like an everyday occurrence," Emerald argued.

"Well, it's not every day that you're attacked in an alley by a violent Kineticist," Yerik snapped, "so maybe we should consider the possibility that these aren't ordinary circumstances!"

Emerald considered this. *[Do you think he's tried to use the gem?]* he asked.

[Your guess is as good as mine.]

"You think someone's using my necklace to try to summon an Outsider?" Dumplin asked in horror.

"No," I said. Once again, everyone turned to look at me.

I wasn't certain, but I had seen the way the boy's eyes flashed. Innocent had known that something was off long before Emerald realized it. The implications were disturbing, but I could guess at their meaning.

"I think the, er, the *Outsider* is already here," I said. "I think it's already in that boy's head. And I think it wants to get out."

Everyone started talking at once, but I was more worried about the hissing laughter in the back of my head. *[An Outsider who's trapped between realms and wants to escape into the material plane,]* Innocent mused. *[What a novelty. I wonder if it will find a way?]*

I sure as every hell hoped not, because it would set a very dangerous precedent indeed.

CHAPTER FIVE

"Do you think this is going to get rid of it for good?" I asked Emerald as he fussed around in the kitchen of the Lute and Goose.

"I don't know that it's possible to get rid of an Outsider." Emerald tipped a spoonful of dried herbs into the pot and reached for a vial.

"Another potion." I peered down into the liquid. "Is this a key element of investigation? Because I'm afraid this is one skill I can't learn."

Emerald snorted. "I work with what I know. And I know plants. So, yes, I'm making another potion."

I hovered around him. In part, I did so because I was genuinely interested in his work. Also, I couldn't leave him. Literally. While I was no longer falling to pieces, experimentation had revealed that my mobility was vastly limited when it came to the marble. I could give him enough privacy to use the privy, but that was about it.

"It's odd," I observed, "that you never mentioned Outsiders before."

Emerald sighed. "Next, you'll be giving me grief for not telling you about dragons. The things you don't know could fill a library, Crim. Hells, the things *I* don't know could fill a library. Well, a bookcase, anyway."

"So modest," I muttered.

He ignored me. "And it's not as if I go around thinking about Outsiders in my spare time. The chances to study them are so slim you can hardly call them 'documented.' For every person who's had a real encounter, there's fifty in a Gwalgofeth sanctuary with delusions of possession. And for each of *them*, there's a priest or paladin rambling on about demons and private hells to scare people into making a donation."

I hopped up and floated onto the counter so that I could watch him work. "Not to be a contrarian, but I'm just now finding out that there's another species of bodiless spirits floating around in the aether." I wiggled my fingers as if to suggest that every mote of dust or slant of spring sunshine might spring to life at a moment's notice. "And we don't know how I came to be."

"Yeah. And?"

"Did it never occur to you that *I* might be one?" I demanded.

Months ago, after the trying events at Emerald's childhood home that led to Innocent's residence in the mind-cottage, I had sworn off trying to categorize myself. In a world where everyone else seemed so intent on doing it for me, the idea of solving the mystery of my origins and uncovering any sort of accompanying label has lost its appeal. And yet, I had been nursing an existential crisis at the thought of my potential demonic nature for hours.

Instead of extending sympathy, however, Emerald only laughed. "Really? *You?* Come on, now."

I crossed my arms over my chest and glared at him. "Why not?" I could not say why his dismissive tone offended me. It wasn't as if I *wanted* to find out that I was a creature of untold mystery and malignant evil.

In a way, though, it would have been nice to know what I *was*. Even if I didn't like the answer.

"Crimson." Emerald left his concoction to simmer and turned to face me. "I will admit, you can be *very* vexing when you want to be. But there are all kinds of disembodied entities wandering around in the world: ghosts, ghasts, spirits, living statues... certain types of constructs can even achieve a facsimile of consciousness. I may not have much firsthand experience with Outsiders, but I *do* know that they're powerful, and that they can tap into magic beyond the scope of any *Aidea* we know about." He shivered. "And, when they latch onto a vessel, they're not exactly respectful of the occupant."

"So I'm weak but respectful?" I asked.

Emerald smirked. "Insulting my wardrobe doesn't count. Besides, we know that I can control you. I won't anymore, but I *can*. Like it or not, I'm quite confident that you came out of here." He tapped his temple. "Outsiders are monsters, Crim. They only look out for themselves."

If that were true, then how could he explain Innocent's obsession with Allure? The trouble, of course, was that he *couldn't*, because he couldn't remember.

I tucked that nugget of information away for later and nodded toward his work in progress. "So if you can't get rid of this thing, then what's the point of the potion?"

"This is insurance," he said. "If the Outsider tries to leave its host, I don't want it coming after me. Theoretically, this should be able to force an Outsider into the open. I'll drink half, and ideally, I'll find a way to get the other half into its host."

"And then we'll have an angry Outsider hovering around," I said.

"Yeah, well. I don't think there's a potion for *that*." Emerald went back to stirring. "But don't worry. I have a plan."

MEL SQUINTED UP AT EMERALD. She had one hand pressed to her mouth and the other resting on the counter. She'd adopted that attitude early in his explanation, and her silent disbelief had only intensified the more he spoke.

"I'm sorry," she said when he was finished. "Let me see if I've got this right. You want to know if I can build a device that can catch an *Outsider*?"

Emerald smiled crookedly at her. "Precisely. And thank you so much for not calling it a demon."

Mel muttered something under her breath and lowered her hand. "Let's say I *could* build such a thing," she grumbled. "I'd have to file a truly absurd amount of paperwork. The Conjury would hear about it eventually. What exactly do you plan on doing with a trapped Outsider anyway?"

Emerald squared his shoulders. "Hand it over to my superior at the Conjury."

I made no attempt to smother my rush of disapproval. *[Is that wise? You know what the Conjury was prepared to do with the citizens of Dyrne. Is handing them a monster the wisest choice?]*

[Actually, yeah.] Emerald absent-mindedly poked the back of his head. *[Because the alternative is keeping a monster in my room at the inn, and that's not happening.]*

He had a point, I supposed, even if I didn't like it, which seemed to be an ongoing theme.

Mel was still mulling his request over. "You're asking for something *really* theoretical here," she said. "I'm not even sure it can be done."

"You told me that the key I showed you could keep something out *or* in," Emerald pressed.

"Sure, with contraband automation! But maybe if I..." Mel's eyes unfocused. "I mean, I'm not saying it would be perfect, but... maybe with a ward... we've got a Fluxist on staff who might be able to help..."

"*Oh.*" Emerald's eyes widened, and he leaned over our side of the counter until he was almost level with Mel's gaze. "Are you thinking of applying Goldbloom's Sixth Theorem?"

"You know Goldbloom?" Mel asked, surprised.

"I do. Most of what I've studied is theoretical, but I figured out how to adapt his Sixth Theorem for lightweaving application. That way, you can recharge an illusion spell without needing an actual *Lightweaver* on hand to do the work."

I had been losing interest in the conversation until he said that, but I shook off my bored stupor. I neither knew nor cared who Goldbloom was, but apparently this theory was behind the spell that kept Dyrne hidden from prying eyes.

"Ooh, that's clever!" Mel exclaimed. She spun her fingers around each other in ever-faster circles. "And I mean, theoretically, an Outsider is mostly *Aidea*, so the mechanism could be self-powering. *Theoretically.* Any time it tried to escape, you could just... *hands of Odologys,* I need to be taking notes!"

While the two of them babbled and Mel began to sketch, I let my mind wander. Sure, we'd figured out what we were looking for. But how in every hell were we going to track an Outsider down?

Unless it found us first.

CHAPTER SIX

"Does it seem suspicious," I asked, "that you and Dumplin were robbed on the same day, and yet we haven't heard anything untoward since then?"

[It most certainly does.] Emerald plodded through the snow on the way to Conjury headquarters. He no longer needed to bandage his head, although there was still a goose egg on the back of his skull that he prodded every so often. *[The good news is that an Outsider hasn't been rampaging through the streets killing everyone in its path, so it could be worse.]*

Three days of poking around the city had yielded us dozens of strange rumors: a young nobleman had supposedly disappeared after a tryst with his lover; there had been periodic rumblings along the wharf that resulted in damage to a handful of private vessels; the castle had been locked down since the ill-fated party that winter; conspiracy theories about the king and the Conjury abounded; and, inexplicably, there had been an uptick in snake bites at the city limits despite the lingering chill. Most of it, Emerald assured me, was probably nonsense, and very little of it was useful to us.

Which left us at a dead end, and me nearly at my *wit's* end, given that I couldn't get more than ten paces away from my friend without getting yanked back into his lap. Why had I ever complained about the length of my tether before?

[Do you think he's been lying low?]

[More likely, he's been stealing illegal trinkets that no one wants to report.] Emerald stomped up the steps of the Conjury building. *[You haven't noticed anything weird, have you?]*

[If you're asking about the gemstone, we've gone over this. If I could sense anyone trying to use it, I would tell you, but we don't even know if it works like that.]

[No need to get touchy. I was just wondering...]

[Well, you've 'just wondered' the same question about three times a day since he stole the emerald. Let me remind you that you're the investigator here, and the only one of us with extensive lightweaving experience. I'm just the poor bastard who has to watch your nostrils quiver while you sleep.]

Emerald yanked the front door open. *[If you think I like this any more than you do, you're gravely mistaken...]*

Our bickering was interrupted by raised voices at the front desk. The secretary, a young man who sported a perpetually bored expression, was watching Commander Finch argue with an elf.

"We're not his *answering* service, and you can't just hang around here until he shows up. I already told you, he hasn't been here in days."

"Him?" the elf asked. "It's the woman *I'm* looking for. About this high, strikingly pretty, human, red hair?"

"I'm afraid they're something of a package deal and—*well*. Emerald." Finch spotted us and crossed her arms. Her whiskers bristled in irritation. "You've seen fit to bless us with your presence at last. What wonderful timing. You've got a message waiting." She pointed to the elf.

"Two messages." The secretary held an envelope aloft. It was stamped with the emblem of the Smith's Guild.

Finch growled.

The elf, however, looked relieved. He hurried over and bowed to me. "I'm not sure if you remember me, miss..."

"From the shop," I said.

Finch's ears flicked.

The tension in the room shifted, and I realized how dangerous a game I was playing. I forced a smile and tried to relax. "Did you find my friend's necklace?" I asked.

"No, but this was slipped under my shop door this morning." The elf held up a sheet of paper, folded in half.

"Oh." I nodded to Emerald. "He'll take it."

Emerald retrieved the note and flipped it open. His eyes widened, and the color left his face. He coughed once before holding it up for me to read.

DEAR SIR,

You were recently approached about a necklace. Please be so kind as to inform the lady who inquired after it that I plan to return it to her friend. I'm certain she will be profoundly grateful for your efforts.

– An Admirer

"OH." I glanced at Emerald in dismay. "You just received this?"

The elf bowed his head. "I came straight away. Not to be indelicate, but you mentioned how grateful you would be for any leads."

"Of course." I tipped my chin toward Emerald. "I believe we can—"

I shivered. Finch was looking at me strangely, and a spark of alarm shot across Emerald's face.

"Sorry," I began again, "I was just—"

Something tugged at my middle, the way my tether did when I reached the end of it, but Emerald was so close that I could have brushed my fingers through his arm merely by extending my own. I placed one hand on my middle and doubled over. The tug wasn't painful, exactly, but I could hardly ignore it.

"Oh, dear," I said. "I don't like that at all."

Emerald reached for me, and the elf bent forward as if to catch me.

[I think we're about to get an answer to your question,] I told Emerald.

And then I was gone.

I WAS GETTING EXTREMELY tired of being yanked about at the will of hostile forces.

One moment, I was bent double in the halls of the Conjury headquarters. The next, I was standing in the middle of a familiar tavern.

The first time I'd visited Dumplin's establishment, it had been packed to the brim with well-meaning Pruvs. At that moment, however, it looked as if a storm had blown through.

Poke lay in a heap by the front door under a broken table. His counterpart was slumped over the bar, unconscious. Every chair in the tavern had been either smashed or overturned and lay close to the wall. The center of the room was almost empty, as if some powerful force had detonated and blown everything outward from its central point. The only things that remained in the middle were two figures and a display box inlaid with silver.

The boy who had attacked us in the alleyway knelt on the floor, pinning Dumplin in place. One hand was on the lambkin's throat, and the other held a dagger that pressed into the faintly furred skin of her jaw.

Dumplin was breathing hard. Tears filled her bright blue eyes. The boy, however, had no expression at all. He was strangely calm, utterly at odds with the room around him. A dozen chains and cords bearing various pendants had slipped from the collar of his shirt and dangled over Dumplin's terrified face. I recognized a familiar green gem among their number.

"Tell us," the boy rasped, "how to open it."

His voice was terrible to hear. I could hear the cracking voice of a young man at its core, but there was another layer to it, as if a second voice was speaking at the same time, something low and rotten and laced with decay.

"Please, you're hurting me!" Dumplin gasped.

"Nothing works," the boy and the thing inside him said. "We keep trying and trying, we have mingled our magics, and still, *nothing works*. But you can help us. You can open it, and *you* can let me out."

I shuddered at the sound of the voice. My movement caught the boy's attention, and he whipped his head up to glare at me with his flat, gleaming eyes. "Hello. Where did you come from?"

I lifted my chin and squared my shoulders. "I'm here to inform you that you're under arrest."

He laughed. Dumplin whimpered as the boy sat back on his heels to study me. "Oh," he said. "Interesting." The hand that had been on Dumplin's throat snaked up to the array of pendants around his neck. His fingers found the emerald. "We never know *what* will happen with the potential we tap from this vessel."

Dumplin curled into a ball and sobbed as the boy rolled back on his heels and rose to his feet. His movements were too smooth to be natural. He stalked toward me, still gripping the gem that had summoned me.

"How do you intend to arrest us?" he asked.

I lifted my chin even higher. "How do you intend to resist?"

He blinked a few times, looking me up and down. "We could break the gem," he suggested.

That stopped me cold. The destruction of the gem was one possibility I had never considered, but it would certainly be an effective means of making my existence *very* difficult. Would Emerald still be able to summon me without it? Would I end up being bound to the marble in his pocket for the foreseeable future?

[You could let me out,] Innocent whispered.

I shook my head sharply. "No."

"You don't think we would?" The boy smiled. "No, you're right. That would be a waste of potential, after all. If she won't help us, perhaps *you* can be of use."

He lifted the gem in his palm and inhaled and exhaled slowly. I felt that shift again, that fracturing of reality that splintered the world into its myriad possible futures. The world around us blurred as Crimsons slipped and moved, as versions of the tables slid across the floor, as dozens of Dumplins reacted in dozens of terrified ways, all to no avail.

And then I was standing where the boy had been, and I was looking at a monster.

The Outsider rolled its shoulders. Its long, skeletal limbs flexed and twisted, and the dark smudge of its withered face opened its jaw. "Oh," it said, and there was nothing at all human about that voice anymore. Only the awful parts remained. It turned on the spot, unfolding its limbs as it straightened up to its full height. The base of its blackened skull nearly brushed the ceiling. "Oh, this is *much* better."

I looked down at my hands. Or rather, the boy's hands, one of which was still gripping the gem.

I could feel the boy's fear in the trembling of his limbs and the erratic thumping of his heart. A sour smell seared the inside of his nostrils; I doubt he'd washed in days. He was terrified.

I didn't mean to do it, he thought. *I didn't mean to call her. It was an accident. I'm sorry!*

Inhabiting his body was a bit like inhabiting Emerald's had been when I possessed him on the riverbank in Upper Bound. I was at the helm, and I was the one who would be making decisions for the pair of us, at least for the moment. I forced his body to take another slow breath and planted his feet.

Gods, it was awful to control someone who was so terrified.

"It is so good to be free. To be the only one in my head." It—*she,* according to the boy's frantic thoughts—rolled its shoulders and stretched its neck. She loped over to the nearest pile of wood that could no longer be called a chair and dug her claws into it.

The chair didn't splinter, but it smoked where her hands closed around it, leaving a charred imprint in the wood. She hissed and pulled back, frowning at her palm. "No good," she said. "Even with my magic, it is not enough to be an illusion." The Outsider stretched, languorous as a cat, and turned back to face me. "But perhaps, without the host... if I can cast *myself*..."

I didn't quite understand her line of thinking, but it was quite obvious that the boy she'd somehow stuck me in was about to meet an unfortunate fate. Sifting through his thoughts was much more difficult than sifting through Emerald's, but at least his grasp of the *Aidea* was easy to summon. The memory seemed to live in his body as much as his mind.

Unfortunately, he was still panicking, and as Emerald had said, I was neither strong enough nor malicious enough to overpower his will entirely. When I tried to move, the boy fought back, and with our combined efforts we managed to trip over our own feet and land in an inelegant heap on the floor.

"I'm trying to *help* you!" I snapped.

"Help me?" The Outsider rose up on her long, skeletal limbs and stalked toward us. "You will help me most by dying. Such a shame, after how close we became... but our time has come to an end, Bram. We are so very close to succeeding."

[Let me out,] Innocent insisted.

I growled and pushed my borrowed body into a sitting position. There was too much magic in play. I didn't understand it.

And it turned out, I didn't like not knowing things.

My anger made me reckless, and I made another attempt to twist the *Aidea* into something useful. The floorboards beneath Bram's hands splintered and sent scraps of jagged wood flying, but it was a poor imitation of what I'd seen him do before.

The Outsider laughed and loomed over me, baring what seemed to be a thousand needle-sharp teeth in a hideous smile. "So stubborn. So desperate. So *weak*." She bent closer and reached her hand toward our throat.

"You are in a garden," said a bell-clear voice.

And it was true. I was still in Bram's body, still face down on the floor, and the Outsider was still standing over me, but the wreckage around us was gone. Instead, a carpet of grass lay beneath me, freckled with brilliant wildflowers.

The Outsider froze.

I lifted my head to get a better view of what was happening. Fruit trees laden with blossoms were surrounded by clouds of bees. Birds sang in the canopy. Vines and stalks jutted upward from the plots around us. It was beautiful.

But it was more than that. I could *feel* the grass beneath the boy's hands, smell the sweetness of spring on the wind, bask in the warm sun on my back. It wasn't the right season, and this place didn't exist, but every one of the boy's senses believed that it was real.

I craned my neck to look around and, in the midst of all that beauty, spotted Dumplin. She was kneeling amid the blooms, her knees folded beneath her, eyes closed, her small hands resting on the ornate necklace like a priestess in an attitude of prayer. Its silverwork glittered in the sunlight. With every breath she took, the purple gem at its center shimmered and winked like a living eye.

"You are in a garden," she repeated. "You feel peaceful."

"The scale." The Outsider shifted toward her, but the creature moved slowly, as if she were not quite sure what she meant to do next.

"The sun is warm," Dumplin went on, in a melodic voice that begged the boy's muscles to relax. "The air is sweet. You are so very, very tired after all your travels. It's time to rest."

The Outsider's head drooped. Her ghastly jaws parted in a yawn. "Yes," she murmured. "A rest."

I was supposed to be doing something, but I had no idea what. Dumplin was right. I *was* tired. Maybe a little nap wouldn't be a bad thing.

"Close your eyes," Dumplin said. "Lie down. You've earned it. There will be time for everything else later."

She had a point. Surely whatever I was supposed to do would keep until later. I had never been tired before, but in my borrowed body, Bram's exhaustion was my own. His eyelids fluttered, and he bit back another yawn.

In the distance, something creaked. Another figure emerged from between the garden beds. I had to rub my eyes before I could make out the details of a large man picking his way through the greenery.

"Emerald!" I slurred in delight. "When did you get here?"

The Outsider stirred, but before it could more than blink, Dumplin said, "The birdsong is a lullaby. A breeze is coming in off the sea." Sure enough, the grass stirred as a cool breath of salt-laden air passed over us.

Emerald knelt down next to me and held up a flask. "Drink this," he said under his breath.

I accepted the flask and sniffed. Bram wrinkled his nose. "Doesn't smell very nice," I whispered back.

Dumplin was still speaking when Emerald tweaked my ear. "Don't be difficult," he hissed. "It's for your own good."

I took a swig of whatever was inside and winced at the taste.

"I need you to be ready," Emerald said. He reclaimed the flask. "The instant Dumplin stops talking, that thing's going to go berserk."

I nodded and tried to sit up. Even through the haze of Dumplin's enchantment, I knew that I had to help Emerald, although what he wanted was a mystery and the means by which I was going to help him achieve it were obscurer still. He approached Dumplin as I tried to rally myself and bent down to whisper into her ear. She nodded and tipped her head back as he lifted the flask to her lips.

Reality came crashing back over us, and Bram's fear came with it. The Outsider roared and leapt upright, snapping her teeth at my friend.

Emerald tossed the empty flask aside and ducked beneath her. I felt the crackle of magic as the Outsider lashed out with a blast of explosive force that made the beams above us sag and splinter. The reverberations of that power echoed through Bram's bones.

[How is it doing that?] I scrambled to my feet. I hadn't meant to ask Innocent that question, but given that my unwelcome passenger had been dispensing advice at random, perhaps I should have started asking questions earlier.

[Bram's magic sparked the potential of the gem.] Innocent sounded bored. *[The Outsider has magic of her own. Bram's casting* her *the same way Emerald casts* you. *The boy is still connected to her, and their power is still intertwined.]*

Emerald rolled out of the way. As the Outsider swiped at Dumplin, Emerald removed something from his coat: a silver object the size of his palm, shaped like two cones with their bases facing each other. I couldn't see the mechanical insides whirring away, but Bram could *feel* it. He was, after all, a Kineticist, and the object Emerald had commissioned was powered by the Hum.

Goldbloom's Sixth Theorem in action, it seemed.

"You would dare?" the Outsider shrieked. "You would force me out, only to trap me? *Do you know who I am?*"

Emerald was too busy flicking the object open to reveal its whirligig heart.

[I can help you,] Innocent promised. *[Together, you and I could defeat her...]*

I'd said no so many times that the answer had grown stale. As the Outsider rounded on Emerald, I did something else instead.

I stepped aside, and let Bram work his magic.

The Outsider screamed as the world shattered. Instead of everything happening all at once, however, things stopped. The world went silent. It was as if I was standing in a room full of mirrors, viewing every possible outcome of the moment at once, while Bram and I stood in the quiet space between them. A liminal space, like the void beyond the mind-cottage.

Bram let out a shuddering breath and looked around. He ignored the many outcomes in which Emerald ended up as a bloody, charred, or flattened mess. He passed over a few where the Outsider retreated, or where she turned at the last moment to kill Dumplin and take her gem. As the possibilities played out before us, I saw so many ways in which it could all go wrong. The device failed. The building collapsed. The Outsider possessed one of the unconscious Pruvs and made her escape.

Amid all those, Bram found one he liked and, before I could think to stop him, he stepped through.

Emerald's arm whipped up, hoisting the device above his head just as the Outsider plunged toward him. Its body bent and warped, collapsing in on itself with a terrible shriek as it was drawn into the mechanism. In an instant, it was gone.

The heart of the device in Emerald's palm whirled and thrummed as he snapped it closed. He collapsed back against the floorboards.

"Well," he panted, turning his head to look at me. "What are the odds *that* would work?"

I happened to know that they'd been very low indeed.

CHAPTER SEVEN

Bram sat in one chair across from Commander Finch, Emerald in the other. I, as usual, stood near the wall and tried my best to be as unobtrusive as possible.

Finch sat with her hands folded, staring down at the device Mel had cobbled together. "All right," she said, in a voice that made it clear she was exhausted, "I'm going to need everyone to explain this again slowly, and in better detail." She pointed her quill at Bram. "You first."

Bram rubbed his palms on the knees of his pants. "Yes, ma'am. First of all, I'm a Kineticist..."

"A Potentialist, specifically, I believe you said?" Finch interrupted, looking over her notes.

"Yes, ma'am. I had just begun my apprenticeship with Lioness Chant. You've heard of her, surely?"

"This may shock you, *boy,* but I don't keep up with every guild craftsman with a prominence title," Finch drawled. "Get on with it."

"Of course." Bram looked as though he was going to be sick. "So, um. Guildmistress Chant was excited about my particular abilities, this idea that I could manipulate the outcome of events. Shuffle the odds. She was curious about whether I was actually glimpsing different possible *realities*, so she set up this experiment to see if she could use my ability to move between... worlds? I guess?" Bram shivered and wrapped his arms around himself. "She was my mentor, so I trusted her, but when we tried, she just, well. She disappeared. It was like she stepped through a door and that *thing* came out. Except, it was her. It wasn't, but it was. *Another* her, somehow, and I don't... it's all my fault..." He let out a choked sob and covered his face with his hands. "And she was linked to me, because of the magic, and she wanted me to help her. She *made* me help her."

Emerald laid a hand on the boy's shoulder, and Bram's babbling trailed off. He hiccuped his way into silence.

Even Finch looked sympathetic. "She was your mentor. She should have known better than to do unsupervised experiments with an apprentice's magic. It isn't your fault."

Bram nodded. After a few moments, he lowered his hands to reveal puffy eyes and a trembling bottom lip. "Th-thank you, ma'am."

"What happened then? After she became that monster?"

"She made me try everything. Different types of *Aidea*, different ways of getting her *out* of me." Bram was shaking so hard that his teeth chattered. "It was like she was still Guildmistress Chant, like it was all part of her experiment, but she was also a prisoner trying to escape captivity that had held her for too long. Sometimes she told me what to do, sometimes she *made* me do it. I think she *liked* it. The novelty of it. That's how I knew it was still her."

Silence descended. With Emerald casting me again, I no longer had any way to interact with Bram beyond normal speech, but I felt awfully sorry for him. No wonder he'd been so terrified when I was in his head. Emerald had once controlled me for a few minutes, and I'd despised him for it. To have a mentor, someone who trusted him, someone who was supposed to *protect* him, do what Guildmistress Chant had done?

If we hadn't already trapped her, I would have wished a far worse fate upon her.

"How long did this go on?" Finch asked.

"Two weeks?" Bram guessed. "Three? I don't know. When she was in charge, I didn't always know *what* was happening. Sometimes I did, and that was worse. And then she'd get all... quiet? Like she was sleeping? That's how I was able to write that letter, to tell you where to find me." Bram rubbed his nose on his sleeve as he turned to Emerald. "Once you got involved, I thought, *At least someone might be able to help...*"

Bram jumped, and I realized belatedly that Emerald had kicked him in the ankle.

Finch's whiskers twitched. "And how exactly *did* you get involved, Emerald Flame?"

"The kid jumped me and stole my lightweaving focus," Emerald said. He pointed to the back of his head. "Knocked me down for a minute. Got me steaming mad. Decided to track him down. Missed some work, but that elf got a lead."

"On your necklace," Finch said drily.

"On my necklace," Emerald agreed. "It was a personal vendetta at that point."

"Mm." Finch glanced down at the table. "Personal enough that, instead of coming to work, you commissioned an experimental enchantment on the sly?"

"I hold grudges," Emerald said.

"Right." Finch made a note with her quill, then sat it aside. "Well, that's clear as mud, isn't it, Inspector?" Her golden eyes flicked toward me, and did my best to appear like a mindless, slack-jawed puppet.

The two men sat very still, awaiting her verdict.

After a few moments, she sighed. "Right. Here's what I'm going to do. Bram's case needs to be taken before the Conjury. If nothing else, we need to make sure that he doesn't accidentally summon another monstrosity from an alternate plane. There are better mentors out there, young man, I assure you." She held up the metal device. "*This* is going into a vault somewhere, probably in Venta Bulgarum, as evidence. As for you—" She pointed one clawed finger at Emerald. "Nobody was killed. No one else has come forward to reclaim their focuses and talismans, and the owner of the damaged property is, for reasons I barely *dare* to speculate upon, not filing a complaint. So as far as my paperwork is concerned, everything you did was aboveboard and Conjury-sanctioned."

Emerald nodded. "Thank you, Commander."

"Remember," Finch warned, "*you owe me*. Now get out, before I change my mind." She turned her finger in my direction. "And take your illusion with you."

Emerald and I didn't need telling twice.

I HAD EXPECTED to find Dumplin's business in a state of collapse, but when Emerald and I returned the morning after the Outsider was captured, repairs were already underway. Dozens of Pruvs were filing in and out through the door, some carrying beams and braces in while others bore the refuse away. Marth waved to us when we entered.

"What a mess, what a mess," he observed cheerfully, dusting off his hands. He held one meaty paw out to Emerald. "I reckon we'd be fit to crack skulls if *you'd* done all fis, but Dumplin says you're fe hero of fe day, 'n she's fe boss, ah? So by my count, you're a *right* summer plum, 'n I won't hear elsewise."

Emerald took the man's hand and let out a grunt of surprise as Marth pulled him into a backslapping half-hug. After an awkward moment, he thumped the man in return and took steps to extricate himself from the embrace.

"Go on," Marth said, pointing Emerald to the back of the room, where Dumplin was giving instructions to a host of adoring Pruv laborers.

The moment she laid eyes on us, she excused herself and trotted over. "I assume you're here to confiscate my contraband," she said.

Poke noticed us and elbowed Doodah, but Dumplin shooed them away with one hand.

"It's upstairs," she said, then reached for her necklace. "I've got the key right here. I hope you don't intend to arrest me, though, as I'm *much* too pretty for prison..."

"Keep it," Emerald said.

Dumplin froze. Her mouth dropped open, but I knew what Emerald was going to say before he said it, and I wholeheartedly agreed.

"Think what the crown could do with a power like that," he murmured, so low that the workers around us wouldn't hear. "Think what the *Conjury* could do."

"You trust me with it?" Dumplin asked. Her eyes betrayed her disbelief.

"I don't know that I'd trust *anyone* with it," Emerald admitted. "But you were under attack, and your first thought was to soothe your assailant. My mentor called that de-escalation, and for most people? That's not their first impulse. So if anyone's going to have an object that powerful, perhaps it's best if it's someone like you."

Dumplin's blue eyes brimmed with tears. She released the silver chain and let the key slide back into her plunging neckline. "Thank you, Inspector. That's very fine of you." She snapped her fingers and raised her voice to a deafening level. "Poke! Bring the inspector his purse!"

Dutifully, the big man trotted over and produced a small bag from the belt of his trousers. He passed it to Emerald, who didn't bother counting it before he made it disappear into one of his many secret coat pockets.

"I'm still willing to offer you a session on the house," Dumplin reminded him. "Either of you."

I shook my head, but Emerald wasn't so quick to answer. I could tell, by the mournful emotion that rolled through our connection, that he was thinking of Tincrown.

"Could be nice to live out a little fantasy," Dumplin added in a wheedling voice.

"I'll keep that in mind." Emerald backed up a step. "Don't make me regret this, all right?"

Poke cracked his knuckles.

"Oh, don't fuss." Dumplin reached up to pat her lackey's arm. "I'm just glad Marsha was right about you. And don't forget, if *you* ever need a favor, I'll be right here. Folks like us have got to stick together, all right?"

[Folks who break Conjury law, she means,] I added silently. I waved to Dumplin before following Emerald back out the front door. **[Is it wise, acting against the Conjury in a city we don't plan to leave anytime soon?]**

[Wiser than letting a dragon scale necklace end up in the hands of someone like Prince Efrain,] Emerald said.

When he put it that way, it was hard to disagree.

"Can we eat dinner together tonight?" Quell asked when Emerald and I returned. "I want to hear about what happened with the Outsider, and Svelte's trying a new recipe tonight. Yerik's been teaching her how to cook and don't tell her I said so, but it's really good. Blare's helping, but he doesn't like it as much as she does."

Emerald looked around the dining room. It was a slow night at the Lute and Goose, and our usual table was unoccupied. "I'd enjoy that," he said. "But only if I have time to wash up first. I couldn't stomach the idea of bathing with Crimson hovering around me on a short tether, and after all that we've been through, I smell like an old foot."

Quell leaned forward and took a whiff, then pinched his nose. "You do," he agreed, with the brutal sincerity of a child. "They're still cooking, though, so you have time. And you're welcome to join us, too, Crimson, even if you don't eat. You can just sit and talk with us, and we can be a... a..." His cheeks flushed scarlet.

"A family," Emerald supplied.

Quell beamed. "Exactly."

"I'll be here," I promised. "But first I need a moment to myself, too."

One of the customers waved to Quell, who practically skipped off to see what the guests needed. How strange it was, to know that we wouldn't be staying at the inn forever, and yet belonged there so fully for the present time.

Emerald went off to draw a bath, while I went to our empty room. It was a pleasure to enjoy the freedom the necklace afforded me, and I promised myself that I would not take it for granted in the future.

In the privacy of the still room, I sat down in my chair, closed my eyes, and slipped into the mind-cottage.

"Innocent?" I asked. "Are you there?"

The cottage was empty, but I could hear scratching in the walls, a sure sign that my prisoner was still caged.

"I was hoping you'd tell me how you know so much about Outsiders."

The scratching stopped.

"Is that what you are?" I asked. "An Outsider? Is that how you knew what was happening before we did?"

Innocent didn't reply.

I approached the wall of the mind-cottage and let my forehead rest against the plaster. "I don't understand you at all. You tried to kill us in the Brotherhood, but you might very well have saved Emerald's life several times over in the last few days. You helped us. And according to Emerald, that's not something Outsiders do." Innocent had let me catch a glimpse of a flashing silver eye through the crack in the ceiling, but that wasn't what its eyes had looked like before I trapped it. The more I thought about it, the less convinced I was regarding its nature.

[What are you, *Crimson Smoke?]* The plaster beneath my palm shuddered and warped.

"I don't..." I balled my hand into a fist and bit my tongue. I was inclined to agree with Emerald's assessment about me. Like it or not, I was nowhere near as powerful as the Outsider we'd fought. I couldn't draw on cosmic magic at a whim. Without Bram's help, the outcome of that battle didn't bear thinking about.

Fighting the Outsider hadn't been like fighting Innocent, something I remembered all too well. If I wasn't an Outsider, then I doubted the shadow-beast was, either.

"I don't know," I admitted. "I'm a prism, I suppose. I'm the person Emerald wanted to be." Saying those words aloud hurt in a bone-deep way that I was unprepared to assess. I pressed on. "I'm the thing that was invited in when my creator almost died."

In truth, I'd concocted half a dozen theories regarding my origin, some of which were contradictory:

I was a wisp of magic granted a half-life by the Middling Godlet.

Or I was a splinter of Emerald's damaged psyche that had gained a mind of my own.

Or I had been created at the moment of Brother Reticent's death and only achieved autonomy when Emerald almost died, too.

Or...

No matter how many theories I came up with, I would likely never get answers. After all, who could tell me the truth with any real authority?

A small fissure peeled open in the wall directly across from me, only inches from my face. On the far side of the fissure, an eye appeared. It wasn't the soulless orb that had greeted me when I first met Innocent. It wasn't the flat, reflective gaze of the Outsider. This eye was warm and bright, a pale brown bordering on gold with little motes of color dancing in the iris.

It was *my* eye.

Innocent blinked. *[I, too, am the thing that was invited in.]*

I stood there for a long time, staring at my twin on the far side of the wall. I tried to imagine the rest of its shape—was it skeletal and lean, like Innocent's preferred form? Or was it indistinguishable from the appearance I was wearing at that very moment? I had thought that Innocent was evil. A monster.

The truth suddenly seemed more complex than that.

Eventually, I pulled away. I closed my eyes and rebuilt the walls between us, mending the cracks and seams in the fortress that would keep Innocent contained. When I opened them again, the wall was whole, the ceiling mended, the cottage pristine.

Without another word, I turned away and slipped back into the Lute and Goose. Then I stood in the mirror, rearranged my outfit into something a touch too gauche for a roadside inn, and went down to enjoy dinner with my family.

A SCANDAL IN KENMORE

CHAPTER ONE

Spring had begun to stake its claim on Kinmore, with the first flowers popping up along the roadside, and the green buds that would become next autumn's apples already pearling in the orchard boughs. I had grown so used to the harsh angles and high contrasts of winter that I'd forgotten how bright and brilliantly green the world could be.

"There's so much *daylight!*" I exclaimed, staring up at the blue scraps of sky visible between the clouds. "Isn't it marvelous?"

"Better than being dark all the time," Emerald admitted. His mood had been subdued in the winter months, and while I suspected that the absence of a certain doctor might be the reason for his ennui, the short daylight hours certainly hadn't helped. My friend was, after all, a Lightweaver. His affinity for long, bright days might not be as acute as mine, but I knew he felt it too.

Even within the city, flowering trees had begun to bloom, bringing welcome flecks of color to the landscape. I was so interested in studying a profusion of white-limbed trees brimming with pale purple buds that I did not immediately note the open-backed cart standing out front of the Conjury offices. It contained several chests, a few crates, and an array of what appeared to be hand-woven baskets, some of which were so large that Svelte could have fit quite comfortably inside. Alongside the cart stood a familiar figure clad in purple and silver silks.

"Commander Finch," Emerald called in greeting.

The irritable Leonhite stood next to the cart, studying a stack of paperwork. "Emerald Flame," she called back. "You're here at last. I expected you yesterday."

"I was busy yesterday," Emerald replied, which was a slight exaggeration of the truth. We had spent the prior day helping Yerik haul down, repaint, and replace the inn's sign out front, as he apparently did every spring. Emerald had done the hauling; Yerik had done the painting; I had offered moral support and an in-depth explanation of color theory which Yerik, at least, seemed to appreciate.

"Well, at least you saw fit to grace us with your presence today," Finch snapped. She dashed off a hasty signature and thrust it toward the driver.

"Didn't know you needed me," Emerald said. "What's this about?"

Finch waved a paw at the cart as the driver stowed the papers and snapped the reins. "Another shipment I'm meant to look over. Gods, it's frustrating. An official in Venta Bulgarum has gotten it into her head that someone's trading secret Conjury intel out of Swoop Oasis. It's only the largest city on the longest trade route on the continent, and they want key outpost commanders to inspect every shipment personally." She flicked her round ears in annoyance. "Which, in this case, makes it *my* problem. As if I didn't have enough to worry about, with Leviathan Loch across the way breathing down my speckled neck all the godsdamned time..."

I felt the pinch in Emerald's gut at the mention of Swoop Oasis, the city in the Nomad Gamut from which Tincrown hailed. I did not think my friend would ever know true peace until we found a way to reunite him with his doctor. I also had no idea how we might go about that, since returning to Dyrne would require going through Upper Bound and would likely raise alarms with the Conjury.

"Sounds tedious," Emerald said, scratching his jaw.

Finch narrowed her golden eyes. "I *know* you're not concerned about my convenience, Emerald Flame."

"Never claimed to be." He lifted one corner of his lips in a fraction of a smile.

Finch huffed. "Are you perhaps concerned about a mysterious disappearance, at least?"

Nothing changed in Emerald's demeanor, but I could *feel* the abrupt sharpening of his intensity. "Disappearance?" he asked.

"Thought that might spark your interest," Finch grumbled. "Come on, we'll discuss this in my office."

I kept my eyes downcast as I followed Emerald through the front door of the building.

[Do you ever find it disconcerting,] Innocent whispered, *[that he views the suffering of others as a puzzle to be solved?]*

I didn't, really. Not when I know how much Emerald suffered, and how much time I spent puzzling over a solution.

"Gorlyn Bracefallow, fourth son of the Bracefallow estate." Finch shoved a small oil painting across the desk. The image was a little larger than Emerald's palm, and depicted a grinning youth with pale skin, red-gold hair, and a constellation of freckles strewn across his cheeks.

Emerald studied the painting. "Couldn't settle for a simple sketch, could they?" he asked.

"Have you met the Bracefallows?" Finch arched an eyebrow and massaged her temple with one clawed paw. The other arm was flung over her armrest at an awkward angle. She seemed utterly exhausted and more short-tempered than usual. "Things are *never* simple with that lot."

"He's been missing for a while, hasn't he?" Emerald asked. "We

—I heard rumors that a young man had disappeared a few weeks back, during that case with the Outsider."

"Did you, now?" Finch's gaze flicked toward me; I, in turn, stared at the wall.

"Nobody mentioned a name, though." Emerald sat back, leaving the painting on the desk between them. Gorlyn Bracefallow smiled up vapidly at the ceiling.

"Not surprising," Finch said. "The old families are close-lipped, and their children have a, hmm. A penchant for indulgence, let's say."

"Ah." Emerald nodded. "So it's not necessarily strange for a young man to wander off for a few weeks."

"Especially not a fourth son," Finch agreed.

[For weeks?] I asked. *[Without warning?]* That seemed very strange to me, but then again, it wasn't as if I could wander off on a whim. Judging by the portrait, Gorlyn was in his teenage years, at least, and older than the three children who were now in Emerald's care. I had only known them for a few months, but I couldn't bear the idea that one of them might vanish without a word. I would be terrified.

"A fourth son might feel it necessary to prove himself," Emerald mused, as much to answer my question as in reply to Finch. "So he might be drunk in a cellar somewhere... or off earning himself a prominence title."

"That's possible," Finch agreed.

"Hmm." Emerald stroked his jawline absently, his eyes fixed on the portrait, and his mind worlds away.

Finch yawned hugely, baring all her teeth and squeezing her eyes shut in the process. On occasion, I forgot how inhuman her anatomy was, but I'd never met another of the intelligent races whose jaws could unhinge to that degree. "I don't suppose you can solve this in a blink, can you? Blame a snake, or something?"

Emerald chuckled. "Not without some evidence. If you had a

body, maybe, but there's no reason to assume he's dead. Is this all you have for me?"

"*You* try getting royals to fill out paperwork," Finch replied.

"I'll want a word with the family," Emerald said. "Think they'll talk to me?"

"Talk, yes. Tell the truth? Only if it suits them. They waited this long to report him missing, which could mean any number of things. They've promised to grant you an audience."

"Lucky me." Emerald smiled grimly. "I'm sure they'll love having a jotunn-born inspector poking around their private residence."

"That's what you've got your poppet for." Finch waved a dismissive paw at me. "Pretty privilege."

Emerald covered a smile with one hand. *[Aw, Crim, she thinks you're pretty.]*

[Ha ha.] I allowed myself the brief luxury of scowling at the wall. *[She also thinks I've got a head full of air.]*

Emerald coughed a few times, and I wished I could scowl at him, too.

Ignorant of our conversation, Finch let out a sigh. "Do try to keep this quiet, won't you? I've got enough to do without the courtiers flying into a kerfuffle."

The copper piping beside her desk clattered abruptly, and Finch reached to uncap the bronze tube alongside her chair. When she saw what was inside, she groaned.

"Keys of Odologys, another pissing shipment." She got to her feet, stretched her back into what should have been an impossible bend, and sighed when a few of her vertebrae popped so loudly that even *I* winced. "That's that, then. Have fun with the Bracefallows."

Emerald rose as well. "Don't suppose you'd want to trade jobs?"

Finch grinned and her whiskers bristled with wicked amusement. "Not for all the crown's gold, Emerald Flame. I'll take the trade goods. *You* can have the courtiers any day."

"How generous of you," Emerald intoned.

If I didn't know better, I would have thought they were on their way to becoming friends.

"I DON'T UNDERSTAND THE TITLES," I said as Emerald and I made our way to the Bracefallow residence. "You and I have prominence titles, earned by our deeds. Well, in my case, *your* deeds, for which I was given credit. But most people take the name of their hometown... except the royals, who take the names of their estates?"

Emerald shot me an amused glance. "Crimson, please. Do you really think that there's a single rule, across all of Dregandresal and the continents beyond, by which people name their children? Or themselves?"

"Well..." I fiddled with the silver pin at my throat. I had once again donned my silver-and-purple day dress, in an attempt to appear more official and Conjury-approved. "I suppose I never questioned it."

"The Conjury has tried to make things simpler from a book-keeping standpoint," Emerald said. "But you can't simply change what people call themselves overnight. There are plenty of people who were alive before the Conjury came to power who have fought to keep their family history intact. And plenty *more* who refuse to acknowledge the Conjury at all."

[Like the people of Dyrne?] I asked, wary of speaking the name aloud.

[In Dyrne, they still spoke to Conjury scouts... Aindreas notwithstanding. There are places in the north, though, like Danilas Freehold, that will resist Conjury oversight until their last breath.]

I puzzled over that as we walked. I had never visited a place where the Conjury lacked a foothold—which made sense, I supposed, given that Emerald worked for them, and I could not stray far from his side. Perhaps it was the spring sunlight slanting pell-mell through the budding branches, or the slow awakening of the landscape beyond the city limits, but I found myself longing to see more of the world. To visit someplace where I would not have to hide my nature.

If such a place even existed.

[If you really wanted a body so badly, there is a way to have one,] Innocent reminded me. *[We controlled Bram. You could have kept him, if you wanted to... gotten rid of the Outsider, taken over his flesh...]*

[That's not what I want, and you know it,] I snapped.

[So you say. But you could touch... and taste... and feel... we could have found a way to finish what the Outsider started...]

"Something on your mind?" Emerald asked.

I started. "What? No. What do you mean?"

"You were making quite a sour face just now." He watched me curiously, and I wondered if he had the slightest clue that there was something *in* my mind. Would Harmony's magic keep him from understanding that anything was amiss? Or could he sense that something was wrong with me, even though I could never explain *what?*

"There's so much I don't know," I complained, which was truth-adjacent if not fully transparent. "Unless you're actively thinking about something, I would have to go digging around in your mind for it, which just seems rude. And might I remind you, we've been here for six months, and we're no closer to finding a solution." *[To separate me. To make me independent.]*

[Right.] Emerald stuffed his hands in his pockets. *[We should spend more time on that...]*

He couldn't mask his reluctance, however. To some extent, I understood that he was in no hurry to be left alone. But shouldn't what I want matter, too?

Not that I had any idea of how to progress, regardless. Even more frustratingly, I had no idea where to start.

CHAPTER TWO

"Gorlyn was always such a good boy." Lady Bracefallow dabbed at the corners of her eyes with a lace kerchief. She was wearing an enormous gown of black silk, trimmed in red lace, that even *I* found ostentatious. I couldn't help but wonder if she'd had the dress made after the grand fete celebrating the prince's engagement. His relationship with Mercedes had ended in tragedy, especially given that most people thought she was dead, but in the months since, I hadn't spotted a stitch of yellow worn by the city's elite, while red had become the reigning color in their palette.

Lady Bracefallow's bottom lip wobbled, and she reached for her husband. "Our eldest three, you know, are *terribly* busy with their duties and obligations, but Gorlyn is the baby of the family."

I forced a smile. "Is that so?"

Lord Bracefallow nodded once. Unlike his wife, his expression betrayed not a single drop of emotion. "We spoiled him."

"*Gods,*" sighed the eldest son, "I'm glad *somebody* said it." Lemuel Bracefallow sat sideways in his chair, with his back against one of the massive wooden arms and his knees draped over the other. His appearance reminded me of Laird Edur Fenguard, but only the worst parts of him. Lemuel's fur-trimmed cloak was lined in silk and decorated with dozens of pins and metals, most of which I assumed were ornamental; Lemuel gave off the air of a man who had never worked a day in his life. His hair was red, like his mother's, but in every other regard he was a perfect copy of his father: sturdy, square jawed, and unsmiling. The second and third sons, Parris and Murdock, might as well have been twins for all I could tell them apart, and so far, they had spent the interview studying the wallpaper.

Lady Bracefallow pressed the kerchief to her mouth and shuddered.

"Now, now, you've upset your mother," Lord Bracefallow intoned.

"That isn't *my* fault," Lemuel snapped. "Gorlyn's the one who ran off and made a mess of things without so much as a note. Meanwhile, *I've* been reviewing the grain yields, Parris has been updating the estate registers, and Murdock's three weeks away from his enlistment date. We're running the house, Murdock's helping the crown keep Leviathan Loch in check, and where's sweet baby Gorlyn? Off somewhere doing Odologys-knows-what with Rilus-knows-who!"

Lady Bracefallow's silent sobs made her shoulders quake.

We had only spent ten minutes in the company of the Bracefallows, and already I wished that my hair was real so that I could begin the process of tearing it out. I felt a bit of sympathy for Gorlyn as I, too, would have fled this family at the first opportunity.

I risked a sidelong glance at Emerald, who sat as still as a stone. A very judgmental stone.

"It must be tiring," I said, "having to count all your wealth." I made sure to keep my smile sweet and guileless as I spoke.

Lord Bracefallow shot me a suspicious glare, but Lemuel lifted both hands to gesture toward me. "*Thank* you! This house has been an ally to the crown for centuries, and one day, it will fall on *my* shoulders to keep the grounds and estates aboveboard. Most of that burden will be mine, unless something should happen to me—"

"Driaweep forbid it," mumbled Parris, plucking at a loose threat in the sleeve of his tunic.

"And Murdock is risking his life to defend our borders." Lemuel nodded to the youngest of the assembled brothers.

I briefly entertained the question of what, exactly, would happen should the house of Bracefallow fall. Would the grounds be divided among their sharecroppers? Would families from the Hives move into the empty building?

I wasn't convinced that the family's decline would be a bad thing. Then again, the crown likely wouldn't allow its wealth to be dissolved so easily.

[If you let me kill them,] Innocent whispered, *[we could find out.]*

I shook my head once, as if the movement might dislodge the shadow-beast's influence and returned my attention to Lemuel, who was still prattling on about the scope of his duties.

"—never once lifted a finger to help." He swept his hand through the air to encompass the whole family. "He's always been happy to benefit from our efforts, but never shows any particular interest in contributing."

Emerald cleared his throat. "Would you say that you resent Gorlyn?" he asked.

Lemuel snorted. "I resent that we're taking valuable time out of our day to discuss his whereabouts. So long as he stays out from underfoot, I hardly think about him."

"Do you have any idea where he might be?" I asked.

Lemuel exchanged a glance with his brothers, then mimed locking his lips and throwing a key over his shoulder.

Lord Bracefallow sighed. "Gorlyn is a bit of a..." He squeezed his wife's hand. "I'll try to put this delicately. He's known since he was small that the title would never pass to him. He's too soft for the army, not a lick of *Aidea* in his veins, and unless some improbable disaster should befall my other sons—"

"Driaweep forbid it." Murdock smirked at Parris, who made a rude gesture in reply.

"—neither he nor any of his future children will hold any social sway. Most people in his position would want to join a temple or dedicate their lives to the service of a deity, but Gorlyn was never very pious."

"Not like Parris," Murdock added.

Parris sniffed and looked down his nose at his younger brother. "I happen to *believe* in the work of Lyric, and there are many ways to serve. Overseeing the estate paperwork on behalf of our family is simply another form of honoring the god of contracts. I know my place, unlike *some* people." He sighed heavily and turned to us. "I'm not sure you're getting the best impression of our family. We're all worried about Gorlyn, but as Papa says, he can be a handful. This isn't the first time that he's gone off for ages on some foolish quest."

I held up my hands, still keeping my demure smile plastered in place. "You'll have to forgive me, but I don't quite follow. Gorlyn isn't here, and he isn't with a temple, so you think he might be...?"

A self-satisfied ripple of emotion passed through my tether with Emerald when Lord Bracefallow replied.

"Gorlyn has always wanted to make a name for himself," he said.

"A prominence title," Emerald said. *[See, what did I tell you?]*

"He wanted to do something grand," Lady Bracefallow blubbered. "Something that would draw the king's att-ttention." Her voice cracked, and she squeezed her eyes shut as two fat tears rolled down her cheeks. "He wanted to do something on his own. Something that n-nobody could refute or lay c-claim to. Nobody but him."

Lemuel nodded. "He stores up the coin from his stipend for a few months and then runs off, slacks akilter, to get himself in another bind. The godsdamned fool goes looking for trouble in the hopes that he will be the brave hero that's needed to set things right." Lemuel rolled his eyes so far back that for a moment I could only see the whites.

"He tried to cross the border into the Uthren Vhald when he was fourteen," Murdock said. "Apparently, he meant to spy on Leviathan

Loch's fortifications. Didn't even get past the first checkpoint before he was arrested. Papa had to petition the king to get him released."

"When he was seventeen, he tried to ride north to the Vapor Plains in an attempt to win the allegiance of the Leonhites. Thought he could succeed where the Conjury had failed. He tried to raise a volunteer corps as he went." Parris shook his head in disgust. "The Conjury picked him up that time. They were afraid he'd start a war if he wasn't careful."

"And he's never careful," Lemuel added.

"I see." I folded my hands in my lap and frowned at Lemuel. "Did he ever tell you what he had planned? Not in detail, of course, but did he give you any hint what his next exploit might be?"

"Not in so many words," Lord Bracefallow said. "I'd have put a stop to it at once."

"He's always been a bit secretive," Lady Bracefallow added. She wiped her nose on her kerchief. "He's reckless, but not stupid."

Lemuel coughed into his fist.

"Could we see his room?" I asked. "In case he left any indication of his plans?"

"Of course." Lord Bracefallow waved to Parris. "Show them upstairs, son."

Parris rose at once and gestured for us to follow. Emerald got up and loped after him, but I lingered for a moment. Whatever else I thought of the family, Lady Bracefallow's distress seemed genuine. "We'll do everything we can to find him," I promised, with all the assurance I could muster. Secretly, I hoped that our investigation would take us out of the city for once.

"I believe you," Lady Bracefallow whispered. "But what if he's... what if he's..."

"He's fine," Lemuel snapped. "And after this, we really ought to cut off his allowance, or hire someone to keep an eye on him." He turned to me. "Maybe that hulking henchman of yours can beat some sense into his stubborn skull."

I turned away before any of them could see my expression of

disgust. I hurried toward the massive stone stairway in Parris and Emerald's wake. Everywhere I looked, I found some reminder of my increasing distaste for the court of Kinmore, be it in the gilded sconces, the satin wall-hangings, or the elaborately carved panels in the ceilings. Ghastly portraits of long-deceased Bracefallows lined the walls, each of them larger than life and scowling down at the viewer with ill-disguised superiority. At least it was apparent that the family tree had branched and forked over the years; following my encounter with the Fenguards, I was wary of portraits that looked too alike.

I could not stop thinking of the Hives. Judging from what his brothers had told us, Gorlyn believed that his legacy would be secured through battle or conquest. What if he dedicated himself to improving his city, and the lives of the people who lived there?

Not that either the king or the Conjury would grant him a title for that.

Parris led us to a door on the second floor of the manor, pushing it wide and allowing us to enter first. Emerald immediately set about studying the books on the shelf against one wall and poking through the papers arrayed in the desk. For the most part, the room was clean and tidy.

"You found it like this?" I asked Parris. Since I could not assist with the physical portion of the investigation, I would do my part by asking questions.

"The staff had already tidied up by the time we realized Gorlyn was missing," Parris said. He rubbed the back of his neck sheepishly. "I'm sorry about Lemuel, he's... under a lot of pressure. From Papa, mostly. We don't all feel the same way about Gorlyn. I'm sure it's not easy, being asked to investigate the disappearance of a young man who's gotten a few months' head start, but he really might be *anywhere*. Papa was furious, said he'd let Gorlyn stay in prison if he got arrested again, that it might teach him a lesson. And he *is* of age. I mean, if he wanted to ride off to the Infested Mountains and, you know, arm-wrestle a jotunn shaman, it really wouldn't surprise me."

He laughed awkwardly and stared at Emerald's back. "I hope that's not insensitive to say."

"Hmm," Emerald grunted, still focused on the desk. His posture suggested that he was too engrossed in what he was reading to respond further, but I could feel his annoyance mounting.

"Is there anyone else that Gorlyn might have spoken to about his plans?" I asked. "A friend? A confidant? A lover?"

"Hmm." Parris scratched his chin and squinted up toward the room's entablature for a moment. "Not that I can think of. He's never shown much interest in girls. Or in anyone, really. He was always more interested in planning his next adventure. Although I did notice that he was watching someone at the last few gatherings, and it made me wonder if he might be more inclined to seek the company of men. Or rather, one man in particular. Have you heard of a fellow named Serkadis?"

Had I been human, I would have choked on my own tongue. At the desk, Emerald stilled.

"We met," I said. "At the prince's engagement party."

"A sad affair, given what came of it." Parris bowed his head. "But if you've met him, you must have noticed that he's a bit, well... *odd*. He comes to every party in the city, slips in late and sneaks out early, always a perfect gentleman but nobody really knows him. And as far as I know, he's never hosted anything at *his* residence, but he gives magnificent gifts at everyone's wedding and birthday parties, so we all keep inviting him."

"And Gorlyn was friends with him?" Emerald asked without turning around.

"They spoke a few times, and they danced at the king's equinox ball. I remember, because Gorlyn *hates* dancing, but he seemed to be enjoying himself."

Emerald straightened up and turned away from the desk. "Thank you," he said stiffly. "We'll be in touch soon."

"Oh." Parris seemed perplexed by the sudden shift in tone. "Well, thank you for coming. I'll show you out."

We didn't speak as Parris led us to the exit. I was reluctant to link my thoughts with Emerald's. The mention of Serkadis had left me out of sorts. He'd made quite an impression on me during our brief interaction at the party, and I was glad that we had an excuse to see him again.

Parris closed the door of the Bracefallow manor house after us, and I hurried to keep up with Emerald, who seemed lost in his own thoughts.

"I suppose we'll need to make an appointment to see Serkadis, then?" I asked. "Do you think he can tell us where to find Gorlyn?"

"Very likely," Emerald said.

I studied his profile as I kept pace with his long stride. "You don't sound happy about that."

My friend wrinkled his nose and, despite the sunshine streaming down between the buildings, he turned up the collar of his wool greatcoat. "I'm not. Because unless I'm very much mistaken, Gorlyn Bracefallow is already dead."

CHAPTER THREE

No amount of pleading and cajoling could convince Emerald to explain his theory.

"But we're working *together*," I whined.

Emerald sat at the desk in our room of the Lute and Goose, writing a letter with painstaking attention to detail. I'd seen him dash off notes here and there, but it seemed that when he put his mind to it, his calligraphy could be pristine. "I know," he said, without looking up from the page, "but I have just enough information to know that I'm missing something. If I'm right, we'll be walking into grave danger, and if I'm wrong..." He paused and lifted the tip of his quill from the parchment. "It'll *still* be dangerous, but marginally less so."

"You think he killed Gorlyn?" I asked. "*Why?*"

Emerald dipped his nib in the inkpot. "That's a serious accusation, Crim. Murder is dire. Self-defense, on the other hand, can have the same result. Given what he said to me at the party, it's possible that he *wanted* me to know that he was in trouble—"

"You spoke to Gorlyn?" I asked.

"No, I meant Serkadis."

"*Serkadis* is in trouble?" I pressed my palm to my forehead, trying in vain to remember anything Serkadis might have said to this effect. "Because he killed Gorlyn? Make it make *sense*, please!"

Emerald executed one last looping swirl of ink and set his pen aside, then turned to me. "As I said, I don't have all of the pieces yet. Perhaps I should have tracked him down sooner, but after everything that happened with Squampf and Mercedes, I all but forgot about him."

I nodded as if I understood perfectly. Truth be told, *I* had thought of Serkadis on more than one occasion, but Emerald didn't need to know that. "Understandable, but..."

"We've discussed the matter of confirmation bias, haven't we?" Emerald interrupted. "I know something about Serkadis that I suspect you haven't put together, but I don't know for certain what it means. I'd like you to arrive at your own conclusions."

"And I can't do that if you tell me what you've figured out?"

Emerald sighed and picked absentmindedly at one of his fingernails. "Crim. When people see that I have jotunn ancestry, they make assumptions, don't they?"

I looked down at my boots. Only a few hours ago, Lemuel Brace-fallow had suggested that Emerald's heritage made him prone to violence. "They do..."

"But *you* don't." He tipped his head to one side. "You have the rare luxury of getting to decide what you believe about people based on how they act. What they say and do, not who—or what—they are."

I stared at him, open mouthed. I had always felt my ignorance to be a barrier to understanding the world around me, not an asset.

"You've seen how I was raised," Emerald went on, looking toward the north-facing wall, beyond which lay the road to the Brotherhood. "Harmony and Modest took great pains to teach me lessons which I've had to spend the rest of my life dismantling. On top of that..." He swiveled back toward me and arched an eyebrow. "You're better at people."

I brightened under the compliment and opened my mouth to respond.

"Don't get cocky." He held up a warning finger. "I made you that way. So here's the plan: I'm writing to Serkadis on your behalf to say you'd love a chance to meet again in person. If he lets you into his home, I'll find a way in and investigate the place, while *you* keep him occupied and have a poke around. After that, we'll have to play it by ear."

"Right," I said. "I'll keep his attention while you do the dirty work."

[*Yes,*] Innocent purred, [*let us observe the killer.*]

[*Emerald's giving him the benefit of the doubt,*] I scolded. I wouldn't be looking forward to spending a few hours in the man's company if I was certain he'd killed someone.

That was what I told myself, at any rate.

I HAD no idea how long it would take Serkadis to reply. Since Finch had tasked us with investigating Gorlyn Bracefallow's disappearance, she wasn't expecting us in the city, and Emerald was once again roped into helping Yerik around the inn.

Since I could be of no use when it came to manual labor, I followed the children instead. Svelte enjoyed baking, and while I could appreciate neither the smells of her work nor the fruits of her labor, I was quite happy to sit on the edge of the counter and watch her work.

"Gotta get the dough... to the right consistency..." She grunted as she leaned her full weight into kneading the bolus of pale dough against the counter. Emerald often looked out of place in the kitchen, given that everything was the right height for Yerik and, therefore, for Svelte. Quell had to reach a bit to look over the counters, but Svelte was perfectly comfortable.

Blare watched her with poorly concealed interest, his eyes flicking between her ruddy cheeks and the straining muscles in her arms. With her sleeves rolled up, it was obvious that her general appearance had changed in the months since she'd left the Brotherhood. She was still heavyset, but her cheeks had lost some of their roundness, and with every passing day, she looked less like the self-conscious child who'd cried and shivered in our old dormitory.

Blare had noticed, too.

"And you gotta get... the texture... right." Svelte paused to tab a towel across her forehead and grinned down at the dough. "I know you can't taste it, Crim, but trust me, this is gonna be my best loaf yet."

I signed what she'd said for Blare's benefit, since her hands were full, then added, "Is this something you've invented?"

"Sort of." Svelte wiped the flour from her hands and took up her own signing. "It's a sourdough base, but I added some new ingredients we found at the market, and the Teguan we bought 'em off of told me he can get more stuff to experiment next time. I've got this idea for a custard, too..."

She was cut off by the swing of the kitchen door and Quell's arrival. "There's a lad at the door. Says he's got a letter for Emerald. Is he in here?"

Svelte sighed and tossed her towel aside. "No, he's helping Yerik pick up a load of new furnishings for the guest rooms. I'll handle it." She scooped her beloved dough into an empty bowl, set it near the stove, and strode toward the door.

I followed her, as did Blare, although we let Svelte take the lead. She strode up to the elf waiting in the middle of the mostly vacant dining room. The newcomer was dressed in a brown uniform of what appeared to be made of oiled canvas. When he saw Svelte, he squinted down his long, arrow-straight nose.

"You can give me that letter," Svelte said, already digging through her apron in search of the coin he'd want as payment.

The elf sniffed and held the letter close to his chest. "This letter is a private delivery for the Emerald Flame—" he began.

Svelte held out her palm, offering her coin to the courier. "I'm his daughter," she said.

The elf blinked. "But..."

"What?" Svelte narrowed her eyes.

"But the Emerald Flame is..." I could see the elf doing a series of frantic calculations. Svelte's dwarven heritage was obvious at a glance, but closer inspection revealed her obvious elven qualities. The Emerald Flame had enough of a reputation in Kinmore that it must have been obvious that Svelte couldn't possibly be his daughter by birth. He cast me a helpless glance. When he saw my red hair, he relaxed.

"I was going to say," he enunciated, "that this letter is a private delivery for the Emerald Flame *or* Crimson Smoke." He retrieved the coin from Svelte, then extended one arm toward me with the letter clutched between his fingers.

Before I could say a word, Svelte plucked the paper from his hands and turned on her heel. The courier glowered at Svelte's back before taking his leave.

Did you know him? Blare signed.

Svelte wrinkled her nose and flicked her fingers against the envelope she held before signing with one hand. "Nah, but I know his type." The gestures of her handspeech were sharp and angry. "*Alder elves.*"

I blink at her, remembering what Emerald had said the day before. "What do you have against alder elves?" I'd seen them around, but the only one I'd spoken to at any length was the shopkeeper who'd helped us track down the Outsider.

"My *dad*," Svelte snapped. "You never met him, but he was as bad as the rest of them. Worse, maybe. Anyway, forget about him." She brandished the letter under my nose. "It says it's for you specifically. Should we open it?"

"Probably n—" I glanced at the looping script and saw who it was from.

Serkadis of Kinmore.

Svelte was right: *my* name was the only one spelled out in elegant lettering. Emerald had intimated that he was going to include my name on the original letter, of course, but this was still the first article of mail I had ever received.

Mail from a potential murderer, I reminded myself. All the same, I nodded. "Yes, Svelte, I think you'd better open it."

We retreated behind the bar, clustering together as we bent over the envelope so that no one else could see. Since I'd revealed my true nature, I had still been *close* with the children, but the dynamic of our relationship had shifted. As we circled up to read a letter that we all knew ought to be left unopened, I was tempted to shift back into my appearance as Vagabond. I could have, of course, but the feeling wouldn't have been the same.

"What does it say?" Quell asked in what, by his standards, passed for a whisper.

Svelte held the card so that Blare could see it while reading aloud, "*Dear Crimson Smoke, I would be happy to play host, and my only regret is that I waited until now to extend an invitation...*" She whistled. "That's a fancy-pants way of saying he likes you."

"What? No. We don't even know each other." I waved her away. "Keep reading."

She smirked at me over the top of the letter before she returned her attention to the note. "*Please do me the honor of calling at my home on the evening of the spring solstice. Yours...* I told you! People don't just go around writing *yours* to strangers." She flapped the paper at me.

I dipped my head and lowered my voice. "Keep your voice down. This is part of an investigation."

"Ah, so you're going to investigate him and then break his heart." Quell nodded sagely. "Very wise."

"That's *not* what is happening!" I hissed.

Blare caught Quell's attention. *Stop teasing Crimson. Look, you're making them blush.*

My hands flew to my cheeks. "I am *not*—"

Svelte stuffed the letter back into the envelope. "Now *you're* the one making a fuss," she said primly, before flouncing away. She and Blare giggled as they returned to the kitchen, taking the letter with them. Quell scurried off to make sure that the half-dozen patrons scattered throughout the inn didn't need anything.

I was left standing there with my hands still pressed to my cheeks, smiling like a fool.

I was going to see Serkadis again.

On my *birthday*.

CHAPTER FOUR

"Let's go through the plan one more time," Emerald said. By that point, we had discussed the plan five or six times already, and given how simple it was, further repetition struck me as redundant.

I held up my hands and ticked the points off my fingers as we walked. "I approach the front door directly while you find some way to sneak around out of sight. You knock, since I can't, and then you hide. I'm let in, we talk, he offers me dinner, but I insist on a tour of the grounds first. I let you know where we are at all times, and you do your best to avoid the staff while poking around in search of... whatever you're looking for." I paused for a moment, just to see if he would chime in and reveal what that might be, but he only nodded. *Not helpful.* "Once you're done looking, you either confront him directly, or I fake an illness and insist that I must leave before supper."

"Right," he said. "We'll sort that part out when we know more."

I turned my gaze away from him and studied the buildings as we passed on our way to Serkadis's residence. Emerald had made no comment as to the date, although I doubt it had slipped his mind. I had been conscious for a year and a day, but that had followed hard on the heels of the lowest point in Emerald's life. It had been nearly six months since he'd forsworn drinking entirely, and he seemed happier at the Lute and Goose than I would have believed, given the absence of a certain doctor. Still, the anniversary could not be celebrated without acknowledging a deep and lasting pain, and neither of us had broached the subject directly.

Serkadis's residence stood at the top of a hill, within the wealthy residential district, but apart from it. The rest of the neighborhood ended at the base of the hill and was surrounded by a low stone wall. A sprawling orchard populated the land between the wall and a high metal gate surrounding the manor itself. The house would be difficult to approach unnoticed, but a child could easily jump the wall and raid the lower orchard, or approach from the unguarded road and make off with the fruit when it was in season. I wondered if Serkadis had designed it that way.

Emerald stayed with me until we were halfway up the slope. As he slipped between the trees, he told me, ***[I won't go far, but it's too easy to see the path from the upper floors. I don't want him to know I'm coming.]***

I approached the tall gate alone. Already I could see a flaw in our plan: there had been no such barrier around Bracefallow Manor. I was wondering what to do next when a voice said, *"Speak your name."*

I looked around for the source of the voice—it was not Serkadis's, I was sure of that, but there was no sign of any guard or watchman. Still, the speaker had been quite close. Further examination of the gate revealed a face sculpted into the ironwork around the latch.

"Crimson Smoke," I said, watching the little face intently.

It *grinned* at me, and the gate swung open of its own accord. I hesitated, wondering what sort of *Aidea* could power a device like that. Perhaps it was the work of an Artificer, like Mel? But even *Aidea* would need someone to charge it, and the gate seemed like it would require a lot more magical fuel than the static illusion that Emerald had placed over the village of Dyrne, or the dancing lights that illuminated the hall of Feynlish Castle.

Perhaps more importantly, I wasn't sure how Emerald planned to make his way through the gate without being spotted. *[There's an interesting bit of magic up ahead... be careful.]*

[I'll figure it out,] he assured me. *[You go on without me.]*

Our plan had already fallen apart, but I could hardly turn back now. Moreover, I didn't want to. Emerald's caution and my nerves, which had troubled me on our walk through the city, were overshadowed by my curiosity. Some great and terrible power lay within the manor house before me, and I was drawn toward it like a moth to flame.

So I went on, leaving Emerald to find his own way through, and approached the massive front door.

The building seemed old, but it was well-maintained. Climbing vines scaled the stone walls, the shutters were painted a rich ocean-blue, and the flowery gingerbread trim made the house look a bit less grim and serious than others we'd passed. A hodgepodge of curves and angles, it had either been renovated or newly built a few years back, judging by its more modern and frivolous features. The building wasn't *small* by any means, but three or four structures of its size could have easily fit inside Bracefallow manor.

For the first time, I wondered if Serkadis lived alone. Did he have a family, perhaps a wife who would greet me at the door? Not that it would matter. Although, he *had* signed the letter *"yours..."*

The gate creaked shut behind me, and I whirled. There was no sign of Emerald behind me. *[Em?]* I asked.

[I'm coming, just give me a—]

"Crimson?"

When I turned back to the house, the door was open, and Serkadis himself stood in the entranceway.

I hurried over. "Your gate startled me," I admitted.

"Ah, yes." He grinned, and the hard lines of his features immediately softened. "I know it's a novelty, but it allows me to feel a great deal more secure. People are curious about me, and it makes them bold. You look magnificent, by the way."

Red and gold were my favorite colors, but I hadn't wanted to wear anything that might be read as a political statement. Given that the nobles of Kinmore had co-opted red to indicate their relation to the king, I'd dressed myself in a flowing overcoat the color of burnished bronze. The coat draped around me like a dress, but it opened at the front with each step to reveal the trousers and high boots beneath. I had spent an unreasonable amount of time deciding how to arrange myself, and I'd hoped to replicate a similar effect to his outfit at the party.

If I was worried that I'd be overdressed, those worries were quickly laid to rest. Serkadis had donned a silver silk coat that buttoned asymmetrically toward one shoulder, and wore loose shimmering trousers that gathered at his ankles. The cut was unusual, but much less provocative than the costume he'd worn to the king's party.

I was only a little disappointed.

"So do you," I said.

Serkadis grinned, and his pale eyes gleamed. "Were you hoping I'd take more of a sartorial risk?"

"Always." I flinched at the crack of twigs in the distance, presumably the result of Emerald heaving himself over the fence somewhere around the side of the house.

"I'm terribly sorry to disappoint you," Serkadis said. "As I said, you look marvelous, but no one who saw you in this would be scandalized." He stepped aside to usher me through the door. "Forgive me, I shouldn't keep you standing in the walkway. My manners are... rusty. I rarely play host." An expression flickered over his features, so swift and subtle I had no chance to read it.

I slipped past him into the house's spacious interior, feeling very wrong-footed indeed. "You don't? How long has it been since you had a guest?"

"Several months," Serkadis said, "and before that... I can hardly recall." The door shut behind us, and he ushered me deeper into the cavernous room. The inside of the house was even more unusual than the outside. I had assumed that the house was three stories high, but the first floor was tall enough for two. Even more oddly, it was nearly empty, with furniture arranged around the walls and no carpets or wood to cover the bare stone floor. A wide staircase led up to the second story, which was supported by beams so massive I could scarcely imagine the trees from which they must have been cut, and a door at the right end of the main room opened into a vast kitchen. An enormous pair of wooden doors stood to our left, but they were firmly latched.

"What do you think?" Serkadis's smile was wry. He held out his arms as he strode to the middle of the room.

"Oh," I said, trying to scrounge up a compliment over the odd construction. "Yes, it's very... open?"

Serkadis laughed. "I am well aware that the downstairs isn't to everyone's tastes, but I'm sure you can see why I don't host many events. Can you imagine what the good people of Kinmore would think of the arrangements?"

"For what it's worth, I don't think much of the other houses I've visited," I said, thinking of Bracefallow Manor.

"No?" Serkadis tilted his head, and his smile gave way to a piercing stare. He folded his hands behind his back and regarded me curiously. "Why not?"

I hesitated.

"Crimson Smoke." Serkadis stepped closer. "I promise I am not usually so demanding, but I implore you to speak freely with me. I do not ask out of idle gossip. I want to know what you *think*. I suspect you have a rather unique way of looking at the world."

"Because I'm not like the other girls?" I blurted. "Please, that's a tired line."

"Are you a girl, then?"

My smile faltered.

"I suspect," Serkadis said, "that you're not like anyone." His eyes never left my face.

Is that what you told Gorlyn Bracefallow? The words threatened to spill out of me, but being that direct wouldn't help our investigation in the slightest, so I swallowed them down. "Are you?" I asked instead.

"Am *I* like anyone else you know?" He chuckled. "Probably not."

"What makes you so special?"

Serkadis hummed. "I'll leave it up to you to decide that."

[I'm over the fence,] Emerald told me. **[Let me know when the coast is clear.]**

Theoretically, I was supposed to request a tour of the house, but given the layout, that wouldn't be effective. I'd need to come up with something else. "You have a beautiful orchard," I said. Would asking him to take a walk through the grounds be feasible?

"I do." He gestured toward the stairs. "It's even more enchanting when viewed from above. Would you like to see, before the light fails?"

I nodded and followed him up to the second floor. A pair of glass-paneled doors opened to a balcony. I waited until he unlocked them and led me through to tell Emerald, **[Clear. But be quick, please... you'll see why once you're inside. There's not a lot of cover.]**

A ripple of affirmation followed. Serkadis approached the para-pet, beyond which the sky had turned a dull gold, bruised along the eastern horizon with ripples of violet and rose. Lanterns and candles were being lit across the city. In the half-light, the sky was trapped on the threshold between night and day, on the day that was divided equally between the two.

"I love this view," he said admiringly. "Something about the quality of the light, don't you agree?"

"I do." I pointed down to a trio of small shadows clustered near the low stone wall. "It seems you have visitors."

Serkadis watched with amusement as one of the shadows leapt over the wall and darted between the trees. "They won't find much yet, I'm afraid. It'll be weeks before anything's in season, and the real harvest won't come in until fall."

"And when it is, will you still watch when they scale the wall?"

"Of course." Serkadis waved to the trees. "It's not as if I can eat it all. I take what I can use, and so will they. Whatever's left will go to the scavengers, or back to the soil."

I studied his profile. "You could sell the excess."

Serkadis wrinkled his nose in obvious disgust. "I could. But to what end? I have more than I need, and not everyone in this city can say the same. If they're desperate enough to steal, then I hardly begrudge them the spoils."

I had no response to that.

"There are those," he added, "that would call me weak for letting others help themselves to what's mine. I'd like to think you aren't one of them."

"No," I murmured. "I'm not."

He smiled at me sidelong as he leaned against the railing. The pale-silver brocade of his coat was stark against his dark skin. Such a muted palette would have left me looking waxy and pallid, but it suited him perfectly.

It's because of his eyes, I realized. In the light of the setting sun, his irises glowed the same pale silver as the thread of his jacket.

"You're staring," he observed.

"Just admiring your tailor's handiwork," I lied.

"Mm." His knowing smile suggested that he saw right through me in more ways than one, but he turned his attention to the cloth, holding it out by the hem to give me a better view of the pattern. "It cost a fortune. I should be ashamed, I suppose, but..." His eyes found mine again. "The wealthy people of this city pay handsomely for garments cut from cloth that is mass-produced in Venta Bulgarum and the eastern provinces. They tend to prefer the newer fashions, too, but I'm a creature of habit. This was made by hand. I happen to know the woman who designed it."

"She's very good," I admitted.

"She is. I like to think of myself not as a mere consumer, but as a patron."

I bent closer to the fabric, admiring the scene that chased itself across the cloth: dragons in flight, looping and coiling between bead-limned clouds.

"Beautiful," I murmured. The buttons, too, were silver, and they likewise depicted dragons.

I glanced up at him sharply. His eyes glinted in the light each time he moved his head, and I noted that the pupils were not round, but faintly elongated and astonishingly black, as if a void lay behind them. It was not the same darkness that I'd observed each time Innocent shifted in the ceiling of the Brotherhood, but more familiar somehow. Not friendly, not malicious, but infinitely deep.

"What are you?" I asked.

In answer, Serkadis lifted one hand toward my face. I flinched away out of habit, but when his fingers passed through a loose lock of my hair, the curl *moved* as if blown by the wind.

Only... wind did not affect me. Nothing did.

I moved back a pace and wrapped my arms around my middle. "What *are* you?" I repeated, but with more urgency this time. "How can... how did you...?"

Inside my head, Innocent howled for blood. If Serkadis was a Lightweaver, he might be able to hurt me, or to hurt Emerald.

"I didn't mean to startle you." His expression was remorseful, but I took another step back. He held up both hands in surrender. "I thought you must have guessed, knowing what you are. Knowing what the Emerald Flame is. I haven't exactly been subtle, Crimson."

I shook my head, retreating toward the doors that led back inside. *[Emerald? Where are you? I think I'm in trouble.]* "I don't know what you mean." Memories of being swept up in the magic of the Black Hollow warred with the dangers of fighting Innocent in my mind-cottage. I had been too free with a stranger, too taken in by my curiosity. Emerald was right. This man was dangerous in ways I didn't fully understand.

"You're a lightweaving," Serkadis said. "Aren't you? But you're not like any lightweaving I've ever encountered before." He studied me with the same curiosity that Emerald might have studied a clue that didn't fit. "You're not *just* a weaving, either. I don't know what to make of that, but I can assure you, I would never harm you. You're not just magic, but neither are you an ordinary person. I admit, I find that quite intriguing."

I squared my shoulders. "What gave it away this time?" I asked, lifting my chin in the imitation of a defiance I did not feel. "And what do you intend to do about it?"

"I expect he plans to blackmail us," Emerald growled from behind me.

I whirled to face him and found him standing in the doorway that led to the terrace. His lips were curled back in a scowl that revealed the shorn-off nubs of his tusks more prominently than usual. His eyes were fixed on Serkadis.

Our host sucked in a breath and ran one hand through his hair. Despite my growing distrust, I couldn't help but notice that his messy appearance somehow made him *more* handsome, which was decidedly unfair.

"That was never my plan," Serkadis said. "I've given you every opportunity to work out for yourself who—or rather *what*—I am. If I'd wanted to blackmail you, I could have done so via letter or babblebird, rather than inviting you into my home. You set off every alarm around my perimeter, I'll have you know, but I have made no effort to stop you." He waved one hand at himself. "And, really, would I have dressed like *this* if I was trying to be covert?"

Emerald huffed and crossed his arms. "I suppose not. But if you'd already worked out what Crimson and I were, you invited us here *alone*, without even a maid or a footman in sight. You have to admit, the lack of witnesses suggests that your intentions are less than honest."

To my consternation, Serkadis stifled a laugh. "I see your point. But you give yourself too much credit, Emerald Flame. I dismissed most of my staff in the autumn, long before I made your acquaintance."

Emerald scratched his chin. "Is that so?"

"I have not invited you here to threaten you, but to ask for your help."

As they spoke, I kept turning from one to the other, waiting for one of them to explain what they were going on about. When neither did, I glared at Serkadis.

"You know what I am," I said, "but you've failed to answer my question. What are *you*?"

Serkadis dipped his head, looking somewhat sheepish, while Emerald rolled his eyes. "Isn't it obvious?" he asked. "He claims no city as his homeland, he avoids meat, he's got creepy eyes, he collects shiny things, is too rich for his own good, and has more magic than he knows what to do with. Also, he dresses like *that*."

Serkadis's ornate silver buttons flashed and the silk thread on his brocade shimmered in the failing light. Below us, three shadows slipped back over the wall and ran off into the city with whatever prizes they'd found.

"He's a godsdamned *dragon*," Emerald rumbled. "And I'm almost positive he ate Gorlyn Bracefallow."

CHAPTER FIVE

"A *what?*" I demanded, at the same moment that Serkadis cried, "I would never!"

I jabbed a finger at Serkadis as I addressed my friend. "That's not what a dragon looks like, is it? Don't they have *scales?*" I nearly blurted out Dumplin's name, but I stopped myself just in time. Serkadis didn't need to know about the necklace our lambkin acquaintance possessed. If he really was a dragon, he might take offense that she'd used dragon parts in the ornament's design.

"They can," Emerald said. He was still watching Serkadis with his arms crossed. I had no doubt that if the alleged dragon made a move, Emerald would tackle him to the floor of the balcony. "Dragons can shapeshift. That's why he needs the big room downstairs... and why the floors up here have to be so strongly reinforced. They can't change what they *are*, just how they look. I expect he weighs thirty times what a normal man does."

"Which is why it would be exceedingly silly for you to start a fistfight with me." Serkadis scowled up at my friend. "If you really thought I was a maneater, then you were unwise to come. Especially knowing that I have more than one means of harming you." As he spoke, he reached out into the air between us and flicked his fingers, as if strumming the strings of a lute. In response, I felt the tug of the tether in my midriff, even though Emerald stood only a few paces away.

"Oh!" I gasped, pressing my hand to my stomach.

Serkadis lowered his hand. "That didn't hurt, did it?" His mouth turned down at the corners.

"No, but... don't do it again." I took another step back.

Serkadis sighed again and closed his eyes as he pressed his fingers to his forehead. "Forgive me," he said. "This is not at all the way I hoped this would go. Will you let me start again?"

Emerald nodded to me. "Depends on what Crimson says."

"Why me?" I squeaked. I was leagues upon leagues out of my depth, floundering in an unfamiliar ocean.

"Because you were taking his measure," Emerald said.

Serkadis raised one eyebrow at me. "Ah. So this was not only a distraction, but a test?"

"Why not?" I snapped. "You were testing us. If you knew he was sneaking around, why not say so?"

"Because I understand why you'd be cautious," Serkadis said. "Let me make you a deal: you can leave now, and I won't stop you, or you can let me explain. But if you choose the latter, I must insist that you stay until my explanation is complete."

Both men stared at me, awaiting my verdict. Serkadis's shoulders slumped under the weight of the secrets he carried. Emerald's mind was locked up safe as a vault. The decision was mine alone.

What did I really *know* about Serkadis? That he had impeccable taste in clothes, which said nothing about his character. For all I knew, Serkadis had been lying about sharing his harvest with his poorer neighbors. He might have even staged the scene just to impress me.

I studied his face, hoping to glean something from a close examination. When Emerald had agreed to let Dumplin keep her necklace, he'd done so because her impulses spoke of her character. A man like

Gorlyn thought the way to win glory was through a show of force. If Serkadis preferred to win my esteem through a display of generosity, that told me something about his heart, didn't it?

Whether that heart was human or not.

"We'll hear you out," I said. "Besides, we owe the Bracefallows an explanation."

Serkadis grimaced. "Very well. I think we'd better start inside, though. Even in twilight, you never know when there might be prying eyes about."

As we returned to the house, I nudged Emerald's mind with mine. *[How **did** you alert him? Didn't you think to check for traps first?]*

*[Of course I did, but dragon magic is... different. It doesn't work the way ordinary **Aidea** does. It follows different rules. Or rather, it follows **hardly** any rules. The Conjury would level this city to get their hands on a rogue dragon, and if you think I'm exaggerating, guess again.]*

Serkadis reached the first floor when we were still a few steps behind, then motioned for us to wait. "I don't usually shift with an audience," he explained. "You might want to stay out of the way so that I don't accidentally squash you in the process." Emerald and I hung back as Serkadis strode to the middle of the room, then turned to face us. He offered me a sad smile, spread his arms, and closed his eyes.

When I rearranged myself, it happened all at once. I was one thing, and then in the blink of an eye I was something else. Serkadis's transformation was slower by necessity, since he had an actual *body* that required rearrangement. Even so, it took a matter of mere moments for his figure to flex and expand. My eyes were everywhere at once as I tried to make sense of the way his silver flesh unfurled.

With the change came a surge of magic which nearly dragged me into its maelstrom. I could *feel* it, tugging at my hair and clothes like a gust of wind. Emerald's eyes widened in alarm, and he gripped his pendant in one fist while making a gesture with the other. His eyes flashed green, and I stumbled back, only there was nothing to stand on. I had no idea what to do; the normal rules did not apply.

So *that* was what Emerald had meant by dragon magic. I'd never experienced anything like it, not even in the in-between realm where I'd made my home.

And then it was over. The magic surrounding Serkadis fizzled out.

I could see why he needed a big ground-floor room. He hardly filled it, even in this new form, but his serpentine tail and elongated neck could have reached halfway across the space if he held both out straight. I could only guess at the span of his huge wings, since they were folded and pressed tight to his body. He swiveled his head toward us, and his silver eyes flashed beneath the crown of silver ore that winked and glinted with every motion of his head. He was brighter than the wall sconces, as if pure radiance spilled out of every scale.

"Aster's sake." Emerald clung to the railing so tight that the wood groaned in his grip.

"What?" Serkadis moved closer and lowered his head until he was eye level with Emerald. He wouldn't be able to eat my friend in a single bite, but two might do it. "Never seen a dragon before?"

"No," Emerald said. "No, I have not." His voice cracked, and the blood had rushed from his face, leaving him pallid and ashen. He was terrified, and all three of us knew it.

"Unsurprising." Serkadis turned to me. "Are you satisfied now?"

I was, in fact, more than satisfied. I was awed. The longer I stared at him, the more clearly I understood that what *truly* astonished me was not the mere fact of his appearance. Magic moved over and through him, an extension of his presence, like another limb. More-over, it was alive.

No wonder I'd been drawn to him. He was made of raw *Aidea*.

Just like me.

"You're beautiful," I murmured, without thinking.

He laughed with enough force to rattle the sparse furniture.

"Thank you. You might be the first person who's ever said that. Not that many have had the chance."

"Then they couldn't really see you," I told him, referring to the swirl and pulse of *Aidea* that radiated from every scale.

He smiled at me, revealing a fortress of teeth. Emerald gulped.

"May I?" I gestured down the steps, and when Serkadis nodded, I approached. I reached one hand outward and upward to his broad, shining chest. When my palm met the metal, it stopped.

I could not feel his scales, precisely, but there was something there: a sensation I had no word for, because it was both so undeniable and yet so unlike anything I'd experienced before. I'd occupied Emerald's body on a few occasions, and spent a few minutes in Bram's. I knew what people with nerves called *cold*. This was like holding a palmful of starlight, cool but bright, a bubbling effervescence that sparked when his *Aidea* met mine.

"You gave Dumplin the silver," I said.

"Perhaps she stole it," Serkadis chuckled.

"No." I pulled my hand away. "It's definitely your magic, and she's much too smart to steal from you and then set up a business in the same city." I looked up to meet his gaze. "Which means that you were testing us even before you extended an invitation. You asked her about us, I assume?"

"When I explain what happened to Gorlyn, you'll understand why precautions were necessary. I had already given the Emerald Flame a few hints out of desperation, but it was comforting to learn that your allegiance to the Conjury is... conditional." He backed away. "Go up to the top of the stairs for a moment, please. I'd like to turn back, and I think it best if you stay out of the way."

I agreed wholeheartedly, given how his first shift had affected me. I sprang up the steps all the way to the second floor and held my ground as he folded in upon himself until he was a man again.

"Much better." He straightened the fall of his coat. "I find it rather unsettling to be my true self in the presence of others, if I'm being honest. Although I suppose most of us feel that way. I'm afraid that this will be a long story, so perhaps we should discuss things in the kitchen. Using that much *Aidea* in one go whets the appetite."

Emerald took a wary step backward.

"Not for flesh, I assure you," Serkadis amended. "I told you, I don't eat meat. Never have. Gods willing, I never will." With that, he turned toward the open kitchen door, leaving us to follow or flee.

Emerald raked his hands over his face. *[What in all the hells did Finch get us into? And how are you taking this so well? He's even more dangerous than an Outsider!]*

[He could be,] I agreed. *[But I think he's chosen not to be.]*

Emerald dismounted the last few steps. *[I hope so.]*

[What happened to trusting my instincts?] I demanded.

[I'm not arguing with you, but...] Emerald held up his shaking hands. *[I don't think I've ever been this powerless, Crim. I've always had my brains, and my size, and my magic, and some combination of the three has always proved to be enough. If he turns on us, I can't defend myself. Or you. Or anyone in this gods-damned city.]*

I understood where he was coming from, but I also knew what dark magic looked like. What it felt like. I'd grappled with it more than once. Hells, some of it lived in my head.

I was beginning to see that magic itself was neither good nor bad. It was a tool that granted power to the wielder, and it made whoever controlled it more of... whatever they already were. Serkadis could have easily used his power to kill the king and rule Kinmore in his stead. He could have declared himself a god if he wanted; I'd seen how swiftly people turned to Allure for answers the previous autumn. If what he wanted was power and control, he could have lived in the finest house in the city, bending people to his will.

And yet, he hadn't.

[Trust me,] I urged Emerald. *[Even if you can't trust him, trust me.]*

If he could have seen Serkadis as I did, he would have understood.

. . .

"Forgive me if I tell you something you already know," Serkadis said. He stood at the long wooden countertop, patiently slicing the vast array of vegetables which he'd brought up from the root cellar. "I don't mean to insult your intelligence, but if your knowledge of dragons comes exclusively from books and lore, it's very likely that some of what you've heard is either myth or propaganda."

Emerald sat on the far side of the counter, watching Serkadis work. My friend was still stiff and wary, but it was impossible to be frightened of someone chopping root vegetables in his shirtsleeves.

Serkadis had removed his coat in our absence and draped it carefully over the back of an unoccupied chair. Was it part of him, as my clothes were, or did he really have a tailor? More importantly, he'd rolled his shirtsleeves up to the elbow, revealing his forearms, which were covered in fine black hairs only a few shades darker than his skin. I could not seem to stop staring at them.

"You're right," Serkadis went on, "that some dragons eat people. Doing so allows them—*us*—to acquire knowledge and power from those we consume. But it changes us. *Punishes* us. Once a dragon has tasted the meat of a sentient being, we become... insatiable." His hands stilled for a moment as he considered the prospect.

"You've abstained, though," Emerald said, glancing down at the dragon's ever-growing pile of finely chopped winter squash. "And not just from the meat of sentient animals, by the looks of things. Do you eat fish?"

Of course he would forget his terror when there was puzzle to be solved.

Serkadis cleared his throat. "It is, quite frankly, my greatest fear. To lose control of my thoughts and impulses would mean losing my *self*. We are nothing more than the totality of our choices, and giving into the hunger would mean I had no choice at all. It seems simple enough to avoid feasting on anything that thinks, but the very definition of sentience is a slippery, elusive thing, isn't it? Rarely is anything in this world so... sharply defined." Serkadis shot me a look. "Lifetimes ago, I and a few others pondered this and thought it prescient to be cautious. Avoid meat altogether and live lives of restraint. But not all of my kin see things that way. Which is why I left. I prefer to live among the mortal races. The way they see things is so *bright,* and it is constantly changing. No generation is quite like the last." He resumed his chopping and peeling. "So I moved here. I found ways to earn a living that don't involve exploiting people—it *is* possible, despite what you may think. I've lived here since before the dragon tiles were installed..."

"Dragon tiles?" I asked.

"Pre-Conjury infrastructure," Emerald said. "A precaution against dragon infiltration. They're mundane ceramic tiles that line the city gates... cheap, but effective. When they're subjected to a certain amount of centralized weight, they break and alert the guards."

I frowned at him. "But wouldn't wagons break them?"

"Nah. A wagon's weight is too spread out. The tiles aren't large enough to have a full cart pressing down on them at one time. But like I said, Serkadis maintains his mass, even as a man."

"And if I was in my dragon form," Serkadis added drily, "they'd notice something amiss without the help of the dragon tiles."

"I wondered how you got around them." Emerald leaned forward to rest his elbows on the counter. "But you *predate* them."

"Indeed. I've lived in this city for, oh, almost three hundred years. I let myself age in one form until it's time to move on. Then I pretend to sell the house, change my shape, and move in again. It's been quite a lovely life."

"But Gorlyn Bracefallow found out," I guessed.

At the sound of the young man's name, Serkadis flinched as if I'd struck him. "Sort of. To be specific, he learned that I'd dismissed all my staff, and started asking *why.* I'm not sure he ever figured out what I was. If you don't mind, I'll hold off explaining that part for a moment. Suffice to say that, yes, Gorlyn learned that I had secrets, and although his guesses were not quite on the mark, he could have ruined me. I was working out a plan to throw him off the scent or, barring that, resolve the situation by some other avenue. I had no idea he would be so reckless."

Serkadis set the knife aside and went to retrieve a large crock, which he swept the vegetables into.

"His death was never my desired solution." He added a few more ingredients to the pot with sharp, almost angry gestures. "One might say that it was not a solution at all. He was convinced that he would be able to earn a title by way of doing something unforgivable. And yet what happened to him can hardly be forgiven, even if Gorlyn was the one at fault." He set the crock on a strangely constructed stove and made a gesture toward the mechanism inside. A fire sprang to life within. More *Aidea*. He could burn Emerald to a crisp if he wanted.

"Are you going to tell us what Gorlyn learned?" I asked.

"No." Serkadis straightened up. "I'm going to show you. I had to do it, given how little I know you, but soon the problem will become more, ah, *acute*. Come with me."

He left his dinner cooking on the stove and led us back into the main room toward the double doors at the far end. When he reached them, he pressed his hands to the latch and closed his eyes. Another surge of *Aidea* was followed by the clatter of tumblers falling into place. The doors swung to, revealing another flight of stairs. This one, however, led down into a subterranean level of the house.

[So far, I believe him,] Emerald said. *[But I don't like the idea of following him into a crypt...]*

[I imagine not, given what happened the last two times,] I replied.

He pulled a face. *[What are you talking about?]*

Ah, right. Thanks to Harmony's meddling, he didn't remember either of his visits to the catacombs beneath the Brotherhood.

[All I'm saying is that if he wanted us dead, or trapped, or

something worse, he wouldn't need to lure us into the basement in order to do it. He'd drag you down there by your ankles.]

Emerald narrowed his eyes. *[Crimson, you are such a comfort.]*

I slipped past him. *[I'm going. You can do what you want.]*

There was no point in maintaining the illusion of walking, so I spared myself the trouble and drifted down the steps in the ghostly manner of a well-dressed apparition. The stairs were wide enough that Serkadis could have traversed them even in dragon form, and they switched back at a landing halfway down. The landing opened to the main portion of the basement, and when I reached it, I was able to see out into the room where Serkadis waited.

I stopped short, and Emerald cursed when he walked right through me. For a moment, we got tangled up in each other, so that my sense became impossible to differentiate from his. Then he was past me, catching his footing on the next step.

"What the hells?" he growled.

I pointed to the lower level. Serkadis stood in the middle of the room. A few paces away from him, arranged on what appeared to be a bunched-up sateen bedspread, lay the most enormous egg I had ever seen. It was easily the size of a young child, and its plated shell glimmered with the same pulsing *Aidea* that had limned Serkadis's other form.

Next to the egg, lying splayed on the floor with one arm extended toward the shell, was a shriveled human form. It hadn't been wearing clothes, and it was so shrunken and decayed that I might not have recognized it as a person. Even the decaying corpses I had encountered in the Cronemire had been more lifelike than the withered husk that lay before us.

The shock of bright-red hair on the corpse's skull confirmed what I'd assumed at first glance.

We'd found the remains of Gorlyn Bracefallow.

CHAPTER SIX

hile I was frozen in shock, Emerald reacted with anger. "Driaweep's withered arsehole, you just *left him here*?" He pointed an accusing finger at the corpse. "For *months*?"

"I can't *move* him," Serkadis said. "He's no worse now than he was when I found him, and I hardly think that reducing him to dust would be a kindness. I thought, if I could leave, at least his family would have something to find." Serkadis dropped into a crouch and pressed his hands to the side of his head, emitting a guttural groan as he did so. "I never wanted *any* of this. But when I heard that someone was trying to smuggle a dragon egg through the port, I couldn't let that stand. Do you have any idea how careful I was? How many minds I had to nudge and shape to make sure that nobody knew I'd taken it? You can't *imagine* the lengths I went to in order to ensure that no harm came to it, and that it didn't harm anyone in the process. I *knew* the risk I was taking, getting involved, but I couldn't... I couldn't simply..." He pressed his hands to his face and let out a muffled scream.

I looked from Emerald's furious face to Serkadis's pitiable

posture and back again. "Can someone explain what happened? Do dragon eggs…?"

"They feed off the life force of everything around them," Serkadis moaned. "It can be draining, even for the parents. But for a *human* to touch it…" He nodded to Gorlyn's shriveled form and let the evidence speak for itself.

"Gods." Emerald shook his head. He dropped down on the top step and stared through the posts of the banister at the egg and the dead boy and the dragon who seemed on the verge of a breakdown. "You really stepped in it, didn't you?"

"Why do you think I took the risk of intimating what I was?" Serkadis snapped.

The answer made me recoil. "Because you knew what *I* was. You thought you could blackmail us, just as Gorlyn blackmailed you."

Serkadis looked up at me. His eyes were puffy and red-rimmed. "In the beginning? Yes. I did."

I turned away. In the grand scheme of things, it was foolish to feel slighted, but seeing him at the party, dressed the way I *wished* I could dress, had shaken and awed me. All he had seen was a mark. A way out of a dire situation of his own making.

Well, sort of. He hadn't wished the egg into being.

[You're being too kind,] Innocent whispered. *[Looking for a way to forgive him. We should trick him, punish him, find a way to take his magic. Imagine what we could do with all that power—]*

"So what's your plan?" Emerald asked. "Find a way out of the city, and then…?"

"There are places I could go," Serkadis said. "Further north, along the trade routes, and then to the coast. The egg is dangerous enough, but a hatchling dragon is like a toddler with the power of an army. A *hungry* one."

[He could free you,] Innocent whispered.

That had me turning on the spot to face Serkadis. "If we help, what will you give us?"

"What?" Emerald squawked. "Crim, we can't—"

"We have a way to help you," I told Serkadis. "Maybe. I see the problem: if you walk out of the city under your own power, you'll break the dragon tiles at the gate. Even if you were willing to risk flying out of the city in your *other* form..."

"The egg would drain my reserves of *Aidea*," Serkadis murmured, almost to himself. "It would be a short flight indeed, and I would have given everything away. Perhaps I could find a way around the tiles on my own, but not with the egg draining me. I can't leave it behind, not after all this."

I nodded. "And if you stay, and that thing hatches, you'll be risking the lives of everyone around you and putting both you and the hatchling in danger. Your options are limited, and time is running out." I crossed my arms. "So I can see why you want assistance, but I'm fuzzy on why we should bother. If we can get you and your egg out of the city, what will you give us?"

Serkadis pressed his palms to his knees and rose to his feet. He seemed more resigned than I had expected. "If you can get me and the egg out of the city, unharmed, I will grant you a boon. Anything within my power."

I shook my head and held up three fingers. "*Three* boons," I said. "One for me, one for Emerald, and one for our... assistant."

[What are you doing?] Emerald stared up at me as if he didn't know me, twisted around in his place on the step.

[If we leave the egg here, more people will die. If Serkadis tries to get it out by himself... more people will die. And if we don't agree to help him, do you really think he's going to let us walk away?]

[And how do you intend to help him?] Emerald demanded.

I raised one eyebrow at him.

"No," Emerald said aloud, "Crim, that's not—"

[We'll let him decide. If he says no, or you come up with a better idea when we're not trapped in a dragon's cellar, then we'll go from there. But you must agree that we have to do something, or else you'll end up like Gorlyn and I'll be absorbed into a dragon's egg.]

Emerald rubbed his forehead. *[I don't want to risk—]* He hesitated. *[For Aster's sake. For all we know, Serkadis, can listen in our thoughts...]*

[Why do you think I'm not saying his name?] I asked.

[I wonder.] Innocent growled. *[I wonder what else he knows. So much power...]*

Serkadis hadn't moved. He stood alongside the egg, breathing heavily.

"Well?" I asked. "What'll it be? Three boons, or nothing at all?"

"If my kin found out that I was granting boons to mortals..." he began.

I shook my head sharply. "Not our problem. I don't like being blackmailed any more than you do. If you'd asked us to help, that'd be one thing. But you tried to use us, so fair's fair."

[When did you get so cutthroat?] Emerald demanded.

[Yes, Crimson Smoke. When did that happen?]

I held my ground against all of them. Innocent was right about one thing: Serkadis presented a rare opportunity for me. Under other circumstances, I would have asked more kindly.

It was *possible* that I was feeling just a tad scorned. And that I'd taken it personally.

Serkadis's shoulders slackened. "Three boons," he said. "But only if we can make it out of the city undetected, with no one the wiser... and with no other loss of life." His eyes found Gorlyn's remains before he turned his face away.

"Perfect." I lowered my hand. "How long do we have?"

"Weeks, perhaps." He turned to the egg. "Maybe less. I have no way of knowing how long it was in the smugglers' possession, or how much energy it was able to absorb while in their care."

"Then I suppose we'd better act quickly. Come on, Emerald." I turned my back on Serkadis and retreated up the stairs.

I had been angry on Emerald's behalf many times, but he was the only person who'd managed to hurt *me* in any lasting way. When Innocent tried to harm me, it was only because harm was in its nature. I had never had my heart broken before, and it was most unpleasant.

Although, in fact, Serkadis was not the real problem. I was angry at myself for letting myself feel anything for him. I wished I could blame the magic.

Serkadis didn't follow us as we retreated into the night. Emerald didn't say a word the whole way back to the inn.

It was just as well. I didn't feel like talking.

CHAPTER SEVEN

"We can't ask him to do this," Emerald said. He'd spent the whole night tossing and turning, and he'd gotten up before dawn in search of a calming drink. At least he bypassed the bar, although the rate at which he'd been downing tea suggested that he was craving something stronger.

"And what do you propose we do?" I stood by the oven and glared at the smoldering coals.

"Find another solution," Emerald grumbled.

The head above the fire made the air ripple, reminiscent of the magic that had shimmered around Serkadis in his dragon form. *[What happens if a dragon hatches in Kinmore?]* I asked. *[How many people is it likely to kill?]*

"Gods." Emerald slumped forward and buried his face in his hands. "I don't know. There's so little information about how the various types differ, and who knows how much of it is real."

"Serkadis was afraid." I circled back around the table so that I could stand at Emerald's side. "It doesn't strike me that someone that powerful would have much to be afraid of, but he said it himself: the loss of control is his worst nightmare. If *he* can't control an errant hatchling, what hope do we have? There's a way to do this without anyone getting hurt, and you know it."

"That's a huge amount of pressure to place on a boy, and a terrible risk—"

"We should at least *ask*."

Emerald snatched up his mug and took a deep pull of his tea without looking at me. "I'm not sure that a magical solution is the answer. He's got more power than anyone or any*thing* I've ever encountered. Why doesn't he just find a creative way to do it himself?"

I reached up to touch a lock of my hair, the one that Serkadis had nearly touched the day before. "I don't think he can."

That time, Emerald *did* look at me. "Meaning?"

"The gate that let me onto the property was the work of an Artificer," I mused. "So was the lock on his door to the downstairs, and the stove."

No matter how deep his distress, Emerald could never resist a puzzle. "Hm. You think his abilities have limits? That makes sense, that he would possess immense raw power, but still needs something to focus it through, just like the rest of us." He reached down to brush his fingers against the pendant.

"And right now, he doesn't have a conduit that will allow him to get out of the city," I added.

Emerald dropped his hand. "But the risk is too high."

"Risk to whom?"

We both spun to the door, through which Yerik had just entered. His hair was tied up under a patterned bonnet and his eyes were only half open. He yawned and rubbed one eye with his knuckle.

"Sorry," he said sheepishly. "I promise, I didn't hear much. It's unusual to hear you two argue like this."

"We usually don't," Emerald said.

[Aloud,] I added.

"Is there anything I can do to help?" In his stocking feet, Yerik padded over to retrieve a mug of his own, then reached for the kettle.

It lifted too easily, and he shook his head. "How much have you had?"

"Not enough to think clearly," Emerald muttered.

Yerik refilled the kettle and returned it to the stove. "Are you going to tell me what's the matter?"

Emerald cast a sidelong look at me. "We have an, mm, *unusual case*. A very powerful client that needs help."

Yerik nodded and crossed his arms. "All right."

"But the only solution we've thought of so far involves Blare," I said.

"Ah." Yerik's eyes opened fully, and his brows pulled taught. "And you said there'd be some risk?"

"There could be," I said.

Emerald frowned and clutched his mug. "There almost *certainly* would be."

"I see." Yerik's eyes drifted upward, toward the rooms above, where the children still slept. "In your opinion, is this client worth the risk?"

"I can't decide that," Emerald retorted.

"I know, and I'm confident you'd leave the final decision up to Blare. But that's not what I'm asking." Yerik returned his attention to Emerald. "It's difficult to imagine that you'd even be having this discussion if the person in question was a sack of pigshite."

Emerald let out a bark of surprised laughter. "That's not something I expected to hear *you* say."

"That's because I don't usually associate with pigshite individuals." Yerik's uneven smile revealed a dimple I had never noticed before. "So I have no reason to talk about them. I remember when we were children, you had no patience for bullies. Has that changed?"

Emerald's smile waned. "My patience has improved, I'm afraid."

"And your sense of justice?" Yerik asked.

Emerald's mouth opened, but he didn't answer.

"I suspect *that* remains unchanged. Or, if anything, strengthened." The kettle began to sing, and Yerik turned away so that he could see to his morning brew. "I don't need to know the details about this client of yours. What you think of him will suffice. Is his cause selfish, or sincere?"

"Sincere," I said. "At least, *I* believe that." Serkadis may have fallen from my good graces, but there was no denying that his motives were at least partly selfless. He was willing to give up his comfortable, stable life in order to protect the life of someone he'd never even met.

Gorlyn Bracefallow could have learned a thing or two, if only he'd approached things differently.

"Emerald?" Yerik pressed.

"I..." Emerald ran a hand through his hair, and his eyes unfocused for a moment. "I think I agree. But I can't be sure."

"The great Emerald Flame, unsure of something?" Yerik teased. "Say it isn't so." He leaned against the counter, sipping his tea and smiling at us. "I trust your instincts, Em. I think you should discuss it with Blare."

"He's a child!" Emerald protested.

I wrinkled my nose at him. "I'm *one*."

"*You're* a magical anomaly." Emerald wagged a finger in my face. "Stop comparing apples to glassberries."

"Was Quell old enough to decide to give up his *Aidea*?" Yerik asked.

Emerald's accusatory finger wilted. "I suppose."

"Then Blare is old enough to decide whether or not to use his," Yerik said. "And I know for a fact that you'll respect his decision more than the Brotherhood ever did."

Emerald sucked in a breath. He wrapped both hands around his mug and stared into its depth, as if hoping he could scry the future if he looked hard enough. "You're right about that."

With Emerald frowning into the dregs of his leaves, and Yerik sipping his tea as he waited for my friend to reach his own conclusions, I found myself wondering how different things might have been if Emerald had never left Kinmore. If he'd been here all along, maybe he could have been happier. Maybe he would never have needed me.

I was of two minds on that front, but if nothing else, I was glad we'd come back.

Blare sat, watching Emerald's handspeech, without giving anything away. Yerik had offered to sit with us while we spoke, and the other two insisted on joining as well. With each successive gesture, Svelte's eyes widened; her cheeks were as white as the face of a full moon, disrupted only by her constellation of freckles.

"Silver dragons are *real*?" Quell squeaked. He looked as if he might topple sideways off his chair. "And they're here?"

"One of them is," I said. "Two, if you count the egg."

The lambkin adjusted his glasses. "But dragons are supposed to be incredibly rare and *terribly* dangerous. Every book I've read about them says so. Between their *Aidea* and their appetites, they can take on armies. And win! I bet he could flatten half the city if he put his mind to it."

Emerald grimaced. "You might be right about that."

Quell leaned forward, his already large eyes magnified by the curve of his lenses. "*Cooooooool.* Can I meet him? I have tons of questions."

"You'll be staying with me," Yerik said gently. "Even if Blare goes. This is dangerous, and distractions won't help."

"Are you calling me a distraction?" Quell pressed a hand to his chest and another to his forehead, pretending to swoon.

Yerik tried to restrain a smile. "Let me rephrase: if you can be quiet for a whole day, Emerald can decide if you go or not."

Quell had never been known for his self-restraint, but at Yerik's words, he closed his mouth, crossed his arms, and looked to Emerald.

"Yerik's right," Emerald said, signing sharply for emphasis. "This *is* dangerous. But as long as we're careful, we'll make the city much safer in the end. And if we're caught, the real danger won't be to you, but to me."

Blare drummed his fingertips against his thigh a few times.

"If you're afraid..." Emerald began.

Blare shook his head and started signing before my friend could finish. *It's not that. I'm pretty sure I've seen scarier things than a dragon.* He snuck a glance at me, and I knew he was thinking of the shadow-beast. *And I* have *been practicing. But this is big, and I've never tried my* Aidea *on anything that big.*

I had learned the year before that Blare was a Stonefeather, which was to say that he could alter the mass of an object when he put his mind to it. The dragon tiles were designed to break under a tremendous, centralized weight. Serkadis couldn't make himself lighter even when he changed shape, as changing into a human form didn't make him truly human. Blare, however, *could.*

"I think you're underestimating how scary a dragon is in person," Emerald said dubiously.

Blare scratched the back of his head and glanced at me again. *Maybe,* he signed after a moment. *But either way, I'm more worried about failing than I am about taking the risk. What would happen if we were arrested?*

Emerald considered this. "Given your age, you'd likely be conscripted by the Conjury as a Castcadesman. Not right away, but they'd keep you under their thumb until then."

That was the Brotherhood's plan for me, anyway, Blare signed. *What else?*

"We could end up on the run," Emerald warned. "If we were found out, and tried to make a break for it, Serkadis might decide to fight back."

At least I'd have someone to run away with. My family got rid of me because I was too much trouble. Blare squinted up into Emerald's face. *Promise me you won't do the same thing.*

Emerald's eyes glistened. *Never,* he signed, unable to force the word past his lips.

He'd been keeping his emotions on lockdown ever since we'd discovered what Serkadis was. In part, I think he was unwilling to admit just how disturbed he was by the whole situation. A lifetime of pushing his feelings all the way down had made it easy for him to put limits on acknowledging his own fears.

Even *he* couldn't smother the surge of guilt and sadness that accompanied Blare's words. He was adept at shouldering his own burdens, but he'd agreed to help Blare carry similar baggage, and that weight was new for him. Abandonment was a wound he couldn't heal, and he knew that all too well.

"You won't be alone," Svelte said. She looped one arm through Blare's, even though it made her subsequently lopsided handspeech more difficult to parse. "Emerald and Crim'll be with you, and so will I."

Quell flailed in his chair, pointing to himself with both hands and nodding frantically.

"Hold on." Emerald held up one hand. "That's not what I—"

"We've never had a home worth defending before," Svelte interrupted. "I dunno about this dragon boon or what Blare wants from it, but I do know that I've never had a home nor a proper family that cared about each other. Anyhow, I'm not going to sit here twiddling my thumbs while Blare saves the day. What if something goes wrong and you need another set of hands? I'm an Arctician. I could be useful."

Quell hunched forward and wrapped his arms around himself.

Svelte leaned toward the lambkin and wrapped her other arm around his shoulder, dragging Blare off balance in the process. "And you never know, you might need someone to talk a guard's ear off as a distraction."

Emerald stared at them as if he'd never seen any of them before.

"Are you going to tell us we're not allowed?" Svelte asked. Her expression suggested that she would not be denied.

"That's not..." Emerald tugged at the hem of one sleeve. "That's not what I was thinking. I've just gotten used to doing things more or less alone."

Let me help, Blare signed. *I* want *to help.*

I'd felt pressured to answer when Serkadis and Emerald looked to me for a verdict, so I could only imagine how my friend felt with five pairs of eyes on him.

"We'll practice," he told Blare. "See what you can do, and how to refine it. I'm not a Stonefeather, obviously, but I know the theory. Let's not make any promises until we have a better sense of your limits."

FOR THE NEXT FEW DAYS, our mornings were spent pretending to investigate Gorlyn's disappearance. We could not very well admit that we knew exactly who had killed him and were working on a plan to smuggle his killer out of the city, after all. In fact, we spent a great deal of our time at the docks, looking into who might have smuggled a dragon egg into Kinmore. But those leads turned up nothing, and Serkadis had told us outright that he'd nudged a memory here and there to cover his tracks. I wondered if Dumplin had a hand in that, given what she was famous for among the Pruvs.

Afternoons and evenings were spent testing the limits of Blare's skill. I was astonished by the progress he'd made since our time at the Brotherhood, even without a mentor. He must have spent a great deal of time studying on his own.

On one of our excursions, I watched in admiration as he used his abilities to make Emerald walk across the surface of a pond on steps so light they barely disturbed the water. By the end of it, sweat poured down Blare's face in rivulets, but he managed to keep all but the soles of Emerald's boots dry until he reached solid land again.

Impressive, Emerald signed. *Keeping the tiles from breaking will require a larger burst of power, but it should only take a few seconds for him to walk across them.*

Blare beamed with pride and wiped his forehead. I, meanwhile, waited until Emerald's back was turned to sign a message of my own.

Who's been teaching you? That was better than anything I've seen you do before.

Blare cut his eyes away from me, toward the pond. *I've been teaching myself.*

I didn't ask how he'd been doing that, but I had my suspicions. And so did Innocent.

My curiosity would have to wait. When we returned to the Lute and Goose, just before dusk, a familiar canvas-clad alder elf was waiting by the bar.

"I told him to give me the letter," Svelte said, with a nasty glare at our visitor.

"My instructions were clear," the courier informed her. He tipped his nose in the air and passed another missive to Emerald. This one looked just like the first, and I craned my neck to read it over Emerald's shoulder.

There was no endearment this time, or affectionate parting message. In fact, there was only one word written on the cream-colored parchment:

Soon.

CHAPTER EIGHT

When our rented wagon approached Serkadis's enchanted gate the following morning, it swung open without bothering to ask our names. Even before the cart passed fully through, Serkadis rushed out to greet us. His skin was more ashen than usual, and his demeanor was pitiable enough that the sharp edges of my anger were softened at the sight.

"You came," he said. "I wasn't sure you would." He raised his eyebrows at the cart full of children and mismatched crates. "And this is…?"

"Our exit strategy." Emerald waved to the cart.

"We're going to help you fill the crates with your stuff," Svelte announced. "That way if someone tries to search the cart, it won't look like we're hauling around empty containers, and we'll have time to come up with a new plan. Plus, you won't have to leave all your things behind, even if you can't take it all with you. And we can hide the… you know"—she mouthed the word *egg*—"in one of the crates so that nobody accidentally touches it. Also, are you the dragon?"

Serkadis dipped into a little bow. "Indeed I am. And you are?"

"Svelte of Kinmore."

"A trusted associate, I assume?" He looked to me for confirmation, but his wry smile wasn't enough to win me over. I was still holding a grudge. When my expression remained unwaveringly cold, his hopeful grin faded.

"Of course we trust them," I said. "We don't make a habit of bringing random children along on cases. You should change. And while you're at it, you should... *change.*" I waved one hand at him. "Into someone the guards are less likely to recognize."

"Excellent point." He waved us toward the house. "I'll get us started. I'm not worried about the majority of my possessions—I have contacts in the city who can arrange for them to be sent onward to wherever I settle next. In fact, it might be better to leave some of the more valuable items. I'd hate to attract the attention of any brigands on the road, given what else we're moving."

We spent the next hour or so packing the crates with items from the house. As usual, my role was a bit more passive than everyone else's. I spent most of my time keeping an eye on Serkadis—I don't know what I was expecting him to do, but I didn't want to be caught by surprise again.

He was, of course, the one to pack the egg. All the while, Gorlyn's remains lay face down on the floor, a stark reminder of what could happen if we failed.

"How do you know it's about to hatch?" I asked.

Serkadis fussed with the nest of linens and bedding he'd arranged to keep the egg safe. "It's hungrier, for one thing. I'm *constantly* drained." He paused in his work long enough to glance at me. "Which is one reason I'm so very glad you came. The last few days have been lonely and difficult. I'm grateful that you and your family are willing to help me..." He gazed down fondly at the egg. "And mine."

I crossed my arms and lowered my head. "We wouldn't have abandoned you. Or Kinmore, for that matter."

[There are a few in Kinmore who deserve to be drained,] Innocent pointed out. *[The prince, the king... maybe even Lemuel.]*

[How can you think that when his brother's corpse is lying ten paces away from us?] I demanded.

[The Bracefallows are no concern of mine. Or yours. Gorlyn's the one who wanted an adventure. I'd say he got what he deserved.]

"The other reason," Serkadis went on, "is the movement. Light won't pass through the shell anymore, and sometimes it shudders of its own accord. I'd rather it hatch somewhere well outside the city walls, where no one will be hurt. Including the hatchling. The one thing most of the stories about dragons get *right* is the subject of dragon blight. An unattended nest can sap the life out of anything that comes near it. I don't know that I have enough *Aidea* to feed more than one." He lifted the egg in his arms so that he might move it, and I would swear he weakened before my very eyes. "Gorlyn's death was a regrettable accident, but if the hatchling had *eaten* him instead..." He shuddered.

I watched him, thinking of the horror on his features when he spoke of losing control.

"I still don't understand how he got in," I said.

Serkadis settled the egg into place and stood upright, rolling his neck and shoulders as he did so. "I am powerful, Crimson, but I am not infallible. I was away on a social call when Gorlyn arrived, and since I had dismissed my former employees to keep them from suffering this very fate, there was no one to stop him."

"So you left the egg *alone*?" I asked, aghast.

Serkadis stepped forward, so that the tips of his boots almost brushed the deflated coat Gorlyn wore. "I was quite sure that the egg could defend itself if necessary. Besides, in order to feed it, I needed to replenish my own strength."

I dropped my arms to my sides. "You feed on—?"

"Not in the way you're thinking," Serkadis said, before I could follow that line of inquiry too far. "I simply require more from life than sitting alone in my home. As I said, I enjoy the company of others. But it will be nice to live with someone who can know both who *and* what I am, even if we'll have to live a bit more simply for a time."

He turned his back on Gorlyn and finished packing up the egg with all the care of a father securing his infant for travel.

"It makes a difference," I said. "Having someone you can be honest with. Someone you can trust, who sees you as you are."

As I said it, I realized what a lonely thing it was to have only *one* person appreciate you. Lying to everyone but Emerald had been isolating. Now we had friends peppered all over: Tincrown, Errol, and Nechtan in Dyrne; Aster, the Sisters, and Burp in Upper Bound; and a growing network of friends and allies throughout Kinmore and the surrounding landscape.

I supposed I couldn't blame Serkadis for his wariness, after all. His circle was smaller than ours, and the stakes of being discovered were higher.

"Crimson—" he began.

"Bring the egg when you're ready," I told him. "You should change in the meantime. Maybe into something that doesn't have dragons embroidered into the fabric, mm?"

Serkadis's face lit up. "I suppose that would be prudent, *after* I load this onto the cart. But I had better shift upstairs so that I can consider my options before your associates ravage my wardrobe."

"*Trusted* associates," I corrected as I left. "And don't you forget it."

When Serkadis emerged from the door of his home for the final time, Quell let out a squeak of surprise before clasping both hands over his mouth.

"I'm pretty sure you can talk now," Svelte said. "You're already here. It's not like Emerald's going to send you back to the inn now."

Quell kept staring at Serkadis's new form. The squat, brown-dappled figure wore a loose, roughly sewn dress—our dragon had chosen to wear the shape of a lambkin, one of the darker-wooled, lop-eared variety. "Hello!" Serkadis chirped in a sweet, high-pitched voice.

It struck me that I'd gotten quite comfortable thinking of Serkadis as a man—but he was something so far removed from manhood or womanhood that such designations were likely unhelpful. As *she* approached the cart, Serkadis gave Quell a wide smile.

"I hope you don't mind," she said. "I thought it would be a good idea to look as unthreatening as possible, and lambkins have something of a reputation."

Given that my primary references for adult lambkinhood were Errol, a moonshiner, and Dumplin, a... whatever Dumplin was, I wasn't sure where the stereotypes of helpless and law-abiding lambkins came from. Perhaps my friends were outliers.

"Besides, I thought we ought to seem related." Serkadis surveyed the children. "If you take the cart, Emerald and I shall walk alongside. And Crimson, my dear, if you could be just a *bit* less conspicuous..." She held her fingers up with only a smidgeon of room between them.

I sized her up. Changing into a bird or a beetle and hiding among the cargo might have been sufficient, but as my anger dissipated, I wanted to stretch my abilities. And, yes, to show off a little, after all the showing off Serkadis had done the other night.

It took me a moment, but in short order I rearranged myself into an entirely new shape. Svelte applauded in delight when I shrank into the form of a lambkin myself. Leaving my Crimson-ness behind was impossible, but if I could be Crimson as a spider or a rat, why could I not be Crimson as a lambkin? True, my wool was redder than most, and I'd taken a few liberties with the fashion of my outfit, but I was confident that I'd pass muster with the city guards.

"Magnificent," Serkadis said. Her eyes gleamed silver, in the way no mortal's ever could.

Svelte smirked and elbowed Blare, who smothered a laugh with his palm. *Magnificent,* she signed, and they both giggled.

Emerald was too busy checking the tracings to notice their

gestures. We'd used a little of the money we'd gotten from Dumplin to buy the cart and the ox that drew it. The cart could carry the egg, but if Serkadis tried to ride along, he'd likely smash through the boards, or else overtax the ox.

"We may have to walk more slowly than usual," she warned. "Shifting forms isn't usually much of a problem, but I've been on the brink of exhaustion all week, and I'll have to stay close to the egg to make sure that it doesn't feed on the rest of you. Especially *you*—" She pointed to Blare. "If the egg drains your *Aidea* while you're working your magic, we won't make it."

Blare shuddered, but he held firm.

Serkadis's gaze softened. "Don't worry. I know what I'm doing. We've bonded by now, and it finds my magic... digestible, let's say. So long as we take a quiet route, we should have no problems."

"Ah, but we're going to take the main trade gate to the north," Emerald corrected.

Serkadis spun toward him. "Not the east?" he asked, referring to our usual route in and out of the city. "It's slower there. The northern gate is always bottlenecked, especially in the afternoon. My former cook complained about it more than once, since she lived outside of Kinmore proper."

"True, but the Conjury's been more critical of shipments lately. They might ask you for additional permits we can't provide, and if you can't cough them up, they'll likely send you back to Conjury headquarters for inspection. They'll have more time and patience for that sort of thing on the less-traveled exits."

Serkadis blanched and rested one hand on the cartwheel as she wheezed. The cart shifted forward under a weight far greater than that of a lambkin. "Oh, dear, an *inspection*..."

"This time of day, the guards to the north will be cranky, hungry, and tired of listening to people complain," Emerald assured her. "And if it comes down to it, I can always tell them I'm with the Conjury and have approval from my commander, although I'd prefer to avoid that if possible." He wrinkled his nose. "Might raise some unfortunate questions with my boss."

"I shall trust your intuition," Serkadis announced. She stood up a little straighter and nodded to Blare. "Please know that, whatever happens, I appreciate your assistance more than mere words can express. And if we do succeed, I am happy to grant you whatever boon you ask, so long as it is within my ability to do so."

Blare nodded. He kept fidgeting, but he smiled when Svelte gave his arm a comforting pat.

"We'll get you out," Svelte said. "Don't worry."

Judging by Serkadis's expression, this was easier said than done.

CHAPTER NINE

Nobody cared about a trio of lambkins and two children hauling junk out of the city. There was too much else going on. Serkadis had not exaggerated the extent of the crowds at the northern gate. There must have been a hundred people ahead of us, all of whom were becoming increasingly irritable.

"What's the holdup?" complained a dwarf that had joined the queue behind us. He was leading a pair of squat oxen which pulled a cartload of old furniture behind them. "I swear, the Conjury's become even more of an arse-pain these last few months. I pay my pissing taxes. Pay my pissing guild fees. Pay the king his fair share, too. Got me bent over a barrel, they have, and still they aren't happy, even when I'm thrice-fu—"

Serkadis turned to him. "Sir," she said primly, "there are children present."

The dwarf glared at her, but the second their eyes met, he softened visibly. "Sorry, ma'am," he said, in an altogether different tone. "Just tryna run a business, and I'm up to my arsehole in fees and paperwork. Er, sorry again." He scratched his chin through his thick beard. "Probably shouldn't say *arsehole* in front of tender ears."

Svelte's face was wine-red from the effort of keeping in her mirth. "That's my people," she said under her breath. "Not those pissing alder elves."

Quell pulled an expression of utter outrage and smacked her shoulder, which only amused her more.

"That sounds terrible," Serkadis told the merchant. "I'm so sorry."

The line advanced a few paces at a time, but it was growing faster than it was moving.

"One more reason not to leave the city," Serkadis whispered to me. "Although I suppose I should be grateful that I get to admire the skyline one last time."

I had never lived anyplace long enough to feel that I belonged there. Serkadis, however, had lived in Kinmore far longer than the lifespan of the average resident. I tried to admire it, too. To see the city as she saw it. As we surveyed the view, shoulder to shoulder, I wondered how many of the other buildings housed secrets that could compare with hers. For all I knew, the city was crawling with gods and monsters.

In a strange way, that notion made me feel more affection for the place.

Emerald had left us behind and was talking with one of the guards. The more distractions, we'd reckoned, the better, and it gave him a chance to keep an eye on us without drawing more attention to us. I could disguise myself easily. A jotunn could not.

Blare was the only one of the children not riding in the cart. He'd chosen to walk behind me as a sort of wall, so that nobody would accidentally bump into me. Or rather, *through* me.

I wanted to sign him some words of comfort, but there was no knowing how many people in the ever-growing crowd could read handspeech, and the gestures would be visible far beyond the radius that a whisper would carry. I settled for an encouraging smile when he lifted his head. He smiled back, but he looked on the verge of being sick.

"Almost there," Serkadis whispered, as much to herself as to me. There were only three carts ahead of ours.

Blare uttered a soft and wordless groan.

And then, at last, it was our turn. The dragon tiles lay beyond us, faded and dark with all the mud and dust left by a day's worth of cart tracks, hooves, and boots. They were just large enough that she would need to take two steps to traverse them. As soon as the guards waved us on, her fate would be decided.

She was still moving forward when a human guard held out an arm to block her.

"Woah, woah," he said, not entirely unkindly. "I need your manifest first, miss."

Serkadis froze. Beside us, the cart drew to a halt.

"A manifest?" Serkadis blinked.

"Got it right here, sir." Svelte retrieved a mess of rumpled papers. They looked as if they'd been passed between a hundred grubby hands. In reality, Emerald had written them up the night before, and the children had found a great deal of amusement in crumpling them up, staining them with tea, and covering them with muddy fingerprints over the better part of an hour.

The guard sighed. "Looks like a weirling's been at them."

"Sorry," Svelte said sheepishly. "I think Brick pissed on them."

The guard wrinkled his nose in disgust. "Who or what is Brick?" he asked, although I got the impression he didn't really want to know.

"Nana's cat," Svelte said, without cracking a smile. "Ever since she had kittens, she's been incontinent."

The guard rolled his eyes. "'Least Brick ain't a person." He turned the pages, seemingly at random, growing increasingly irritable at the sight of the illegible scrawl. "Clothing, books… what the hells does *this* say?" He held the manifest out toward Serkadis and me.

I squinted at the paper. "Teakettle," I translated.

His lip curled. "Teakettle?" he repeated. "How can you be sure?"

"It says so, plain as anything," Serkadis added sweetly.

"What in every hell is taking so long?" the dwarf behind us snapped. "I've got places to be!"

I bit back a smile. Emerald had been right about the atmosphere. Everyone was eager to move on, even the guards. The guard was only two pages from the end of the manifest. Then he would pass it back to Svelte, and we'd move on, and Blare would succeed, and—

"I don't know this signature," the guard said.

The smile froze on my face. "What?" *How would he even know?* Emerald had scrawled an incoherent name at the end of the paperwork in the hopes that it would look enough like something, but not enough like anything specific, to pass muster. An official Conjury stamp covered half the letters. It should have been enough.

"You've got one signature on the trade permit, but the rules've changed. Everything going in and out of the city needs a secondary approval, which means either a second affidavit from a commanding officer, or a voucher from the relevant guild. I don't suppose you have a letter from the Craftsman's Guild notary?" He looked at each of us in turn.

"No," I said, since Serkadis looked as if she might swoon. "Nobody told us."

"Makes sense." His smile was thin, but the veneer of politeness remained in place. "It's a new policy. The king approved it just last week."

Last week. While Emerald and I had been prowling the docks, Finch had been receiving new orders. I suppressed a scream of hysterical frustration. After all our planning, our plan's downfall would come in the form of *paperwork.*

[Emerald,] I thought, ***[you'd better get over here.]***

"I suppose that means we'll have to go back and arrange that," I said aloud.

The guard shook his head. "Nah, we can do an on-site inspection. Elfreth can do it, over there." He indicated the guard Emerald was talking to. "Just step aside so that I can process the fellow behind you." He nodded to the irate dwarf.

"About time," the dwarf grumbled.

Serkadis swayed on her feet, looking terribly pale. If she swooned, I couldn't catch her.

[Cause a scene,] Emerald told me. *[I'm coming. Just buy some time.]*

That was something I could manage. I puffed myself up to my full lambkin height and planted my fists on my hips. "See here, we've been waiting for ages. My wife's exhausted." I nodded to Serkadis. "The children have been out here for hours. If you're not going to let us through—"

The guard sighed. "If you'll just step this way."

I jabbed a finger at his chest. "I *pay my pissing taxes*!"

"Exactly!" the dwarf bellowed. "And I've lost half a day's pay wasting time with the king's new orders! If he wants to see my papers, he can get down here and examine them himself!"

His outrage was echoed by other people in line, who took the opportunity to air their own grievances. The guard clutched the manifest tight in one hand. He must have felt the tide turning against him, because his other hand groped for the pommel of his sword, but the guard was stretched thin. If a riot broke out, the few guards on duty would be overwhelmed within minutes.

Over the clamor of the crowd, Quell's voice broke like a bell through the storm. "Daddy!" he wailed. "I gotta go! I've been holding it in for*ever*!" After several days of silence, it was as if all the sound he'd been storing up burst out of him at once. He wrapped his arms around himself and began to wail at a pitch that would have sent Brick running for the hills, if only the cat had been real.

The guard seemed on the verge of caving, and Emerald was only paces away from coming to our rescue when someone bellowed, *"That's enough!"*

Bringing a whole crowd to heel with a single utterance required a particular brand of authority that few living souls possessed, but even an irate crowd of merchants could be intimidated by the arrival of a Leonhite. I recoiled as Commander Finch appeared from the guardhouse by the gate and stalked over to us, with all of her teeth bared. Her claws were out, and the gleam of fury in her eye communicated loud and clear that she would not tolerate anything but total obedience.

Emerald froze. Serkadis leaned toward me, and even Quell fell silent. The stillness that swept over the crowd was instant and total.

"What's the problem?" she snarled at the guard. The resonant timbre of her voice made the very air tremble.

"Their manifest." The guard thrust the paperwork out to arm's length, as if he was afraid that Finch would tear him limb from limb if given the opportunity. She was certainly capable of it, and she looked more than prepared.

She ripped the already beleaguered papers out of his hand and examined them. She opened her mouth to speak when her eyes settled on me.

Since the first day we met, I had played the part of a ghost in her presence. I had gone to great lengths to give her reason to think I was nothing but a mindless illusion. She had *certainly* never seen me in my present form, but the moment our eyes met, I became convinced that she *knew*.

Her head swiveled on her neck like that of an owl until she spotted Emerald only a few paces away. It swiveled back to examine the cart, the children, and the assortment of crates.

[She's been on the lookout for smugglers,] I thought. *[Em, what if she thinks we're involved in whatever the Conjury's trying to stop?]* We had unintentionally placed ourselves at the confluence of every trouble that plagued the city.

[In that case,] Emerald replied, *[we're done for. She'll bring the whole force of Conjury law down on our heads. They'll find out that we're smuggling a dragon and an egg, covering up for a murder...]* His thoughts devolved into a series of curses so foul they would have made even Dumplin blush.

Having taken in the whole tableau, Finch turned back to the

guard. Her whiskers trembled as she spoke. "You're the one who stopped them. Because of the paperwork?"

The guard nodded. "Yes, ma'am."

Aster help us. He was going to get a medal. He was going to be promoted to captain of the watch while Emerald was led off in chains.

"You held up all *these* people," Finch said, "over *this* paperwork." The resonance in her chest deepened to a growl.

"Y-yes?" the guard repeated, with noticeably less confidence.

She shoved the stack of papers in his face. "Whose signature is that?" she snarled.

The guard appeared as confused as I felt. "I don't... I don't know..."

"*It's mine, you imbecile.*" She shoved the paperwork against his chest, rumpling it even further and tearing it where her claws pierced the parchment. "They work me to the bone. Triple, *quadruple* my responsibilities with no extra pay. Tell me to hand-check ship-ments that have already been approved. And now you're going to make me come out here and *verify my own signature?*"

With every word, the guard curled further in on himself. "Yes, Commander. Sorry, Commander." He pushed the paperwork back into Svelte's hands. "Move along, then..."

Finch turned on her heel and stormed back to the guard house. As she passed Emerald, she glared at him but didn't utter another word.

Relief and confusion dueled for dominance as we stepped forward. A sweat broke out on Blare's brow, and the tension in his shoulders and the joints of his fingers suggested that keeping a dragon from breaking ceramic was a great deal more difficult than making a jotunn walk on water. His lips pursed into a little "O" of effort, and he exhaled in a long, unsteady breath.

Only when Serkadis took her two steps over the tiles without so much as cracking them did relief win out at last.

CHAPTER TEN

The towns and villages of outer Kinmore gave way to farms, which in turn gave way to forests. We chose a way that the other carts eschewed, hardly speaking as we did so. Svelte guided the ox, while the rest of us reveled in the shocking fact of having gotten away unharmed.

An hour outside the city, we drew off to one side of a country road, where Blare proceeded to have a delayed attack of nerves.

"You did it!" Svelte grabbed him by the shoulders and shook him. "I'm so proud!"

I did, Blare signed. *I still don't believe it. I thought my heart was going to crawl out of my throat, I was so scared of that cat-lady!*

"Adrenaline can help you channel *Aidea* in short bursts." Serkadis signed as she spoke. Perhaps I shouldn't have been surprised that she knew handspeech. She'd been alive for hundreds of years, after all. "But I admit, I may have had a hand in your success."

You lent me some of your power? Blare asked.

"I amplified yours." Serkadis shrugged one shoulder. "Which is not quite the same thing. You have great potential, should you choose to pursue study of the *Aidea* in the future."

Blare's smile was so wide that his face could barely contain it as he signed, *Thank you.*

"I'm only stating a fact."

"Well, *I* want to state a fact too," Quell announced. "Which is that we make an excellent team, but I don't know that I'm cut out for adventuring. I like books, thank you very much. When that Leonhite lady came out to yell at us, I almost *died.*"

"That was your boss, wasn't it?" Svelte asked.

I nodded. "Well, *Emerald's* boss, but technically yes."

"I wonder why she helped us." Svelte considered me. "I think she recognized you. Do you think she was lying to cover for you?"

"I don't know," I admitted. We'd had several unusual interactions with Finch lately, and I thought she might be hiding a secret or two of her own. "I'm glad she did, though."

"As am I." Serkadis reached up into the cart and retrieved one of the boxes. "If you'll excuse me, I find that I'm not entirely comfortable in this form at the moment." She withdrew into the nearby woods. I took the opportunity to return to the more familiar shape of Simone.

"Didn't you like being a lambkin?" Quell asked.

"You made a pretty adorable one." Svelte pulled Quell into a loose chokehold and rubbed her knuckles against the top of his head. "Not as adorable as our special little guy, but—"

"Get off!" Quell squirmed out of her grasp, nearly knocking his glasses off as he did so. Once he was free, he ran his fingers through his wool. "You're gonna mess up my hair!"

Emerald and Serkadis reappeared at the same time, one from the road, one from the trees. Emerald jogged toward us while Serkadis returned his box to the wagon. He was his usual human self again, although he'd donned dull, ordinary clothes rather than his trademark finery.

The first words out of my mouth were, "Did you talk to Finch?"

"No." Emerald wiped the back of his palm across his forehead to dash away the sweat. "And I plan to keep it that way for a few days at least. Better to stay out of her way, I think."

"She did seem pretty cranky," Svelte agreed.

"In the meantime," Serkadis said, "I suppose you want your boons. Who knows if our paths will ever cross again. Better to ask for them now, I should think. Blare, what can I grant you?"

The boy frowned and tugged on the bottom hem of his shirt. Whenever he was nervous, he needed something to do with his hands.

"That's easy," Quell said. "He wants his hearing back, don't you?"

Blare's mouth pursed, and his brows pulled together.

"No, he doesn't." Svelte nudged Blare. "You wouldn't want to change yourself, would you?"

Blare shook his head. *I don't think I do. If we were still at the Brotherhood, maybe that's what I'd ask for. Brother Harmony would want me to. But I'm not sure I'd like it, and I don't think I'd want to change something so important about myself permanently just for other people's convenience. It might make things easier, but...*

We waited while he groped for the right words.

I wouldn't want to hear all the time. Maybe some of the time? Is that possible?

Serkadis crossed his arms and let his eyes wander over the fields. "Maybe," he said. "I'm not sure it counts as a boon, but I have an Artificer on my payroll who has managed a clever trick or two. She might be able to come up with a device that could do that. Something you could use when you wanted to, and remove when you felt like it. I can write to her, if you'd like. And I'd pay for whatever she designs."

Blare nodded. *A sometimes-thing. Something I could choose. Yes, I'd like that.*

"Marvelous." Serkadis turned to Emerald. "And you?"

"Nothing," Emerald said.

"Really?" Serkadis asked. "There's *nothing* you want?"

"Nothing I'd want to change," Emerald said. "Doesn't seem worth the risk."

Serkadis dragged the pad of one thumb over his bottom lip, while I watched a tad too intently. "You're limiting yourself," he said. "If I might offer a suggestion?"

"If you want," Emerald said. "I doubt it'll change my mind, though."

Serkadis made a strange gesture, too fast for me to follow, and held out one hand to Emerald. A single silver scale, roughly the size of the pendant Emerald wore to cast me, had appeared from seemingly nowhere.

Emerald whistled. "Dragon scale, huh? That's dangerous stuff."

"*Powerful* stuff," Serkadis corrected. "You saw fit to leave a certain necklace with a mutual friend because you trusted her. I happen to believe you'll use this appropriately. Or maybe you'll find someone you deem more deserving of its power. That's not *my* choice to make. Take it or leave it."

Emerald stared at the scale for a long time before reaching out one hand. Serkadis tipped the scale into his open palm, against which it appeared considerably smaller.

"I'm sure you'll find a worthwhile use for it," Serkadis said. At last, he turned to me. The kindness in his eyes cut me to the quick. "And you, Crimson Smoke. I know what you want."

In his voice, my name gained new weight. "You do?"

"Freedom." He waved to Emerald. "The choice to go or stay. The independence to chart your own course. Even if you change nothing about your life, it would be *your life,* and not his."

I took an involuntary step closer. The last of my anger melted away. "Yes. *Please.*"

"I make no promises," he said. "But I will try. Emerald, if I may." He extended his hand again, waiting patiently as my friend removed his necklace and handed it over.

Serkadis cradled the verdant jewel between his upturned palms. He closed his eyes.

It did not happen all at once. Even when it began, the first thing I felt was a chill. A breeze on my cheek. I thought it must be the same surge of power that had accompanied Serkadis's transformations, but then it died, only to return in tandem with the rustling of the trees along the roadside.

It wasn't magic I was feeling. It was wind. *Real* wind. The breeze carried the tang of salt without the rotten, piscine undertone I'd once experienced on the docks. My hair moved with it, as did my skirts, and I let out a shriek of excitement that made the muscles in my throat tighten. I clapped my hands, and my palms made a sound when they met. I took a breath. A breath within my own lungs. My heart thudded with excitement. *I had a heart.*

The rush of sensation was almost too much to bear, and I cried out again, turning my face skyward so that I could feel the warmth of the spring sun on my cheeks. Real tears, *wet* tears, gathered in my eyes, blurring the world a little.

Only, the world never stopped blurring. As my sight faded, I could hear my friends' voices calling out to me, as if from very far away. From underwater. The brisk kiss of the breeze deepened to a terrible chill that raised gooseflesh on my arms and made my teeth chatter. I tried to breathe and found that I could not. Instead, icy water rushed into my lungs.

I choked and sputtered, but there was no air to be found, only more water—water that buoyed my limbs in slow motion and made my hair float around me like loose seaweed, red as the sunset, red as blood. The only source of light in that terrible place came from far away, fractured with ripples. The water was brackish and tasted of decay.

I tried to swim, to rise, clawing toward the surface in desperate search of air, but I was weighed down, dragged by the current, by the eddies of tainted water where the swamp met the sea, my shoulders heavy with the weight of my coat, which felt as if it was weighed down with stones—

And then I was on my hands and knees, back on the road to

Kinmore, sobbing into thin air I could no longer feel. My hair hung loose and lank around me, but I no longer had lungs. The ache in my chest was something else entirely.

"Crimson?" A slight warmth on my shoulder startled me, and I looked up to find Serkadis kneeling beside me with one hand brushing against the illusion of my arm. "Are you all right?"

"I..." I pressed my hand to my chest. Aside from being a bit bedraggled, I felt just as I always had. "I think so?"

"I'm sorry." He held out the gem. "I don't think I can do what you want. I tried, but you faded until you almost disappeared, and I don't think I should push it any further."

"Oh." I looked around at the others. "Did I?"

"You really did look like a ghost," Quell said. "It was creepy."

"Is that... all that happened?" I sat back on my heels, and only then dared to look at Emerald. I knew what I'd experienced, and I prayed to every god—Aster, the Middling Godlet, the Crone, even Guise if he was listening—that Emerald had not been forced to relive what I had just experienced for the first time.

The only emotion he evinced, however, was concern. Whatever Serkadis's magic had done to me, it was mine and mine alone.

"Well, thank you for trying." I forced my tone into a semblance of cheerfulness and got to my feet. Serkadis handed the necklace back to Emerald, who clasped it around his neck once more. It occurred to me that when Bram had pulled the chain from Emerald's neck, I'd vanished. Then again, Bram hadn't been a silver dragon. Serkadis's power must have continued to cast my illusion without interruption.

It was a relief, to think logically rather than fall apart. I could see why the practice held such appeal for Emerald.

"Is there anything else I can offer you?" Serkadis asked.

I shook my head. "Nothing I can think of." I was in no rush to try any more experiments which might yield a similar result.

"You'll have to think of one for later," Serkadis said. "And if we meet again, you can ask me then."

I rearranged my hair with nothing more than a thought and nodded my agreement. "Next time," I told him. "You owe me."

With that, he turned to the children. "Thank you again, trusted associates," he said. "I'll write, or send a babblebird, when we're settled in. I should get going before the light fails."

The five of us watched as he approached the ox standing in the cart's traces. When he first reached for the beast's head, it shied away from him, but the second time it let him loop his fingers around the ropes at its neck and lead the way.

"We should go, too," Emerald said. "We'll have to take the long way to avoid entering the city again tonight. I'll deal with Finch another day."

"I'm starving," Svelte announced. "When we get back, I'm eating *two* dinners."

"Can you carry me?" Quell asked. "My legs are tired."

"You were riding in the cart with me, lazybones! If your legs need anything, it's a good stretch..."

While my family went one way, I stood still for a moment, watching Serkadis walk the other. He looked back once and smiled, lifting a hand in farewell, and I waved back.

[Why didn't he see you?] I asked Innocent. It was a question that had troubled me since I first learned what Serkadis was. *[How come he could feel my magic, but not yours?]*

[It's obvious, Crimson Smoke.] My passenger's voice was smug. *[He looks at you, and he sees us. He knows I'm here, but he thinks I'm part of you. Because I am. The longer I live here, the more comfortable I get.]*

Behind me, Emerald called my name. "I'm coming," I replied, as I hurried to catch up to my family.

A CRIME OF FASHION

CHAPTER ONE

Commander Finch stood over the kneeling form of my companion and shook her head. "If you tell me it's another godsdamned snake," she said, "I'm going to have an extra-large oubliette made special in the castle dungeons just for you."

Emerald leaned over the swollen, purple face of the dead man, whose limbs were contorted at such unbelievable angles, I could only imagine he'd died in excruciating pain. "If you don't want me to solve the case, why did you call me in?"

Finch pinched the shallow bridge of her feline nose between two fingers and sighed. "Fine," she said. "Walk me through it."

Emerald rose to his feet. He folded his hands behind his back and surveyed the room. "Consider the room first, Commander. Sturdy walls, a single door locked from the inside, an undisturbed window both barred and latched. How might one gain entry to the room without damaging the structure?"

Finch raked one hand down her face and rolled her eyes back in her head as far as they would go. "I can't *wait* for you to tell me."

I bit back a smile. I had no idea why Finch had gone out of her way to protect us at the city gates during Serkadis's escape, and neither she nor Emerald had alluded to it once. Instead, a subtle shift had taken place between them, so that they had become something like…

Well, like actual *friends*.

Emerald began to pace the room. "The whole place is secure, no one in the rest house admits to having heard a scuffle or anything out of the ordinary, and the room next to this one has been unoccupied since the former mistress of the house passed on three years ago. When the unfortunate merchant retired last night, he was quite well. And now…" Emerald paused for effect and made a sweeping gesture toward the corpse.

"Now he is quite dead," Finch intoned. "Will you get to the gods-damned *point*?"

"Eventually." Emerald pointed to the floors. "The house is heated from below, which means the only vents are in the flooring." He bent to point out the decorative wrought iron vents on one side of the bed. "Perhaps they might have been removed, but their screws are still in place, and it would take someone very small and very clever to not only fit *through* the vents in order to make their escape, but to secure them firmly in place once they were gone. Which leaves…?"

Emerald's bright eyes bounced from my face to Finch's and back. I volunteered nothing, in part because I always played the role of a mere illusion in Finch's company, and in part because I had no idea where he was going with this little demonstration.

Finch sighed in a pitiful manner, but she looked around in search of an answer to my friend's question. Her eyes settled on the silk bell-pull beside the bed and climbed toward the ceiling, where it disappeared through a metal fixture fitted into the wall.

"Oh my gods, you think a snake crawled through there." She pointed up the hole. "Let me guess… The bell-pull from the other bedroom connects to the same opening. So someone snuck in there last night, induced a snake to climb the bell-pull in the adjoining bedroom, through the gap in the wall, and down *this* rope into the bed where this poor fellow slept. When it was done, it returned to the other room by the same means."

I stared at her, unable to keep my mouth from falling open as her theory took shape.

Emerald squinted at her. His incredulity was obvious, but it appeared to stem from a rather different source than mine. "Are you *serious*?"

Finch glared right back at him. "It sounds like the sort of nonsense you'd come up with."

Emerald rubbed his temple with two fingers, as if fighting off a headache. "Finch, please. For one thing, how would someone induce a snake to climb a bell-pull, slip into a bed in the adjoining room, bite a man, and then shimmy back to its master?"

Finch wrinkled her nose. "*Aidea*? Maybe an Augur wanted to take him out of the picture?"

"And nobody noticed someone breaking into or out of the house with a venomous serpent in tow?" Emerald asked.

Finch sucked her teeth. Her chest rose and fell a few times, but in every other regard, she was perfectly still, almost preternaturally so. She would have made a terrifying soldier. As it was, she made a terrifying boss.

"Commander Finch?" A young, bespectacled woman poked her head through the door. She wore the purple and silver livery of the Conjury, and her tight curls were pinned back from her face, revealing high cheekbones. "I have the staff downstairs waiting for your interviews whenever you're ready."

"A moment, please, Aaliy." Finch beckoned her inside, although she was still watching Emerald with that huntress's stare.

Emerald pickled idly at the nailbed of his index finger. There was a subtle tilt to his lips, a quietly smug attitude that I would have noticed even without the benefit of our mental tether. "There is one other flaw with your snake theory," he said.

"Go on, then," Finch growled.

Instead of speaking, Emerald took his time righting himself, strolling to the corpse, and kneeling down again. Finch's assistant let out a squeak of horror as my friend lowered one hand to the man's neck and used two fingers to tilt his head to one side. The dead man's throat was so badly swollen that I could not, at first, work out what he wanted us to see.

"How exactly did this killer snake murder him," Emerald asked, "without leaving a mark upon his person?"

To say that the victim was hardly petite would be an understatement. In life, he would have stood shorter than my associate, but not by much. Nevertheless, even hours after his death, his features were so swollen and warped that I could not be sure whether the portrait hanging across the hallway from his bedroom door was painted in his likeness or someone else's.

Emerald sounded far too pleased when he said, "He wasn't."

Out of habit, I turned my head to meet Emerald's eyes. With Aaliy in the room, it would make sense for Emerald to resume manipulating me in order to save face in front of a low-ranking stranger.

"Wasn't *what*?" Finch demanded.

"Wasn't killed by a snakebite," Emerald said. I had never seen my friend so smug. "He was poisoned before he entered the room."

"Oh, come now, you're taunting me." Finch pressed her round ears back against her skull.

"My dear commander." Emerald rose to his feet. "First you tell me that I mustn't, on any account, blame a snake for this man's death. Then, when I do as you ask, you claim I'm having fun at your expense. Is there no middle ground with you?"

Finch's upper lip peeled back from her formidable canines. "Emerald Flame, I swear by all the gods…"

"I never said a snake was involved. That was your guess. Points for creativity, I suppose." He waved to the bell-pull. "As I was saying, there is no way in or out, so unless a serpent decided to execute the most complicated and unlikely murder in the history of Dregandresal, there is another explanation."

[The scout on Kovin Isle was killed in a locked room,] I thought.

Emerald paused. *[Yes, by someone who had to be present in the room. One can't strangle a man from afar, Crim, not without the aid of Aidea. It is, however, perfectly possible to poison him, and... well, just look at the corpse.]*

I stared down at the dead man. The flecks of spittle at the corner of his mouth were pale pink; had he bitten his tongue as he choked, or had whatever poisoned him made him bleed internally? Either way, it was horrifying to witness, a stark contrast to the fresh folds of his attire. The robe he'd died in looked new, and although I knew Emerald would have called me shallow for it, I thought it a shame that he'd died in such expensive clothes, in which he would no doubt be buried as well.

Finch pointed a clawed finger at the dead man. "So someone poisoned him, he fled to his room, and died alone after locking himself in? To put some distance between himself and his murderer?"

"It may not have *been* a murder, Commander."

"You think that might have been an accident?" she demanded.

"Judging by the swelling, it's entirely possible that he ingested something to which he had an extreme allergic reaction," Emerald said. "Although I wouldn't rule out deliberate poisoning, I've never seen a poison that could do this. The swelling, the rash on his chest... the most common poisons will make a man die in agony by shutting his organs down."

"An *allergy?*" Finch snapped. "You think he died of an allergic reaction?"

Emerald clapped his hands together. "Let's say, for the sake of argument, that the deceased was allergic to a particular ingredient. The cook is overworked, she forgets that he can't eat, say, wildfell brightcaps. She makes a mushroom stew for dinner, and everyone else eats from the same pot, but no one else gets sick... and suddenly the master of the house is choking on his own supper, blue in the face... He flees to his room and locks the door behind him..."

"And the rest of the staff cover for her." Finch's eyes were unfocused.

Aaliy cleared her throat. "I don't mean to interrupt, Commander, but the cook mentioned that she's a new hire. She's only been working in the house for a few months. Isn't it possible she might not know if her employer was allergic to something?"

"Even *he* might not have known," Emerald said. "Perhaps the poisoning was accidental."

"Gods." Finch shook her head. "Assuming you're right, I doubt we'd ever have worked that out. I suppose I should go talk to the household staff, then, and see what we can determine. Come along, Aaliy."

She turned on her heel and strode out into the hallway. Her assistant paused just long enough to cast me a curious look. I nodded sagely and waved her farewell.

[I thought the dramatic reveals were supposed to be my job,] I teased. When Emerald had originally conceived the concept of an illusory partner-in-crime-solving, he'd made me his mouthpiece. According to him, most people didn't take an intellectual jotunn seriously, but that didn't seem to be a problem when it came to Finch.

Maybe people didn't take an intellectual Leonhite seriously, either.

[It would have looked odd if you suddenly got chatty in front of Finch,] he pointed out. He was still looking down at the body, rubbing the pad of one thumb across his bottom lip in thought. I sincerely hoped that was not the same hand with which he had prodded the corpse.

[Of course. There is not even the smallest *part of you that enjoyed showing off in front of Finch.]*

Emerald cast me a sidelong glare. *[It's all part of the game, Crimson.]*

I resisted the urge to roll my eyes. *[What game is that?]*

[Do you know who this man is... or was?] Emerald tilted his chin toward the corpse.

I thought this rather an abrupt change of subject, but to humor him, I leaned forward and squinted at the man's remains. *[I've never met him, I don't think.]*

[Nor have I, but his name is known to me. Faldwell of Kinmore. He made his reputation buying and selling silk and fine lace, first as a trader, and then by opening a textile factory in the merchant district. Rumor has it that he was not always... trustworthy among those he perceived to be his lessers.]

I lifted my head sharply. *[Meaning...?]*

[That several young women have been let go over the years after claiming that he took liberties. I don't know the details, but it might provide a motive. It might also explain why the old cook left.]

I had felt a great deal of sympathy for the man until that point, but after this particular revelation, I beheld him with new eyes. *[You don't think it was an accident?]*

[I'm merely a consultant on the case. I gave Finch several possible explanations that would explain the evidence, and now it's her job to prove which one is right.] Emerald turned away. *[The cook has plausible deniability. If the rest of the staff ate the same meal as Faldwell, she could easily claim that she forgot, or that Faldwell never mentioned his allergy in the first place. If it ever goes to trial, the magistrate will find it almost impossible to prove her guilty. Short of bringing in someone like Viet of Vows, I suppose, although the Conjury would never waste his skills on such a paltry case.]*

I took one last glance at Faldwell's pathetic remains. Knowing that he had not been a good man in life, and that his death might well have been delivered to him by those who'd suffered under his employ, I was left with one question: did he *deserve* what had happened to him?

Was his murder justified?

I thought not. But then again, I could not be sure of the extent of his abuses.

Still turning the matter over in my mind, I followed Emerald into the hall. *[Where are we off to next?]*

Emerald groaned and passed one hand over his eyes. *[Don't remind me.]*

[How can I remind you of something I don't know?]

[You do, too, know. Starting this afternoon, I'm keeping my promise to Yerik.]

We were almost to the front door when I realized what he was referencing. I could not contain my burst of mirth, although I was aware that it was a faux pas to cackle at a murder site.

After months of badgering on Yerik's part, Emerald had agreed to sit for his portrait.

CHAPTER TWO

"Do we have to do this out here?" Emerald fidgeted against the cushions of the worn armchair that Yerik had set up for him along one wall of the Lute and Goose's dining room.

Yerik looked up from his sketchpad. "The lighting in here is perfect! And I need to be nearby, anyway, in case it gets busy again. I can't leave the running of my business to three unattended minors, no matter how reliable they may be."

"Fine, but..." Emerald squirmed again.

The lunch crowd had already disbanded, but an unprecedented number of people had lingered over their drinks to watch Yerik work. The canvas he would be using stood along the wall, as yet untouched, while he decided on the perfect composition.

The final portrait was intended to match the one of Coirpre that hung over the bar. Yerik had wheedled and pleaded for ages for Emerald to sit for a matching portrait, but it was only when he stooped to guilt—*"I've been providing room and board for months, and I only charge you a pittance, surely this isn't too much to ask..."*—that my friend finally agreed.

"Maybe one of the upstairs bedrooms?" Emerald suggested.

Yerik scoffed. "With those pathetic little windows? I think not."

I hadn't heard Svelte come up behind me, so her laughter was rather startling. "Watch out, Yerik, I think he's trying to get you alone."

"I am not!" Emerald insisted.

Yerik's cheeks darkened at the implication. "Svelte, really, you have *such* an imagination."

Svelte caught my eye and shook her head. "Clueless," she muttered, and turned back to the bar. From the kitchen came the clank of dishes, and the chatter of Quell's high voice punctuated with long silences, presumably while Blare signed his answers. It occurred to me how comfortable we'd grown in Kinmore.

Svelte's attempts at playing matchmaker were amusing enough, but I suspected that she had personal reasons behind her efforts. We never spoke of leaving, but Tincrown was always on Emerald's mind, and I was sure there would come a time when we made our excuses and departed. Svelte must have known that this arrangement, however cozy it might be, was only temporary.

She did not want to leave. And what better way to arrange that we would stay forever than for Emerald and Yerik to agree that things were perfect just as they were?

I was more than fond of Yerik, but I was certain that would never happen. Not simply on Tincrown's account, either. Emerald hadn't said as much, but agreeing to sit for the portrait felt like a concession: we would be moving on eventually, and in this way, we'd be leaving something behind.

The door of the Lute and Goose opened, revealing the familiar face of the alder elf courier who had delivered Serkadis's letters. His eyes narrowed when he spotted Svelte, but to my surprise he strode directly to her and held out two envelopes.

"These are for Miss Crimson," he announced. "Although I reckon I ought to hand them off to *you* in order to avoid another squabble."

Svelte sneered at him and slapped a few coins into his hand, while Yerik and Emerald observed this exchange with interest. The courier counted them twice, dropped the coins into his pocket, and loped off. When he opened the door a second time, he was nearly brained by a large object sailing through the front door. Svelte cried out and reached for a broom, hefting its handle before her like a javelin, but the object in question turned out to be a large bird with a sturdy beak and small black eyes. The bird circled me twice, then landed on the arm of Emerald's chair.

"Roots of the high tree." The courier pressed one hand to the breast of his oiled canvas coat. "Damn talking fowl nearly take out my business, then my eye..." He shook his head a few times and retreated backward through the door into the afternoon sunlight.

I had encountered babblebirds twice before. This one was substantially larger than the others, and it paused to scratch its chin with one foot before saying, "Crimson Smoke and the Emerald Flame."

"I'm the Emerald Flame..."

"Wait!" I exclaimed, for I had recognized the voice as that of Serkadis, and I was sure that the silver dragon would not want his private affairs announced in a public dining room.

It was too late. The babblebird puffed itself up importantly and said, in a perfect imitation of Serkadis's lilting voice, "We are quite settled. Thank you so much for your help. I hope we shall meet again on the shores of the Northward Sea, but until then, know that I am grateful. Yours, Silverskin of the Furling Weald."

I relaxed at once. I should have known that Serkadis would have taken precautions to hide himself and his identity. In sending this message, he had not only communicated his safety, but given us a way to find him again in the form of his new identity. I wondered how he'd adjusted his appearance in the meantime, and whether the egg had already hatched.

Emerald, too, seemed relieved. "Thank you," he told the babblebird. "Message received."

The babblebird bobbed its head up and down a few times until

Svelte produced a small biscuit from the pocket of her apron. The babblebird flew to her shoulder, accepted the treat, and allowed her to carry it to the door. It cawed in midflight, and then it was gone.

"Interesting message," Svelte observed upon her return. "Silverskin... that's quite a name. Blare will be glad to learn that everything turned out all right. As for these..." She lifted the two envelopes. "This one's from the Bracefallows."

Emerald sighed and extended a hand. "I'll take that." Officially speaking, Gorlyn's case was still open, and we'd spent the better part of six weeks tracking down evidence and reporting back to his family. In fact, when Serkadis made arrangements for his belongings to be shipped to his new residence, someone had boxed up Gorlyn's remains. Emerald's idea was that, if and when we could determine who had been smuggling a dragon egg through the city, we could "discover" Gorlyn's remains on their property. The Bracefallows would receive closure, and the smugglers would be brought to justice. Until then, he spoke with the Bracefallows every week or so to keep them abreast of the case.

I knew the lie weighed on him. As he slid the envelope into an inner pocket of his greatcoat, the lines around his eyes deepened. Faldwell might have deserved his fate, but Gorlyn certainly hadn't.

[How do you know?] Innocent mused.

I ignored the question. "And the other letter?"

Svelte studied the envelope. "It's for you. And for what it's worth, it smells like..." She lifted the paper to her nose and sniffed experimentally. "Like perfume. *Real* flowery. I bet you anything a *girl* sent this."

Emerald held out his hand for it, too, but Svelte pulled back.

"This one's not for you," she admonished. "It's addressed specifically to Crimson."

"A lady's writing letters to Crimson?" Yerik asked.

"I can't think why." I moved around behind Svelte to read over her shoulder. "Oh! It's from Rubi!"

I was met with nothing but blank stares.

"Rubigold Stonewall," I explained. "We met at the... at the palace."

Emerald flinched. The memory of Squampf's death was another sore spot.

"See why she's writing," I urged.

Svelte opened the envelope and unfolded the parchment within. "*Dear Crimson Flame, I did so enjoy making your acquaintance at the party last winter, in spite of everything. I know that you must be terribly busy solving the city's problems, but I am wondering if you might be available to come to a ladies' tea at the House of Thorns...*"

Emerald gagged. "A social invitation? Not a chance."

I was not so quick to dismiss the letter, however. "Yerik," I asked, "do you know where the House of Thorns is located?"

"Of course." Yerik pointed vaguely toward the front windows. "It's in the northeast corner of the city, almost due north of the Hives. The estate abuts the palace."

"Not too far, then." I made a show of rubbing my chin. "And since Emerald will be spending the next few days sitting for his portrait..."

"You can't go alone," Emerald reminded me.

I turned up my nose at him. "I'm the only one who's invited, anyway. Besides, it's a *ladies'* tea."

He rubbed his forehead. "No, Crim, I mean you *can't* go alone. Do I really have to spell it out? It's a tea party. You'll be expected to *drink tea.*"

"Ah." The problem became clearer. When I traveled with Emerald, we could do a wide array of things I could not, such as opening doors, lifting up cups, or any number of other mundane tasks for which a physical body was required. My excitement waned.

"I could go," Svelte blurted. She pressed the letter to her chest so hard that the parchment crumpled. "It's a ladies' tea, and I'm... well, I'm close enough. I could pretend to be Crimson's handmaid, fancy ladies have things like that you know, and I'd be able to help. Of course, I'd need a nice dress, but sometimes people leave the change and Yerik lets me keep it, so I'm sure I could get *something* without too much trouble..."

Emerald appeared quite taken aback by her enthusiasm. "Why go to all that effort for a tea party?" he asked.

"Because it would be the first time in my life I'd be allowed to do something *fancy*," Svelte said dreamily.

"And besides, this letter might be more than it seems," I added. "Rubi knew us by reputation. She might be writing because she needs help."

Emerald relented. "I suppose. And since I'll be otherwise occupied, I can't really complain." Never mind that he'd already complained a great deal about sitting for the portrait. "Svelte, I'll leave the correspondence to you."

Svelte beamed. When one of the guests thumped his mug on the table and called for a refill, she practically skipped away.

Emerald flopped back in his armchair and pressed one hand to his forehead. "All right, Yerik." He spoke in the grim tone of a veteran soldier being sent off to fight in yet another fruitless war. "Let's get this over with."

EMERALD RETIRED to his room after an early dinner, and I went with him to help him review the notes we'd taken during the course of our smuggling investigation. There wasn't much to go on, and I quickly grew bored and irritable.

Which was why, when Yerik knocked on the door, I was relieved to set the case aside for a moment.

"We're in the middle of something," Emerald complained. "And you can't tell me that the light's perfect *now*."

"Actually, I'm here for Crimson," Yerik said.

Emerald puffed out his cheeks and returned to his work. "They're all yours."

I followed Yerik downstairs, noting how gingerly he closed the door of our room behind him, out of respect for Emerald's work.

When I tried to ask him what he was after, he shook his head and waved for me to follow.

Svelte and Quell were still at work, along with a young woman from a nearby farm who worked for Yerik when time allowed. She winked at us as Yerik retrieved his cloak from a peg near the front door, and the two of us departed without explanation.

"Am I being kidnapped?" I asked cheerfully as we made our way down the front walk of the inn.

Yerik laughed. "No. I need a consultation, but it's the sort of thing Emerald can't help me with, I'm afraid. Only your expertise will do."

"Is that so?" I asked, secretly flattered that I could be thought to have expertise in *anything*.

"A few weeks ago, I took the children to a tailor," Yerik explained. "She's hardly the finest in the city, and she's quite young, but her prices are reasonable. Someday, I'm sure she'll catch the eye of a patron, but for now she's affordable. And since she has the children's measurements, I thought it would be a nice opportunity to surprise Svelte with a gift."

I pressed my hands to my cheeks. I had been consulted many times, but always with the understanding that I was Emerald's associate, or even his employer. Nobody had ever come to me on my own account, and certainly not to discuss the subject of my greatest passion. "Yerik. Am I to understand that you've come to me for *fashion advice?*"

His booming laugh echoed across the fields and startled a herd of sheep into raising their wooly heads in unison. "Exactly. Svelte was so excited about the idea of having something nice to wear that I can't help myself."

"That's very... *fatherly* of you."

Yerik sobered. He fiddled with the clasp of his cloak as he led me toward the nearby row of shops. "I know that Emerald is the chil-drens' *legal* guardian, but the two of you are away so much that I... I suppose I have come to think of myself in that capacity, yes."

For the second time that day, I tried to imagine what would happen when we left.

"You know," he said abruptly, "I'm aware that Emerald's not made for city life. Not that we're in the city proper"—he waved to the fields and gardens that surrounded us—"but you know what I mean. He hasn't asked, but if he decides to leave, I'd be happy for them to stay with me. Children deserve a stable home. A place where they feel they truly belong. Neither of us had that when we were young. When Emerald goes, I hope that he'll at least give them the choice to stay."

I walked in silence with my hands clasped behind my back. We had almost reached the shop with the woodcut of a needle and thread hung above the door when I spoke again. "For what it's worth, Yerik, I think you make a marvelous father."

He turned his face away from me. His voice cracked as he told me, "You don't know how much it means to hear that."

The subject of fathers was a tricky one, I knew, especially for the former wards of the Brotherhood. I let Yerik have a moment to collect himself as he pushed open the door of the tailor.

The building was humble, but I was taken in at once by the bolts of brilliant fabric that lined the walls, and the headless dress forms which displayed samples of the seamstress's work. The fabrics were not as fine as the ones the nobles wore, but they were bright and cheerful, and the careful beadwork on the finished samples elevated them to something truly special.

Perhaps because of the late hour, there was no one to greet us, so Yerik and I took our time perusing the shelves.

"I have something in mind," Yerik said. He withdrew a folded drawing from an inner pocket of his cloak. "Although I'll be the first to admit, I don't know a *thing* about fashion."

He was spreading the paper flat on the counter when the sound of raised voices made both of us jump. I could not make out the words, and the argument didn't last long. A curtain in the back corner of the shop was flung open, and a hooded figure emerged, walking with purpose. The woman's face was covered, but I could tell from her posture that she was angry. She didn't stop to acknowledge us as she stormed through the front door, slamming it behind her.

A second woman emerged from the back room. Her fine brown hair was coming loose from its braid, and her eyes were red-rimmed and puffy. When she saw us, she straightened up a little and forced a smile onto her delicate features.

"My apologies." She swept over to us. "I didn't realize anyone was here."

Yerik frowned at the door through which the angry woman had vanished. "Are you all right, Vasilika?"

"Oh, you know how it is." The tailor laughed woodenly. "Difficult customer. Some people are *so* hard to please. Are the children happy with their new clothes?"

Yerik relaxed and adjusted the picture so that both Vasilika and I could see. "Yes, but I'm hoping you can help with a special order. I know it's short notice..."

"For that girl of yours?" Moment by moment, Vasilika's smile became more genuine. "Oh no, long sleeves? For a girl her age, at this time of year? You must be joking."

I pretended to lean against the counter. "Thank goodness *you* said it. I wasn't sure how to broach the subject of that dowdy neckline."

Yerik held up both hands in defeat. "Forgive my ignorance. I told you I was hopeless! I've been wearing a variation on the same outfit for nearly twenty years."

"Yerik, my dear." Vasilika laid one hand on his shoulder. "We know."

For the next half hour, we discussed color, cut, and decoration. Vasilika laughed almost as easily as Yerik—and yet every few minutes, without fail, she glanced toward the front door, no doubt thinking of her difficult customer.

CHAPTER THREE

Svelte eagerly wrote out a letter which I dictated to Rubi the next morning, accepting the invitation to visit and asking for details. When I spoke to her again that afternoon, however, she was distraught.

"I was hoping I'd have enough," she said, counting out the coins she'd managed to save in the months she'd worked at the tavern. "But I asked Miss Vasilika how much a dress would cost, and..." She shook her head and fell silent.

"You can wear something you already have," I suggested, although the temptation to reveal Yerik's plan was almost too great.

"Of course." Svelte tucked the coins away again. "I'm used to making do. I don't mean to complain."

She was quiet for the rest of the day, going about her chores with less enthusiasm than usual. Emerald, too, was in a sullen mood. The weather didn't help; it was a gloomy, dreary day, business was slow, and everyone around me was sulking. For symmetry's sake, I sulked, too.

. . .

THE MORNING OF THE PARTY, just after opening, Vasilika strode through the door with a package under one arm. Svelte and Blare were wiping down tables while Quell mopped, and when she saw the tailor, the girl lifted her head in surprise.

"You're here awfully early," she said. "What can I do for you?"

"Nothing at all." Vasilika set the package down on one of the tables and stepped back. "I've brought you something."

Svelte tiptoed toward the package as though it might contain a serpent—of the venomous variety. Yerik, who had moved his efforts from sketchpad to canvas, kept messing about with the paints, although I could tell he was watching the proceedings from the corner of his eye. Svelte gave the twine around the package a tug, and gasped when the wrapping fell open to reveal a folded dress in sapphire blue. She ran her fingers over the beadwork and lifted her eyes to Vasilika's face. "For me?" she squeaked.

Vasilika nodded.

"But... the money..."

"You're too young to worry about that." Yerik abandoned his paints and came over; Emerald followed after him, none the wiser about what was happening.

Svelte's bottom lip wobbled. "But..."

"It's a gift," Yerik said.

Svelte let out a loud sob and launched herself into Yerik's arms. She sniffled against his shoulder while he patted her hair.

"Thank you," she said, her voice muffled against the material of his shirt. "I've never... nobody's ever..."

Yerik kissed her forehead. "I know."

She pulled away suddenly, wiped her tears against her palms, and snatched up the parcel. "I'm going to try it on!"

"Let me come with you, in case it needs any last-minute alterations." Vasilika followed Svelte up the stairs, pausing at the landing to wink over her shoulder at us. Her mood could not have been more different from the night we'd visited her shop.

Quell leaned on his mop as they vanished into the upper floor.

"It's just a dress," he muttered. "Dunno why she's got to be all emotional about it."

The lambkin wasn't facing Blare, but the devices that Serkadis had commissioned from the Smith's Guild meant that Blare heard anyway. He nudged Quell with his shoulder, shook his head, and signed. *It's not just a dress, and you know it.*

Roused by the voices from downstairs, the inn's other customers began to emerge from their rooms, prompting a flurry of activity including the steeping of tea and the serving of breakfast. I was the only one who noticed when Vasilika reemerged from the upstairs rooms. She waved goodbye to Yerik as she passed, but it was me she approached for a whispered conversation.

"I think Svelte could use a bit of encouragement." She smiled knowingly. "You remember how it is to be that age."

Of course, I remembered no such thing, but I nodded. "How could one forget?"

Reassured that Svelte was in good hands, Vasilika departed, leaving me to mount the stairs and approach the door of the children's room.

"Svelte?" I called.

From inside, a defeated voice said, "Come in."

I checked both ways to make sure that no guests were present before slipping through the door like a ghost. Svelte was standing in front of the mirror, hands on her hips, glaring at her reflection.

I did not often visit the children's room unless I was specifically invited, but the three of them kept it as neat as their old dormitory in the Brotherhood, although they had more possessions now. The beds were made, although there was a dimple at the foot of one of them, suggesting that Vasilika had perched there for a moment while she and Svelte spoke.

"Is something the matter?" I asked.

Svelte huffed. "No."

I drifted closer. "Forgive me if I express just a *touch* of skepticism. You don't seem pleased. Don't you like it?" I asked.

"I like the dress," she said, but in a manner that suggested that something else was the matter.

Following Vasilika's lead, I sat on the edge of the bed, although I did not disturb the sheets with my presence. "I think you look rather fetching."

She wrinkled her upturned nose and glared at the girl frowning back at her from the glass. "*I* think I look more like a bouquet of wilted bluebottle. Blue ain't my color, I don't think."

"I thought you'd like the hue."

"The color's not the problem. It's my favorite color."

I had thought so, and in fact, I had been the one to suggest it. "But it's not *your* color?"

"Makes me look a bit like uncooked dough, don't you think?" Svelte prodded her full cheeks, then held up her mostly exposed arms and wiggled them a bit.

It was my turn to frown at the mirror, albeit for a very different reason. "That's Guise talking." *Or Brother Harmony,* I added silently. *Guise never whispered insults in Svelte's ear, but the Brothers did...*

Svelte froze with one arm raised and the fingers of her other hand pinching the soft flesh beneath her bicep. I saw the change in her expression as my words sank in. "Oh," she murmured. "I reckon you're right."

"*I* think the color brings out your eyes. As for the cut, I believe it suits you." I hesitated a beat before adding, "In fact, I envy you."

She snorted and turned to look me up and down with the matter-of-factness that I had only ever encountered among children. "*Right.*"

"You think I'm lying?" Not many people knew what I was, but in Svelte's company I could be perfectly honest. I folded in on myself, rearranging my form into the familiar shape of Sibling Vagabond. "Yes, I can look however I want." I changed again, this time into the form of a small ginger cat. I howled once, then stretched upward again into the shape I'd only experimented with in private: a halfway point between Simon and Simone, with my hair falling in coils over shoulders exposed by the scooped neck of a dress that rivaled anything I'd seen in the king's court, and stubble dusting my jaw.

The girl's eyes popped wide.

"I am always myself, Svelte, but I can't eat cakes or slam doors or feed sugar to the king's horses." I pulled back into the appearance I'd worn before, although the color in my cheeks was higher than it had been at the outset of the conversation. "I can't hug my friends, or smell the ocean, or..." I stopped short at the memory of Serkadis's fingers catching a lock of my hair, and how strange it had been to feel *real* to someone else. How novel.

And how lonely, in the aftermath of his departure, to know that I must go back to being nothing but a phantom.

Svelte nodded slowly. "Well, that's a mixed bag. 'Cause I'll tell you what, the waterfront smells like week-old shite and rotten fish more often than not. And you can't go hungry when you don't need to eat. So I expect there's loads of people who'd be happy to trade places with you, but..." She turned back to the mirror to study her reflection. "But yeah, I suppose you're right about the word of Guise. Nothing I do would ever be *ordinary* enough for him, so I might as well stop trying." She ran her hands over the skirt and straightened up. "I wonder what this lady of yours will think."

"She's hardly *my* lady," I retorted. "Anyway, don't worry, Rubi's lovely. She'll adore you."

[Crim?] Emerald thought from downstairs. *[There's a coach here for you.]*

I got to my feet again. "Are you ready?"

Svelte ran her fingers through her hair a few times, straightened up, and smiled experimentally at her reflection. "That'll do."

I paused to change my outfit, rearranging my attire into the blue dress I'd come to think of as Emerald's apology dress, the one he'd conjured for me after our first fight in Dyrne. "There. Now we match."

On our way out, we were beset by Svelte's small crowd of admirers.

"Goodness!" Yerik cried. "You look lovely." He swept in to give her a farewell hug. "Have a wonderful time.

"You look like a *lady*," Quell said. He adjusted his glasses to get a better look at her, then nodded his approval.

Only Blare hung back, with his lips slightly parted, a faint blush just visible on his umber cheeks. *You're beautiful, Svelte,* he signed, almost shyly.

Svelte's usually pale, freckled skin was immediately suffused with pink. *Thank you*, she signed back.

That color brings out your eyes.

The rest of us, Quell included, did our utmost to pretend that we didn't notice their clumsy flirtation, although I heard Emerald's low chuckle from across the room.

[Oh, stop it,] I scolded. **[You're just as obvious when you're flirting.]**

That was enough to knock the smug smile off his face. Fortunately, he didn't respond in kind to taunt me for *my* lack of subtlety around a certain dragon.

Then again, subtlety was not a quality I'd ever claimed to possess.

CHAPTER FOUR

S velte pressed her face to the glass and whistled as Rubi's home came into view. "Your lady's got deep pockets, doesn't she?"

I rolled my eyes at her. "Stop calling her *my* lady. You remember her title, don't you?"

My young companion's smile turned impish as she pulled back from the window. "Are you worried I'm going to embarrass you in front of your posh friend?"

I let my silence and my arched eyebrow speak for me.

"I know how to bow and scrape and speak fancy," Svelte assured me. "And ladies' maids are supposed to be seen and not heard. But I *do* hope she has some nice cakes. Rich people have the best food, and they *always* take it for granted."

When the carriage stopped, Svelte opened the door and made a show of helping me down. Unlike the royal coach I'd taken that winter, this one was drawn by a quartet of dapple-backed, fine-boned deer. They flicked their ears and turned up their noses when Svelte held out her hand to them before trotting away at the snap of the driver's reins.

"I like the horses better," Svelte said.

Given Rubi's title, I could only assume that the estate we'd been brought to was the House of Thorns. There were certainly a number of roses in the sprawling gardens, but the whole place was a riot of color. We made our way up the wide paved walk, stopping here and there to admire the various blooms.

"I didn't know roses came in so many colors," Svelte marveled. "Do you think there are people whose whole job is to invent new colors of roses? And why is that shrub trimmed to look like a weirling? Oh, Crimson, *look at that house.*"

She scurried ahead of me, in exactly the way a ladies' maid wouldn't, and I followed on her heels with a bit more trepidation. A ladies' tea sounded like a pleasant pastime. But where were the ladies? When I looked over my shoulder, not a single other carriage was in evidence. Had we somehow come on the wrong day? No, that couldn't be right—Rubi had sent the carriage. None of it made sense.

We had not yet reached the front door when it was flung wide, and a familiar figure emerged from within.

"You're here!" Rubigold Stonewall exclaimed.

She clearly expected me to grasp her hands in greeting and fling myself into a girlish and enthusiastic embrace. I was forced to shy away from her, and her face fell at the rejection.

"Of course I am," I said, and smiled in what I hope was a reassuring way. "You sent a carriage, so you must have got my letter."

She nodded as she tucked one of her loose, pale curls behind one ear. "I know. But sometimes people say things they don't mean, and one is left to drink one's tea alone."

Rubi had clearly gone to great lengths to look lovely. Her rose-colored dress was ornamented with silk flowers, more of which were pinned to her hair, which had been carefully curled and cascaded along her cheek and over one freckled shoulder. She must have spent ages getting ready, and yet she moved in the same way Emerald often did: as if she were too large, and too much, and was rather embarrassed that anyone was looking at her.

"I wouldn't miss this afternoon for anything," I told her, perhaps a *touch* more vehemently than I felt. I was being completely honest when I added, "I've been looking forward to it."

Rubi's face lit up again, and her posture unfurled like a fiddle-head. "Have you really? So have I."

"You look beautiful," I added.

Her cheeks flushed the same shade as her dress. "It's a new dress," she blurted.

Svelte cleared her throat, and Rubi jumped at the sound. "My goodness! I didn't realize you'd brought a guest."

"I hope it's not an imposition," I said. "This is my..." Svelte was staring at Rubi with such unabashed fascination that I could not imagine passing her off as anything so commonplace as an employee. "Cousin," I decided. After all, there was some resemblance between us, right down to the red hair. "She's visiting from the country, and I didn't want to leave her alone."

Svelte dipped into a polite curtsy, which revealed that beneath her fine dress she was wearing plain work shoes. "It's a pleasure to meet you, Rubigold Stonewall, Thirteenth Heir of the House of Thorns, Future Wardeness of Fallow Lakes."

Rubi hid her smile behind one hand. "How formal! That's quite unnecessary, you must call me Rubi. I'm afraid I missed your name."

Svelte froze. I had grown so used to her name that I had long since forgotten that it was a thinly veiled reprimand. No wonder she'd scowled at herself in the looking glass.

"I-it's Sveta," she mumbled.

"It is my pleasure to meet you, Sveta. Of course you're welcome to join us. The more, the merrier! Please come in, the cook just brought up a *lovely* tray of teacakes." She waved us through the front door and closed it behind us.

Stepping into the sitting room, I was faced with two things for which I was entirely unprepared. The first was the grandeur of the room itself. Thorny vines were carved into the hardwood beams above our heads, the silk wallpaper was patterned with buds and blossoms, and even the furniture was upholstered with a rose motif.

"The House of Thorns," I murmured, remembering Rubi's title.

She laughed as she settled into one of the large, plush chairs. "Who can resist a theme?"

Whoever had decorated the room had taken things to the extreme, but my larger concern waited on the sitting-room table. A gilded samovar stood alongside two conical glass cups, emblazoned with—what else?—gold-painted roses. A dozen beautiful iced teacakes waited on a nearby tray, alongside two matching plates.

Two of everything.

So much for my plan to disappear in the crowd of women. Evidently, I was the only guest who'd been expected.

"I'll get another set of dishes," Rubi said, and hurried over to a glass-fronted display case bristling with dishes.

Svelte dropped heavily onto one of the sofas and leaned back to admire the ceiling. She straightened up when Rubi returned.

"Do you take sugar?" Rubi asked, fussing over the table. "I don't know how things are done in Venta Bulgarum." She wrinkled her pert nose in distaste. "I've heard some of them put a sort of fruit juice in their tea. Or even *milk*." After scowling at the samovar for a moment, she seemed to realize her faux pas and blushed again. "Of course, if you two want milk, I'm sure we can find some...!"

"No milk," I said firmly. If I could have wheedled myself out of accepting the drink at all, I would have done so. I perched on the sofa alongside Svelte.

"I'll take it however you like it, miss," Svelte said agreeably. She was eyeing the teacakes critically, although she kept her hands folded in her lap.

"Go on, take one." Steaming tea splashed into each of the cups in turn as Rubi served us.

Svelte used the silver tongs to serve me first, then took one of the little cakes for herself. The moment she bit into it, her eyes rolled back, and she smothered a small groan.

"They're good, aren't they?" Rubi asked.

"I wish I knew how to bake like this." Svelte nibbled at the remainder of the cake. "It's so *light*."

"I'll give the cook your compliments." Rubi added a bit of honey to each of our drinks, then sat down across from us, tucking her feet under the hem of her dress. "I'm so glad you came, Sveta. I thought it would be just Crimson and me sitting here. Not that it would be such a bad thing..." She glanced at me again, then lowered her eyes to her drink.

Her words confused me all the more. "I thought I was the only one you were expecting."

She laughed airily. "Well, it's not as if you were the only one I *invited*... but you're the only one who wrote back."

Svelte almost dropped her plate and had to bend over to catch it before the delicate porcelain hit the floor. "What? You mean you invited other people, but they didn't come?"

Rubi lowered her cup back to the table without having taken a sip. She had gone rather pale at the question. "It's nothing to worry about. Give them a few weeks and it will blow over."

"What will blow over?" Svelte asked.

Rubi wilted. "You haven't heard? I thought everyone in Kinmore knew."

"I'm hardly at the center of the city's social sphere," I said wryly.

"You don't have to talk about it if you don't want to," Svelte assured her.

Rubi ran her palms over the dress. Her complexion was even more sallow than it had been a moment prior. "You remember Lady Isabella of Tenbridge Sound?"

I shuddered. "I wish I didn't."

Svelte's eyes bulged at my poor show of manners, but Rubi managed a laugh. "Yes, she's... she's *quite memorable*, isn't she? She's got her eye on this young man who's visiting his grandmama for the season. *Everyone* has been fawning over Basco all summer, but he and Isabella are, um, *involved*. The trouble is, he and I have been spending a great deal of time together..."

With each word, Rubi trembled. A sheen of sweat had begun to break out on her forehead.

"Do you fancy this Basco fellow?" Svelte asked.

Rubi shook her head. "We're just friends."

Svelte and I exchanged a knowing look.

"It's true!" Rubi insisted. "Nothing's happened between us, but he's privately confessed that nothing's going to happen with Isabella, either. He doesn't like her, because, well..."

"Because she's so memorable?" I asked drily.

"Yes, exactly." Rubi offered a shaky smile. Her hands were balled in her lap. "And since I'm not the only one throwing myself at his feet, I... *Goodness,* is it warm in here?"

I couldn't answer the question, but Svelte shook her head. "I think it's lovely, but I could open a window if you—"

Rubi lurched upright. One hand grasped at her skirt, while she used the back of the other to wipe the sweat from her brow. I had thought Rubi merely nervous and awkward in our company, but when she looked around the room with unfocused eyes, I realized that something was, in fact, terribly wrong.

"Forgive me," she murmured. "I just need..."

Her eyes rolled back in her head, and she pitched forward across the table, sending cups, dishes, and teacakes scattering in every direction. Svelte screamed, and I sat there frozen, unsure of what to do. Rubi was still moving, although there was an uncontrolled jerkiness to her movements that reminded me horribly of the seizure Blare had suffered during our tenure at the Brotherhood of Guise.

[This is more fun than I thought it would be,] Innocent whispered.

"Shut up!" I barked, forgetting that I alone could hear him. "Svelte, what should we do?"

The girl had already put aside her shock and rushed forward to pull Rubi off the table. She dragged her into the middle of the room, on the rose-patterned carpet, away from the furniture and broken dishes.

"I'll keep her like this. You get help." Svelte, too, had gone terribly pale, but I thought it must be more from alarm than anything else. Ice crystals were already forming in the air around her head; her control over her Arctician *Aidea* tended to slip in times of high stress.

[Unless something was poisoned...] Innocent mused. I thought of the dead merchant, Faldwell, whose face had swollen so badly in death that his features were unrecognizable. *[Svelte ate the teacakes, Svelte drank the tea... they might both be dying, and there's nothing you can do at all, you'll just have to sit here and watch, the way Humble and Allure and Steady sat and watched Reticent burn...]*

"CRIMSON!" Svelte bellowed, loud enough to startle me out of my shock. Rubi lay on her side, arms flung at strange angles, gasping for breath. Her eyes rolled back, and spittle foamed at the corner of her lips. She kept trying to speak, or perhaps to breathe, but the only sound that came from her chest was a thin, ragged wheezing sound that stutter-stopped each time her lips moved.

I sprang up and raced from the room, leaving Svelte in the presence of a woman who, for all I knew, might be dying, at a party I had brought her to, thinking it would be a pleasant afternoon.

CHAPTER FIVE

Svelte sat on the loveseat, her blue party dress rumpled, her arms wrapped around her knees, eyes puffy and swollen. A small snowdrift had gathered around her while she cried, and it was gradually melting into the sofa's floral upholstery.

"I don't understand." She blotted her eyes on the kerchief Finch had handed her. "She was fine when she greeted us, and then... as we kept talking, she got worse, until she just collapsed."

"You did very well," Emerald said gently. He and the commander sat in armchairs across from her, both of them looking quite sympathetic. In the hour since they'd arrived, several somber members of the household had cleared away the broken dishes and spilled tea. The room looked almost as tidy as it had when we arrived, a sight entirely at odds with everything that had transpired since our arrival. There was nothing at all tidy about the events that had unfolded there.

And yet, the House of Thorns stood strong, despite the fact that its heir was still fighting for her life in the rooms upstairs.

"She's lucky," Finch said, "that you're quick on your feet, young lady. The physician says she might have choked to death if you hadn't been there to keep her on her side."

"My, um, my brother." Svelte wiped her eyes. "He's had something like that happen to him a few times. Will she be all right?"

"The physician is with her now," Finch said. "I'd send you home, but the physician wants you to stay here until he can be quite sure you won't suffer the same effects, just in case it was something in the food."

Svelte nodded and tucked her chin between her knees, breathing hard.

I wished that I could comfort her, but nothing I could have said to put her at ease would have been strictly true. I could not promise her that Rubi would be safe. I could not promise that *Svelte* was safe. I could not even put my arm around her to offer her the comfort of a physical touch.

Emerald looked utterly exhausted, and he kept running his hands through his hair as he watched Svelte sink into herself.

"I'm sorry I wasn't here," he said at last.

Svelte hiccuped. "Wouldn't have mattered." She squeezed her eyes shut. "I've seen sick folk before, you know. You can't lightweave illness away, and you can't fight it with fists, 'cause Guise knows I tried when things with Blare were at their worst..."

"He would have been able to do *something*," I blurted.

Finch arched an eyebrow at me.

I ignored her. Let her think Emerald was using his poppet to comfort a frightened girl, or assume that I was some subconscious voice in Emerald's mind looking for the right thing to say. We would make our excuses later if necessary. For the time being, only Svelte mattered.

"You shouldn't have had to face that alone," I said. "Without someone who could do the hard part. You shouldn't have had to stay here while I ran off."

"Someone had to go," she said. "Someone had to stay. You got them to send for a physician, and that's what she *really* needed."

I lifted my shoulders toward my ears defensively. "Yes, but I shouldn't have left you—"

Svelte uncurled from herself just enough to reach one arm toward me. She let her hand hover over mine, not quite brushing the place where my hand would have been, if I had one. "I reckon that's Guise talking," she whispered.

I had never believed in Guise, but I suppose Emerald had, which meant that even before I was myself, I'd been part of something that Guise's messages of conformity had tainted. Svelte wasn't mad at me, but that didn't stop me from being angry with myself. I should have been able to do more. I should have been able to do *everything*. My job was to protect the people I loved from every bad thing that might come their way, and anything less than that was a failure on my part.

Perhaps that belief would bear further examination at some future date, but I didn't have the stomach to unravel it just then.

Finch was leaning forward, one elbow braced against her knee, her chin in her palm, observing the conversation with the same rapt intensity that most people reserved for the theater.

The silence ended abruptly with a knock on the front door. Someone in the hallway went to answer it, and the sound of two voices—men's voices, judging by their timbre—wafted from the front hall. This was followed by the click of bootheels on stone, and a creak of hinges, as the newcomer was shown into the sitting room.

Finch and Emerald both turned in their chairs, as the entryway to the sitting room was behind him, but Svelte and I had an excellent view of the man as he entered.

He was tall and fit, with pin-straight black hair that fell nearly to his waist. He had high, fine cheekbones, and unbelievably large eyes the color of the midnight sky. I was about to ask his name when I saw, from the corner of my eye, that Svelte was staring at him with open-mouthed awe, and that the color was bright in her cheeks. A quick survey of the room revealed that she was not alone.

Emerald was staring.

Finch was staring.

I inclined my head to the newcomer. "You must be Basco."

The young man nodded solemnly and stopped beside Finch's chair. "I heard that Rubi was feeling unwell. I came as soon as I could. Not that there's anything I can do, but I couldn't just sit at home and wait for news."

Emerald cleared his throat. *[Who in Aster's name is Basco?]*

[A friend of Rubi's. She was telling us about him when... when she collapsed.]

[And you knew it was him, because...?]

I pretended to cough into a freshly conjured kerchief. *[Because she mentioned that everyone she knows has been throwing themselves at his feet, and the three of you seemed more than prepared to do the same.]*

Emerald snapped his mouth shut and crossed his arms. "Pull up a chair," he grunted in Basco's general direction. "We'd like to ask you some questions."

"Questions?" Basco appraised my friend and Finch for the first time, and his posture immediately shifted. "You're with the Conjury. What's the Conjury doing *here*? I thought Rubes was having a party?"

Finch seemed to have recovered her sense of propriety and was no longer gawking at the man. "She was, until she... took ill. Am I to understand that you and '*Rubes*' are close friends?"

Basco flushed and went to retrieve another chair, pointedly avoiding all eye contact. "Indeed. I've only been in town for a few months, but we've grown close in that time. She's one of the few people I've met in Granny's circle who's actually *nice*."

Emerald laughed, and then tried to pretend he hadn't.

"Well, it's true." Basco sat down and got comfortable. "Things are very different here than where I come from. For one thing, there's no Conjury presence in Danilas Freehold." He nodded toward Finch. "Not to get political, ma'am."

Finch's nose twitched. "Tell me, then, as Rubigold's friend, would you say she has... enemies?"

Basco chuckled. With every moment in the chair, he seemed to expand, in the way that only young men were wont to do. Unlike Rubi, he had no compunction about taking up as much space as his comfort required. "Enemies? Good grief, no. Can you imagine disliking Rubi?"

"I think Lady Isabella can imagine it," I murmured.

Basco's smile slipped. "Yes, well. Name one person Lady Isabella *does* like."

"You," Svelte blurted. "Rubi said so."

The young man shook his head. "Maybe she likes the idea of me, but it isn't the same thing. Yes, all right, I suppose there are people who don't care for Rubi, but they're the ones missing out."

Finch's eye twitched. "Young man, if you could be a *bit* more helpful..."

Basco looked up at her in surprise. "Helpful? What do you—?" His eyes widened in understanding, and his whole posture shifted. "Madame, is this an *investigation*?"

"Well, I'm certainly not here for a tea party," Finch rumbled. She pointed to herself, then Emerald, waving her paw back and forth. "Do we look like the sort of people your young lady might invite in for a drink?"

Basco studied them for a long moment. "Yes, actually," he said. "I wouldn't be surprised at all. Rubes isn't particularly... that is to say... she's more interesting than other people, and I suspect you are as well. I've never seen a Leonhite this far south. But if you're here in a more official capacity, does that mean that what happened to Rubi wasn't an accident?"

Finch licked her lips.

"Celestriona's dripping—" Basco caught himself and pressed a hand to his mouth. "Oh, no. *No.*" He leaned forward and gripped his temples, staring at nothing in particular, looking rather haunted. He sucked in a breath and let it out, slow and shuddering. "This is all my fault."

I raised my eyebrows at Emerald, who only shrugged.

"Did you poison her?" Svelte wiped the back of her hand beneath her nose. She was still curled up on the edge of the sofa, watching Basco with open curiosity. Her panic had faded, to be replaced with her usual matter-of-factness.

"What?" Basco shook himself. "No, no, I would never." His eyes found mine, and he let out another heavy sigh. "You were asking if Rubi has enemies. I get the impression that she was always a social outcast, but things have gotten worse since we became friends. You see, my grandmama is quite insistent that I get engaged to this... uh, *young lady* I don't like very much at all."

"Lady Isabella," I said, recalling what Rubi had been about to say before her grand collapse.

Basco nodded. "Isabella, on the other hand, seems perfectly happy with the idea. Apparently, this is all something our families worked out when we were younger, something I knew nothing about until I arrived in Kinmore a few months ago. But we..." He paused, licked his lips, opened his mouth, and closed it again.

I understood the difficulty. He was a young man of good manners speaking about a lady to whom he was informally engaged. I had no such investment in niceties. "Isabella is a terrible person, and you want nothing to do with her."

Basco laughed awkwardly. "Well... you said it, not me."

Emerald tilted his head. "You know her?"

Finch maintained her composure, but her golden eyes flicked toward me, and there was a question in them. How could *I* know Isabella, if Emerald didn't?

Because I am not what you think I am. I could hardly admit it, but Finch had already proven that she was an unpredictable element, and so far, she had made no mention of my slip-ups and tells. Rather than acknowledge her curiosity, I nodded to Emerald.

"We met at the same party where I met Rubi. She made a lasting impression." ***[Picture a younger, more feminine Dirkus.]***

Emerald wrinkled his nose. ***[Ah.]*** "I take it she and Rubigold aren't friends?"

Basco shook his head. "I don't think they ever were, but Isabella has taken offense at my disinterest, and she blames Rubi for it."

"And she, in turn, has turned the other ladies of Kinmore against Rubi," I guessed.

Basco nodded.

"Oh." Svelte shifted her feet off the sofa at last. "That's why nobody else came to her party."

The pained grimace on Basco's face was reply enough.

More voices from the hallway made us all turn to the door. A moment later, the elven physician strode through. Her hair was pulled back in a tight braid that reminded me a bit of Calla's usual style, and her demeanor suggested that she would suffer nobody's nonsense.

"She is alive," the physician said. "Although if you have any notion of questioning her, it'll have to wait."

"Alive?" Basco squeaked. "Was there any danger she *wouldn't* be?"

The elf turned cold eyes on the young man. "Had I been delayed even a quarter of an hour, she would no longer be among the living."

I had thought Basco understood the danger, but of course he had not been there to see what Svelte and I had experienced. The whine that emitted from him was as pitiable as that of a kicked dog. He curled in on himself and pressed his hands to his face as he muttered something incomprehensible.

Finch looked upon him with pity. "Do you have any idea what brought it on? An allergy, perhaps?"

Emerald glared at the back of her head.

The physician snorted. "Hardly. Unless you reckon that everyone alive is *allergic* to redfallow."

"Redfallow?" Emerald asked. "What variety?"

The physician seemed both taken aback and pleased by the question. "I have no way of knowing that for sure, but the broad-leaf variety is a common problem for farmers in the area. If the sheep get into a patch of the stuff, they can sicken and die within hours unless they're treated. I recently had to treat a fellow who walked through a stand and nearly went into shock that evening. Even brief contact can irritate the skin, but prolonged exposure or ingestion can be fatal. Although it's not too difficult to treat, as long as you can diagnose it."

Emerald nodded along with her explanation. "But it would *look* like an allergic reaction...?"

"Oh, it'll make you puff up like you wouldn't believe," the physician said, almost cheerfully. It struck me that Emerald had found another kindred spirit, someone who loved her work so much that she could separate suffering from her fascination with its cause.

Not all of us could do the same. "It causes seizures, too, doesn't it?" Svelte asked.

The physician's smile vanished. "Not precisely. It inflames the body, causing the veins of its victims to—"

Svelte bit her bottom lip. I believe we all remembered at once that she was a child who had witnessed something horrible, and that no matter how much sense she had displayed in the moment, the events of the afternoon had been more trying for her than for the rest of us.

"It doesn't matter," the physician said hastily. "What's done is done, and you appear to be no worse for wear." She strode over to Svelte and placed her hand on the girl's forehead, then felt beneath her chin and along her neck. "No inflammation at all. You're free to go."

"We should *all* go," Finch said. "I'll pack up the cups and plates and have them sent to the Alchemist's Guild—"

"Wearing gloves," Emerald reminded her. "Broad-leaf redfallow is just as dangerous to those who touch it as those who ingest it."

Finch narrowed her eyes. "I don't carry spare gloves on me at all times, you know."

"I do." The physician produced a pair of thin, plain white gloves. "I made sure to wear them when I was examining Miss Stonewall; they're enchanted to neutralize any toxins they come in contact with. Just be sure to toss them when you're done. Redfallow can be quite nasty. It's the oils in the leaves that are the trouble, you see, so even when you can't *see* anything, they're still dangerous."

"Leaves?" Svelte glanced at the samovar. "Oh, no, the *tea*! I didn't drink any!"

"Nor did I," I added grimly, as an explanation took shape in my mind.

Finch hummed. "No, you wouldn't have."

I turned my head to meet her gaze and lifted my chin. "But what are the odds of that, Commander? It was a tea party, after all. One might expect the guests to consume that particular beverage."

Finch lifted one brow. The shift in coloration on that part of her pelt was subtle, but even so her expression of surprise and understanding was easy enough to read. "If I was going to poison someone, I'd make quite sure that none of my friends attended an event where said poisoning was going to take place."

I nodded my agreement.

"Gods," Basco murmured. He dragged a hand down one side of his face. "Do you think...? Isabella?"

"That's a serious accusation," Emerald told him. "One that I don't think we're prepared to make."

"But one you'll want to investigate," Basco said. He seemed so lost and helpless that, for a moment, I thought he might topple sideways off the chair. "You *have* to let me help."

Finch sniffed, and her whiskers quivered. "I think we can handle this on your own, thank you."

To my surprise, Basco sniffed right back. "Really? Are you going to arrest Lady Isabella and bring her in for questioning? I think not. I may not understand everything to do with the Conjury, but I know that there is tension between the elite of this city and your employers. If you're seen to be harassing a titled heir, you'll have the whole court up in arms. The situation is fraught as it is, following the... the unpleasantness this past winter. I expect it would make your job a great deal easier if I paved the way for your investigation."

"And how do you intend to do that?" Finch asked wryly.

"I'll throw a party. Tomorrow." Basco's vacant dismay was becoming rapidly replaced by newfound certainty. "Grandmama loves the idea of a spectacle. A last-minute party with a limited guest list. Nobody will be able to resist." He squinted at Finch and Emerald. "A masquerade. I'll invite everyone from Rubi's guest list, everyone who didn't come."

"People will think that's suspicious." Emerald scratched his jaw. "And whoever's responsible will likely want to avoid scrutiny."

Basco shook his head. "No. They'll think it *salacious*. They snubbed Rubi over this nonsense with Isabella. Trust me, I've been observing them for the last three months, and there's nothing these people love more than proving that they're better than everyone else."

All of us gawked at him.

He smiled sadly and lifted one shoulder. "That's why I enjoy Rubi's company. She's the only one who wouldn't sacrifice their friends and family on the altar of *reputation*." This last word he spat out with abject disgust.

"A party." Finch smirked. "I can't think of the last time I was invited to a court party. Oh, wait, I can. *Never*. Far be it from me to miss such an exclusive event." She dug her elbow into Emerald's side. "What about you?"

"I wouldn't miss it," Emerald intoned in the flattest, deadest voice imaginable.

"Very good. Tomorrow." Basco got to his feet and straightened his coat. "For Rubi."

CHAPTER SIX

"You know," Svelte said, straining her muscles as she kneaded the dough of her newest culinary project, "I never realized how much I hate your job."

I perched on the edge of the counter and swung my feet back and forth, occasionally forgetting to stop them in time and letting them pass through the cupboard below. Svelte had barely slept the night before, and I should know, as I had spent the night watching over her. I had rearranged myself into my form of Sibling Vagabond—not that it changed anything substantial, but I always felt more like one of the children in that form. Things were rapidly becoming more complicated, as the "children" would soon cease to be children themselves. They were on the cusp of something I would never experience, a significant and lasting change that would always elude me.

I envied them.

"Why is that?" I asked.

Svelte paused so that she could wipe her forehead on the small towel flung over one shoulder. "It's all misery and dying, isn't it? The adventure parts were fun, even with the shadow-man. Scary, but exciting. But yesterday... I thought Rubi was going to die. And I thought I'd be sitting right next to her when it happened. It was horrible." She went back to the dough, punching it with her fists this time. I'd seen her do this before, but not usually with such force. "Somebody did that to her *on purpose.*"

"But our job is to stop people like that," I pointed out.

Svelte cast me a sidelong glance. "Most people try to *avoid* horrible situations."

Innocent chuckled. *[Yes. And others ask the darkness to take up residence in their heads.]*

I turned my face away from Svelte and frowned. *[I didn't invite you. I beat you, and now you're trapped.]*

[Call it whatever you like. I'm still here.]

Emerald shoved through the kitchen door. "Morning," he grunted.

"I believe people traditionally wish each other a *good* morning," I called.

He stomped over to the stove. "I'm just being a realist. Where's the tea? Didn't anyone make any?"

Svelte paused mid-knead. "No. After yesterday, I..."

"Right." Emerald straightened up. "Wasn't thinking. Crimson, stop messing around. We need to go into town and talk to Finch."

I leapt off the counter, rearranging myself into Simone as I did. "See you later, Svelte. Don't think too much about it, all right? Rubi's safe now, and we'll catch whoever did this."

On the way out, I couldn't help but pause in front of Yerik's partially painted canvas. He had started with Emerald's outline, but he was a long way from adding any specific details to the portrait, although there was no mistaking my friend's sullen, slouched posture.

[Can't imagine why anyone would want that on their walls,] Emerald thought as he stomped toward the door.

I suppressed a smirk. **[I just wonder where he'll position the goose.]**

. . .

FINCH WAS ALREADY SCOWLING when we entered her office. Her assistant, Aaliy, was hovering near the desk while Finch read through a long document written in neat, miniscule script.

"That's two theories we've had to throw out," she snarled at Emerald. "Allergies, and now redfallow. Utter piss."

Aaliy fidgeted.

Finch made a sharp gesture at her. "Go on, get out. I'll tear the inspector a new one in private."

The girl bolted for the door, murmuring some semblance of a polite greeting to us as she fled.

"What's wrong with the redfallow theory?" Emerald asked as he settled in his usual chair.

Finch shoved the paper across the desk toward him. "See for yourself. I brought everything to the Alchemist's Guild, just to make sure nobody would bungle the job, and do you know what was in that samovar?"

Emerald looked up from the report without moving his head. "Not redfallow, I take it?"

"No!" Finch slapped her paw down on the desk. "Not a leaf of it! The chemist made quite a production of the fact that it was a tisane, not proper tea, whatever *that* means. But no, it shouldn't have been poisonous. They took samples from the cups, too, looking for whatever oil that physician was on about, but there was nothing out of the ordinary."

"But the young woman *was* poisoned." Emerald dropped the report between them again. "And surely the physician would know what poisoned her, since she was able to administer an antidote in time."

Finch threw herself back into her chair, arms crossed, sulking like a petulant child. It would have been rather endearing, if she didn't have *quite* so many teeth. "I'm sure I don't know. Perhaps this case is entirely unrelated to Faldwell... although we've questioned the staff, and not one of them seems to know a gods-cursed thing..."

"And if we're going to question the staff at the House of Thorns, we'll need to know what to ask," Emerald mused. "And since the tea wasn't the problem... Hm."

"Hm," Finch agreed.

The two of them sat back, gazing up at the ceiling with nearly identical frowns, while I watched from my usual spot in the corner.

[Faldwell,] Emerald thought. *[A textile merchant, found dead in his room. A member of the old court, poisoned at a party. Nothing obviously in common, not even the circumstances, except the manner of poisoning itself...]*

I waited for some stroke of brilliance to pull him bolt-upright in his chair, but nothing did. He sat there, rubbing his palms across the thighs of his plain trousers. They were the same clothes he always wore, although Yerik had finally bullied him into purchasing several additional pairs.

"*Oh!*" I exclaimed, as the idle thought sent a series of revelations spinning into place. "Oh, I've got it!"

It was the first time I had spoken aloud to Emerald in Finch's office. In the past, I had always remembered to play the part of a blank illusion, a mindless scrap of light awaiting orders. At my sudden outburst, Finch startled so badly that she hissed and dug her claws into the wooden arms of her chair.

Emerald shot me a disapproving sidelong glance. "Sorry," he said. "My subconscious can be... hard to control at times."

"Of course." Finch released the chair, which was now rather mauled. "Does this mean you've worked it out?"

Emerald pursed his lips. *[Might as well tell me. Maybe if you've got a good explanation, we can distract her from your odd behavior.]*

[I think I do. But I need you to ask Finch something first.]

Emerald's eyebrows rose at the question, which he relayed to the commander. "What became of Faldwell's body?"

"It's in the cold room on the lower floors," Finch said "Why?"

"We're going to take a look at it." Emerald got to his feet. "But before we do, we're going to need another pair of those physician's gloves."

I HAD ENCOUNTERED the Aideatic system of cold storage back on Kovin Isle. There, the facility had been little more than a hut in the harbor, kept cold by the enchantment of Arcticians like Svelte.

Kinmore's facilities were somewhat more advanced. Instead of being left in plain wooden boxes with scrawled labels, corpses were placed on what looked like stacked, sterile shelves. They were laid out on slabs that could be removed from the racks, covered with purple and silver silks—an odd use of the Conjury colors, but presumably an indication that they were in the care of the organization for the time being—along with detailed labels that could be cross-referenced with their files.

The human woman sitting at the desk beside the front door was reading a novel, and she didn't look up as we walked in. She was perhaps in her sixties, wearing an elaborately tied scarf over her hair and shoulders which matched the rest of her Conjury uniform.

"I hope you don't have another one for me today, Commander," she said, even as she turned a page.

"We're here to look at Faldwell." Finch strode toward the slab where the dead man in question lay.

Her arm was already outstretched to pull the sheet back when I exclaimed, "*Stop!*"

Finch froze.

Having already spoken in front of the Arctician on duty, I reasoned I might as well keep going; we had a reputation to maintain, after all. I hurried over to Finch with my hands behind my back. "Don't touch him. If our theory is correct, you won't want to risk putting your hands on him." I tipped my head toward Emerald, subtly enough that the Arctician would be unlikely to notice, but in the hopes that Finch would take my meaning. Or take *Emerald's* meaning, since she assumed he controlled me.

Finch narrowed her eyes. "And what exactly *is* your theory?"

[Yes, Crimson,] Emerald thought irritably, **[I'd like to know as well.]**

Standing there in silence while I explained my theory to Emerald would look just as odd as if I spoke aloud, so I fell into the character that Emerald had in mind when he created me, the one person that he'd wished he could be in public: the showman.

I swept over to the corpse and waved my hand above the blanket covering his body. "Yesterday, the physician said that redfallow was poisonous if ingested... *or if it touched the skin.* According to the Alchemist's report, nothing that Rubigold Stonewall consumed was poisoned. And yet she was poisoned nonetheless."

Finch crossed her arms and tapped one booted foot on the floor. She was watching me with the same blatant irritation she had shown Emerald the other day, which I took to be a good sign. If she believed that we were, in essence, one and the same, she might simply have accepted that I was an extension of Emerald's personality. "Get to the point."

I turned to the Arctician. She still held the novel in place, but she hadn't turned another page. No doubt she was listening in. "Do the Alchemists ever test remains as well as objects? Do you know who would have handled him when he was sent here, or since he arrived?"

She set her novel aside. "I know who brought him in. As for the rest, we've been waiting for a priestess of Lemda to come and bless him before we touch him. There's an *order* to things, otherwise we'll get ghosts, and then the paperwork *triples.*"

I was tempted to ask about the frequency of hauntings she'd encountered, but it was not the time. "Could you please send for whoever handled him before?"

"I'm not your errand-girl," the woman retorted, but she got up anyway, and left us alone in the quiet, chilly chamber. At least this time I'd remembered to make it look like I was breathing. As soon as the Arctician left, I stopped pretending and resumed my usual blank, poppet-like expression.

Finch eyed me for a moment. "Where are you going with all this?"

Emerald took a step forward, but Finch waved him off.

"Let's give your *subconscious* a chance to explain," she said drily.

Emerald squeezed his eyes shut and rubbed his forehead. *[Well, now you've done it, Crim. She's noticed something's off. I hope you have a plan for explaining this away, because if she's worked out what you are, there will be a dozen hells to pay.]*

I wasn't so sure. Finch wasn't the only one with suspicions, and if she did ever try to threaten us, I had the beginnings of a countermeasure tucked away in my back pocket, so to speak.

In the meantime, we only had a few hours before Basco's impromptu party, and I had a theory to prove. "Are you aware of the rumors surrounding Faldwell?" I asked.

Finch tilted her head. "Around his death?"

"Around his treatment of people who he deemed beneath him."

"Ah." Finch grimaced. "I wasn't before, but after talking to his staff, it seems that there were a lot of people with... motives."

"When we discussed his death before, we thought he must have locked himself in his room *after* falling ill. But what if we were wrong? What if he was poisoned after he entered, by something that was waiting for him inside?" *[Get over here, Em, and lift the corner of that sheet. Carefully.]*

[I'm not your errand boy, either.] Emerald strode over and lifted the sheet by its corner, revealing the dead man. He looked just as he had before, although his swollen face was turned away from us. I was glad of that. After seeing Rubi suffer so, I didn't want to imagine that it was her, lying here in the cold, waiting for answers that might bring her some measure of justice but would never bring her back to life.

"Do you see anything noteworthy?" I asked.

Finch peered at the corpse. "Nothing's different, not that I can tell."

"Look at what he's wearing," I said. "The robe is new. It looks like the first time he's worn it."

[Your obsession with clothes is astounding,] Emerald remarked.

[I know that you don't care about fashion, but in this case, it has allowed you to overlook a possible means of murder.] "The physician said that redfallow's oils can linger in fibers, and they will remain potent even after the leaf itself is no longer present. Faldwell worked in textiles. He wouldn't think twice about putting on a new dressing gown. And if the article itself was poisoned..."

"Then whoever did it wouldn't have to be in the room with him," Finch finished. "And none of his staff would be any the wiser."

Emerald nodded to Finch, as if the whole thing had been his idea from start to finish. "Do you see? Faldwell was poisoned by his own goods, the very clothes for which others suffered so terribly to make. A bit of poetic justice, don't you think?"

"And Rubi said that her dress was new," I added. "She ordered it for the party, so it was the first time she wore it. I remember her saying so."

"Gods." Finch stepped back from the corpse, and Emerald released the sheet. "I wouldn't have thought of that."

[Nor would I,] Emerald admitted grudgingly. *[At least, not until someone else was stricken down. I'd have needed more of a pattern.]*

[Good thing you have me, then.] I winked at him with the eye Finch couldn't see.

The cold-room door opened, and the Arctician returned with a pair of Conjury agents. "There you are," she said, scooping up her book again.

"Is there a problem, Commander?" one of the agents asked.

"Not with your performance," she assured them. "But the investigators have questions."

"May I see your palms, please?" I asked.

The two men presented their palms. One of the agents looked perfectly ordinary, while the other's were swollen and red.

"Had to scrub my hands three times to make the tingling stop," said the one with the swollen hands. "Don't know what happened. Haven't gotten a rash like that before. Figured it must be something I ate."

"Do you remember how you moved him onto the slab?" I asked.

The man with unblemished hands nodded. "I took the ankles."

"And I lifted his shoulders."

[There you have it,] I told Emerald. *[The one who came in contact with his dressing gown got a bit of the poison on him, but not enough to make him sick, and he washed it off in time to avoid anything worse.]*

Emerald reached up to scratch his jaw, paused, and lowered his hand again. *[I should probably do the same, just in case. Good work so far, Crimson, but...]*

He asked his question in silence at the same time that Finch uttered it aloud. "But why would someone with a grudge against Faldwell act against the House of Thorns as well?"

"I don't know," I admitted. "But I have an idea of who we might ask."

CHAPTER SEVEN

Vasilika's door was unlocked when Emerald and I arrived. Finch had promised to send for a chemist to test Faldwell's clothes, and Aaliy had been dispatched—with suitable gloves—to retrieve Rubi's gown, but I was quite sure of my theory.

I was less confident that the incident Yerik and I had stumbled into the night he ordered Svelte's party dress was related to our case, but I could not quite dismiss my suspicions. If nothing else, Vasilika might at least be able to introduce us to the city's other tailors and seamstresses.

We found her kneeling by one of the forms, measuring the cut of a new skirt. "Oh!" she exclaimed, her face lighting up with a brilliant smile when she recognized me. "How was the party? Did Svelte settle in?"

Emerald ran his tongue over the stump of one tusk. *[This conversation's on you, Crim. Since you won't tell me what you're thinking.]*

[As if. You just don't care about clothes—you think it's all frivolity and pride. I think you're just jealous that I finally solved a

puzzle before you did.] I approached Vasilika and lowered my voice, though we appeared to be alone. "The dress was lovely. The party, not so much. I have to ask you something, and I'm afraid it will be a personal question, but I hope you will trust I have good reasons for asking."

Vasilika draped her measuring string over her shoulders and clasped her hands in front of her. Even when she was serious, there was a smile in her eyes. Beyond her talent with a needle, I suspected that some of her success came from being good with people. As disillusioned as I had grown with Kinmore in general, I was increasingly fond of this little hamlet beyond the wall.

"Any friend of Yerik's is a friend of mine," she said. "How can I help you?"

"Have you ever had dealings with a merchant named Faldwell?"

As my question, the brightness in her eyes winked out. Her shoulders curled to her ears. "Of course I did," she said dully.

"Unpleasant dealings?" I pressed.

Vasilika passed her hand in front of her eyes. "I assume you're investigating his death."

Emerald and I nodded. She might not have answered the question outright, but I had my reply all the same.

"A moment, please." Vasilika slipped past us toward the front door, which she locked behind us. "I would prefer that what I'm about to say stay between the three of us, if possible. I understand that you have a job to do, but this is—" She trailed off, staring out the window at the warm, bright world outside.

After a long moment, she withdrew to the room beyond the curtain and returned with a bottle. "Would either of you like a drink?"

I shook my head. Emerald waited a beat before saying, "No." It was not quite the truth, as I could tell that he wanted one very much, and perhaps always would.

"Then I hope you'll forgive me a moment of weakness." She

poured herself a generous glass of the pale amber liquid and returned to perch on the stool near her current project, facing us. "So. Faldwell. You're heard the rumors?"

"I have," Emerald said darkly. "But I'd like to hear it properly. From someone who was there."

Vasilika took a sip of her drink. "At the start, there weren't many of us, and the conditions were decent. But as his business grew, he brought on more workers. Started hiring younger, too, mostly from the Hives. People who wouldn't complain when he lowered their wages."

"Or did anything else," Emerald murmured.

Vasilika took another, deeper draught from her cup. "Exactly. I left before the worst of it, but I know some who stayed, or were hired on later. When I heard he was dead..." She swirled the last measure of her liquor, staring into its depths. "I won't say I was happy. Thinking about that man never will never bring me a scrap of joy. But the *relief.*" She shivered. "I suppose I shouldn't be saying this to Conjury investigators, but knowing that I'll never encounter him again, that I'll never look up from my work to find him standing at my door, is a gift. Driaweep can have him." She tossed back the last of her drink. It must have been potent, because her eyes watered as she swallowed.

"I'm sorry," I murmured.

Vasilika wiped the back of her hand across her mouth. "Why? It's not an uncommon story. Kinmore is built on tales like mine. Besides, I got out." Her expression softened, and her earlier brightness returned. She spread her hands out to encompass the shop. "I'm happy now. I have my own shop, and I answer to no one. I'm lucky. And Faldwell got his, in the end. Is it true that he was murdered?"

I opened my mouth to respond, but Emerald got there first. "Where did you hear that?" A good question, since that information was hardly public. Until today, the Conjury had not known the cause of his death.

Vasilika's hands tightened on her skirts. "From a stranger. I had the most unusual encounter the other night. Someone came in, asking about my relationship to Faldwell. She seemed to know who I was, and she kept asking if I did it, or if I knew who did."

I rocked back on my heels. "Your difficult customer."

The seamstress frowned at me. "What? *Oh!* That's right, you were here when she left. I never saw her face, she was awfully careful about that, but she said... that is, she knew that I had cause to detest Faldwell. She said she'd ruin me if I was lying to her, but I had no idea what she was talking about. I didn't hear the news of his death until afterward, but whoever she was, she must have known that someone killed him."

[Do we believe that?] Emerald asked. **[Do you?]**

I might have been more skeptical if I hadn't been there to witness the end of the exchange myself. It was possible that Vasilika was lying, but two things tipped the balance in her favor.

The first was her honesty. She had been forthcoming with us when asked, and I was convinced that her distress was real. If she was hiding something, why would she admit her history with the dead man? She had no reason to think that we knew *how* he died, since only a handful of us were aware of the means of his death.

The other point relied on my judge of character, and in this I felt quite confident.

"Are you aware that there was another attempted murder in the city yesterday?" I asked.

Vasilika's eyes widened. "A *related* attempt?"

"Indeed. At the party Svelte and I attended."

She cried out and pressed her hands to her mouth. "Oh, *no*. Is she all right?"

Emerald stiffened. **[How does she know about Rubigold?]**

[I doubt she does. Or rather, I doubt she cares about Rubi and the court.]

Sure enough, Vasilika wiped a fresh spill of tears from her eyes.

"That poor girl, after everything she's been through. Please tell me she wasn't hurt."

"Svelte's safe at home," I assured her.

"Oh, Celestriona's blessings." Vasilika produced a kerchief from her pocket and blew her nose. "I'm glad to hear it. But someone else was—?"

"Not beyond saving. Are you familiar with the House of Thorns?"

The seamstress thought about it for a moment. "I know the name, of course, but nothing else."

"They've never commissioned your work?"

Vasilika emitted a watery laugh. "Goodness, no. I've never made anything for the likes of them. Many of the ancient houses have their own tailors on staff, and the cost of materials alone is exorbitant."

I studied her current work in progress. "You have the skill, I think."

"But not the inclination." Vasilika refolded her kerchief and tucked it away. "I have no desire to be under a rich man's thumb ever again. I'd rather live modestly and freely than feel I had no recourse but to bend to my employer's will."

I understood what she was saying about Faldwell, although her words struck another chord as well. I, too, longed to live simply and freely. I was happy enough in Emerald's presence, but I would never be able to choose another life. I was glad, for her sake, that she could.

[I believe her,] I told Emerald. *[She was worried about Svelte yesterday. I don't know her well, but if she was planning to do something terrible to Rubi, I don't think she would have sent Svelte off to bear witness to such a thing. Nor, for that matter, would she have been happy to see me go to the scene of her impending crime.]*

[I agree.] Emerald bowed to Vasilika and thanked her for her time, while adding to me, *[Perhaps we'll learn the truth tonight at Basco's party.]*

. . .

On our way back to the Lute and Goose, Emerald and I debated the identity of Vasilika's mystery visitor.

"Do you think she was trying to stop whoever killed Faldwell?" I asked.

"Or to blackmail the person into helping her poison Rubi," Emerald suggested.

"Ooh, *that's* interesting. Do you think it was Isabella? But how could she have gotten away with it? I mean, she could hardly have a dress delivered to Rubi's house with no explanation and expect her to wear it."

"Maybe she wanted to know *how* it was done, and planned to pay off someone in Rubi's household to apply the redfallow oils to her dress. Although I'm inclined to think that whoever did this was eager to avoid incrimination. There's a reason people consider poison a woman's weapon. Violent attacks give the aggressor power over their victim. Poison, however, is about achieving *results,* not dominance."

I wrinkled my nose. "That's a grim assessment. Besides, Lady Fenguard had no trouble getting her hands dirty."

"Yes, well." Emerald chuckled. "If this line of work has taught me anything, it's that people will do whatever they believe necessary. And like Basco said, the court runs on reputation."

"So the courtiers will do whatever they deem necessary in order to protect their standing," I finished. "I see the logic. At any rate, if we find Rubi's attacker tonight, she'll likely lead us to Faldwell's killer."

We reached the walkway of the Lute and Goose at the same moment that the elven courier emerged from the door.

"There you are," he sniffed. "Had to leave your things with your *assistant.* At least I didn't run into that gods-cursed bird again." He strode past us to where his mount—one of the lovely little deer that had pulled Rubi's carriage—waited for him.

"Thank you!" I called, as much to draw attention to his perennial bad manners as to express my genuine gratitude.

The inn was packed with guests, so Emerald and I made our way upstairs to take shelter until the dinner rush ended. "Dunno what I'm going to wear to this blasted masquerade," Emerald griped. A large package and a hastily scribbled note from Finch waited inside the door to our room; Svelte must have tossed them there for safe-keeping. "Good news. The chemist confirmed your theory. Good thing, too. Can you *imagine* if Rubigold had accidentally worn that dress again?"

I shook my head.

[Oh, yes you can,] Innocent hissed. *[You can imagine it, because it would be just like before... twitch and foam and blood and gasping. There are worse ways to die, you know. It could end in fire, like it did for Reticent when your master and his little friends killed him.]*

As Emerald tore into the package, I squeezed my eyes shut. *[Shut up. You're not being the least bit helpful, so bite your tongue.]*

[Unhelpful? Like you, you mean, when you watched Rubi topple and writhe? When you let Svelte help her, because you couldn't do anything? Are you calling me *useless, Crimson Smoke?]*

"Oh, *hells.*" The sound of a package hitting the floor made me open my eyes. Emerald stared down at the parcel in horror, holding his hands up as if he'd burned them. "Dammit, guess that answers that question. *Shite.*" He turned and barreled out of the room, hands held aloft as he charged into the shared washroom across the hall.

The package lay, half open, with a froth of lace and brocade spilling free of its wrapping. There had been a note among the packing paper, but it had slipped free when Emerald tossed the whole box aside. It lay, face up, on the floor of our room, revealing the careful, blocky writing on its face.

CRIMSON SMOKE—

• • •

I WASN'T *sure you'd have anything appropriate to wear tonight, so consider this a gift. I look forward to seeing you again.*

WITH GREAT ANTICIPATION,
   Basco of Danilas Freehold

CHAPTER EIGHT

Commander Finch was waiting for me outside the doors of Basco's family manor, although I didn't recognize her at first.

"Crimson," she hissed as I approached.

Her appearance was startling, although I wasn't sure what I'd expected her to be wearing. I'd never seen her in anything other than her Conjury uniform. If I'd given the matter a moment's thought, I might have imagined her in a dress of some kind, not long robes stippled with hand-stitched flowers and an enormous plaster headdress.

"Goodness." I squinted at her. "What are you supposed to be?"

"The Green Woman," Finch snapped. "It's all I had on hand."

"You had this, what, lying around in case of emergency?" I eyed the unsubtle costume. It was, admittedly, beautiful. Although it struck me as the sort of thing one might wear to a festival in which a sacrificial victim would be strapped down to an altar and bled dry in the name of some obscure god.

Although maybe such things were less common than personal experience had led me to believe. My experience in the Cronemire made it hard to tell.

"I could hardly dress like you," Finch retorted, indicating the low-cut gown that Basco had sent to our room earlier in the day.

It was, of course, not the dress he'd mailed. When I rearranged myself before leaving the Lute and Goose, I had copied the dress right down to the details of the delicate beadwork. In the darkness, the dress was black, but when it caught the light, it glittered in a dozen colors: a rainbow trapped in a shadow. Sort of the opposite of my situation with Innocent, come to think of it.

I looked down at myself. The low front and plunging back of the dress left a great deal of illusory freckled skin on display, despite the long matching gloves. If Finch had worn a dress like that, her dappled pelt would have been exposed instead. Either way, I couldn't imagine her dressing as I had. The regalia of some unfamiliar goddess of the wilderness suited her nature far better than high fashion.

"You're here alone?" she asked.

I shook my head and pointed to the shrubbery, just outside the circle of lamplight, answering as though I were under Emerald's control rather than my own. "I'm over there."

Emerald shifted between the shrubs. Until that moment, he had blended in perfectly.

Finch nodded. "So you are. I take it you'll be staying out here and sending Crimson in alone?"

"I'll be too recognizable," I said. "Crimson stands a much better chance of coaxing the truth out of people." *[Crimson also hates talking about themself in the third person.]*

[Crimson can get over it,] Emerald shot back.

"I should tell you..." I lowered my voice and inclined my head toward Finch's headdress. "Someone tried to poison me. Or rather, they tried to poison Crimson. Someone sent a dress to the inn tonight, with a note... signed by Basco."

Finch sucked her teeth. "Cogs of Odologys, that's sinister. You think it really was from him?"

"I think if he sent a dress to Rubi, she'd have worn it willingly, and we didn't get the chance to ask her." I had been surprised by how quickly Basco thought to organize a party. Now, I found it suspicious.

Emerald had decided to do a bit of his own snooping, but he'd also decided not to tell Finch about his plans to break and enter, tossing around the phrase *plausible deniability*. At his urging, I told Finch, "If you need help, Crimson will let me know. Of course, they can't be poisoned, but they can let me know if you need help."

"They?" Finch asked me. No—of course she wasn't asking *me*. She was asking Em. I was just a poppet. I didn't have preferences, or an identity that deserved respect. I was a prop. A convenience.

"She, for tonight," I said. It was the closest I could bring myself to tossing away the language that had fit so comfortably, even if Harmony was the one to bestow it. "I switch this little illusion so freely that I sometimes find it easier to think of Crimson in neutral terms. For tonight, she is Simone of the Road. Speaking of which, perhaps you'd better not let on that I work for the Conjury."

"People will still recognize... them. Crimson, I mean." Finch tipped her chin toward me.

A lace mask had been included in the parcel, but my hair would have given me away regardless. I had debated hiding it under a scarf like the one the Arctician wore, or under a hat of some kind. In the end, I decided against it. "Someone at this party is a poisoner. If they recognize me, there's a possibility they will give themselves away by observing me."

"You, Emerald? Or you, Crimson?"

I couldn't picture the Leonhite's exact expression beneath her mask, calculated and observant. "Maybe both. Although I doubt they'd have sent a dress if they knew about the lightweaving. It's certainly not made in a jotunn's size." I nodded to the front door, eager to escape the confusion of having to speak about myself as if I were not present. "Shall we go in?"

Finch bowed and let me lead the way to the two liveried bodyguards who flanked the doors. My name was enough to gain us entrance. The doors of the manor were flung wide, and Finch and I were led through to a reception hall, which the whole of the Lute and Goose could have easily fit inside.

I suppose I should have gotten over the opulence of Kinmore's great houses, having been inside so many. The building Finch and I entered was just as grandiose as the Bracefallow manor, but more tasteful, and far less aggressively on-theme than the House of Thorns.

"Basco's grandmama has excellent taste," I whispered to Finch.

"Basco's grandmama has too much damn money," Finch whispered back.

Just as Basco had promised, the party was exclusive by Kinmore standards. Sixty or so people were in attendance, engaged in games and gossip, or dancing to the music played by a pair of bards in the corner of the hall. I was somewhat disappointed to note that neither of the players wore green. I knew a few of the people by sight, if not by name. Very few of them were as committed to the concept of a masquerade as Finch was, the vast majority opting for half-masks like the one I wore. The only two people I knew by name, though, were Basco and Isabella, who were engaged in what I supposed passed for genteel dancing in Kinmore. There seemed to be a lot of predetermined steps involved, and very little touching. Or smiling. Or enjoyment of any kind, if their facial expressions were anything to judge by.

"Do you recognize anyone?" I asked Finch.

Beneath her plaster headdress, Finch sniffed. "Oh, believe me, I'm familiar with this lot. You see that couple dressed as foxes? The shorter one tried to bully me into shutting down the main thorough-fare for their wedding a few years ago. As if I could put the whole city on pause for a day, just for her convenience! We nearly came to blows. Fortunately, her wife is much more sensible."

I peered at the couple with interest. My only close female friend was Svelte, and despite our brief stay in the Sisterhood of the Crone, I found the personal lives of women to be something of a mystery.

"And those four, in blue?" Finch went on. "The parents moved here from Ambervin—they're just as rich as anybody else, but apparently it's the wrong *kind* of money." I could practically hear Finch rolling her eyes beneath her mask. "They're doing their best to marry one of their girls into a title."

"I didn't realize that there was a *wrong kind* of money," I murmured, forgetting for a moment that I was supposed to be Emerald, and that Emerald would likely know enough about the hierarchy of the city that he wouldn't be surprised.

"Oh, believe me," Finch rumbled, "there's a wrong way to do everything in this city. Come on, I'm getting a drink, and then we can keep gossiping about all these stuck-up bastards and their petty squabbles."

I followed her toward the spread. Something about her words stuck with me. *[Emerald,]* I asked, *[what do you know about marriages in the court?]*

[Not now.] There was a strain in my friend's reply. *[I'm halfway up to the damned window, and this is* not *an easy climb.]*

For once, breaking and entering wasn't my job. It would have been easier for me, of course, but I had another role to play tonight.

I watched the faces of the crowd, half hidden by their masks. Most people ignored me, although a few of them seemed taken with Finch's Green Woman costume. Only one person tracked my movements across the room, a woman in a striking purple gown. Her face was fully obscured by a full mask, capped with dyed feathers. I was about to ask Finch if she knew the woman's name when Basco hurried over.

"Crimson!" he said, keeping his voice low. "You're here. And is that... Finch?" He pointed to the disguised Leonhite, who was sneaking finger sandwiches under the lip of her mask at that very moment.

"It is." I forced a smile. "She's the Green Woman, apparently."

He looked me over. "And what are you supposed to be?"

[Dead,] Innocent sang. *[You're supposed to be dead, just like Rubi was supposed to die. You could let me out. Return the favor. I won't be so subtle as poison, and I will be ever so tidy. Not a witness left...]*

"A crow," I blurted. "I'm a crow."

"Don't you think it's a bit *drab* for a party?" Isabella sidled up to us and raked her eyes over me. Her dress was pale gold, while Basco's silk outfit shimmered iridescent silver in the light of the wall sconces. "A common crow? What an ill omen."

"And your costumes are good luck?" I asked.

"Isn't it obvious?" Isabella's smile was mirthless. "I'm Ianna of the Oases. He's Regis of..."

"Glacial Walk." Emerald had told me the story once, on our way out of Dyrne. He'd been feeling sentimental at the time. I knew that Basco was disinterested in their union, and Isabella's tone suggested that the feeling was mutual. "Two lovers, destined to spend their lives apart." I lifted my eyebrow. "You've dressed like that for good luck?"

"We've dressed like two most famous lovers who ever lived," Isabella corrected. "Basco, dear, will you fetch me another drink?"

Behind her back, Basco made a not-so-subtle gesture that suggested I should use the opportunity to interrogate his fiancée before hurrying away.

[Basco asked what my dress was supposed to be, Em.] I offered Isabella a pained smile. *[What if **he** wasn't the one who sent it?]*

[Maybe was trying to put you off the scent.] Even through our link, Emerald sounded distracted.

[He sent a letter with his name on it, and then tried to throw me off the scent? How does that make any sense?]

[Sorry, give me a moment. I'm in the family's private quarters, and I nearly fell to my death twice getting up here. Let me look around before a maid or someone walks in.]

The silence with Isabella was growing tense. I needed to say something, or I would lose the chance to speak to her. "So…" I began.

"Stay away from him." Isabella's dispassionate expression soured, and her voice dropped an octave. "I see what you're doing, trying to imply that he doesn't belong with me. And I *know* you're friends with that simpering clod from the House of Thorns. But Basco was promised to *me*." She produced a fan seemingly from thin air and waved it alongside her face. The angle of her wrist suggested that she was not overheated, but rather, concerned that someone in the gathering would be able to read her lips or overhear us if they passed too close. "If he breaks off this engagement and turns to *her* instead, I will die of shame."

I, too, produced a fan, this time from *literal* thin air, and mirrored her pose. "Am I to understand that you'd do anything to avoid losing to Rubi?" I asked.

Isabella sneered. "As if I could *ever* lose to her. She tried to throw some hideous little tea party just yesterday, and nobody went. But look." She twirled her fan to indicate the room. "They're here. Because Basco and I matter. Because people listen to me. The House of Thorns has long since lost favor with the court. Basco is simple, but he's not that stupid. Rubi would be a terrible match for him. He might as well marry a krub."

I had met several krubs, and liked all of them more than I liked her. "I rather think Rubi the better catch."

Isabella scoffed. "She's a disgrace, and she knows it. Why else wouldn't she be here tonight?"

"I expect she's still recovering from being poisoned," I snapped.

Isabella stopped fanning herself. "What?"

"She was poisoned," I repeated, but with less vitriol this time. "At her party."

"Poisoned?" Isabella shook her head slowly. "No. Her party was canceled. I convinced all my friends not to go. Gods, is she so pathetic that she threw a party for *herself*?" She laughed and shook her head. "That's the most tragic thing I've ever heard. I'd poison myself, too, if I was her. She should have done us all a favor and done it properly."

I gawked at her. "You're a terrible person. Do you like *anyone*? Do you even like Basco?"

"I like his family's reputation," Isabella informed me. "And his grandmother likes my money. Opposites attract, didn't you know? Once we're married, we'll be the only family in Kinmore with trading access to Danilas Freehold... and I'll be able to save this musty old house from being sold away piecemeal." She looked around the hall with open disdain. "So, like I said, you can stop advocating for your little friend. Even if Basco wanted to break off our engagement, his family would never let him."

If I'd had blood, it would have drained from my face. Instead, I'm sure I didn't remember to blink for the next ten seconds at least. Basco hadn't told us about his family's change of fortune. Perhaps he hadn't wanted to reveal his troubles.

Or perhaps he didn't know about them in the first place.

[Oh, dear, Emerald, I think I've worked it out,] I thought.

[I think I have, too,] Emerald said. *[I've found—]*

But what Emerald had found, he didn't say. Instead, a silence followed. Not a distracted silence, but a terrible one, sudden and deep and profound. I had never experienced a silence like that.

"Finch!" I cried, lurching away from Isabella. "Come with me!"

To her credit, Finch responded immediately. She ripped the Green Woman mask off her head and tossed it aside as I bolted from the room. Isabella screamed, guests scattered, and Basco called my name, but I would not be slowed. I forgot to move my feet, forgot to pretend that I was short of breath or to arrange droplets of sweat on my forehead. I *flew*.

I was not the only one. I'd never been in a fight with Finch at my side, and so I had never seen how swiftly she could run. She kept pace with me as I navigated the warren of the mansion's many hallways, following an internal compass that pointed, always, to the source of my illusion. The source of my existence. The beating heart of the man who brought me into being, my truest and dearest friend.

I should have vanished, I thought. *If she hurt him, I should have vanished. But if she killed him…*

It was too terrible to contemplate. I had wanted freedom, but not at this cost. Emerald's safety was a price, perhaps the *only* price, I would not pay.

At the end of a long hall on the mansion's second floor, a door stood ajar. Seeing our destination, Finch lunged ahead in a great burst of speed and burst through. I was right behind her.

It took me only a second to take in the tableau before us: Emerald, lying sprawled beside a desk, with papers and ledgers scattered in drifts like fresh snowfall; the candlestick lying just beside him; and the woman in purple bent over a rolltop desk with a vial clutched in her gloved hands.

Finch was on her in an instant, yeowling so terribly that I could say, from firsthand experience, it would have put an Outsider to shame. She collided with the woman at a full tilt and knocked her off her feet into the bookshelf behind her. Tomes rained down on them, obscuring their tussle. The woman in purple fought back with admirable recklessness, but she was no match for a fully trained Leonhite commander, even an unarmed one. To my relief, I saw that the little bottle had fallen harmlessly to the plush carpet alongside the desk. I had no doubt that the Alchemist's Guild would find redfallow oil inside.

I was more concerned about Emerald. I rushed to him and laid my hand across his back, hoping to feel some sort of spark. Even when my fingers passed through his skin, I couldn't feel anything from his mind, but at least he was breathing.

Alive, but unconscious.

So how was I still there?

Basco, flanked by a handful of guests—mostly men—arrived at last. The young man was breathing hard, but he still managed to choke out a cry of shock.

Finch had wrestled Emerald's attacker to the ground. In the scuffle, the purple mask with its crown of feathers had been knocked aside. I could only see a sliver of the woman's face, since Finch was sitting astride her back and grinding her face into the carpet to subdue her.

"Gods and Outsiders," Basco panted. "Grandmama? What's going on?"

CHAPTER NINE

"I'm sorry I can't be more entertaining." Rubi struggled to sit upright against her wall of pillows. "I would offer you some tea, but we wouldn't want a repeat of last time."

"You don't need to entertain us," Svelte assured her. She rearranged the skirt of her party dress and plucked absentmindedly at the beading. "We just wanted to be sure you were all right. I needed to see for myself."

"You're a sweetheart, Sveta." Rubi's cheeks were sallow, and rather narrower than before, but her smile was still radiant. "I'm lucky to have you as a friend."

Svelte blushed with pleasure. "Are we friends, miss?"

"Of course." Rubi tilted her face toward me. Her blond curls spilled across the pillowcase, bright and sleek in the sunlight that filtered through the casement. It had rained for two miserable days, but that morning had dawned bright and clear, as if her well-being and the weather were intertwined. "Any cousin of Crimson is a friend of mine."

"I'm sorry about Basco," I told her. "Has he been by to see you?"

Rubi sighed. "No. He left for Danilas Freehold this morning. He

292

wrote a terribly long and apologetic note, but he felt so guilty about what his grandmother had done, I don't think he could stand to be in the same room as me."

I nodded my sympathy, but Svelte huffed. "He's a rubbish sweetheart, then."

Rubi laughed. "We were never sweethearts. Only friends. Which is what makes the situation so absurd... getting rid of me would hardly have made a difference in his engagement."

"I'm glad he's not marrying Isabella, at least," I mumbled. I hadn't told anyone the terrible things she'd said about Rubi, but I wouldn't soon forget them.

"He deserves better." Rubi stared out over the grounds of the House of Thorns, in the direction of the newly empty manor house where her friend had spent the summer.

"You *are* better," Svelte insisted. "You're more than good enough for him!"

"That's kind of you to say, but we would never have ended up together. He's not the sort of person I'd be interested in courting." It was Rubi's turn to blush, and she took great care not to keep her eyes averted from the present company. "I'll miss him. I don't have many friends in Kinmore."

"You've got two," Svelte announced. "And you could have more. Come visit us at the inn sometime. Or we'll come to you. Yerik would ask a million questions about all these old paintings."

Rubi tilted her head. "Who's Yerik?"

Svelte faltered. "My... my papa. He loves painting."

"Oh, is he your brother?" Rubi asked me. "Or your sister's husband?"

I had no idea what to say to that. After opening and closing my mouth a few times, I finally answered, "Neither. Our family is... complicated. We're a rather mismatched set."

"I'd love to meet them all." There was a softness, a rawness in her expression that made me realize Rubi had never mentioned her family, other than when announcing her title. No parents had come running when she collapsed, no sister had waited at her bedside, no brother had burst forth to defend her. She hadn't even had friends who cared enough to attend her party, aside from the two of us.

Svelte realized this at the same time I did, and she lifted her chin. "Write to me when you're feeling better. I'll bully my dirty brothers into dressing like civilized people for once."

Rubi swallowed. "Thank you. Both of you. I owe you my life."

"We'll visit again," I promised. "Whenever you like."

We stayed and chatted a while longer, until Rubi began to drift off. As we took our leave, I wondered about introducing her to Vasilika—not out of some desire to matchmake between them, but because I thought both women could use a friend. It would be nice to make people happy for once, rather than just prowling into the ruins of their lives and picking up whatever pieces remained.

Emerald was sitting in his armchair in the dining room of the Lute and Goose. The physician who treated his injuries had insisted that he remain still and quiet for several days. Emerald had refused to stay properly bedridden, and Yerik had been equally insistent that he remain within the confines of the Lute and Goose for the time being. After a great deal of negotiating, Emerald had agreed to stay put until the portrait was done.

"How is she?" he asked when Svelte and I entered.

"Lonely," Svelte said.

"But much better than I feared," I added.

"Excellent. You just missed Finch's assistant, by the way. She said they've caught the tailor responsible for Faldwell's death. It was someone who used to work in his horrible factory." *[Another story like Vasilika's,]* he added privately, since neither of us had any desire to share what she'd told us in confidence. "Dame Glasshaven blackmailed her into revealing her methods, although how *she* knew that Faldwell had been murdered still isn't clear."

"Glasshaven?" I repeated.

"Basco's grandmother."

"Basco Glasshaven?" I pulled a face. "Gods, that's ghastly."

"I doubt he'll inherit the title now," Emerald said. "By the sounds of it, there's nothing much left to the family name."

I wondered how many of the city's old families were living far beyond their means. Perhaps in another generation or two, the old houses would fold. I also wondered if that might be a good thing.

Svelte went upstairs to change into her work clothes, while I meandered over to where Yerik sat, engrossed in his art. "Oh, look at that!" I exclaimed. "You've finished Emerald."

"You have?" Emerald leapt to his feet. "Aster's blessings, I'm finally free!"

"I'm not done," Yerik protested.

"He's painting the background now," I noted.

"Which means I no longer have to sit for it, eh?"

Yerik jabbed his paintbrush at me and hissed, "Traitor."

"Come on, Crimson. We've got an errand to run." Emerald sprinted toward the door before anyone could catch him.

"What I still don't understand," I mused, "is why she thought she could get away with poisoning me and leaving you unharmed. Why send a dress for me and nothing for you?"

"Oh, that's easy." Emerald turned off the main thoroughfare, toward Bracefallow Manor. "She thought you were the only threat. Her intellectual equal. If anyone could work out what she was doing, it would be you, not your grunting, puerile henchman. She must have panicked when she saw me going through her ledgers. There are plenty of people who don't think jotunn capable of learning to read."

I pretended to gag. "Between her and Isabella, I suspect Basco will be better off in Danilas Freehold *without* a title."

"Undoubtedly." Emerald looked up at the manor and sighed. **[All right, when we talk to the Bracefallows, here's what we'll say:**

we've been busy with another murder case, we were waiting to hear back from a contact in New Wrighton about a ship's manifest, and we suspect Gorlyn is off at sea somewhere. That he stowed away on one of the Trader's Guild vessels.]

[How long do you plan to drag this out? Now that, um, Silverskin is safely settled.]

[We'll come up with something soon. I still want to figure out who was smuggling that dragon egg.] We mounted the steps to the front door, and Emerald paused to straighten the fall of his shirt before rapping his knuckles sharply against the door three times.

We waited a full minute before one of the footmen opened the door. "I beg your pardon, Inspector," he said to me, ignoring Emerald entirely. "Forgive the delay. The house is turned on its head today."

He ushered us through to the sitting room, where we were waylaid at the door by Lemuel Bracefallow.

"Don't know what the Conjury pays you for," he sneered. "We might as well not have contacted you in the first place, for all the help you were."

"Were?" I repeated. Apprehension slithered through me. We had Gorlyn's remains. Serkadis had told us he was safe. What could we have missed? "I'm not sure what you mean."

"Who is it, Lemmy?" Lady Bracefallow called from within the salon.

Lemuel stepped aside as his mother approached. Every time I had seen her, she had been dressed in black, prone to weeping, and desperate to be reunited with her youngest son. For once, she was smiling. She'd exchanged her mourning clothes for a lavender day dress. She was as happy as I'd ever seen her.

"Oh, you've timed this visit perfectly!" she exclaimed. "I'm so happy to say that we no longer have need of your services."

"You don't?" I was fully aware that I was not even living up to babblebird standards when it came to repeating what I'd been told, but I was at a loss.

Emerald choked as he peered into the room. *[Crimson. Look.]*

Lady Bracefallow held out one arm. I'm sure she said something, but I had no idea what it might have been, because in that moment, I was knocked nearly as senseless by the sight before me as Emerald had been by Dame Glasshaven's well-aimed candlestick. Seated in one of the many chairs, between his brothers Parris and Murdock, was Gorlyn Bracefallow.

In the flesh and smiling and very much alive.

[Oh,] Innocent whispered. *[Look at this. Things are finally getting interesting.]*

THE TALE OF THE INNOCENT VICTIM

CHAPTER ONE

Commander Finch looked up from her paperwork. "Are you even reading those files I gave you?" she asked.

Emerald, in fact, was not. He sat slack jawed, staring at the wall before him, his eyes slightly unfocused. He had been doing that a lot lately.

Gorlyn Bracefallow was dead. We knew that for a fact. And yet, Gorlyn Bracefallow was alive. We had seen that with our own eyes.

And there had been no way to make enquiries about how such a thing was possible without admitting that we'd tried to cover up his untimely demise.

"Emerald." Finch snapped her fingers in front of my friend's nose. "Emerald Flame. Hello?"

"I'm reading them," Emerald mumbled.

Finch rolled her eyes. "Go home. You've clearly taken one too many blows to the head in the line of duty. Maybe it's a good thing that Mentalist is coming to analyze us."

That, finally, startled Emerald out of his reverie. "Mentalist? What Mentalist?"

"You really *aren't* reading the files." Finch reached over to tug the neglected papers out of my friend's grasp. "Conjury headquarters has taken a particular interest in the health and well-being of this office. Which, for the time being, includes you."

If Emerald hadn't been sitting, he would have fallen over. "*What? Why?*"

Finch puffed out her cheeks as she rearranged the papers into some semblance of order. "The Conjury is concerned that there may be a traitor in our midst. There have been, shall we say, discrepancies." She said it casually, as if this was no cause for concern... never mind that it threatened to turn our world on its head.

Emerald and I could not share a glance in Finch's presence, but a current of deep concern flowed between us, although his had a different flavor from my own. I was concerned about the handful of times—and counting—that Emerald and I had directly defied Conjury directives, never mind how many times we'd done things they'd never thought to make rules about. I very much doubted that there was any law stating, *Conjury agents shall not smuggle accidental murderers through the city gates, especially not when said murderers are dragons.* Likewise, *Conjury agents shall not leave invaluable magical artifacts in the hands of freelance lambkins* was probably a given, even if it had never been set down in ink.

Even worse, a Mentalist might be able to undo Brother Harmony's work. Not only would that bring to light Innocent's existence and Emerald's involvement in Reticent's death, but the revelation could do incalculable damage to my friend's well-being.

[So kill the Mentalist,] Innocent supplied unhelpfully.

"Any idea what they're looking for?" Emerald asked, his voice as deceptively casual as Finch's had been. He plucked at the hem of his shirt, as if plucking a stray thread, although none was visible.

"They're concerned about things being smuggled out of the city. After all, Kinmore abuts the Uthren Vhald, which has so far resisted Conjury influence." Finch kept rearranging the papers again and again. Like Emerald's gesture, it might have passed as inconsequential, except that her movements bordered on the compulsive.

"So Venta Bulgarum's worried that someone is defying orders?" Emerald asked. *Pluck. Pluck. Pluck.*

Finch nodded. "Someone on the inside," she said. The files hissed against one another.

[She's going to threaten him,] Innocent warned. *[She's going to blackmail him, let him take the fall.]*

That gave me pause. *[The fall for what?]* I asked, despite the fact that I did my best to ignore Innocent whenever I could.

My unwelcome passenger hissed. *[And you call yourself an investigator.]*

Emerald plucked. Finch shuffled.

"Oh!" My voice echoed off the walls of the small room, loud enough to make them both jump. "They're looking for *you!*"

Emerald stared at me as if I'd announced to him that I'd only be dressing in yellow for the foreseeable future. Finch recoiled and bared her teeth, flattening her ears back to her skull.

"Sorry." I lowered my voice to a stage whisper. "I'll be quieter. But I've been wondering why you didn't say anything about me, even though you obviously noticed that something was odd. And that's why you helped us get through the gate a few weeks ago. You didn't want to draw the Conjury's attention to *us,* because you're already doing... something? Illegal, I assume?" I frowned at Emerald. "Although I'm not... *oh,* all those manifests they've had you reviewing! You're clearing exports from the city, aren't you? No wonder you didn't want those guards to start questioning manifests with your signature on them!"

A deep, resonant growl was coming from Finch's direction, although it seemed much too big to come from her body. Her pupils had narrowed to slits, and they were fixed on me. Beneath her claws, the arm of her chair groaned.

"Crimson," Emerald said, with more crispness and gentility than usual, "could you please stop making the angry Leonhite think we're blackmailing her? Let me remind you that, if she decides we're a threat, I'm the one who'll be on the receiving end of her ire."

"Oh!" I held up both hands and waved them in front of me in what I hoped was a placating manner. "No, no! Sorry, Commander, it's not like that at all. I just put it together, although in hindsight you've been giving us hints for ages. All that talk about *wildesprigge*, and the way you didn't ask too many questions about the Brotherhood, and... and all that." Perhaps it was best not to list out all the dubious activities we'd engaged in right under the commander's nose.

Said nose twitched a few times as Finch's eyes darted from my face to Emerald's and back. "Your subconscious again?" she growled.

"No." Emerald dragged one hand down the side of his face and rolled his eyes toward the ceiling. "I'm afraid that's all Crim. They're a little slow on the uptake."

This time, it was Finch and I who goggled at *him*.

"You knew?" the commander asked. She sounded a bit strangled, as if her windpipe wasn't quite up to the task of proper speech. "Since when?"

"Since I saw that shipment of baskets you approved," Emerald said. "I can *read* Leonhite, you know."

Finch drooped forward toward the desk. The fight went out of her. "So that's why they're coming," she mumbled through her fingers.

"Gods, no," Emerald said. "You think I alerted them? That I wrote a letter to Venta Bulgarum telling them what you'd done? I have no interest in being more thoroughly examined, either."

Finch was still for a long moment. Then, quite slowly, she lifted her head. "You really didn't?"

"It would make me a damned hypocrite, don't you think?"

I watched the volley of their conversation with interest. At this lull in the conversation, I lifted my hand, as if I was still a child in the Brotherhood classroom waiting to be called upon.

"Yes, Crimson?" Emerald crossed his arms over his chest, and he crossed his legs at the ankle, leaning all the way back in his chair.

"I've missed something." I lowered my hand. "Leonhite writing?"

Finch frowned. She pointed between the two of us. "So you don't… just know things?"

"Sometimes I do." I shrugged one shoulder. "But I miss a lot."

"Huh." She blinked a few times. "Fascinating."

Emerald puffed out his cheeks. "Leonhites hail from a steppe to the North of the Nomad Gamut. There aren't many trees up there, so instead of writing using paper and ink, or even little marks in stone or clay, the oldest version of their language is communicated through patterns in basket weaving. I assume that the Conjury has been concerned that information is being passed by notes or other objects hidden inside shipments of trade goods, but you're able to communicate via the objects themselves. Clever."

Finch hummed. "I'm surprised you know that. Our language is one of our most closely guarded secrets. And you can *read* it?"

Emerald nodded. "Passably. I've spent time in the Vapor Plains."

Finch looked as if she had five hundred more questions in the queue, but after opening and closing her mouth a few times, she finally asked, "Why didn't you say anything?"

"Because," Emerald said, "it was none of my business. I'm independently contracted to the Conjury, and they don't pay me enough to stick my nose into Leonhite espionage. Sounds messy. Not my problem."

I clapped, then I used the fingertips of my pressed-together hands to point to the commander. "So, to recap: Finch is smuggling Conjury information northward, and we'd just as soon not know the dirty details." I pointed to Emerald in the same fashion. "We have no outstanding loyalty to the larger organization, and we want to keep my nature a secret." Which was an understatement, but if we were going to stay out of Finch's business, I wasn't going to blab all of *our* secrets. "So have we agreed *not* to blackmail each other, or…?" I trailed off, although I did raise my eyebrows in anticipation of their replies.

Emerald reached one large hand across the desk. "I'll keep your secret if you'll keep mine. The fact that they haven't sent Viet of Vows means they're not certain of anything. We can find ways to cover for each other."

For a moment, Finch hesitated. "They were going to, actually. But he and his partner were held up by some surprise business at the Temple of Celestriona out past BelaMontis. It got out of hand and... well, the administration settled for the next best thing."

Emerald frowned. "Shit."

Finch nodded and ran her claws over the stiff fur on the back of her neck. "They're sure *something* is amiss. I have no idea how much they know or how invasive this Mentalist will be. It may not be possible to hide everything. Including this conversation."

"I'm confident in our abilities to obfuscate," Emerald assured her.

She lifted one hand toward his, but still seemed unconvinced. "Have you ever encountered a Mentalist?"

"No," Emerald said. And, oh, Aster's meadows, I wasn't going to say anything about *that,* no matter how much Innocent cackled in the back of my psyche. "But if it can't be helped, it can't be helped. We both knew the other's secrets, more or less. At least now they're out in the open."

[That's right,] Innocent taunted while they shook on it. *[Because they're both smarter than you.]*

[And yet I'm the one who imprisoned you,] I retorted. *[How miserable it must be, to have been defeated by such an inferior intellect.]*

Innocent had no response to that.

*[I **can't believe you didn't tell me about Finch,**]* I complained as we made our way back to the Lute and Goose. *[**How much of that basket-writing did you get to read?**]*

Emerald stuffed his hands in his pockets. *[**I don't know what you understand, and what you don't. I bet if you'd looked more closely at the designs, you could have read them yourself. You seem to understand** other **languages I know just fine. As for what they**]* *said, I could only see the sides facing us. The writing system is circular, so you'd have to see the whole basket to know what it said.]*

[But you got the gist...]

[From her, and from a former acquaintance. You remember what the Bracefallows told us about Gorlyn trying to go north? The Conjury has made incursions into Leonhite lands before, but they never last. It's difficult territory to conquer, even more difficult to live in, and the Leonhites have the advantage. For now.]

We crossed through the eastern gate, across the dragon tiles that I had barely noticed before we helped Serkadis escape. The more time I spent in Kinmore, the more I realized just how large the world was, and how small I was within it. Every person we passed, every employee and shopkeeper, every resident of the Hives had their own history, their own interests, their own motives. I was lucky, perhaps, to have spent my formative days in Dyrne, in relative isolation from the madness of the port city. And Kinmore was only a tiny fraction of the continent of Dregandresal, which in turn was only a single landmass on a larger world...

"There's so much I don't know," I murmured aloud.

Emerald sucked his teeth. "Frustrating, isn't it? Makes it damn near impossible to learn everything." He sounded genuinely put out.

[And yet, you didn't press Commander Finch for details.]

[She has people she's trying to protect,] Emerald reasoned. *[Same as we do. If I thought she was plotting an attack, I'd feel differently, but I think she's just trying to keep the people she loves out of the Conjury's grasp.]*

[Why not fight, then?] I asked. *[Why are the two of you pretending to work for them, if you don't believe in what they're doing?]* This was a topic we'd danced around more than once, and I never felt quite satisfied with Emerald's answer.

[Because as long as I work for them, even if I don't wear their colors, I can be sure that there's one person in their ranks who has people's best interests in mind. Working for them grants me access

to spaces from which I would otherwise be barred. The Conjury's goal, theoretically, is to keep people safe from dangerous magic-workers. If Serkadis had been forced to fight his way out of the city, how many people would have been hurt or killed?] Emerald cocked his head. *[We're still keeping people safe. We just... found another way.]*

I wasn't sure how I felt about this reasoning, either. On one hand, it was hard to refute, since I'd been complicit in many of the actions in question. Even when we'd made mistakes, I believed in the sincerity of our intentions. On the other, if people like Emerald and Finch kept their heads down and worked within their approved framework, how would anything ever change? Weren't they just ensuring the success of an institution they didn't really support?

Emerald had accepted input on plenty of things. We'd compromised in ways that ensured we were as close to equal as we could be, so long as I was bound to him. The one aspect of our lives to which I had never agreed, or at least assented, was our relationship to the Conjury. Emerald had made his choice regarding his alliance. Left to my own devices, I wasn't convinced that I'd align myself with the powers-that-be. But so long as the two of us were a set, what other choice did I have?

It all led back to my desire for autonomy. After Serkadis's failed attempt to free me, however, the outlook for that eventuality was grim.

Our wanderings brought us back to the Lute and Goose. It was still late morning, thanks to Finch's early dismissal, and was just beginning to drizzle. The overcast sky threatened more rain to come, which would likely result in a quiet night at the inn. Locals tended to stay home during bad weather, and the trade caravans that frequented the rooms moved in cycles. We were due for a bit of rest.

Emerald pushed open the front door just as the rain began in earnest, pounding against the large windows that faced the nearly empty road.

Yerik stood behind the bar, taking stock of his inventory. He looked up from his notes when we entered and flashed a welcoming grin.

"Ah, here they are." He motioned to a pair of cloaked figures sitting at the table that Emerald and I most often frequented. Apart from a trio of regulars clustered by the dormant fireplace, they were the only guests in the dining room.

Emerald stopped and turned to the strange pair. "Were you looking for us?" he asked.

"Ah, yes. The Emerald Flame. I've been looking forward to meeting you." The smaller of the two figures lowered his hood.

The false Gorlyn Bracefallow had come to call at last.

CHAPTER TWO

Emerald approached the table warily. His posture betrayed very little of his tension, but I felt it through our connection: sharp and irregular, like the strike of hailstones on a suit of armor.

"Good afternoon," he said. He straightened his shoulders a little, rising up to his full height. When he slid into the chair between the two interlopers, he spread his knees, taking up more space than was necessary. A reminder, perhaps, of his size. He'd behaved quite the opposite in Finch's office, when he wanted to assure her that he was no threat.

The false Gorlyn had made a mistake. I could still hear Yerik puttering around behind the bar, and children's voices emanating from the kitchen at the back of the inn. These strangers had brought the fight into our territory, where our people resided. I was rather shocked to discover just how furious this made me. Not because of Emerald's loyalty, not due to Innocent's predatory tendencies, but because *I* loved this place, with its faded floors and silly paintings and ever-present air of welcome.

My family lived here. Whatever game this man was playing, he'd chosen the wrong opponent.

My emotions must have bled through the tether, because Emerald looked up at me in alarm. I, however, only had eyes for the man pretending to be Gorlyn.

He simpered at me and waved to the remaining empty chair. "Please. Sit."

I simpered right back, although I suspect a bit of Innocent's feral nature bled into my smile. "I'm perfectly content to stand, thank you. What brings you two to the Lute and Goose?"

[Easy, Crim.] Emerald patted his knee, the way I suspect he would have tapped my shoulder if he could. *[Let's see what we can learn from him.]*

[All that pretty red hair,] Innocent whispered. *[He'd look even prettier with a bloody throat to match.]*

Gorlyn—since I had nothing better to call him, I settled on the name of the dead boy for the time being—steepled his fingers. "They say you should never meet your heroes," he mused, "but in this case, I couldn't help myself. You two were kind enough to go looking for me when I was lost. Now, Mummy and Daddy are so *pleased* to have me back, they'll let me do anything I like. Sleep in my plush feather bed, stroll through the halls, buy whatever I want on the family credit. I'm ever so glad I came back from..." He made a show of pausing and tapping one finger against his cheek. "Where was it, Whale Bone Island? Perhaps New Wrighton? I forget what your falsified manifest said, but either way, I'd much rather be back home. I really should be thanking you two."

Emerald's hand balled into fists.

"Oh, piss off with that *mummy and daddy* shite." Gorlyn's companion waved a dismissive hand in the air. They sat slumped over their mug, and their face was obscured by their hood, but their stature made me think they must have dwarven blood. "Nobody's fooled by it."

Gorlyn smirked across the table. "We don't need them to be

fooled," he said, in a slightly softer voice. "We need them to know who we're messing with."

"And who is that, exactly?" Emerald asked.

Gorlyn tilted his head to one side. He ran his tongue over one canine. "You haven't worked that out yet? These local heroes, I tell you, Sal. They never live up to the hype."

I had been too busy trying to work out how someone would make themselves look exactly like the dead boy long enough, and accurately enough, to fool his family. It hadn't yet occurred to me to question his motives for doing so. While he was chattering away, I was observing the subtle disconnect between the movement of his lips and the sound of his voice; the way his chest didn't rise and fall with his breath, the ruby set in the silver cuff about his wrist.

He lowered his voice and fixed his cold eyes on Emerald. "We're the ones your friend Serkadis stole from."

Emerald's breathing hitched. "You're with the crew who brought the egg to Kinmore." The *dragon* egg, he meant. The one that had killed Gorlyn, and which we'd helped Serkadis smuggle out of the city.

"Aye," the cloaked figure agreed. "That cargo would have made us quite a haul."

"We'll make up for it," Gorlyn said. He kept his voice low enough not to be overheard by the handful of possible witnesses, but loud enough that we could make out every word. "Now that I have access to Bracefallow Manor, I've got all sorts of plans. At first, I thought about robbing those bastards blind, but then I realized what a huge opportunity this is. As the youngest of the Bracefallow heirs, I can open doors for our little venture that we never dreamed of before."

I lifted my hand to the back of Emerald's chair, ostensibly to brace myself, although in reality I was more interested in showing a united front. "And you're telling us all this because...?"

The cloaked figure moved his hood aside, and for the first time, I caught a glimpse of his face. He was indeed a dwarf, although like none I'd ever seen before, with skin as white as parchment and small black eyes which showed no iris. "Because we'd really hate for you to make trouble for us," the dwarf said, as if he was pointing out the obvious solution to a logic puzzle, and not making a veiled threat. "We could handle it, mind you, but it would make things messy."

Gorlyn nodded. "Bring trouble to my home, raise the alert with dear old Mummy and Daddy, and I'll bring trouble to *yours*." He nodded meaningfully toward the back-of-house, where our mismatched family went about their tasks, unaware of the conversation that unfolded between us.

"Lovely place," the dwarf added, looking around the inn. "Strong beams. Old wood. It's been standing a long time, I reckon, but under the right conditions, this place would go up like a matchstick."

[Crack his chest open,] Innocent singsonged. *[Scrape the meat from his bones. No one threatens what is ours.]*

Emerald's mind was astonishingly quiet, still as the surface of the sea at night—right before a storm rolls in. "You might want to choose your words more carefully," he said. "In certain circles, what you just said might be misconstrued as a threat."

The chattering group by the fire had fallen silent, and though Yerik's back was still turned to us, I was certain he had overheard enough of the conversation to draw his own conclusions.

"It *was* a threat," the dwarf growled. "Stop sniffing around the docks. There are more where we came from."

Emerald's lips curled back in distaste, revealing the shorn-down nubs of his tusks. His eyes, normally a deep green, flashed with the same strange glow that I'd observed in full-blooded jotunns. "What an interesting negotiation tactic."

[We're not putting up with this, are we?] I asked him.

[We most certainly are not.] He sized up the two men, assessing which of them was the greater threat, and which one we ought to strike against first.

I made the decision for him. Usually, I was useless in combat, but I had a move of my own. Back in Upper Bound, a fellow named Hudson had thought I was a Lightweaver using illusion to disguise my true appearance to steal the identity of Crimson Smoke. At the time, I'd been frustrated by his suspicion. In hindsight, it had proved to be a valuable lesson.

I reached across the table toward Gorlyn, with some half-baked notion that I might snatch the illusion off of his face. To my surprise, I felt the warmth and give of his skin beneath my fingers.

Perhaps I should have expected it. Illusions, whether cast by Emerald or by someone else, were made of the same stuff I was. They were real to me. I grasped at the illusion and yanked hard, the way someone might yank a tablecloth aside without disturbing the dishes atop it.

Gorlyn's disguise came free. For an instant, it hung limp in my hands, a loose sack of skin and hair. Disconnected from its caster, it soon faded to nothing. We were left staring at the young woman who'd been concealed beneath the disguise.

She was wearing the same clothes as the illusion, although they fit her differently than they'd fit her Gorlyn-shape. The shoulders were slack around her narrower frame, her chest and hips were rendered shapeless by the excess of cloth, and unlike Gorlyn's strawberry-blonde hair, hers was dark and shaved close to the scalp, presumably so as not to interfere with her disguise.

Despite their obvious differences, she and Gorlyn were of a height. When she spoke, her voice was deep enough to mimic the young man's. She pointed across the table at me and twisted her narrow features into a snarl. "The Crimson Smoke's a gods-cursed *Lightweaver!*" she spat.

Not quite accurate, but close enough. And now that we could see her real face, she had lost her element of anonymity.

Her companion, Sal, lurched to his feet. With a pop of magic, twin flames exploded in his open palms.

Chaos erupted in the dining room. The three regulars hopped to their feet, but instead of racing for the door, they turned their ire on Sal and the former Gorlyn. One lifted a chair over her head and charged forward, yelling in Pruvhathayn as she pelted toward the flaming Thaumaturge.

Emerald grabbed the Lightweaver by the collar and yanked her off balance. Behind us, the door to the kitchen opened. I heard Blare's wordless scream of anger, and then Quell shouting something incoherent. I turned just in time to see the two hurl an enormous bucket of water, carried between them, toward the Thaumaturge.

They were too far away for the attack to be effective... or so I thought. I hadn't counted on Svelte standing behind them, her blue eyes glittering like frost under starlight, or the sudden motion of her hands. At times, it was easy to forget that she was an Arctician, and a powerful one at that, but I was reminded of that fact once again as she gestured to the small wave of water. Some of it hit the floor and froze to the boards, but the rest turned to icicles that shot through the air toward the would-be arsonist. It sliced his sleeves and exposed hands, and it made him fall back a pace.

Unfortunately, ice wasn't a particularly effective weapon against a roaring fire. The Thaumaturge cursed, only momentarily inconvenienced.

Then the charging Pruv hit the ice. She lost her footing, and—chair still raised like a battering ram—collided with the dwarf. They were both carried forward, through the window, and out into the pounding rain.

Emerald was still holding the Lightweaver, although now that he had her, he didn't seem to know what to do with her. She, alas, did not hesitate. She twisted in his grasp, nimble as a cat, and pulled free. In the same movement, she drew two thin, curved blades from her belt. Another advantage to the mismatch between her whipcord figure and the sturdier build of the man she'd been impersonating: she could carry hidden weapons on her, concealed beneath her illusory dimensions.

She swiped at Emerald, who was forced to retreat. His reach was greater, but the blades as long as her forearms more than made up the difference. He dropped into a crouch, dipping back with each slash. I had no doubt that he was waiting for the perfect opportunity to strike and catch her off guard.

But he'd forgotten about the sheet of ice on the tavern floor.

The moment his boot hit the slick surface, he stumbled. The smuggler saw her opening and lunged.

I screamed. Svelte screamed. And, for some reason, the smuggler screamed, too. She stopped short of my friend, dropped her blade, and pawed at her chest. The fine silks she'd stolen from the Brace-fallow household revealed a dark and rapidly growing stain around the metal bolt that protruded from her ribs.

Standing in the door, framed by the dark sky and the driving rain, with a small puddle forming around his boots as water dripped from the flaps of his oiled canvas uniform, was the elven courier who had vexed Svelte for the better part of a year. He clutched a small crossbow in both hands, with its channel aimed at the injured woman.

"Roots of the Great Tree," he murmured. "What in all the hells did I just walk into?"

He seemed utterly stricken by his involvement in the strange scene. The Lightweaver gasped as she toppled sideways and gradually fell still, her mouth open, her wide eyes fixed on the beams of the ceiling above.

So it was that Gorlyn Bracefallow died a second time.

CHAPTER THREE

While Emerald examined the remains of the dead smuggler, Svelte and Yerik shepherded the courier to an armchair. Svelte went to fetch him some tea, while Yerik and the other guests stepped outside to see what had become of the Pruv and the Thaumaturge.

The courier seemed dazed. "I've held that crossbow more times than I can count," he said to no one in particular. In his shock, he looked much younger than I'd previously assumed. "I've even fired it a few times. But I've never..." He shook his head and ran his fingers through his hair. "This is supposed to be the *quiet* route."

"I'm sorry." I sank toward the seat of a nearby chair. "But for what it's worth, I'm grateful that you intervened."

[We didn't need him,] Innocent complained.

I ignored it.

Svelte emerged from the kitchen with a mug of some steaming beverage and a platter piled high with pastries. "Didn't know what you'd like," she said sheepishly. "So I brought two of everything."

The courier seemed to remember his disdain for her and sat up straighter. "That's not at all necessary..."

"Svelte." She set the mug down and stuck out her hand. "And don't be an ass. We're friends now."

The courier stared at her hand for a long moment before extending his own. "Feverfew. Of Thumb River Basin."

"Nice to meet you, Feeve," Svelte said. "Now, have something to eat. I thought you were going to keel over on the spot, you went so pale."

The elf sputtered. "*Feeve?*"

I left them to it and went to crouch beside Emerald. Yerik returned with a muddy, bedraggled Pruv in tow and led the woman straight to the bar for a pick-me-up on the house.

"Find anything interesting?" I asked in a low voice.

"Nothing useful." Emerald passed one hand over his eyes. "Driaweep's pickled pecker, what a mess."

"Colorful epithets aside, do you have the slightest idea what to do now? A dead Lightweaver in the Lute and Goose doesn't look good for us. At least the weird-looking dwarf should stand out."

Emerald's brow furrowed. "Weird dwarf?" he asked.

"Didn't you get a good look at Sal?" I asked. "I'm sure that's not his real name, but he wasn't a Lightweaver, and this one was too busy with her own disguise, so I assume that was his real face."

"I didn't get a good look at him," Emerald admitted.

I described my brief glimpse of his face.

"Sounds like a Brimstone dwarf. They tend to be a bit... distinctive. They tend to live strictly underground. I wonder what he's doing this far south?" The question was hardly out of his mouth before he nodded in understanding. "Probably an outcast, if he's working as a smuggler. You're right, he should stand out in a crowd, but no doubt he's got some safehouse to run back to. I bet my arse they aren't registered with the Conjury."

"No bet," I said at once. "Keep your arse to yourself. I'm sure you're right."

Emerald choked on a laugh just as Yerik and his Pruv guest came over to speak to us.

"Sorry I lost 'im," the woman said. "Hit my head hard on fe cobbles, 'n he fought like fe greased wassail inna crab trap, he did."

Wassail? I mouthed to Yerik, who only shrugged.

"No one can blame you for letting a Thaumaturge slip away," Emerald assured her. "Thank you for the help. We weren't prepared for an attack like that. You might want to make yourself scarce, though. We'll have to alert the Conjury, and they'll have questions for anyone they know to be involved."

The Pruv nodded sagely. "You're a right turnip on harvest day," she announced, and threw back the rest of her sizable drink before making a swift departure.

"Speaking of the Conjury." Feeve flicked crumbs off of his wet oilcloth. "I completely forgot the real reason I came." He produced a letter from his pocket and waved Svelte away when she tried to pay. "I reckon I should stay until you can send for someone, since I'm the one... responsible, but you ought to see this first."

Emerald plucked the letter from his fingers and unfolded it. "Wonderful," he grumbled. "Just what we need."

I peeked over his shoulder. "What is it?"

He held up the paper to show me the missive written in Finch's sharp scrawl.

The Mentalist had arrived a day early and was already making his rounds at the head office. This blackmail attempt and ensuing battle couldn't have come at a worse time.

Fortunately for us, our blackmailer had been careful to cover their tracks when they approached the Lute and Goose. Nobody outside of our little circle had seen the dead Lightweaver's disguise.

As her remains were laid out on a slab in the Conjury's cold room, it occurred to me that her death presented another problem. Emerald and I had been able to buy ourselves time in our investigation of Gorlyn's disappearance by pretending he was off somewhere on a Feynlish shipping vessel. By all appearances, he had come home, only to vanish again.

[I hope you have a ready explanation,] I thought. *[One that won't drag poor Feeve even deeper into our mess.]*

Emerald only nodded. His mind was spinning like clockwork beneath his cool exterior.

As before, the Arctician in charge of maintaining the temperature of the cold room was flipping through a novel and doing her utmost to ignore us. I caught a glimpse of the title on the cover this time: *The Kineticist's Secret Baby*.

Finch shoved through the door, with another figure in purple silks trotting along at her heels. I started at the sight of a swamper elf, another rare sight in Kinmore.

"Basel, this is the Emerald Flame. And Crimson Smoke, obviously. Emerald, Crimson, this is Basel of Clearfall. Our visiting Mentalist." She bared her teeth at us in what might be charitably called a smile, if one was feeling *extraordinarily* philanthropic. "Sorry that you have to arrive during this mess, Basel."

The elf shook his head, making the tight twists of his hair bounce around his pointed ears. "I don't expect you to drop everything on my account," he said. His voice was unexpectedly soft, with a slight accent that took on a subtly different cadence than the local Osmarian. "I'm happy to observe for now. Please carry on just as you would without my presence."

Finch's eye twitched. "Of course. Excellent. Now then, Emerald... that courier was only able to tell us how things *ended*. Who is this, and why was she trying to stab you?"

"I don't know who she is, exactly. But she was trying to impersonate Gorlyn Bracefallow. I suspect she was trying to take advantage of the young man's absence by stepping into his shoes. She's a Lightweaver."

When he offered nothing else, Finch prompted. "And she was trying to stab you because...?"

"Because we saw her at Bracefallow Manor the other day and

recognized her as a fraud," I explained, following Emerald's lead. "She was afraid we'd out her to the family, so she came to threaten us into silence."

"She came. To threaten you. Alone?" Finch pointed at the corpse. "That seems... ill-advised, given her size."

"She had a friend with her," Emerald added. "A Vultitian, trained in Thaumaturgy. He threatened to burn the place down."

Finch squeezed her eyes shut. "Two unregistered *Aidea* users, working together? That doesn't bode well."

"That's why we're here," Basel reminded her in his soft, lilting voice. "The Conjury exists to stop individuals like this."

"True enough." Finch loped over to the corpse's side and studied her. "Can you describe the Thaumaturge?"

"Nope," I said.

"Never saw his face," Emerald added.

"He kept his hood up," I clarified. "We only heard his voice, and he didn't say much."

Finch kept her back turned to Basel, but we could see her eyes, and the warning frown she directed toward us. "Is that so?"

"Don't worry, Commander. We'll take care of it. After all, that's what we do." I hooked my arm in front of my chest in a jaunty display of confidence.

[Too much,] Emerald warned. *[And don't forget, Basel knows exactly what you are, even if the Arctician by the door doesn't.]*

[Right.] I lowered my arm but kept the smile on my face. I didn't have enough of a sense of Basel to know how to play this. *[I'll just be quiet then.]*

"I'll leave the investigation to you, then," Finch said. "But I think we ought to post a couple of guards at the Lute and Goose until this Thaumaturge is caught."

"Really?" Emerald seemed taken aback by the suggestion. "You'd do that for me? For us?"

"Of course. Your family was threatened, Emerald." Finch seemed confused by his surprise. "This isn't the first time they've come into the line of fire, so to speak, as a result of your work for the Conjury. At least this time there's something I can do about it."

Basel nodded enthusiastically. "Oh, I quite agree." He whipped a tiny notebook out of the front of his robes and began to take notes, still talking as he scribbled down his findings. "An added guard will provide peace of mind for the two of you, and they may catch the assailant if he makes another attempt to threaten you. It's the wisest choice all around. If nothing else, it should alleviate some unnecessary stress while you pursue your case."

All four of us stared at him. Apparently, this pronouncement was even more interesting than the Arctician's novel.

"Right," Finch said. "That settles that, I suppose. I'll reach out to the Bracefallows and inform them of this development, and I'll assure them that you're hard at work solving this case."

Basel held up one finger. "Not *too* hard at work, though. I'm afraid I'll need at least an hour of your time tomorrow. I'll be conducting introductory sessions with all of the staff, and that includes you. Given the importance of your case, I'll defer to your schedule, but I must insist that you make time for me."

"Of course." Emerald dipped his head in acknowledgement. "I... look forward to it."

Basel grinned. "You don't need to lie to me. In fact, I'd much prefer you didn't. Tomorrow, then." He turned to Finch. "Now, Commander, if I might have a word..."

The two of them left the cold room, and Emerald waited for the door to close before he followed.

"Well, he's something else," the Arctician intoned. "Seems nice enough, for someone who's planning to poke around in our brains with invasive magic."

"Right," Emerald said. "Excellent choice in reading material, by the way. It's a slow burn, but the payoff is worth it in the end."

The Arctician chuckled as she returned to her book. "Oh, I know, love. This is my fifth time reading it."

CHAPTER FOUR

There were a few hubs of information in the city, but only one that favored us especially.

"Well, look what the spirit dog dragged in." In the midst of her fully refurbished bar, surrounded by patrons who looked upon her with the same quiet wonder generally reserved for houses of worship, Dumplin preened. She was ensconced in a lambkin-sized chair on top of one of the many circular tables littering the room. "Two of my favorite customers. Have you come to call in that favor, Emerald Flame?"

"Not exactly." Emerald looked around at the hundred or so tipsy Pruvs jammed into the relatively small establishment. "Can we talk in private?"

"Of course, love." Dumplin snapped her fingers. "Someone let me down."

The assembled crowd jostled for the honor, and Dumplin was handed down to floor level, where her admirers parted to make way for her and for the pair of us as well. Her bodyguards met us at the stairs, but Dumplin shook her head and motioned for them to stay where they were before climbing the steps to her private offices on the third floor.

"Are you sure I can't interest you in a private session?" She pointed to the case where her amethyst necklace was displayed. "Offer's always open."

"I'd prefer some information, if you have it." Emerald lowered himself gingerly in one of the chairs.

"Oh, don't worry, sweetheart, those seats can take a bit of wear and tear." She directed a salacious wink my way. "What do you want to know?"

"We're looking for a smuggler," I told her. "Might go by the name of Sal. A Thaumaturge. Do you know him?"

Dumplin's amusement vanished in a blink. "Is he a Brimstone dwarf, by any chance?"

"That's the one." Emerald settled deeper into the chair and looked relieved when it held his weight.

"Everybody knows Salvation," Dumplin spat. Her floppy ears trembled with rage. "He used to bully me, back when I was new to the city. He and Garland operate a dockside racket, and they make life miserable for those with nothing left to lose."

"Garland?" Emerald echoed.

"That's the name they give," Dumplin explained. "I don't know much about them, although the stories people tell make it sound like they're a shapechanger. *Everybody* has a story about Garland, but nobody knows what they look like. It's made them a bit of a legend around here. The bad kind, the one parents tell their children at night to keep them in line. *You never know if Garland's watching,* that sort of thing."

"The Lightweaver," I said.

Dumplin's lips parted, and her eyes darted between Emerald's face and mine.

"I think we may have killed Garland this afternoon," Emerald said.

I opened my mouth to clarify that we hadn't actually done the killing, but thought better of it. If word got out that Feeve had killed a big player in Kinmore's underground, it would likely put him at risk.

"Good for you." Dumplin's vehemence made Innocent purr in approval. "I wish to Pulchradune you'd gotten them both, though. Salvation's the dangerous one."

"That's really his name?" I asked.

"Oh, course not." Dumplin raked her fingers through her expertly fluffed wool. "Nobody gives their *real* name in this gig. But it's the one he goes by. Lends him an air of mystique. I tell you what, Emerald Flame. I'd never go toe-to-toe with Salvation, but if you brought him to his knees, I'd finish what you started. If you wanted to make him disappear, I mean."

I pretended to cough into my fist. *[What was that you said about her tendency toward de-escalation, Em?]*

"He must have done something pretty awful to make you feel that way," Emerald observed.

Dumplin licked her lips. "He likes to make an example of people. If someone in the Hives steps out of line, he'll punish them. With flame."

I pressed my hand to my mouth. I understood her meaning well enough, and that would have been sufficiently terrible. But in a densely packed neighborhood like the Hives, burning one apartment would surely result in burning the ones around it, too. Other families might be trapped inside, and those that fled would lose everything. "Why haven't you told us about them before?"

Dumplin gave me a pitying look. "You're a sweet thing, Miss Crimson, you really are. Do you genuinely believe that two smugglers are the worst problems we're facing in the city? Hm? And if I did tell you, and you didn't catch 'em fast enough, what would become of me? The Conjury has its priorities. The rest of us have to look out for ourselves. And there's no telling where Garland might be, or what they might overhear. Or at least, there wasn't. But now..." She reclined, spreading both arms over the back of the chaise. "Now you've made things interesting."

"Do you know where he's likely to go to lick his wounds?" Emerald asked.

Dumplin hummed. "If I tell you where to find him, I don't want the Conjury getting involved. If word gets out that I'm squealing to the establishment, I'll become a pariah overnight."

Emerald pointed to himself. "Am I not the establishment?"

Dumplin rolled her eyes. "Hardly. You're a good local boy. One of ours. And this city takes care of its own. So what do you say? You and me, we handle this *my* way. The Hives' way."

My friend sat in silence for a long moment, tapping a drumbeat against the plush arm of his chair with his right hand. *[I hate politics.]*

[I suppose you shouldn't work for the government, then,] I rejoined.

He made a rude gesture in my direction. "If I say no?"

"Then I can honestly tell you I don't know where to find him, and good luck proving otherwise." Dumplin's saccharine expression returned. She studied her exquisitely manicured fingernails. "I know when I'm in over my head. That's what you love about me, darling."

More silence followed. I felt the exact moment when my friend caved. "Fine," he said at last. "If you find him before we can, we'll do things your way."

Dumplin, ever the businesswoman, held out her hand for a shake. "Let me put my boys on it. Come back tomorrow night. Sunset."

"So you *do* know where he is," Emerald grumbled.

"No, but I'm confident in my abilities to find him in the meantime. Don't take this the wrong way, sweets, but I have more friends in the city than you do." Dumplin hopped to her feet and led us back to the door. "Don't you worry your pretty little heads. By tomorrow night, I'll have sniffed out where that rat is hiding, and we'll settle the matter for good."

CHAPTER FIVE

asel balanced a pair of spectacles on his nose and looked down at his notes. "I must say, Emerald, I've been looking forward to this discussion. Oh, my apologies... may I call you Emerald? Is that presumptuous?"

Emerald shifted on the couch in the Mentalist's temporary office. "Sure, it's fine. What have you been looking forward to, exactly?"

Basel crossed his legs and propped his notes against his knee. "Well, you're a fascinating case, aren't you? Your situation is quite unprecedented."

Emerald shifted again. "Right. Because nobody expects a jotunn to succeed in my line of work."

Basel tipped his head back and laughed. His mirth seemed sincere. "Oh, I understand that feeling more than you might think. How many swamper elves work for the Conjury? But believe it or not, that isn't what I meant. You were a prodigy. A Castcadesman from the age of majority until your, hm, poorly documented departure. That was around the same time you earned your prominence title, wasn't it?"

There could be no mistaking the increasingly sullen set of Emerald's shoulders. "The two events were... related."

"I know how to read between the lines." Basel tapped his quill against the paper. "And your illusion earning a title of its own, that's also quite unusual. Speaking of which, how would you feel about dispelling it during our chat?"

Emerald looked over his shoulder at me. "I'd prefer not to," he said. *[Although if he insists...]*

[I understand what's at stake here,] I assured him. *[If you're going to send me away, at least give me enough warning to make sure I can go to the mind-cottage first.]*

Innocent growled. *[So obliging. Too obliging. We could simply eat the Mentalist and be done with it.]*

Murderous tendencies were one thing, but I was curious about how an incorporeal shadow-beast might go about eating someone, though I thought it better not to ask.

"I see." Basel made a note. "And why is that?"

"I find their presence comforting."

"*Their.*" Basel made another note. "So you've assigned your imaginary friend a gender identity, but not a static one."

"It—" Emerald batted his hand back and forth between two ends of an implied spectrum. "It switches. Based on what I need at the time."

"Oh, goodness, there's so much to evaluate here. I'd love to explore that more, but I'm afraid our focus here is rather narrower in scope. I see here that you've recently adopted three young people from the orphanage where you were raised. Why is that?"

Emerald's mouth dropped open, but no sound emerged.

"Take your time." Basel lowered his pen and directed all of his attention to my friend. "I'd like an honest answer, please. I'm willing to wait for it."

"Well, they... they deserved better." Emerald seemed bewildered that those words had emerged from his mouth. "Better than the Brotherhood could offer."

"Better than what *you* experienced, you mean. And you believed that you could provide a suitable alternative."

"I knew that I was willing to try, and that the Brotherhood was not." Emerald leaned forward on the cushions. "Are you threatening to take them away?"

"What? No!" The swamper elf's eyes widened, and he snatched the spectacles off his face. "That would be a horrible thing for me to do! No, I'm simply noticing a trend in your sense of justice. Finch's reports suggest that you put a great deal of pressure on yourself to do the right thing, even when it isn't easy. Going back through old records, I've noticed that even in your earliest cases, you regularly risked your own health and safety to ensure the well-being of complete strangers."

Emerald snorted. "You make me sound like a hero. I'm not."

"I never said you were. But I would go so far as to say that you're a man who *aspires* to heroism. A noble aim, certainly. But I suspect it's a lonely one." Basel wagged the feather end of his quill toward me. "Lonely enough that it might warrant inventing an imaginary companion to fill the void, hm? Someone who can never leave you, the way your parents did."

Emerald shot to his feet. "We're done here."

"I meant no offense, Emerald." Basel's voice was kindly. "You've had many people let you down. The Brotherhood. The Conjury. Every blood tie, every institution that swore to protect you failed in that very aim. I'm concerned that you're operating under the belief that you can *earn* love and loyalty through impeccable performance."

My first impression of Emerald, my first conscious memory, suggested an immovable figure made of solid stone. Solid, unbreakable, and steadfast.

I knew better now. Coldness and inflexibility had been forced upon him by the Brotherhood when Harmony saddled him with that word, that name. In the end, it nearly killed him.

"Is this part of your investigation?" Emerald's mouth was set in a ruthless line, his eyes shuttered, his shoulders squared. "Or can I go now? Or maybe you'd prefer to poke around in my head and just *take* what you want."

Basel nibbled his thumbnail. "I wouldn't. I swear. Between you and me, there's no real evidence of any wrongdoing here, and the rumors—they really are only rumors—started before you returned to the mainland. I have to keep everything aboveboard, but if you want to leave, you're free to go."

"Thank you." Emerald turned his back on the elf and strode to the door.

"Think about what I said," Basel called after him. "You're worth more than the value other people place on your work, Emerald Flame."

Emerald fled into the hall and slammed the door behind him, giving me barely enough time to slip through. Perhaps Basel didn't need my act to be convincing, but Aaliy was standing in the hallway, arms crossed and shoulders hunched.

"If you said anything to him about Finch—" she hissed.

Emerald stormed past her without uttering a word.

"We didn't," I whispered. "Of course we didn't. But you... know?"

"I'm her assistant." Aaliy's posture unwound. "I'm not stupid, I can put clues together when I need to, but she's the best boss I've ever had. Don't tell her I said anything, right? I don't want her to worry."

The door behind us opened again, and a rather frazzled-looking Basel emerged. "Oh, hello, Aaliy. Are you ready for our session?"

Aaliy nodded as she slipped past me, while I went the other way, each of us focused on the well-being of the people we would do anything to protect.

EMERALD DIDN'T GO to the Hives. He fled toward the Lute and Goose in silence, his mind cut off from mine, his eyes fixed dead ahead. I didn't try to speak to him. There was nothing to say.

I believed with my whole heart that Basel meant well, but I

wished he'd kept his mouth shut. The subject of Emerald's parents was an old wound, perhaps the *oldest* wound, and the Mentalist had no way of knowing how much it had almost cost my friend.

The Castcadesmen Finch had posted at the inn tried to greet us, but Emerald ignored them. He slammed through the front door and took the steps two at a time until he disappeared into the upstairs hall. I let him go. We could talk when he was ready.

"What happened?" Yerik asked.

"We met with the Mentalist." I rolled my eyes. "Ten minutes in, he starts asking Emerald questions about his parents."

Yerik grimaced and leaned both elbows on the bar. "Oof. I had one fellow do that the first time we had a private dinner together, and I've literally never spoken to him again. It's one thing to talk when you're ready, but having that sprung on you is..." He shook his head, incapable of verbalizing how painful the topic could be.

"I'll leave him to think for a bit," I said. "He'll let me know if and when he wants to talk." That hadn't always been the case, but by now, I trusted Emerald to set his own boundaries with me.

I was also feeling the tiniest bit guilty. I was supposed to be the one person who could never leave him, but I had been desperate to do exactly that. After Serkadis's attempt failed, I was gradually resigning myself to the facts of our circumstance, but I had made no secret of my desire for freedom. That must have hurt Emerald more than I cared to consider.

I pushed my maudlin reflections aside and surveyed the room, which was oddly packed for the early hour. "You're doing a brisk business today, I see."

Yerik immediately brightened. "Oh, yes. Everyone heard about the fuss yesterday, and they came to defend the inn, bless them."

On closer inspection, the packed house bristled with weapons of every variety, from pitchforks and scythes leaned against walls to knives and trowels tucked into belts. No doubt there were a few *Aidea* users in the crowd as well.

Dumplin was right. Even in the outskirts, Kinmore took care of its own.

DUSK WAS FALLING by the time Emerald reemerged from his room. The prior day's rain had given way to a humidity so thick that it clung to the windows and seeped through the canvas-covered hole in the wall of the tavern, which awaited a replacement pane. Despite what I inferred to be an undesirable heat, based on the attire and general stickiness of the guests, Emerald wore his black overcoat, the one that allowed him to blend into the night.

"Come on," he told me, making no mention of the conversation with Basel. "We have an appointment to keep."

CHAPTER SIX

The atmosphere of Dumplin's establishment was markedly different from our last visit. The front door was closed, with Poke and Doodah—gods, it made so much more sense now that I knew that they used pseudonyms—standing guard at the entrance. They waved us through to where a small army awaited us.

The crowd was not, as I had anticipated, composed entirely of Pruvs. I recognized a few other faces in the crowd, although two in particular drew my eye. Oreia, priestess of Lemda, sat cross-legged on the steps to the upper floors, sharpening her blade. Alongside her, dressed in similar robes and ceremonial mail, was a young woman with kohl-lined eyes and a clean-shaven head.

"Merced—?" I began, then stopped short. Surely, shouting her name in public was a terrible idea.

The young woman turned to greet us. Her face was narrower than it had been, and she moved like a warrior rather than a sheltered princess now. Still, she smiled when she saw us and lifted her hand to wave.

"You're still in the city," Emerald said as he approached.

Oreia snorted. "Brilliant observation, Inspector."

"I wanted to stay," Mercedes said. "It was my choice. I decided to serve the people. Not as some figurehead, but as one of them. This is my home." She lifted her chin proudly, as if daring us to argue.

Well. She'd grown up, apparently. There was no more talk of bardic college, at any rate.

Emerald studied her. "Seems risky. You're not that hard to recognize."

Mercedes inclined her head. "I trust my goddess, and my sisters, to keep me safe. And I think a time will come when I serve a greater purpose. Efrain and I have unfinished business."

If only Squampf could be here to see who she was growing into, I had no doubt he'd have happily bent his knee in service to her. If and when the time came, I didn't envy the prince his comeuppance. I was proud of her conviction, and pleased that I had played some small role in it. Everything we did rippled outward: we had changed the course of the city, and its future would continue to evolve.

It had been so long since I experienced hope that it took a moment for me to recognize the emotion.

"Lemda is a goddess of justice and protection," Oreia reminded us. "Even if someone recognizes her, and the crown tries to reclaim her, they'd have to go to war with the temple to do so. I say, let them try."

In the center of the room, Dumplin clapped her hands to draw our attention her way. I couldn't help but notice the heavy necklace glimmering at her throat. "I think this is everyone we're expecting. My boys were clever enough to sniff out Salvation's hiding place, and thanks to the Emerald Flame, the dwarf's just lost his biggest ally. Garland is dead." She paused, allowing for the cheer that followed her words, before proceeding. "Tonight, we'll put an end to the man who's terrorized us for years, the man who once gutted Kettle Alley—"

A dozen members of the crowd boomed, "For Kettle Alley!"

"The man who torched a tent city in the Beggar's Pass!"

"For the Beggar's Pass!"

"The man who—"

"*Dumplin! Miss Dumplin!*" A small human girl of six or seven pelted through the front door, pursued by a red-faced Poke.

"Sorry," he panted. "She's a slippery little thing, slid right by me..."

"That's all right, sweetheart." Dumplin turned her attention to the child, who was shaking so badly she could hardly stand upright. Mercedes rushed to her and knelt at her side, holding the girl steady as she sobbed.

"What's the matter, little one?" she asked.

"I-it's the Undercroft, miss." The girl leaned into Mercedes's arms and scrubbed at her swollen eyes with one knuckle. "It's b-b-burning."

Our usual routes through the city brought us within sight of the Hives nearly every day, but we rarely traversed them. I had walked its edges, but the paths of its interior were unknown to me, and the names of the boroughs Dumplin mentioned sparked nothing in my memory.

So it was that my first trip into the Hives was in the midst of a group of calloused laymen and battle-ready priestesses, led by a lambkin entrepreneur seated on the shoulders of one of her many admirers. The sight would have been funny, if the circumstances hadn't been so horrifying.

I could not smell the smoke, but I could see it framed against the summer sky, illuminated from beneath by the flames from which it rose. Even from a great distance, we could hear screaming. At first, I thought that it emanated from the burning building itself—a horrible thought, given how far away we were—but I soon realized that the rest of the Hives were in turmoil as well. Residents were fleeing the conflagration with bundles on their back and children in tow.

"Where are they going?" I asked Oreia as we wended our way through the increasingly narrow alleys.

The priestess's visage was pale and cold, like the face of one of the moons on a frigid winter night. "They're getting out while they can. If the fire spreads, the Hives will burn to the ground. It's happened before. The streets are too narrow, the houses built too close, and I doubt anyone from the city's authorities will bother to get involved until tomorrow at the earliest."

"But..." I turned my head to watch as a boy, no older than fifteen, hurried past with his baby sister on his back. The little girl was laughing, as if the whole affair were a game, unaware that she might be homeless by morning. And that, even then, she might be considered one of the lucky ones. "But surely the crown..."

Oreia spat into the gutter. "The people living here are too poor to pay taxes. I promise you, the king is standing in the window of his high tower right now, watching with no more alarm than a farmer watches rats drown themselves in the river to escape a blaze he set." She forced her way forward in the crowd, leaving me behind to make my own way.

[Emerald, please tell me that isn't true.] I fell back to keep pace with him. *[Finch will come. Finch cares. She's... she's not like that, is she?]*

[And what'll Finch do?] Like Oreia, his expression was one part anger, one part resignation. *[She can't put out a fire on her own. She can't fight a Thaumaturge on her own. We need to focus on stopping that dwarf before he burns anything else.]*

[Yes, Crimson. Let's stop *him.]*

As usual, I didn't dignify Innocent's comment with a response.

By the time we reached the Undercroft, the smoke was thick enough to make Emerald choke. We had passed the last of the evacuees, but there were still plenty of people who'd stayed behind to help. When they spotted Oreia and Mercedes and the other priestesses of Lemda, they flocked toward us, in search of guidance.

"What happened here?" the priestess demanded.

"A Thaumaturge forced his way into one of the apartments," one man replied. "Threatened to kill the folks inside if they didn't keep quiet. He was trying to lay low. Said his partner got taken by the Conjury, and he didn't want word getting out."

"It was my cousin's apartment!" a young woman added. "I could hear their fighting through the walls next door. He was in there for hours, but then my cousin tried to leave for his night shift at the dockyards... people need to eat, you know, but the Thaumaturge wasn't having none of it. They fought, and then..."

"Please, help us." A woman with elven features grabbed Oreia's elbow. "My sister's still trapped inside with my nephew, and he's only six..."

As the pleas and explanations came in from all directions, I retreated to Emerald's side. *[He didn't know that Garland was dead.]*

[Must have worried she'd squeal under interrogation. If she did, their usual hideouts wouldn't be safe.] The fire was reflected in Emerald's eyes, orange on green, a forest ablaze. *[We've got to find him, Crim. Tonight.]*

He didn't voice his worry: that there were people still trapped inside the rubble, people he could help, given the chance. He could be of physical assistance.

I could not.

[Stay here,] I told him. *[Help Oreia and Dumplin organize the rescue. I'll find Sal.]*

Emerald turned his head toward me. *[You can't stop him on your own.]*

[But I'll be able to find him faster than you can. I can fly, I can walk through walls, I can navigate the streets more easily than you. And I won't burn. When I do find him, I'll tell you where to go. We can ambush him, and he won't see it coming.]

[Or you could let me have him,] Innocent whispered. *[I know what to do with those who let their power lead them astray...]*

[All right.] Emerald nodded. *[That's a good plan, actually.]*

Oreia was already giving directions, and the priestesses under her command fanned out, dispensing tasks to the gathered crowd. In all the chaos, it was easy enough to slip away unnoticed and fold myself into the shadows between the narrow streets.

The moment I was sure I was unobserved, I rearranged myself into a redwing blackbird and took to the skies of the burning district.

CHAPTER SEVEN

I did not confine myself to one form as I roamed the half-abandoned streets of the Hives. I changed as it suited me, swiftly and with little fanfare, sometimes taking to the sky, sometimes squeezing between walls, sometimes slipping underground to explore the network of sewers and pipes beneath street level. At times, I changed to make my form more discreet in case I was spotted; at others, I did not bother. Speed was my foremost aim.

Innocent, as always, observed my actions. *[This is good. This is how a predator hunts. You are learning, Crimson Smoke.]*

I did indeed feel predatory. Rather than fading as I circled outward from the source of the fire, my anger only grew. These people had so much to lose, and Sal so little to gain. What was the point of taking what scraps these people had earned? Personal enrichment? From what I could tell, Sal's actions made the city worse for everyone. From the egg that had killed Gorlyn and caused Serkadis to flee, to the names Dumplin had called out before we set forth, to the inferno behind me, all of it was an indictment.

And not only of Sal. It seemed to me that every person, in every position of power, big and small, was focused on the wrong things.

What was the point of them? Of *any* of them, if things like this could be allowed to happen?

[To serve their own selfish ends,] Innocent concluded. *[To profit enough that they can turn their backs on those they're meant to serve.]*

In my anger, I failed to avoid a flock of startled skipgulls, which was how I found my target at last. The gulls were panicked, fleeing from something that frightened them more than the scent of smoke.

I changed form midair, to the in-between shape I'd come to favor, halfway between Simone and Simon. Light as a shadow, I landed on my toes, crouching on the edge of a roof overhanging a street below.

The dwarf stumbled along below me, his ragged, scorched cloak hanging in tatters from his shoulders. He'd been injured, likely in the fight with the man whose apartment he'd commandeered as well as his unplanned departure through the window of the Lute and Goose.

[I found him, Em.]

[Where are you?] my friend asked at once.

[I'm not sure, but...] I tried to send him a picture of the place, noting details like the painting on the side of one building, the abandoned hogpen in an open lot between a tannery and a textile factory, and the aborted alleyway beyond. *[Can you see that?]*

[Not exactly, but I think I can describe it well enough for someone to recognize. Stay with him. We'll be there soon.]

I prowled along the edge of the roofline, following his progress. If I could find some way to lure him into the dead-end alley, I could keep him from disappearing again.

[And if your friends come? Then what? He'll try to burn them. Do you think a man like that will give up so easily? That he'll let them take him alive? A cornered beast knows he has nothing left to lose. But you and I, we can't be burned. We can end this now.]

[No.] Sal was almost to the mouth of the alleyway. If he passed it, I might miss my chance to corral him.

[Such interesting morals, Crimson Smoke. You treat your unsullied hands like the king treats his wealth: a prize to hoard and treasure, but to

what end? You will risk your friend's lives so that he can be... what? Arrested? If he is taken by the Conjury, they will wield him like the weapon he is. If you let Dumplin and Oreia take him, they will dispatch him anyway. Death will come, to him or others. I'm only suggesting that you skip the middleman.]

I paused on the corner of the roof. Emerald wouldn't approve of the idea Innocent had put forth. At least, I didn't think he would. And I couldn't ask him, since any discussion of Innocent was wiped from his mind the moment I broached the topic.

And yet, hadn't I *just* been questioning my adherence to Emerald's moral code? His unwillingness to take real action against those who kept their boot on the city's throat?

[He threatened to burn your home. Your family. Your best friend. You have seen that it was no idle threat. Protect them. Protect the Hives. If you won't let me do it, let me teach you how.]

I knew Innocent was bloodthirsty. I knew it craved violence. But this was different, because even without its mutterings, I felt another, deeper drive.

My job was to protect Emerald. It always had been. Hitherto, I had believed that my role was to be one of unerring goodness, at least as I could quantify it. But Oreia was good, too, wasn't she? And she was willing to do whatever it took to dispense justice in Lemda's name. I did not serve the Middling Godlet, precisely, but its nature, like mine, was one of duality. Of balance.

Innocent might call what I was about to do a departure from my morals, but I preferred to think of it as a departure from my usual methods.

Sal had already passed the mouth of the dead-end alleyway. I rearranged my costume to the one Garland had been wearing when Feeve killed her and leapt over the street below. It would have been an impossible jump for most people.

But I was not most people, after all.

Sal stopped and looked up. "Who's there?" he demanded. Flames sparked to life in his palms. "Show yourself!"

"Sal?" I called. I made my way to the roofline at the end of the alleyway, pitching my voice lower to match Garland's baritone, and trying for a bit of her accent as well. "Sal, is that you?"

I floated down to the ground, lingering near the back wall of the alley. After a moment, Sal reappeared, backtracking to find the source of the voice.

"Garland?" he called. "Where the shite have you been? I thought the Conjury got you."

"I can look after myself," I said. "Looks like you've had a rough night, though, Sal. Was that your handiwork I saw earlier?"

[Good, lure him closer. Pull him into the trap.]

I didn't bother explaining to Innocent that I was genuinely interested in the matter of Sal's guilt. Just because *a* Thaumaturge had set fire to the Hives didn't prove *this* one had.

"Thought they got you." The fires in Sal's hands burned out, plunging us into darkness, so that only moonslight and starlight illuminated the alley. "Thought you'd use intel to buy 'em off and buy their mercy. Pissing *jotunn.* Did you know that red-haired bitch was a Lightweaver?"

I shook my head. "Not until it was too late. Are you hurt? You took a nasty tumble out of that window."

[Yes, come closer, show us your wounds. Show us where it hurts.]

"Between that and the big bastard I got into blows with earlier, I'm not at my best." Sal sighed. "Come on, *Lord Bracefallow,* we've got to get out of here. Our cover's blown. I say we go back to that mansion, take what we want, and burn the place to ash before sunrise. We're as good as done for now. Might as well make a run for it. Maybe head east to..." He stopped suddenly. "Hang on, how did you find me?"

I took a step forward. "I followed your handiwork."

"Like shite you did." He turned back to the mouth of the alleyway. "The Conjury *did* take you, didn't they? This is a trap. You've walked me into a trap, you little—"

I darted past him to block the mouth of the alleyway, hemming him in. I had already noted the rough masonry of the walls around him, which would be hard to burn. No doubt he'd try, but even if he set them aflame, he wouldn't be able to flee through wreckage the way he would if they were made of timbers.

I lowered my hood and let him see my face. In an instant, his fingers blazed again.

"You," he spat. "Crimson pissing Smoke. Guess you're not a genius after all, or you'd realize fire's *my* domain." He flung a fistful of flame at me, which of course passed right through me to fizzle out on the cobbles behind him, still caked in mud from yesterday's rainstorm.

"Yes." I took a step closer. "Me."

And I rearranged myself into twice my normal size.

Sal yelped and stumbled backward until he hit the stone wall behind him. "What in the hells are you?"

"You know exactly who I am." I bent forward with a smile, rearranging it until it was much too wide for a human face. "I'm the one who's here to save the city from murderers like you."

"No. Please..." Sal raised his arms, using the flames to ward me off, although he must already have realized it was useless. "Please."

"Please, what?" I glowered at him. On the rare occasions when Emerald spoke through me, I had no control over my voice. I became his poppet. It was different, with Innocent. The shadow whispered in my ear, but the words that I uttered were my own, and I spoke with the conviction of my own self-righteousness. "You've hurt people. *On purpose.* And for no good reason. You've done it again and again. You've had the choice to stop, but you—" I shook my head. "You just. Kept. *Going.*"

I loomed over him. The moonslight at my back cast a shadow toward him, only it wasn't mine: the long limbs, the boney neck, and the long snout were those of the beast I carried within me.

Perhaps that should have frightened me. Truth be told, I was too angry to care.

"This is what I don't understand," I went on. "You have enough.

All of you. The king sits on his throne surrounded by more wealth than he could spend in a lifetime, while his people starve in the streets. The Conjury hole up in their distant city and send their agents out to do more harm than good. And you... what good are *you*?" I rested my elbows on my knees and glared at him. The shadow I cast stretched longer, reaching toward him with its skeletal fingers. "You have the power to help those without *Aidea*. To upend that balance of power. You can make warmth from nothing. And instead, you pedal pain. Why?"

Sal whimpered. He shrank away from me, from *us*, and pressed his back to the alleyway wall.

"I asked you a question," I growled. "I expect an answer. Why?"

"P-please." Drops of spittle flecked his lips. "Please, have mercy."

"Why should I?" I replied. "To whom have *you* shown mercy?"

He blubbered incoherently. The sight should have inspired pity, but it only made me angrier. He didn't deserve kindness or forgiveness. The Conjury and the crown were happy to let people like him run free, so long as he didn't threaten the *social order*.

My anger changed me, and my form changed with it.

I had long since proved that it was not possible for me to become something other than I was. Whatever form I took was part of me. An aspect of myself. Crimson-as-a-man; Crimson-as-a-woman; Crimson-as-a-bird; Crimson-as-a-toad.

I let myself become something else. Something I had never been before.

I became Crimson the monster.

My limbs warped and stretched, becoming impossibly long and hideously jointed, while the illusion of skin sunk tight to my phantom bones. Perhaps, when the Crone overtook me in the Black Hollow, she had left a bit of herself with me in the form of dripping black-capped toadstools that sprouted from what remained of my clothes. Scarlet armor formed itself around my midriff like dragon scales. The dark, red liquid from the toadstools dripped down my bony arms and crept along my not-skin of its own accord, in defiance of gravity's usual law.

The change didn't hurt, but I felt it in a way that I had experienced no other transformation. Becoming this thing, some strange amalgamation of monstrous parts, meant accepting that monstrosity was part of me. Emerald had always feared and reviled anything that might be construed as beastliness. Crouched in that alley, I embraced it.

When I spoke again, my voice was low and fractured, as if many tongues were speaking at once. "You believe you cannot be caught. You consume and corrupt at will. You act as if you are above the law. And perhaps you are." I craned my serpentine neck until my face was only inches from his. "But I am not the law. And you are not above *me*."

Sal blubbered at my feet. The fire in his hands had gone out. He said nothing, asked nothing, didn't even bother to beg anymore. He only wept.

I reached toward him, extending one hooked claw toward his chest. Perhaps I could force an image into his mind, the way I had done with Aindreas back in Dyrne.

Or perhaps Innocent was right, and I could do more.

"Crimson?"

I startled at the sound of a familiar voice and froze with the tip of my claw only inches from Sal's shoulder. I had not heard Emerald's approach, but nevertheless, he stood there, flanked by Oreia, Dumplin, Mercedes, Poke, and Doodah.

"Emerald!" I picked my voice into something light and welcoming, and hastily rearranged myself into my usual, inoffensive form. "You found me in time!"

I had no idea how long the others had stood there, or what they had heard. Oreia, at least, was focused on Sal, and she loped forward to grab him by the back of his neck and press his face into the dirt. She bound his hands behind him, then passed him off to Dumplin's bodyguards.

"Good work," she told me. "We'll take it from here."

They bore Sal away. Mercedes fixed me with a long, wary look before following the rest of them off to gods-knew-where, to do gods-knew-what. I trusted their judgment on that regard.

Sal had harmed the city, and the city took care of its own.

I hurried over to Emerald's side. "Should we go back to the fire and try to—"

Emerald held up a hand. "We'll talk about this later," he said, and turned his back on me.

That wasn't fair at all. I hadn't let Innocent out. I hadn't laid a finger on the dwarf—yet. We'd taken him without anyone else being hurt. What right did Emerald have to be mad at me?

Except that he'd spent his whole life trying to prove that he wasn't a monster, and I'd spent most of a year harboring one right under his nose. It was changing me. Besides, it had been a long night, and the work wasn't done yet. He was probably just in a hurry to get back to the apartments and help the survivors.

Yes. That was it. Or at least, that was what I decided to believe. As we made our way back through the winding warren of the Hives, I tried not to take his silence personally.

[For what it's worth,] Innocent whispered, *[I thought you were magnificent.]*

CHAPTER EIGHT

Finch, Aaliy, Basel, and a handful of Castcadesmen had joined the relief efforts by the time Emerald and I returned, though only Finch and Basel wore their Conjury uniforms. Their skeleton crew was far outnumbered by members of the local guilds, who had swarmed into the neighborhood and were using a variety of devices to put out the flames, temporarily reinforce collapsing beams, and rescue survivors who were still trapped inside.

In the end, only one building was leveled, with the buildings nearest damaged beyond repair. I was limited to directing newcomers toward the stations where they would be most useful—a necessary task, I supposed, but one that still felt inadequate in the wake of so much destruction.

Just as Oreia had predicted, dawn arrived before the king's guard did, although even their belated support offered a bit of relief. Those who had spent the night pawing through rubble were dead on their feet.

"Come with me," Finch told the Conjury members. "We'll set up bunks at headquarters, and I'll arrange for someone to feed us. There will be more work to do tomorrow, I promise."

Ash-flecked and weary, we withdrew to the relative safety of headquarters. While everyone else sought out a place to sleep, I approached Finch.

"Give me something to do," I begged in a low voice. "I can't touch anything, but I can't sleep, either. You might as well put me to use."

"Gladly." Finch led me toward the front desk, but stopped shy of the young man who was usually in charge of greeting visitors. "I'm not going to ask for too many details at the moment, but... off the record, the person who did this..."

"Is taken care of," I told her. "Off the record? Lemda's justice is swift."

The tension around her eyes relaxed, and her ears perked up. "Off the record, I'm glad to hear it. We'll sort things out tomorrow. Well, today. *Later.*" She yawned so wide that I could see every tooth in her mouth. "People will be coming by to ask for information. If they want to talk to me, tell them to piss off. If they want to know how to help, tell 'em where to go. Got it?"

I nodded. "Got it."

Emerald didn't even try to find me before he fell asleep.

OVER THE NEXT FEW DAYS, news trickled in. First, that the smuggler's hideout had been found. Sal's body was discovered inside, his throat slit apparently by his own hand.

I wondered if that was true. I wouldn't have put it past Oreia to convince the man to do it himself. Or maybe Dumplin had found another use for that necklace of hers.

There were other things found in the hideout as well. Proof, for example, of Sal and Garland's plot to defraud the Bracefallows, in the form of stolen items, forged documents... and Gorlyn's remains.

"It's almost suspicious how neatly that was resolved," I told Finch when she informed me of this development.

"Really?" She twitched her whiskers. "Makes perfect sense to me."

Emerald kept to himself, filling his days with manual labor in the Hives and spending his nights on a bunk at the Conjury headquarters. He avoided Basel, which I more than understood. He avoided me, which I did not.

[I'm not the one who killed him,] I complained to Innocent. *[Emerald is the one who brought the priestesses to arrest him. All I did was keep him from escaping.]*

[It's very unfair,] Innocent agreed.

I was not thrilled that the only one I could turn to for support was the monster living in the walls of my mind-cottage, but at least *someone* agreed with me.

Stepping through the door of the Lute and Goose should have felt like coming home. I was certainly pleased when the children rushed out of the kitchen to greet us.

The place was no longer packed to the brim, the number of diners now returned to a more standard quantity. Two women rose from a booth by the window to greet us.

"I'm sorry to hear about everything that happened in the Hives." Rubi did, indeed, look utterly distraught. "Is there anything I can do?"

"The temple of Lemda is raising money to help the survivors rebuild or relocate," I said. It was one of the lines I'd uttered dozens of times over the last week.

"*I* can send money," Rubi agreed.

"And I expect there's a need for clothes?" Vasilika added.

I smiled at her, pleased by her willingness to help. "Of course."

From the corner of my eye, I saw Emerald and Yerik discussing something in low tones. Emerald headed into the kitchen, leaving me to do the talking.

I joined Vasilika and Rubi at their table to share what I knew of the events in the city, albeit a highly editorialized version. The official report, as it were.

When Emerald emerged from the kitchen and headed for the stairs, I made my excuses to the ladies and followed him. He'd avoided me this long, but he could not ignore me forever.

"It's good to be back, isn't it?" I asked. "I've missed this place. Maybe we should stay for a few days, let you get some rest, before we go back to—"

Emerald opened the door of his room, *our* room, and stepped inside. The door slammed in my face.

I froze where I stood. The door between us was no obstacle to me. I could dart through it without a thought, as I had done many times before.

The door was not the problem. Even if I stepped into the room beyond, there would still be doors between us, ones I couldn't see, but which I had helped erect.

If I followed him, we were going to have a fight. I knew it. Words would be said that neither of us could take back, and although I didn't know what they would be, I was not ready to find out.

When I said that I wanted to be free of our connection, to be my own person outside of his sphere of influence, I hadn't meant this. I didn't fully understand the problem, or how to make it right.

He would come to me when he was ready. Until then, I had friends waiting for me downstairs.

I turned back to the stairs and left the door stand, untouched, where it divided us.

THE DEATH OF THE BARD

Emerald raced along the waterline south of the dockyards. He wasn't built for speed, but neither was the man ahead of us; though he boasted no visible jotunn ancestry, the man was thickset, broad shouldered, and heavy.

By all appearances I, too, was running. There was no real benefit to pulling ahead, although if I wanted to, I could have flown toward our attacker. If we'd been alone, I might have tried to block his way, just to see what he would do, but there were far too many witnesses. If we were going to catch him, my friend would have to be the one to do the catching. So I stuck to Emerald's side and pumped my arms and legs for all I was worth. I even pretended to sweat a little.

To our left, the low warehouses of the dockyards obscured the skyline. Some people were alarmed by our presence, but a fair number of them watched our passage with little more than mild interest.

To our right, a reinforced wall cut down from the walkway into the whitecaps beneath. There must have been a real shoreline there before, but whatever the landscape *had* been was covered by layers of stone built up to support the seawall, and held in place with a metal grid that was no doubt enchanted.

[A little faster,] I urged. *[You've almost got him, Em. Quick, before he—]*

Too late. The man swung around and dropped to one knee, pressing his hands to the path below him. I couldn't see what he did to activate his *Aidea*, but the ground below us shook, and Emerald stumbled.

"Oh, dear," I murmured. "Not again..."

When the little group of Castcadesmen and soldiers had tried to accost Bale of Kinmore, he'd refused to go quietly. In fact, he'd nearly brought a whole section of the city down with him, and he seemed prepared to do so again.

Seismic *Aidea* made the seawall tremble, and Emerald dropped into a crouch as the ground beneath us shook. The metal grid buckled near where the fugitive crouched, and small stones began to tumble through into the whitecaps below.

"Emerald..." I warned.

I was facing the wrong direction, so I heard the crack first, and the screams that followed. Uphill, a building broke apart as a fissure opened in the ground, shattering the foundation and sending a jagged rupture deep into the earth.

"Gods," I murmured. Calling on a single divinity seemed insufficient. This was quickly becoming a disaster worthy of a pantheon.

Emerald would not be deterred. He leaped across the ever-widening chasm and charged toward the Shaker.

At the same time, a trio of Castcadesmen burst forth from an adjoining alley. One of them lifted her hands, clad in gloves lined with metal insets, and a static crackle filled the air. The pop of the resulting spark was loud enough to make me flinch.

Bale's focus was broken by the yellow-gold snap of electricity that zinged from her gloves through the salt-soaked air. He was blasted off of his feet, and the rumble of the land settled.

Emerald tackled him a moment later, and it was all but over.

The three Castcadesmen wrestled the downed man into submission and bound his hands behind him. A few more agents, most likely those without *Aidea* at their command, caught up and surrounded them, crossbows at the ready. They dragged Bale to his feet and hauled him away.

"Impressive work," I observed.

The Sparkmage who'd summoned that electric snap looked up in surprise. She was young, I thought. Younger than I looked, certainly, and not *so* much older than Svelte. Her amber cheeks warmed at the praise.

"Th-thank you, Crimson Smoke." She executed a formal bow. "I thought it best to stop him as soon as possible, before..." She turned her attention to the damaged buildings, and the deep crack in the earth through which seawater already washed. "I was afraid I'd kill him if I was too far off—the spark's a bit hard to control, you see. But I didn't want to risk any more damage to the city."

"Are you from here?" I ask.

The Sparkmage's chest puffed up with pride. "Born and raised. I grew up near the Hives. Nana always told me that if I studied hard enough, and became a Castcadesman, I could make something of myself one day. Like... well, like you. And him." She tipped her chin toward Emerald, who was deep in conversation with one of her fellows. "He started as a nobody, too, didn't he? But these days, you can be a nobody from Kinmore and still be a hero. I hope to earn my own prominence title one day." She dipped her head. "Begging your pardon, miss, but I ought to stick with the prisoner." With that, she turned and jogged away.

I watched her until she, along with about half of her squadron and their prisoner, withdrew toward the heart of the city. The rest stayed behind to notate and begin repairs on the damage Bale had done.

If only things were simple. Some days, it was easy to hate the Conjury. Others, I was reminded that—like any organization—it was made of up of groups of people, and very few of them were truly evil.

Was the Conjury defined by its rotten core? Or could it truly be changed, over time, but the small actions of its most sincere members?

[Intent does not matter when the heart is rotten,] Innocent rumbled.

Personally, I suspected that nothing, not even the net worth of the Conjury, could be summarized in a single aphorism.

"Crimson!" Emerald waved me to his side. "Come on, there's nothing more we can do here. Let's let the captain get on with his work."

The captain in question sneered at Emerald's back and muttered something under his breath as we departed, before spitting on the ground at his feet. I wondered who he despised more: the rogue Shaker who'd nearly collapsed the seawall, or my half-jotunn friend?

I realized then just how tired I was of Kinmore. In some ways, the city had been good to us, but in that moment, I longed with all my heart to be gone. Back to Kovin Isle. Or northward, perhaps, to meet Captain Finch's people in the Vapor Plains. Northwest, to see Basco in his home in Danilas Freehold. East, in search of Serkadis, to learn what had become of him.

Anywhere else but the city that was wearing Emerald down, slowly but steadily, like the seawall after years of salt surf and summer storms.

THREE DAYS LATER, we sat on one of the pebbled beaches east of the city. Yerik had closed the inn for the morning. It was an especially fine day, and Rubi had insisted that it was too good to spend indoors. She had offered to bring the children on her own, but Yerik had decided to come along, and he coaxed Emerald to join our little outing.

Blare and Quell played in the waves, while Svelte and Rubi walked along the waterline, collecting sea glass and shells and laughing about something only they could hear. I sat in the sand, enjoying the play of light on the water, the gold-flecked motes of sand that fractured among the rigid spears of sea grass with each breeze, the brilliance of the waves that rolled in from an endless blue horizon to lap at the shore.

Behind me, Emerald and Yerik sat in silence, although I could feel the storm brewing in my friend's mind. A thunderhead, despite the cloudless day that heralded the end of summer. Soon, the days would grow shorter, and the nights would stretch long.

"You're leaving soon," Yerik said, sounding more matter-of-fact than I would have guessed.

Emerald snorted. "And where do you think we're going to go?"

I couldn't feel the sunlight that shattered on the surface of the sea, but his words warmed me. We might not be on speaking terms these days, but he still said *we*, and that was something.

"I don't know." Yerik leaned back on his elbows to watch the boys stumble through the surf, laughing, as a larger wave came in. "But I run an inn, remember? I know wanderlust when I see it. I'm surprised you've lasted here this long."

Emerald used one hand to shield his eyes and turned to study our friend, our host, our... whatever Yerik was. More than a companion, I thought, but I knew no word in Osmarian for the not-quite familial ties that bound us to him. "You thought I'd leave sooner?"

"You aren't happy here," Yerik said, as if that was obvious.

"I'm as happy as I've been anywhere else," Emerald said. That, I thought, was true. Although the bar was pretty low in that regard. "Even with my... with Tin... even the last place I lived, I could never see myself staying permanently. Kinmore has enough to keep me occupied."

I didn't share what I was thinking, that his *occupation* was not the road to contentment. I recalled what Basel had said about Emerald making himself valuable in order to earn the respect of his peers. Nothing he did would be enough to change the minds of those who saw him as less than a person. And even if they did, what then? I could not imagine that the approval of the world's Dirkuses was his ultimate aim.

Yerik must have been thinking along the same lines I was, because he flicked a few pebbles across the beach before sighing. "When I was a boy, I wanted nothing more than a home where I felt secure. I made that for myself, Em. And now I have more than I could have dreamed, and I know more or less what tomorrow will look like, and that's good enough for me. If every day was like today, I'd have no complaints." He cast a shrewd, sidelong eye at my friend. "But you? You wouldn't. I understand that. So, I'm glad we had this last year. I know it's almost over. All I ask is that, when you go, you at least tell me first. No sneaking off in the dead of night, all right?"

Emerald hummed and returned his attention to the beach. "I promise."

Svelte and Rubi had turned back toward us, still laughing. In the surf, Quell tripped, and Blare hauled the lambkin back to his feet.

The word I'd been looking for came to me at last, the Osmarian word for the thing Yerik had become to us.

Anchor.

And it made me sad to think of the rope that bound us to the seabed slowly fraying, day by day, until it inevitably gave way.

CHAPTER TWO

" I know you don't like meeting with me," Basel said, his everpresent smile plastered on his cheerful face. "I promise, I won't go prying again. I wanted you to know that I've cleared you as a cause for concern in my notes."

Emerald lifted one eyebrow. "Thank you." The second word lilted upward, taking on the tone of a question.

"Your work has been exemplary," Basel went on. "The Conjury was unlucky to lose you as a Castcadesman—" He stopped, then shook his head. "*Unlucky.* Pardon my phrasing. The Conjury was stupid and careless when it came to how they treated you. For what it's worth, the commander who released you from service is no longer an officer. Times have changed in Venta Bulgarum. I understand that you're doing well for yourself in your current capacity, but I've recommended that if you *do* ever decide to return to Conjury service, you should be considered for a leadership role."

Emerald's other eyebrow joined the first. "You did? Even with...?" He waved over his shoulder to where I stood, slack jawed, in the corner of the room.

Basel smiled wryly. "We all find coping mechanisms, Emerald, and there are worse options. Some men with your history would turn to drink... or worse."

Emerald, who had turned to drink *and* worse, fidgeted in his chair.

"I'm not sure what sway my words hold, but at any rate, I'm very pleased with what I've seen of your work. You're dedicated, and I believe that you genuinely value the well-being of the citizens we serve." Basel closed his notes. "And there you go."

Emerald rose from the chair in increments, as if waiting for Basel to spring some nasty, last-minute surprise on him. "Thank you," he said again. When the swamper elf waved goodbye, Emerald fled, with me trailing like a ghost in his wake.

It had become Rubi and Vasilika's custom to meet at the Lute and Goose once a week to discuss ways in which they might put Rubi's vast wealth and Vasilika's intimate knowledge of city life to use. At first, it was only the two of them, but by and by, they'd made friends among the inn's regulars. One of their weekly meetings was in full swing by the time Emerald and I returned home following Basel's all-clear.

"...not interested in throwing money at the problem in the name of a temporary solution," Rubi was saying.

"What if we offered a stipend to tradesmen willing to take on untrained apprentices from the Hives?" Vasilika asked. "Give the youth a chance to learn a trade."

"Like a scholarship?" Rubi asked thoughtfully. "That's an interesting idea. Might step on some toes in the guilds, but I think we should be able to handle that."

"Or you could offer loans, without the crown's interest rates," a man suggested. "It's nearly *impossible* to open a business without the funds on hand, and the king's rates nearly double a man's debt over the course of a year."

Rubi wrinkled her nose. "I like the idea, but I don't know that I can manage account books like that all on my own."

"So don't," a woman put in. She was wearing plain clothes and a half-cape with a deep hood, but she'd thrown it back to reveal her face. Mercedes of Kinmore was becoming a regular sight in the Lute and Goose. "Let the Temple of Lemda handle the bookkeeping. That way you can stay anonymous as well. The king won't take kindly to a noblewoman putting a dent in his coffers, but he can't say anything about the temple doing it."

"And then you could petition other anonymous donors," a dwarf from one of the guilds added. "Speaking of scholarships, I'm sure the guilds would be willing to open more spots for students if they had the resources..."

The conversation continued as Emerald and I settled in a far corner.

"Good grief," I said under my breath. "I think we may be witnessing the start of a revolution."

"I'm impressed with your friend." Emerald nodded to Rubi. "She's got more substance than I would have given her credit for." He didn't meet my eyes when he spoke, but it was better than the silent treatment to which I'd been subjected lately.

A loud thumping at the inn door startled the company into silence. When the sound repeated a moment later, one of the Pruvs got up and went to the door to open it.

The babblebird, which had evidently been waiting outside, waddled through the door like an oversized skipgull hunting a tide-pool. It looked around before croaking, "Crimson Smoke and the Emerald Flame."

Emerald went to retrieve the bird and set it on our table. "I suppose it's another message from... Silverskin," he murmured.

The conversation on the other side of the room resumed, but Svelte and Quell—who had been seeing to the needs of the guests— came over to listen. Even Yerik made no attempt to hide that he was interested in the forthcoming message.

"Go on, then," Emerald said.

The babblebird ruffled its feathers and tipped its head sideways to examine us with its beady eyes. It opened its mouth.

The scream that emitted from its beak was loud enough to drown out any conversation around us.

"*Oh, Emerald!*" it wailed. "*I'm dying... I don't have long for this world, and with my final breaths, I must insist that you avenge me!*"

Every head in the room swiveled toward our table. Svelte's jaw dropped. Emerald groaned and buried his face in his hands.

I would have known Coirpre's voice anywhere.

"*Sabotage! Deceit! Oh, woe is me! Here I lie, on the outskirts of Venta Bulgarum, fending off Driaweep's grasping hands. I don't know how much longer I have, but I beseech you, please find my shriveled remains at the Boar's Cradle and render the justice only you can provide. I beseech you...*" The babblebird let out a shrill, lingering gurgle that was no doubt part of its message, and which seemed to go on interminably, causing Emerald to slump ever deeper in his seat. At long last, the bird went silent, looking mightily pleased with itself.

"Well," I said into the ensuing silence. "That was... quite the performance. Very in-character."

Svelte looked up from the babblebird in alarm. "You know who this is from?"

"Oh, we most certainly do." Emerald shot a pointed look at the massive painting of Coirpre that hung behind the bar.

Quell was studying the bird intently, as if he was afraid that it might explode. "He's faking, right? I mean, whoever sent this message wasn't actually being murdered."

Emerald rolled his eyes. "Of course not. He just wants attention. Absolute pain in my..." He trailed off and rubbed his temples. "Venta Bulgarum. Really? What has he gotten himself into this time?"

The rest of the assembled guests continued to stare.

Emerald got to his feet. His chair scraped across the well-loved floor. "Svelte, would you please be kind enough to give this messenger a reward of some sort, before it decides to subject us to another rendition of that awful farce?"

"Where are *you* going?" Svelte asked.

"To pack." Emerald flapped a hand at the bird. "And to write some letters. It seems Coirpre wants to meet us at the Boar's Cradle, and that's at least a two-week journey on foot."

Quell dropped the mug he was holding. The clay shattered at his feet, leaking the dregs of room-temperature ale across the worn wood. "You're leaving?" he asked.

Emerald seemed to realize the implications of this for the first time. His smile was sad. "I am. That man is a terrible actor and a worse bard, but Crimson and I both owe him our lives."

Svelte darted away and returned with a broom to sweep up the broken crockery. She was careful to keep her face turned so that we wouldn't see the tears welling in her eyes, but I knew they were there.

I also knew, but did not say, that we would have been leaving soon anyway. Coirpre's message was the excuse that Emerald had been waiting for.

The one we'd both been waiting for, if I was being honest.

He began by writing letters: to Dumplin, to High Priestess Oreia, to Finch. The latter was a cursory note explaining his imminent departure, but he spent a great deal of time decorating the top of the paper with a set of symbols written in a spiral pattern. It was rather pretty and would mean nothing to most people who might see it in passing, but in the Leonhite language, it warned her to be careful and promised to keep her secret. After his signature, he added a little sketch of a flowering weed, *wildesprigge,* rising tall among a patch of grass.

"We won't say goodbye to her in person?" I asked.

Emerald shrugged. "What is there to say? I'll ask Svelte to post these letters with Feeve tomorrow. By the time she reads this, we'll already be gone."

"Svelte will be staying, then?" I asked softly.

"I'm sure she will. She's happy here, like Yerik. They all are. I'm sure they'll stay." Emerald sealed the last envelope and got to his feet.

"Emerald." I waited for him to look at me, but he did not. Instead, he began opening drawers and gathering his things. "Emerald, can we talk?"

"About what?" he demanded.

"About why you're avoiding me?"

"You know why."

"Because—" I rubbed my temples. "Because of what you saw in the alley? When I cornered Salvation?"

He grunted. "Exactly. See, you do get it."

"I promise you, I don't. I didn't hurt him. I didn't kill him, any more than you did by bringing Oreia and Dumplin to him." We still didn't know for certain whose hand had been holding the knife, but I remembered that Dumplin had been wearing her necklace the night of the fire. The more I thought about it, the more I was convinced that Sal *had* been the one to slit his own throat. What Dumplin had shown him, however, I could only speculate.

[You would have, though. If you'd had more time, you would have found a way to hurt him.]

Innocent was probably right, and not just because it had wanted to hurt him so badly. Threats and violence were not outside my realm of expertise. I had threatened Aindreas when I visited him in confinement. If I could have made him bleed, I think I would have.

Perhaps Emerald knew that. And perhaps that was the source of his anger, but until he said the words aloud, I could not be sure.

"Explain it to me, please." I perched on the chair, with my legs crossed and my hands folded in my lap, as demure as a schoolmarm. "Explain why you're angry."

"Because of what you became. Because that isn't how we do

things!" He stuffed his spare trousers in the bag without bothering to fold them.

"And how do we do them, exactly?"

"By the book." His shirts, socks, and undergarments were shoved unceremoniously into the bag as well. Even his grotesque yellow suit, which had been languishing in the bottom drawer, seemed fated to accompany us. "Respectably. We have to follow the rules—"

At these words, I snapped. "Whose rules, exactly? The rules set by the Conjury, which you've happily broken in, let me think, *every single case we've investigated thus far*? The rules of the crown, which we have deliberately undermined on more than one occasion? Or perhaps you mean—"

"*My rules.*" Emerald slammed the bag down on the bed and leaned his full weight against the frame. "I know you weren't there for everything I've been through, that you won't understand, but there are rules I've had to follow my whole life, in order to survive in a world where I'm *never* welcome." He let his head droop forward against his chest, and even in his profile I could see his pain. I could also see how deeply he believed every word he uttered. "I've never seen you become that... that thing, whatever you want to call that shape you took in the alley, but you can't do it again. It was..." He shook his head.

"Terrifying?" I suggested. "Dangerous?" When he did not respond I added, "Ugly?"

Emerald made a sound like a wounded animal. "*Monstrous.*"

I fell silent, turning the word over and over in my mind, examining it from every angle. "Why is that the rule?"

"Because that's the one thing I can never be," he said. "And I made you. Like it or not, Crim, I made you. You were supposed to be the best parts of me. And if you can become monstrous, then..."

Then so can I.

"Ah." I crossed my ankles and twirled a lock of my hair around one finger. "I see."

"Good. Then you know why you can never do it again."

He went on packing. The bag that Tincrown had given him as a parting gift soon groaned at its leather seams. Emerald was doing his best to fit his last shirt inside when I spoke again.

"I don't agree."

He froze. "What?"

"I understand what you're saying," I told him. "And I understand that you had to find a way to survive. But look at it from my perspective. You still work for people you had to hide your lover from. People who, after fifty years in power, have not made the world safe for him... or for you. If you can't challenge the Conjury, how can you expect anyone else to do it? And if nobody does, how can things ever change? You're entitled to make your own choices, but so am I. And if scaring the piss out of a monster by showing him his own reflection is one of the few ways I can fight back, then I can't promise that I'll never do it again."

Emerald dropped onto the end of the bed. "Crimson..."

"If you won't fight back, then I must find my own way."

"Fight back?" my friend repeated. He closed his eyes. "You don't know what you're asking of me."

"I have an idea. But in truth, I'm not asking you anything. I'm not sure that your old rules serve you anymore, if indeed they ever did. Either way, they are not *my* rules. And since you and I are..." I waved a finger between us, as if tracing the invisible line of our tether. "*As we are,* I suspect that you share similar doubts about what we've witnessed in the course of the last year. How much longer do you plan to work for the Conjury? Honestly?"

Emerald covered his face with his hands. "I can't think about this right now."

I got to my feet. "It's *all* I can think about lately. I suppose we'll have plenty of opportunities to discuss it later, though. I'll leave you to finish your packing." With that, I sailed toward the door, and onward through it, out into the hall.

Usually, I was careful about stepping into the open, but I hadn't bothered to check the hall this time. I was, therefore, quite alarmed to find Blare standing in the hallway, looking profoundly guilty.

Did you... I started to sign, then realized that asking him in handspeech if he'd overheard anything was an absurd question. He wasn't wearing Mel's amplification devices, so that couldn't be the reason for his glum expression. *Did you want something?* I amended.

I have to tell you something. Or, show you. He gestured toward his eyes, although he would not look at me. *And I really hope you won't be angry with me.*

Should I get Emerald?

Blare shook his head. *No point.*

I put aside my annoyance with my friend and followed Blare into the children's room. My curiosity mounted as he knelt down to fumble beneath the bed. The box he withdrew was an unfamiliar one, but when he opened it, I flinched. Inside lay a small collection of items taken from the Brotherhood of Guise.

Innocent tapped at the walls confining it. *[No wonder he had Emerald's marble. Clever little thief.]* The shadow-beast sounded almost... affectionate.

The majority of the box, however, was taken up with an item that I'd never thought I'd seen again. On my last visit to Brother Modest's office, I'd noticed that the old spellbook—the one containing the ritual that led to Reticent's death—was missing. I'd assumed Harmony had destroyed it once and for all.

I'd been wrong.

"You kept it?" I murmured as I sank to the floor beside Blare. When he didn't answer, I realized my error and repeated my question in handspeech.

At first, I just wanted to make sure that no one else found it, Blare explained. *But then... well, Quell's been translating it. There are some strange old spells in here, and I think they might be really powerful. There are a few that make me think—* He stopped and swallowed hard. The subtle bulge in his throat bobbed. Since when had he started to look more like a man than a boy? *I think there's something in here that might help you become, you know. Your own thing. Like you asked Serkadis to do for you.*

"Oh," I said. "Oh." After what I'd been through during that attempt to free myself, I wasn't sure I wanted to try again. And certainly, after what had happened to Reticent, I was wary of the book's contents. But it *was* very old, and very powerful.

It was also the book that had called Innocent into being. Might it, therefore, contain a way to be rid of my unwanted shadow?

Svelte told me what happened downstairs. Blare's frantic signing pulled me back into the moment. *She said that you're leaving and going to Venta Bulgarum. She and Quell want to stay here, with Yerik. She assumes that I do, too.*

But you don't? I signed.

Blare shook his head. *Quell gave up his Aidea. Svelte only wants to use hers to bake things. They're happy here. I want... more. I don't know what, yet. I don't care about power, and I don't want to work for the Conjury, but I want... I want to go with you. To Venta Bulgarum. I'm more like Emerald than Yerik, and if I stayed here, it would be for Svelte and Quell's sake. I love them, Svelte especially...* His throat bobbed again. *But I don't want to stay forever. If you take me with you, maybe I can help you get free, or find someone who can.*

I wasn't sure if he meant that I would be freed from Emerald or Innocent, but it hardly mattered. *If you want to come with us, then come. I'm glad you told me about this, but...* I remembered, again, what Basel had told Emerald that first meeting. *You don't need to be useful for us to want you. I'll talk to Emerald.*

Blare's smile lit up the room. It was almost enough to banish the shadows that seemed to linger around the old book balanced in his lap.

CHAPTER THREE

Our last morning in the Lute and Goose was a somber one. Svelte cried when Blare told her he was leaving, and Quell bawled so loudly that he had to excuse himself to the kitchen to calm down. Yerik left the doors locked for our last meal together at the largest table in the room.

"You'll be careful, won't you?" Yerik asked. I wasn't sure who he was talking to, but when no one else answered, I made my voice light.

"Of course," I said. "We're going to see Coirpre, after all." I gestured to the pair of paintings, with the smiling man in green seated alongside Emerald's new, dour portrait. "I'm sure he's gotten himself into another absurd scrape. Fleeced another merchant caravan, maybe. Tumbled into a year-long contract with a robber-baron. The usual."

I was the only one who laughed, although to his credit, Yerik tried.

We lingered while Yerik and Svelte assembled as many supplies as we could carry with us. Quell hugged Blare around the waist, and Emerald around his knees.

"Don't forget me," he begged Blare. "Don't forget any of us."

How could I? Blare signed.

The lambkin's eyes flicked toward Emerald, a reminder that forgetting wasn't as difficult as any of us would like it to be.

Svelte squeezed her brother until his eyes watered.

"You've got your dragon scale?" she asked Emerald. "And your marble, in case your necklace gets stolen again and you need another way to summon Crimson?"

Emerald nodded. "I have everything. Next time we come through, you'll have to show me your new recipes."

Svelte hugged him, too. When that was done, she stepped away and wiped her eyes on her sleeve, baring her teeth in a watery smile. "Have a grand adventure, you three."

Yerik bid Blare farewell, but he hesitated when it came to Emerald. He seemed taken aback, but pleasantly so, when Emerald yanked him into a sincere embrace.

"At least you've got that godsdamned painting to remember me by," Emerald said.

Yerik chuckled. "I'm not the one who forgot I knew you. Crimson, keep an eye on them. I know these two will be a handful."

We gradually withdrew to the front door, promising to write letters and send babblebirds. We all swore up and down we'd visit within the year. They were not empty promises. At least, they were not meant to be.

I did not know it then, but fate—or perhaps the gods—had other plans. Emerald and I would never walk through that door again.

EMERALD HAD SAID that the trip might take two weeks on foot. Fortunately, we were not forced to walk the whole time. On the fine days, we could sometimes catch a ride on a passing cart in exchange for a few coins. There were passenger wagons, too, that would carry us between towns if the drivers were of a mind to offer. Some were reluctant to welcome a jotunn aboard. Others were pleased with the security he offered, or knew the two of us by name and reputation.

The landscape around us changed gradually. As we made our way northeast, the rolling hills gave way to more rugged terrain and denser forests, where the turning leaves were further along than they had been in the south. At some juncture, we crossed the border between the Kingdom of Feynlish and into Osmaria, although I knew this only because of the change in colors of the pennants hanging from the village rooflines.

While we traveled with groups, Blare wore his amplifiers more often. When it was just the three of us, he mostly stored them in a pouch at his belt. Emerald and I pretended that our lingering silence was a normal part of our travels together, and I doubt Blare noticed the difference, but I did. I wished that we'd discuss old stories over the fire the way we had on Kovin Isle. I wished he'd speak to me at all.

His tongue was still, and the link between our conscious minds stayed closed.

Maybe Coirpre will fix him, I thought, as I stood watch in the night. There was no reason for us to sleep in shifts, since I never needed rest. Emerald and Blare should have been the best-rested travelers on the trail, if only Emerald would sleep properly.

He rarely did.

Because I'd expected to spend two weeks on the road, I was caught unawares by the sudden appearance of an inland sea barely a tenday into our travels. A mountain rose along its shores, so high that it stood head and shoulders above the surrounding land. Every inch of its slope was built up, with the most impressive buildings at its peak. The settlement dwarfed Kinmore both in scope and grandeur, even from afar, and would have left me breathless were I not perpetually so.

I did not need anyone to tell me where we were. Emerald had been dreaming fitfully of Venta Bulgarum for days. It was beautiful and terrible to look upon, and I could only imagine what it would be like to walk its streets.

I'd thought myself immune to wonder. Apparently, I was not yet as jaded as I'd let myself believe.

THE BOAR'S Cradle sat well outside the city walls, and it was—to put it kindly—an absolute cesspit.

"Gods." Emerald used his shirt to cover his nose. "This stinks worse than Kinmore Harbor."

Why would your friend want to meet us here? Blare's dark complexion was enough to disguise when he blushed, but the stench of the Boar's Cradle was sufficient to turn him ashen with disgust.

Because our friend is trouble, I signed back. *And probably in trouble.*

He'd have to be, Blare replied, *to choose a place like this on purpose. I miss the Lute and Goose.* He meant it as a joke, but there was more than a grain of truth beneath the surface.

"You!" The bartender let the bottle she was holding slam against the bar as she jabbed a finger our way. "I know who you are."

Emerald rolled his shoulders, like he was expecting a fight.

But the barkeep wasn't pointing at him. Her eyes were fixed on me. Like the rest of the Boar's Cradle, she looked hard-used. Five parallel scars raked across her face, as if something the size of a bear had taken a swipe at her nose and very nearly gotten to keep its prize. Her dark hair was cut close to the scalp. She had the sort of leathery toughness that either spoke to long years of hard labor or not-so-long-years of constant battle.

"You, there, the pretty one!" she snapped. "I know who you're looking for." She gestured from me to the back corner of the tavern. "Have a seat. I'll let him know you're here."

"Er." I looked around, already regretting that we hadn't rented a room elsewhere for Blare before coming to this wretched place. "Thank you?"

She waved me off, and the three of us picked our way across the floor. Blare's boots made a wet, sticky sound with each step, as if he was wading through a shallow bog and not traversing a tavern floor.

There was a window near the back table, and when we chose our seats, I found myself sitting closest to the glass. Outside, dusk was just getting comfortable, and the city on the mountain had begun to glitter with tiny golden lights from its thousands upon thousands of windows.

"It's magnificent, isn't it?" I murmured.

Blare nodded, but Emerald shrugged. "If you like that sort of thing. Hopefully we can settle whatever Coirpre wants from us and move on without setting a foot inside."

And go where? Blare asked.

Emerald shrugged again. "Anywhere but here."

"*Ah! My good friends!*" A familiar blur of golden hair, cornflower-blue eyes, and verdant garments flung himself into the booth alongside Emerald. Coirpre paused to take in Blare's presence. "And my *new* friend!" he added with more cheer than a place like the Boar's Cradle warranted.

"Why the hell have you brought us here?" Emerald growled.

Coirpre pressed a hand to his chest. "Getting right to business, are we? No welcome at all?"

Emerald raked a hand through his hair and turned his back toward the window, wedging himself into the booth at an odd angle so that he could get a better view of Coirpre. "Hello, Coirpre. Glad to see that your very convincing death rattle was all a ploy. Now, would you please be so kind as to tell me why, in the name of Driaweep's withered jewels, you've dragged us here?"

Coirpre patted Emerald's arm. "Leave the poetry to me in the future."

Emerald shot me an incredulous glance. For just a moment, we were on the same team again. *Aster bless Coirpre for that.*

"I brought you here for the terrible service," Coirpre said. "And the rancid atmosphere." He winked at Blare, who laughed under his breath. "It's the one place this close to Venta Bulgarum that the

Conjury agents never visit. I'm sure you can see why. And if the babblebird had been intercepted, anyone who knew the area would find it entirely plausible that I'd been stabbed here and left to die on the floor. See, I'm not as stupid as you think I am."

That was certainly *one* way of looking at it.

"That explains why you brought us *here*." Emerald slapped his hand on the table. "Not why you brought us *here*." He gestured over his shoulder to the glittering city beyond the glass.

"Ah, yes, I'm getting to that." Coirpre sat back as the barkeep arrived to deliver four heavy mugs. He smiled at her and placed a coin in her open palm. I caught a flash of silver before it disappeared into some secret pocket of her clothes.

"Awfully expensive for beer that I'm sure none of us will be drinking," Emerald deadpanned.

Coirpre passed the mugs around. "First of all, it isn't beer. There's a *child* present, and I know you don't drink. They're empty. What I'm *paying* her for is cover, and to make sure that nobody interrupts us."

I leaned across the table. Emerald's excitement blended with mine. "You've got a case," I said softly.

"Indeed, I do. One that I'm sure you'll want to take on." Coirpre lifted his empty mug and pretended to take a sip. "But first, let me tell you a story about a remote island I once visited to the south."

Emerald flinched and closed his eyes. "*Shite.*"

"You've heard of it, then?" Coirpre asked. "Kovin Isle only recently came under Conjury control, but I'm told it's lovely this time of year."

"Oh, no." I lowered my voice. "Coirpre, what happened?"

"There were rumors," he said, "of a lost town, destroyed by a natural disaster. But then, one day, it suddenly reappeared. Apparently, there was an old man who'd used magic to hide the town from the Conjury, but he died quite suddenly. Something to do with his heart, I believe."

The pang that went through me was very close to painful.

Nechtan had been using magic to hide Dyrne from sight. Magic *we'd* taught him. Because he was invisible, I'd never had a true sense of his age, and it hadn't occurred to me that he might not live long enough to pass his knowledge off to someone younger.

Emerald leaned his elbows on the table and hid his face in his hands.

"It's all very hush-hush," Coirpre went on. "Nobody knows exactly what happened, but a handful of people were arrested. The rest got away. Now, there are all sorts of rumors, but I happen to have spoken to a young woman who works for the Conjury prisons. Lovely lady. She's very good at her job, but she drinks like a fish, and when she does, she talks. According to her, there are three people being kept beneath Venta Bulgarum as we speak, awaiting interrogation. The other two are in transit to the *Aidea Nulda*. Supposedly, some of them are—"

"Invisible," Emerald said.

Only five prisoners... it could have been much worse. We'd been afraid that if the Conjury found out about Dyrne, they'd find a way to use the villagers to accomplish their own ends.

Even five was bad news, though. And it didn't help that any of them might be coerced into telling the Conjury about Emerald's involvement in the cover-up.

"So you've heard," Coirpre murmured.

"About the village," Emerald said. "Not about the arrests."

Blare was watching this exchange with obvious interest, but I'd have to explain the significance of it all later, in private.

"Who did they arrest?" I asked. "Do you know?"

"The two headed for the Nulda are men, apparently," Coirpre said. "That's all my contact could tell me. But the ones here? I can tell you all about them." He waved his mug toward the window. "Two of them are a couple, and the woman is with child. Quite far along, by the sounds of it. I believe they're waiting to see how her child comes out. The man is quite ordinary, but she's a bit, erm, lacking in the *skin* department."

[Kristine,] I thought, horrified.

[And Parian.] I hadn't expected Emerald to respond, but apparently our little spat was nothing in the face of this new nightmare. ***[And their baby, who will certainly be invisible. All the children of Dyrne are at first.]***

That's only two, Blare signed.

Coirpre cocked his head and looked to me for an explanation.

"He said, that's only two people. You mentioned a third."

"Yes." Coirpre set his mug down with a hollow thump. "The woman, as I said, was in no condition to flee. Her husband was loyal enough to stay behind even though it meant his certain capture." Coirpre paused, either to choose his words or for dramatic effect. "As was her doctor."

Emerald groaned and shuddered so pitifully that even the other guests, who seemed disinclined to pity, frowned in sympathy.

"Tincrown is in Venta Bulgarum?" I whispered.

Coirpre nodded. "Locked away in the Conjury's cells."

"But..." I turned to Emerald. "But we can't let him stay there. Or Kristine, or Parian. We have to get them out. We *have to.*"

For all his talk of rules, I knew Emerald could not let this stand. His fingers parted, revealing one bright green eye. *[We do.]*

Blare made another gesture, but not in handspeech this time. He simply pointed to Coirpre and raised his eyebrows, then held out his hands as if waiting for something to be placed in his upturned palms.

"You want to know if I have a plan?" Coirpre asked.

Blare nodded.

"My young friend." The bard leaned across the table and grinned almost as wide as I had in the alley, when I was looming over Sal. His eyes flicked toward the window again, and the godsdamned city on the far side of the grease-flecked glass. "I thought you'd never ask."

[We're staying, aren't we?] I asked Emerald. After all his talk of rules, I was no longer sure.

I needn't have doubted him. There was one person for whom

Emerald would do anything, and he was locked away only a stone's throw from where we sat. My friend could bluster on about being ordinary all day, but when it came down to it, he had never managed to be as cold and unyielding as he pretended.

He stared out the window for a long time, then he turned his face toward me and met my eye. ***[We'll find a way. I don't care what it takes. Even if it kills me. Even if I have to give up everything to make it happen. Even if I have to do something terrible along the way. I'm not letting them have him.]***

From behind the walls of my mind-cottage, Innocent purred in delight.

K.C. and I truly hope you enjoyed this Heavenfall novel. We love Crimson and Emerald as much as we hope you do.

Interested to read more in this world? Sign up for our newsletter at: rileyrookhouse.com/subscribe

Find a link to it and many other Heavenfall titles on RileyRookhouse.com

Acknowledgments

From K.C. Norton: Writing this series always means dredging up a bunch of emotional debris I'm not quite ready to look at, mudlark style. My sincere appreciation to everyone who's helped me sift through the mud in search of the good stuff.

In addition to the usual suspects, I want to give special thanks to John Andrew Quale, better known as Prince Poppycock. My appreciation, in fact, to everyone whose gender identity (or gender expression) can best be described as "Yes, And..." Especially for younger people, I know it can be hard to see what's going on in the world right now. You're not alone. We're in this together, with our powdered wigs, makeup, and 17th-century silk high-heeled shoes.

From Riley Rookhouse: I'd like to give thanks to all the usual suspects: Amy and Ami for our long bouts of plotting—I owe them so much; Diane Callahan, Story Garden's lead editor; and the Zanesville crew who inspired Heavenfall in the first place.

We have an amazing team over here at Story Garden. I couldn't ask for a more creative and reliable writer than K. C. Norton, who turned an idea I had decades ago into reality, creating characters with such depth that they have become living, breathing people in my mind. I often say that K.C. opened up an emotional vein and bled this story onto the page. You can see it in every word she crafted and every wound she exposed to make these characters more than the sum of their parts.

We're grateful for Angela Traficante's thorough copy editing. Our compliments also go out to the book cover illustrator Hannah Elizabeth who can finally add this cover to her portfolio. As well as letterer James T. Egan of Bookfly Design for his assistance on the cover.

We can't wait to share the rest of the stories in the Crimson Smoke and the Emerald Flame series. And thank you, dear reader, for reading until the very last line.